TRIBAL HONOR

TRIBAL HONOR

T.G. BROWN

TG
THRILLER
Publication

For my Aunt Liz.
Rest in peace.

CHAPTER
ONE

Better the devil you know than the devil you don't. The people in Marvin Bingham's life would learn that knowing the devil didn't do much good either.

Marvin was driving a 1983 dark green Ford pickup. The engine roared down the highway on a lovely, sunny spring day. Marvin was in his late twenties. In his front passenger seat was his wife, Sharon.

Sharon was in her thirties, but she had been diagnosed with stage-four liver cancer. It wasn't a matter of if she was going to die; it was a matter of when.

Marvin stole a sidelong glance at his wife of four years and felt a familiar twisting knot in his stomach. The idea of living without her made him contemplate taking his own life. Marvin had spent years not feeling any emotions, and Sharon showed him that he could feel again. She'd revealed that things could be different for him.

Marvin wasn't anything special. He knew that. Marvin stood around five foot ten and was barely visible if he turned sideways. His arms resembled noodles, and he'd worn reading glasses since he was in middle school. When he met Sharon at an AA meeting, he'd thought she was beautiful. Marvin charmed her with his quips and remembering that chivalry wasn't dead. He couldn't believe it when she agreed that they could get sober together. The rest was history.

Sharon coughed, and Marvin rubbed her back with one hand, leaving the other on the steering wheel. It'd been hard on Marvin to take care of Sharon for the past couple of months after she was diagnosed with cancer. Marvin stuck it out, enduring the long nights of misery, seeing the woman he loved suffer. He hated the sounds of coughing and hacking.

"We'll be back home soon, honey," he said. "You'll get your beauty rest. Not that you need it."

Sharon cleared her throat. "We should go watch a movie tonight. I want to go out."

"The doctor said if you want to have any chance of beating this cancer, you gotta sleep as much as possible."

"I ain't beating this cancer, Marv."

"Hey now! Don't talk like that. We're gonna get through this."

A tear slid down her cheek. "I can't keep going to sleep early in hopes that a miracle will happen... I wanna live out my last days having fun. I want to do something fun with you... Like we used to when I was healthy."

"Damn it, Sharon. You can't give up on me like this! We're gonna beat this cancer if we do what the doctor says."

"You're in denial, Marv. I'm gonna die. But before that, I want to have some fun. Is that so much to ask?"

"Is it too much to ask for you to keep fighting?" His voice ratcheted up. "This isn't easy for me either. We can go to the movies when the cancer has gotten out of you!" His white skin turned red.

Sharon turned her face to the window and started to whimper, her weeping interrupted by coughing.

Marvin looked over, feeling guilty. He even felt that he might have overreacted. Right up until he crashed the car.

Tires screeched on the pavement ahead. Marvin ripped his gaze away from Sharon and slammed his foot on the brake, but the truck skidded into the car in front of them.

The accident rocked Marvin and Sharon, snapping their necks forward and then back. The pickup didn't have airbags. Marvin caught his breath and looked over at Sharon. She appeared okay.

"Are you all right?" he asked.

"Yeah. Are you?"

"I'm okay. Wait here."

Marvin got out of the pickup and went to talk to the other driver. Traffic on the highway had come to a dead stop due to another accident a few miles up the road. Police cars had blocked the route. Luckily, Marvin was able to slow the vehicle enough to minimize the damage. Both vehicles were operational, but Marvin's pickup had a nice dent on the front bumper, and the other car had a dent in the back bumper.

The other guy was a jerk, but he didn't want the accident on his insurance so they agreed not to report it. Marvin was steaming as he climbed back into the truck. They sat still, as traffic didn't move. He didn't say a single word to Sharon who had at least quit obsessing over going to the movie theater.

———

Finally, they made it back to their cheap, rundown house in Jericho Nation. Marvin parked the truck in their driveway and shut off the ignition.

"I'm sorry," she said.

Marvin didn't reply.

She continued, "I know it's been hard on you to not have a drink... especially with taking care of me. I just wanted you to cut loose and to be able to do it with me."

Not have a drink echoed in his ears like gunshots. His knuckles popped as he squeezed the life out of the steering wheel.

"Shut the fuck up, Sharon!"

Marvin stormed into the house. It was a one-bedroom home in

a new housing development, but it hadn't been cleaned in months. Dirty dishes filled the sinks; kitchen counters had month-old stains on them.

Marvin slammed through the house to the littered garage. He grabbed a bottle of whiskey that he'd been saving. *Fuck sobriety.* He tore open the bottle and started chugging.

———

Sharon made her way inside. Walking was excruciating, so it took her five minutes to walk from the gravel driveway to the front door, about ten yards. The gravel walkway had nice large rocks edging the path.

When she trudged in, Marvin had the TV on. He was sitting in a recliner in the living room with the bottle of whiskey in one hand and the remote in another. Sharon glanced at the bottle. Her eyes showed concern. Marvin raised the bottle to her.

"Here you go! You wanna have some fun? Why don't you have a few drinks? This will be fun! Go out with a bang!"

Sharon hacked again.

"Can you please stop?" She turned away. "I'll go to bed early."

"Oh, no, you won't. You'll drink with me! Since you're so intent on quitting and letting this cancer win. Let's get fucked up!"

Sharon didn't reply and took a few steps toward the bedroom.

"Don't you fucking walk away from me." Marvin launched himself out of the recliner.

Sharon would have moved faster, but she couldn't. She limped down the hall. Marvin chucked the remote against the wall as hard as he could. It shattered into several pieces.

"I said, don't you fucking walk away from me!"

Sharon stopped with her back to Marvin. She closed her eyes and rested her hand on the wall. Marvin marched over and pressed the bottle against her cheek.

"Here... have a drink."

The bottle was half empty already. She said nothing and shook her head no.

"No? You don't get to say no. Drink."

Sharon said nothing.

Marvin grabbed hold of her neck and tipped her head backward, tilting her mouth toward the ceiling. He poured the whiskey all over her face. Sharon tried to shake loose, but she was too weak.

"Please," Sharon tried to say as she gargled on whiskey. "Please.... stop."

Marvin noticed the booze dripping down her face to her clothes and onto the floor.

"Fucking waste of good whiskey! What, you don't want to 'have fun' anymore?"

"You made your point."

"I don't think I did."

Marvin grabbed her head and slammed it into the wall. Sharon's legs buckled, and she collapsed. Marvin kicked the crumpled woman on the floor twice more.

"You dumb fucking bitch! Do you know what I've given up to be with you? And you want to quit! All I hear is you talking about wanting to give up. Why the fuck am I doing this then? Do you see what you've done? Made me wreck my truck. Made me relapse! Just because you want to quit. Fine, quit then. If you really want to quit. Don't fight back. Just let me beat you like the quitter that you are."

He cracked her another time in the ribs. Sharon used all her strength to put her hand up. Marvin loomed over her and stared into her eyes.

"Fucking pathetic." He walked away.

"Need..."—another cough—"... need help."

"Of course you need fuckin' help," he snarled. But he turned back and helped her to her feet.

"I... can't see," she mumbled, staggering.

He ignored her.

"Do you need help getting the groceries out of the truck too?"

"No... I got it. Then I'll go to bed."

"Good."

Sharon slowly walked back to the front door. She opened it, took a step, and tripped on the door frame. She fell headfirst onto a stone the size of a football. The side of Sharon's head smashed into the rock. Her body was motionless.

Marvin stood five feet away, a bottle of whiskey in hand.

"Sharon?"

No response.

"Honey? Are you OK?"

No response.

Marvin dropped the whiskey bottle on the floor. He sprinted to Sharon's body. Her head had landed on the rock in exactly the same place Marvin had smashed her into the wall. Her eyes were open. Marvin saw blood pouring from her head onto the gravel path.

"No. No, no, no! Please, no—Oh God, no!"

Marvin cradled Sharon's body in his arms as her blood trickled onto him.

He burst into tears.

"Not like this! Not like this!"

Marvin was wailing. Uncontrollable emotions went through him.

His neighbors ran over and saw him holding her.

"Call 9-1-1! Call 9-1-1!" Marvin shouted. "Someone please help us!"

He gazed into her vacant eyes.

"I didn't mean it, baby. I didn't mean it. I love you. Come back to me..."

CHAPTER
TWO

I sometimes stare at myself in the mirror. Not in the kind of way that you'd think. When I was growing up, my father told me, Warren, if you can look yourself in the mirror and be proud of the man you are, you're doing something right. If you're not, then you're doing life wrong.

Sometimes I believe the job I do makes a difference. Maybe save a life or two. For that, I gaze at myself in the mirror proudly. Yet a part of me doesn't feel like I'm a good man.

A part of me struggles not to cave someone's skull in whenever the opportunity arises. I know that's wrong, but I can't help it. It's just the way I feel.

One cold, wet, December day in 2019 was the last time I remember when I held it together. When the facade was impenetrable.

I had just come back from visiting my parents, as I did every Monday night. If it weren't for my parents, I'm not sure what side of the legal fence I would've landed on.

When I was young, I got into fights a lot. I got suspended from school numerous times. My mother and father taught me to never start a fight, but always finish them. I have to admit, when I was younger, it didn't take much for me to "finish" a fight.

Staring at my reflection on that December night, I could hear my dad's voice in my head.

"You have to control your rage, son. Or it could get you in a lot of trouble when you're older. You're a good man. Don't let your rage end you and what you stand for."

I'm trying, Dad.

There is a metaphorical crossroad I find myself at every time I wear the uniform and badge. One direction points me to law and order—the "correct" way of doing things. The opposite direction points me in the way of a vigilante. The way that would undoubtedly end in my demise and the loss of everyone I hold dear.

I flicked off the light switch and stopped staring at myself in the mirror like a narcissistic prick. I had to get some form of sleep, which was getting harder and harder to get. There were too many dark memories in my head, waiting to come back to life as soon as I closed my eyes.

My bedroom was a complete disaster. Clothes and random items were lying all over the place, like a hurricane of clothing. There was also a woman who did fashion modeling sleeping in my bed, who I paid no attention to. The deed was already done; not much else for us to do. I'd hoped she'd distract me from the dreams that awaited me, but that never worked.

Before I flicked my bedroom light off, I sat on the edge of the bed, contemplating whether I should attempt to sleep or wake the girl in my bed for round two. To be honest, I don't remember her name. All I could tell you was she was Brazilian and barely spoke English.

As I was trying to decide, the police vest hanging in my closet caught my eye. I glanced at it for a second. I was going to have to go back to work soon. I'd been a tribal cop on the Jericho Nation Reservation for six years and I had developed good survival instincts. I learned that you should always trust your gut. My gut feeling was telling me something terrible was going to happen. It was like a gift and a curse. I couldn't explain it. All I could do was feel it. I stared at the vest.

A reckoning was coming, and that reckoning had a name. Marvin Bingham.

CHAPTER
THREE

Graveyard shift brings out all the zombies, they say. Well, this guy was nothing compared to the monster I'd meet later in the night. That son of a bitch, Marvin Bingham.

Anyway, I found myself face to face with a guy who looked like the undead. This guy was six-foot, the same as me, and about seventy pounds lighter than my six-foot, two-hundred-pound frame. The Latino male, around twenty years old, standing in the middle of the traffic zipping along Highway 18. He was wearing nothing but a pair of jeans. It was thirty degrees.

We in police work call this a clue, meaning that this guy was probably using some sort of controlled substance. Methamphetamine, cocaine, heroin, and so forth. It wasn't hard for people to obtain drugs on a tribal reservation. I knew this guy from previous contacts in my career. He wasn't usually this hyped up. He must have got a bad batch of drugs. I always forgot his name though, yet he never forgot mine.

I was attempting to de-escalate a volatile situation with this guy, but it wasn't working out so well. He decided to yell out a loud war cry and charge me.

"Fuck you, Warren Lawson!"

Well, Dad, I didn't start this fight, but I'm sure as hell gonna finish it.

He stepped in and swung a wide-arcing, knockout blow of a punch. I saw it coming a mile away; a blind man would have. I ducked under the punch and swiveled my body behind him in one swift movement. I wrapped my arms around his waist, spun, and dropped my body weight, taking him to the ground in a tight circle. He hit the asphalt face-first, splitting his lip.

I was on his back, effectively pinning his chest to the ground. Blood spewed from his lips as he started to flail. Then I saw him reach into his waistband.

Weapon.

He bucked furiously, gaining just enough room to pull out a switchblade knife. He rotated his body toward mine and swung wildly at my throat. I hopped back to dodge the blade. Then I parried the attack, kneeling and grabbing his wrist to control the hand holding the knife.

Keeping my knee planted on his chest, I bent his arm in a way that it shouldn't, using a modified wrist- and arm-lock technique. I twisted until he screamed, his shoulder popped, and the knife dropped with a rattle to the asphalt.

I turned and socked him square in the nose, then grabbed the knife and tossed it into a nearby drainage ditch. I rolled him onto his stomach and gained control of both arms while pinning him to the ground. I'd just gotten the cuffs on him when I heard my radio sounding off.

The dispatcher was frantically checking my status. I didn't know it at the time, but my radio accidentally keyed up as I was fighting the Latino guy.

"I'm code four," I assured the dispatcher.

A Kirk County deputy came on the radio and advised me that he was en route. The deputy was part of a specialized unit called the "Mobile Crisis Response Team." Their duties were negotiating with people having a mental crisis. They were often referred to as MCRT for short.

I got the guy to his feet and into my patrol vehicle and waited for backup.

CHAPTER
FOUR

MAY 21, 1995, WILLAMINA, OREGON

I t had been eight years since Marvin had lost the love of his life.

Long after the cops came the night Sharon died, Marvin had clutched her body. He didn't remember how long he held her. Hours. Police had declared it an accidental death. Technically it was, but Marvin knew it was his fault.

Sharon had put Marvin in her will before she died. Sharon gave Marvin all her money, savings, and assets. Anything of value that she owned went to Marvin when she passed.

Marvin received thousands. He lived pretty well for a guy without a job for about five years.

Marvin spent every day after Sharon's death drinking any alcoholic beverage he could find. Sharon had been the only thing that kept him from becoming the darkness he craved. With her gone, what was the point of trying to be good?

But he realized that he needed a job to support his drinking habit.

The neighboring town to Jericho Nation was called Willamina. It was a small, hard-nosed logger town. Marvin went down to the local mill and was hired a few weeks later. A lumber job in the

Jericho Nation/Willamina community was about as secure a job as you could get. The forests went on for miles upon miles.

He operated machinery; it was good honest work. Marvin made friends with a few coworkers. After work, they'd go out for beers at the local bar in town, Vivian's.

The bar was nothing fancy, but it got the job done. Truck drivers, loggers, and known low-end criminals kept it in business. It was the type of bar that only sat about five to ten people per night, and that was fine for its customers. There was a pool table, wooden floors, and wooden stools to sit on.

Marvin was out at Vivian's with some of his friends on May 21, 1995, after working long hours. They were going to get some time off for the weekend. Marvin was drinking a bottle of imported beer, playing pool with three other people.

"Marv, did you hear about Diana?" one of his friends asked.

Diana was one of the upper management employees for the lumber company. Marvin had only seen her a couple of times. He'd met her on the day he interviewed for the job. She had the same beauty Sharon had.

"No, I didn't. What happened?"

"She's sick, man... Like real fuckin' sick."

Marvin placed the edge of his pool cue down and laid it on the table next to the white cue ball. He lined up his shot and hit the white ball into the solid yellow ball, which missed the corner pocket.

"Sick? How so?"

"She's got cancer... Real bad, too. She might only have a year or two to live."

"You shitting me?"

"No, man... I heard she stepped down from her position today because of it."

"Does she got anyone to take care of her? Y'know, help her out?"

"Not that I know of... I think her kids live across the country. They might not even know yet."

"We should be helping her out."

"How are we gonna help, Marv? You know how to beat cancer now?"

Marvin's friends didn't know about what happened to Sharon. He remained silent as he watched his other two friends lining up their shots.

Marvin took another drink of his beer. "No, I don't know how to beat cancer... but I wish I did."

———

Diana lived outside of town on a nice five-acre property in between Willamina and Jericho Nation. It was nice and quiet out where she lived, just the way she liked it. She had gone through two divorces and she wasn't even in her late forties yet. Diana was forty-five but had a substance addiction, alcohol mostly, though she couldn't stop smoking to save her life. She promised that she would stop, and she did—for a few days.

The smoking caught up with her and she ended up with lung cancer. She'd grown up in the Willamina community. Out in Willamina or Jericho Nation, there wasn't much to do but drink booze or use some substance to have fun. Yet, it was her home, and she liked the people in it.

It was the morning of May 22. The sun was up early; at nine a.m. it was getting warm, but the light breeze felt nice. The birds were chirping, and she could see traffic already getting heavy on the highway from her house. Diana had a gravel driveway that was about two hundred yards from Highway 18. Green fields surrounded the house.

Diana stood on the front porch of her nice three-bedroom, two-story house looking at the blue sky, and beautiful vegetation of the area. The green grass of western Oregon was something to marvel at.

An old beat-up Ford pickup turned into her driveway.

Who is that? she wondered. She squinted; as the truck got closer, she could see it was green, but she still didn't recognize it. Eventually, the vehicle came to a halt about twenty yards away from her front porch, and the tumultuous engine went silent.

She saw a tall, skinny male with glasses get out of the driver's seat. He was alone, and nothing about him seemed threatening at all. Diana thought she might weigh more than him, and she only weighed 140 pounds, standing five foot four.

The guy reached into the Ford truck and grabbed a basket from the front passenger seat. In the basket were beautiful flowers and several types of candies and fruits. As the man approached she vaguely recognized him, but didn't know from where.

"Hello there," the man said. "My name's Marvin... Marvin Bingham. You might remember me from when I interviewed for a job at Hampton's a month ago."

"Oh! That's where I recognize you from. I knew you looked familiar."

Marvin inched closer and stopped walking about five feet away from the deck. He noticed a cup of coffee in her hands. He didn't want to make her uncomfortable, so he remained standing at a healthy distance. Marvin gazed at Diana's long, black, windblown hair.

"I just wanna say, I'm sorry for barging in on your private time like this... I just... I heard about you leaving the company from some guys... I heard you were sick and living on your own, so I wanted to bring you this." Marvin raised the basket to her.

"That's for me?"

"Yes, ma'am, it is, if you'll have it."

Diana's bottom lip started to quiver as she felt a flood of emotions rush through her body in an instant. Even Diana wasn't sure where these emotions were coming from. A tear welled from her eye as she responded.

"That's—that's the nicest thing anyone has ever done for me."

Marvin stepped up onto the deck with Diana and handed her the basket. She was speechless.

"Thank you, thank you so much. This means a lot to me."

"Yeah of course... I, uh... know a little something about what you're going through. I've seen what it does to a person. It isn't something anyone should have to take on alone."

"Did you have cancer?"

"No... my wife Sharon did. She died eight years ago... I held her in my arms as she went."

"I'm so sorry."

"It's OK, I wanted to let you know that you weren't alone in what you're going through. I'll help you any way I can."

Blown away by his kindness, she stuttered, "I couldn't... I couldn't ask that of you."

"You don't have to. I'm offering."

Diana considered this for a moment. She had nobody that could help her. The cancer wasn't bad yet, but she knew once she started doing treatment, it would get a lot harder. Diana's family had moved on to different spots in the country. The more she considered Marvin's offer, the more she realized she couldn't beat this alone. Yet, a part of her didn't trust this guy.

"How'd you know where I lived?"

"I asked one of the upper management guys that knew you, told him I was going to drop off a package to cheer you up. They were for it, so they told me where you lived."

If the man didn't seem so pathetic himself, she may have been more alarmed. She could feel herself release the tension in her shoulders the more she got to know the man. Maybe this guy could be easy to boss around, she mused.

"I'm glad they did... But are you sure you wanna help me through this? This is a tough thing you're offering to do."

"I know how hard it is... But a part of me feels like I failed my wife years ago. Now, I just want to make sure I don't fail anyone else going through what she went through."

"You might be the sweetest man I've ever met."

"And you might be the most beautiful woman I've met."

She smiled. She liked the flattery.

Marvin added, "You were always nice to me whenever you

saw me. Even though I was just a lower-level lumber guy... You were polite and waved to me. I appreciated that."

"Well... I got a few ex-husbands that would disagree with you about the nice thing," she quipped. "Are you sure you want to do this?"

"One hundred percent sure."

She grinned, and he smiled back.

———

As he watched her turn and walk toward the house, Marvin wondered, *Is this my shot at redemption?*

CHAPTER
FIVE

Marvin moved in with Diana. The first month was nothing short of spectacular. Diana would give him a list of things to do around the house and Marvin did them without hesitation.

They had separate bedrooms, and Marvin still worked at the lumber mill. Marvin wasn't getting paid at all to help her. Diana had offered to pay him several times, but he refused. Marvin advised her that he was only doing what a good friend would do.

Marvin and Diana made it a tradition to go on walks together once a week. Sometimes Marvin would take her to the beach and they'd walk together, looking at the waves. The Oregon coast was beautiful in the summer. Other times they walked around Diana's property or drove to town and strolled around there.

Marvin and Diana got to know each other best during the walks. Marvin opened up about Sharon for the first time in eight years. He, of course, left out the details that led to Sharon's "tragic accident."

Diana told him about her ex-husbands. Diana had a history of dealing with abusive men who managed to charm their way into her life. Diana said she knew Marvin wasn't that type of guy from the moment she laid eyes on him.

The hardest part was the doctor's visits that he would take her to on a weekly basis. The doctors got less and less ambitious about Diana's health. Diana tried to stay positive about the cancer, but Marvin noticed it was weighing on her.

The night of June 22, Diana was starting to feel the expected health effects of the chemotherapy. Diana and Marvin were lying in the living room together watching a movie. The movie ended and Diana rose to go to bed. When she stood up, she got light-headed and fell to one knee, and almost face-planted into the ground.

Marvin reached out and caught her. "Diana! Are you all right?"

She said nothing; she felt like she was in a daze. Diana wasn't sure what happened.

"Here. Let me help you to your bed, all right?"

Diana nodded in agreement. He wrapped his arm around her torso and lifted her to her feet. She limped to her bedroom, leaning on him the entire time. Marvin assisted her to her bed. Diana crawled under the covers.

"Do you want me to get you some water?" Marvin offered.

"No... I'm OK."

"All right, I'll be right out here if you need anything."

Marvin started to walk out of Diana's room. Marvin took a step out into the hallway and heard her say.

"Marvin..."

"Yes?" He turned.

"Could you—could you lie down with me tonight? I know it's a weird request but... I'm scared I won't wake up and I don't want to be alone."

"Hey now... you'll wake up tomorrow. It's just a minor setback, OK? But yes, I'll stay with you tonight."

"Thank you, Marv."

"Any time."

Marvin slid in under the sheets next to Diana. She cuddled her head on his chest and stayed close to him. Marvin's heart started pumping as he thought maybe she was interested in him as more than just a friend. Marvin's arms embraced her.

"I'm not going anywhere," he assured her.

She smiled, closed her eyes, and took a deep breath. If she wasn't going to wake up tomorrow, at least she went to bed with a smile on her face. Marvin closed his eyes, and they fell asleep together.

The next morning they woke up and Diana seemed better. The pair spent another day together. The day flew by as it always did. It was nightfall before they knew it. Diana went to sleep, while Marvin was wrestling with his inner demons.

Marvin bought a fifth of whiskey earlier in the day while on a grocery store run. When she went to bed, he sat in the dark living room, drinking from the bottle. He felt guilt for the first time in a long time. Like Sharon was looking down on him, saying, "You replaced me? How could you?"

Marvin drank until the bottle was empty. Marvin helped himself to a couple of beers in the fridge of the kitchen. He drank six more of those and was drunk enough to finally pass out.

———

In his dreams, Sharon haunted him. While he slept, he relived a memory of him being bullied in high school. A couple of high school jocks beat him up after school. He relived the memories of everyone calling him a freak because he didn't play sports or because he liked certain things that others didn't. His father having a drunken rage, night after night. He and his brother hid from him as he searched the house for a belt to beat them with. His father was a big hulking man, his mother was the opposite. He got the physical features of his mother, which made him easier to pick on.

Marvin lived a life of being an outcast... until he met Sharon. For a second, the nightmarish dream felt like a dream worth having. Then the dream changed from Sharon's beautiful smiling face to her screaming at him.

"YOU KILLED ME! YOU KILLED ME!"

Marvin tried to plead with Sharon, but his words fell on deaf ears. Sharon continued to shout.

"YOU KILLED ME AND THEN YOU REPLACED ME!"

———

Diana woke up in the middle of the night. She heard a commotion in the living room. She crawled out of bed and slept-walked toward the incoherent sounds coming from Marvin.

"Marv?"

She could overhear Marvin talking in his sleep down the hallway from her bedroom.

"I'm sorry. Sharon, I'm sorry I killed you."

Diana went down the hallway and found the living room light. She switched it on. Marvin was thrashing around in his sleep. Diana contacted Marvin and shook him hard, waking him up. Marvin let out a loud holler as he came to.

"Hey, you're OK... You're OK, it's me, Diana."

Marvin was breathing hard and sweat covered his body. It looked like he just ran a marathon in record time.

"I'm sorry... I was having a nightmare."

"I heard. Was it about Sharon?"

"How'd you know that?"

"You were talking in your sleep."

"Oh, God... I'm so sorry." Marvin blurted as he wiped the sweat off his face.

"It wasn't your fault." Diana hugged him. "You're a good man, Marvin. She knew that too."

Marvin rested his face on Diana's shoulder. Diana was kneeling next to him on the floor. He hunched forward from the chair he was sitting on and hugged her back.

Marvin moved his head away from her shoulder. His face was directly in front of Diana's.

"Thank you," he said. "You changed my life."

"I'm the one that should be thanking you. I thank God every day for meeting you."

They smiled at each other. Marvin's heart started to thump again, just like the night he held her in his arms. He leaned his head forward and kissed Diana on the lips. She gripped his face and kissed him back.

———

A week later, Diana and Marvin met with a couple of lawyers. Diana had a will that would leave her kids with her inheritance, but she changed her mind. Marvin deserved it more than anyone in her life. He had proved to her that he cared for her more than anyone she'd ever met. Marvin tried talking her out of it, reassuring her that what he did wasn't about money or an inheritance. Diana wouldn't hear any of that kind of talk. Just like that, Marvin was looking at an even more sizable inheritance.

CHAPTER
SIX

I waited for the MCRT Unit to respond and speak with the mentally ill guy who attacked me. I was ready to get this guy off my hands. About ten minutes after the fight, a Kirk County Mobile Crisis Response Team deputy pulled his patrol vehicle behind mine. I'd pulled onto the shoulder of the highway so I was no longer blocking traffic.

I knew the deputy, his name was Brent Cardwell, and he had been a deputy for around thirty years. He was nearing retirement but still loved the job. He was a large man who towered over most, at six-five, a bulky two hundred fifty pounds. He was a man who his peers respected. We got out of our vehicles to talk.

"Sounds like you had a bit of a scuffle. You all right?" Cardwell asked.

I replied, "Yeah, I'm good."

"Where is our emotionally disturbed person?"

"In the back seat of my car. He had a knife earlier, but I took it away from him. It's in the front seat."

"Copy that... Glad you're safe, War." People always call me 'War,' as a nickname. "Tell me about your contact with him."

I told him what was said, how the fight went down, and what

my concerns were. Cardwell had a therapist that rode with him as an attachment to the MCRT Unit. He asked me if it was safe for her to contact the male. I explained that it was safe because he was secured in handcuffs and had been checked for weapons... but that she should talk to him through a window to be on the safe side. Cardwell agreed.

Cardwell strolled back to his patrol vehicle and motioned with his hands to the therapist riding in his patrol vehicle. She was seated in the front passenger seat. I saw her slip out of the seat and step out under the light of a street lamp nearby. She was wearing a tactical vest that was yellow and black, which was the same colors as the deputy's uniforms.

She was small, maybe five one or five two, with platinum blond hair in a ponytail. Her eyes were brown, her skin pale, and she couldn't have weighed more than 115 pounds. Her body type resembled a gymnast or a ballet dancer.

The therapist walked over to talk to Cardwell for a minute. I stayed at my patrol vehicle and watched. I tried not to make it obvious that I was checking her out, but it was becoming harder by the second. I glanced down at the ground and then away from them. I felt raindrops coming down from the cold winter sky and the breeze of cars passing by.

"Hi, there," she said in a friendly tone. "I'm crisis clinician Ashley Bradford. How can I help?" Her calm and sweet demeanor made me feel so comfortable I forgot that I had been in a fight a few minutes prior.

"Nice to meet you, Miss Bradford, I'm Officer Warren Lawson." I extended my hand, and she shook it in a firm, professional manner.

She wanted to hear more details about the person we were dealing with. I repeated the story to her as Cardwell stood by and listened. As I finished up the story, I saw that both she and Cardwell had a smirk on their faces, but I didn't know why.

"Is his name Julio by chance?" she guessed.

"You know, we didn't really get around to exchanging names,"

I responded, "I've seen him a few times but I don't remember who he is."

She looked back at Cardwell. "I bet it's Julio."

"I bet you're right."

Cardwell and Ashley went to the back seat of my patrol vehicle. Cardwell opened the back door. He and Ashley called out, "Julio! How're you, man?"

"Hey, guys! My nose is a little fucked up, but I'm a'ight. Where have you been? I needed you earlier!"

Julio's demeanor completely changed. I waited, getting drenched by the Oregon rain. Ashley talked to Julio as if they were neighbors who'd known each other for the past twenty years. They laughed and talked about Julio's personal issues. She learned that he'd stopped taking his medications. Fifteen minutes later, Julio was cooperating and asked for a ride to the hospital. Cardwell took Julio out of handcuffs and escorted him to their patrol vehicle. I stared at Ashley in disbelief.

"So just like that, we're cool? Guy draws a knife on me and he gets a free ride to the hospital?" I asked.

"No... He'll undergo a different solution. Julio has severe mental health issues which make him completely delusional... He sees things that aren't there... I know this because he's a patient at Salem County Hospital and has been diagnosed with dozens of mental health issues. Julio can't think long enough to plan and commit a crime. He can't think long enough to remember to flush the toilet. What I'm trying to say is he can't be charged with a crime because he doesn't have the mental capacity to knowingly commit a crime."

What she said made sense, but I didn't like it. For all I knew Julio took a bad batch of meth and was taking it out on the nearest cop. However, she seemed confident in what she was saying. Cardwell trusted her, I could tell by his demeanor.

"Officer Lawson... I know it's hard, but this is the best way to deal with him. If his case wasn't so serious, I would be completely on board with locking his ass up." She gazed into my eyes. "I hope you know that your actions saved his life today. You could have easily killed him, but you didn't. His family and I appreciate that."

I should have caved his skull in a little more...

"Yeah, I guess so, Miss Bradford. I'll defer to your better judgment."

"Please, call me Ashley. Makes me feel old when people call me Miss or Ma'am."

"You don't look a day over twenty-five."

She smiled. "I like you, Officer Lawson. You're reasonable and give great compliments."

"You can call me Warren."

"All right, Warren. Deal."

A couple of Harley Davidson motorcycles drove by us in the two-lane. It was a nasty day, so I was surprised to see bikers out riding. They were part of a gang. I noticed Ashley staring at the bikers like she had a fascination with them.

"Is that what does it for you? Bikers?" I inquired.

"Oh, well... yeah. Once upon a time, this girl dated a biker or two," she admitted.

"Oh boy, it must be like Niagara Falls down in the southern lady parts right now."

As soon as I made the joke, I regretted my choice of words. Maybe I was too comfortable with her after all.

She laughed, and I felt a small bit of relief. Ashley replied, "How'd you know?"

We shared a laugh, "Have we met before? You look familiar."

"I used to work at Salem County Hospital in their crisis unit. You brought in a guy who tried to kill several cops... Then I had to provide therapy for that jackass."

"Ah, yes. I remember now... You know, that same asshole was connected to some pretty bad bikers... Just some food for thought. Cops might be a better choice in my opinion."

She scoffed, "Oh, I'm sure you think that."

I chuckled. "Just looking out for my work colleague."

"Gee, thanks."

Cardwell finished up his conversation with Julio at their patrol vehicle. He waved over to Ashley and said, "Come on, let's get this man to the hospital."

"Well, that's my cue. Gotta go. It was nice talking to ya."

"Hey, hold on," I said.

"Yeah?"

"Could I get your number? You know... in case I need to call you for more help with mentally ill subjects in the future."

"Smooth. Yes, of course."

I handed her my cell phone, and she dialed her number. She told me to text her my name so she could get my number in return. Then, she got into the patrol vehicle with Cardwell and they escorted Julio to Salem County Hospital.

CHAPTER
SEVEN

Diana wasn't showing any signs of getting better. Marvin expected this to be the case. When Diana's children learned that she had willed her life savings to Marvin, they thought he was strange and untrustworthy. Why would Marvin come into her life after she was diagnosed with cancer? He had to be there to get money out of the deal. Diana didn't listen to these allegations because all she could see was Marvin's undying loyalty to her.

After Diana went to bed, Marvin spent his nights drinking any alcohol he could. Marvin quit his job and used some leftover money to buy whatever he wanted. In fact, he found himself getting excited about when Diana would go to bed so he could feed his habit.

Marvin tried to go to sleep sober multiple nights. Each time he was plagued by nightmares of Sharon, telling him he failed to nurse her back to health. The nightmares only vanished after he drank a couple of bottles of whiskey.

Sharon was a reminder of everything he hated about himself. Marvin had a rough childhood. He often thought about how his father beat him, his brother, and his mother daily. Marvin's father always told him he was a worthless pussy growing up. He swore he'd never be like the old man, but as he got older, he grew ever closer to becoming what he hated.

Living with that many bad memories stored in your head is like watching a water pipe about ready to burst from too much pressure. It's bound to happen, and it's going to be a mess. Sharon once made a joke that Marvin couldn't hurt a fly. Marvin took that as an insult. So he slapped her with the back of his hand to prove her wrong. That's what his dad always did. That's how Marvin was taught about men gaining the respect of a woman.

———

Months went by. It was Halloween time in the year 1995. Marvin was helping Diana with everything. Including bathing her. Diana was undergoing chemotherapy, and she had lost her hair in the process. She was no longer the pretty butterfly Marvin saw when they first met. The emotional roller coaster of someone going through cancer is unbearable and nobody should have to go through it. Marvin had gone through it twice. However, that wasn't the hard part for him.

They were in the bathroom of Diana's house. Diana was sitting in the bathtub, naked, as Marvin rubbed a yellow sponge on her back. Marvin couldn't hide his alcoholism anymore. He carried a bottle of Jack Daniels everywhere he went in the house like it was important for his survival. Yet, he was kind enough to share it with Diana.

"Did you think you could save me?" Diana asked, with a slight slur in her speech.

Marvin stopped drinking from his bottle and handed it back to her, "I hoped I could."

"Do you take care of me because you think it will help you get over the death of Sharon?"

"I thought that."

"Do you still think that?" Diana took a swig and handed the bottle back.

"No, Diana, I don't." Marvin chugged out of the bottle some more.

Diana started sobbing.

"Oh, no... Not again, God damn it. No more fucking crying!"

Diana turned around to face him and slapped the water in the bathtub. The water splashed into Marvin's face.

"Fuck you! You have no idea what this is like!"

"Oh, I don't? I think I have some sort of idea."

"So you had cancer now, did ya? No, your wife had it. Not you. So you DON'T know."

"Real fucking nice, Diana. Since none of this is hard for me."

"Oh, poor Marvin! You chose to take care of me and be a part of this."

"Yeah, because I wanted to change your life! I wanted to help you get past this!"

"There is no getting past this! It's fucking cancer, Marvin! Nobody gets past this! Do you have some fucking God complex? Thinking you can just cure me of cancer with nice kisses and bubble baths? Give me a fucking break."

Marvin's face turned red, his jaw clenched. He had no reply, so he decided to take another long chug of his Jack Daniels. *God complex? I'll show you a god complex.*

"I don't understand why the hell you're treating me like a piece of dog shit but I've had about enough of it," Marvin slurred.

"Oh, you've had enough of it? What are you gonna do, big man? You couldn't win a fight against a one-armed Helen Keller, you pussy."

Marvin felt the rage. The powerlessness of not being worthy. His need to let the darkness come out. He wanted to smash the bottle across her head to get her to shut up. Then he thought against it. *She's acting out because of the cancer, it's not her.*

One side of Marvin was trying to reason with him and remind

him that it was important to stay calm. *Don't repeat the mistakes of the past, make a new ending.*

The other side of Marvin didn't want any of that. Marvin felt a satisfactory feeling of imagining caving her head in with the whiskey bottle. He pictured the power he would feel. Proving her wrong. Getting her money after she died and not having to take care of her anymore. He could move and get out of the shitty town of Jericho Nation.

"You want a God?" He said, "How about the *devil*, you worthless cunt."

He savagely gripped her head and shoved it under the water of the bathtub. The tub was full. Diana kicked and grabbed for Marvin's hand. He put down his bottle of Jack Daniels and placed his other hand on Diana's chest. Marvin rose and leaned his weight down onto Diana.

He held her underwater for a couple of minutes. His adrenaline pumped, and a red haze of rage rinsed over him. Diana fought the best she could but had no strength or stamina to do so. He fixed his gaze on her the whole time. She screamed from underwater, bubbles flowed out of her mouth, and the water muffled her voice. Her body squirmed all over the white-colored tub, getting water all over Marvin's clothes. He continued to drown her, getting more aroused by the second. He watched the light go out in her eyes and realized it was done. Diana was dead.

Marvin stood and looked down at Diana's body. He took a moment to realize what he'd done. He waited for the crushing regret and guilt that had followed Sharon's death, but it didn't come. He felt accomplished. Marvin took a drink from his Jack Daniels bottle and wiped his lips. The bottle was almost empty.

He had to make this look like an accident.

He turned on the faucet to overflow the tub. Then, he dunked Diana's lifeless body underwater. Marvin took a deep breath and went to the washing and drying machine. He made sure his clothes were washed and dried Then, he went out and did some yard work. He was sure to make contact with the neighbors so they could back up his story later with the police.

About one hour later, Marvin made a 9-1-1 call from the telephone in the house. Marvin put on a performance for the dispatcher.

"Please send help! My girlfriend cut her wrists. I—I think she's stopped breathing! I think... I think she's dead... Oh god! Please send someone to save her!"

———

When medics and police officers responded to the scene, Marvin played the role of a grieving boyfriend. He told the cops that he was doing yard work when Diana went to take a bath. Then he found her in the tub, dead. They asked questions about Diana, and Marvin answered them calmly. Marvin felt a rush, lying to the police officers and getting away with it. When the officers learned she had cancer, they didn't suspect little ole Marvin of anything criminal. All Marvin had to do was fake a couple of cries for them, and he was off the hook.

There was no evidence that proved his story was false either. The kids tried fighting for the will in court but ultimately lost. The children argued that Diana's mental state wasn't right when she changed the will; however, there were signed documents between Diana and her lawyer that said otherwise.

Marvin Bingham collected the money that Diana left behind for him months later. Then, he was gone.

CHAPTER
EIGHT

My shift wasn't done after dealing with Julio. Later that night, I responded to a call at the White Salmon Casino. Most of the criminals in the county hung out at the local casino, and I got to deal with most of them. There wasn't a night that went by that we didn't get a call from that damn casino.

Dispatch contacted me on the radio. There was a domestic disturbance on the gaming floor. Dispatch didn't have many details for me, other than a female was seen shoving a male and both appeared to be around sixty years old.

I drove to the main entrance. The outside was orange and white with the White Salmon logo of a wolf jumping over a mountain.

The casino was a hundred thousand square feet of indoor space, surrounded by paved parking areas. Inside were multiple restaurants, slot machines, several table games areas, and an event center that could hold thousands of people. There was also a 550-room hotel attached to the casino.

I parked my patrol vehicle under a large awning, mentally preparing myself to investigate one of countless domestic disturbance cases destined to come my way. I noticed people walking in and out of the casino. Some were smoking cigarettes near the main entrance. Others walked out toward one of the several parking lots. The glass doors were well polished with the White Salmon Casino logo on the middle of the door. I grabbed the golden handle and entered.

Upon entering the casino, my brain was instantly stimulated by the number of lights inside the place. There were bright orange pathways on the carpets, meshed with dark blue coloring around the orange pathway. The ceiling was well-lit with orange lights, covered by expensive orange-colored chandeliers, interspersed with blue lights to match the flooring colors.

This casino was the pride and joy of the Confederated Tribes of Jericho Nation. It employed several tribal members and had made the tribe lots of money over the years. The casino was so nice, it didn't make sense for it to be in a place like Jericho Nation. Yet it has been there for years and will continue to be there long after I leave.

I went to a podium area where I knew I'd find casino security officers at all hours of the day or night.

"You here for the domestic?" asked a disgruntled older security officer in a white uniform shirt and black pants.

"Yeah, can you point me in the right direction?"

"Let me contact the supervisor working on it. It'll just be a second."

"Thanks."

I waited as the security officer talked on his radio, advising his boss that Tribal Police were at the casino. His tone of voice and body language screamed, *I fucking hate my life.*

"The supervisor will be with you in a moment. Subjects are still on casino property."

"Copy that."

A minute or two later a tall, skinny guy wearing an all-black suit with a red tie and nice black dress shoes approached me.

"Hey. A couple of our officers are talking to them on the

gaming floor right now. You want me to take you to them?" he asked.

No, I think I'll just let them sit for a couple of minutes while I drink a beer... Of course, I wanted him to take me to the people involved. Why else would I be here?

"Yeah, that'd be great."

"All right, follow me."

We zigzagged through the crowd on the gaming floor to the other side of the casino. I observed an older gentleman, talking to a security officer, gesturing with his hands. A Native American woman around the same age was not talking much. She was sitting on a chair near a slot machine with her head down; she looked sick. I guessed that the man was pleading his case to the security officer that the police didn't need to get involved.

"Hello, I'm Officer Lawson with the Jericho Nation Tribal Police Department. Can I speak with you for a second?" I said to the sixty-year-old male.

"Sure you can. Can we talk somewhere a little more private though?"

"Yes sir, there is a medical room nearby that is nice and quiet."

"That works for me."

Security escorted the male and female to the medical room as I followed. The old woman got out of the chair like it was the hardest thing she had to do. Like she was lifting a semi-truck. She looked like she was gritting her teeth every step of the way. They both reeked of alcohol. It was hard to tell if the female was really sick, or just really drunk. My nose caught something that smelled similar to a rotted dead animal, but I couldn't tell where it was coming from.

As we entered the medical room, I explained it was standard protocol for a police investigation for me to speak with them one at a time. The male said that they understood, but I doubted the female understood much of anything that was being said.

Her face was blank. Her eyes opened, but nothing was registering. She had dark tan skin with dark brown eyes and black hair.

Her hair was graying a little, and she appeared to be short and scrawny. Although her skin was predominately brown, she looked a bit pale.

The male was tall, skinny, white-skinned, wore glasses, and came off as the nerdy type. He liked to talk, that's for sure. He talked the whole way to the medical room from the gaming floor. The male covered about five different topics during the two-minute walk.

I asked them who wanted to talk to me first. The male was quick to speak, but the female grunted out a single word.

"Me."

The word was barely coherent, so I asked her again if she wanted to talk to me first. She nodded. It was like pain and happiness battled for supremacy with every facial expression.

"All right sir, if you don't mind, could you wait outside the room as I talk to her, please?" I suggested.

"Why yes, of course," he responded.

I left him with the security officers and opened the door for the woman. The stench I'd smelled followed her into the room. I wondered when she'd last showered. She walked slowly, and like she was in pain, so I assisted her to a chair.

The medical room was ten-by-ten, with white linoleum flooring. There were a couple of cushioned stools in the middle of the room and cabinets around the periphery. I motioned toward a stool for her to sit down on. She sat on one and I sat on the other. I detected a heavy scent of Axe body spray. The spray seemed to be an attempt to mask the smell of alcohol and rotten animals.

"All right, ma'am. First things first. Do you have any identification on you?"

It was always good practice to identify who you were dealing with from the start of an investigation. You never know. If I learned anything over the six years, I'd been a police officer, it was that people are never what they seem.

The female gazed at me and smiled, but didn't reply. I started to think that she might not speak English.

"Do you speak English? Do you understand what I'm saying?"

The lady didn't answer for about twenty seconds and then grinned once again. She nodded her head up and down again.

"What's your name?"

The woman kept smiling at me. Like she was nervous because she didn't know what to say. I felt like somehow my words were lagging as if we had a bad internet connection. I fished out my wallet and showed her my Oregon driver's license.

"Do you have one of these? Can I see it please?"

I held the license up in front of her face for another twenty seconds. Then she started to nod with excitement.

"Yes, yes!" She rummaged around in her pockets. She was wearing black sweatpants and a blue hoodie. She was checking everywhere and finally found her wallet in her front hoodie pocket. She raised the wallet in the air to me with excitement.

"Here, here!"

I confiscated the brown leather wallet and opened it. I found her identification in one of the pocket slots. I read her name, Susanna Holt. She had a listed address in the tribal housing area of the Jericho Nation Reservation. She was a longtime tribal member. Her date of birth suggested that she was in her sixties, but she looked thirty years older.

I wrote down Susanna's identification card information in my notebook. I put the card back into her wallet and handed it back.

"Thank you. Now... did you get into a fight with your significant other tonight?"

No answer. She smiled wide, nodding her head from side to side. Her eyes started to close and then rapidly open. When her eyes opened, she would see me and be startled by my presence. This process repeated itself a couple of times. I kept asking questions, in hopes that I would get some sort of answer. I did my best to hide my frustration, but it was challenging.

"Are you injured?" I inquired.

"No."

The frequent grimaces on her face said otherwise. I noticed her pupils were dilated which made me wonder if she was mixing narcotics with the alcohol.

"Who's the man with you tonight?"

"Bad man... very bad man."

"Bad? How is he bad?"

"Bad man."

"Bad how?"

"Not good."

"What's not good?"

"Him."

"I get that, but I need to know why you're saying that."

No answer. More nodding off to sleep and then waking back up surprised to see me. Not only would she wake up surprised, but it also seemed like she was frightened.

"Did you and the bad man get into a fight tonight?"

No answer.

I decided after about fifteen minutes of that process; I wasn't getting anywhere. Susanna was either too intoxicated, too sick, or mentally ill; possibly both. I asked her to wait outside, escorted her out, then indicated that the male should step inside. The male seemed happy to comply and sat on a stool. I stepped out and spoke to security for a minute and asked them what they knew about the domestic disturbance.

Security officers told me that Susanna and the nerdy-looking male were seen at the buffet in the casino. Susanna stomped away from the male and he followed. Susanna turned around and shoved him away from her. That's all they knew. Security officers only knew of the altercation because a casino surveillance employee caught the incident on camera.

Back in the medical room, I sat down on another stool about three feet away and in front of the man. He smelled even more like alcohol than Susanna, but the rotting smell had left with her.

"So you know why I'm here tonight talking to you, right?"

"Yes, I think I do. It's about a disagreement between Susanna and me, correct?"

"Correct."

"First things first. Do you have any identification on you?"

"No, I don't."

"How were you able to buy alcohol without identification?"

He paused for a second, in deep thought, "Son of a bitch, you're right... Man, I must have had too much to drink tonight. Thank god for buses, am I right?" He chuckled to himself as he dug into his pockets. He wrenched out his wallet, found his identification card, and handed it to me, "Here you go, sir."

I looked down and read the card. His name was Marvin Bingham.

I examined the identification card. 1960. Old enough to be my father. So far, I was able to hold a conversation with him, anyway. Marvin and I were polar opposites. At six-foot, two hundred pounds, I had a very low body fat percentage. This Marvin guy was a few inches shorter, weighed about a hundred and fifty pounds, and had a very low muscle percentage. Light gray to white hair; dark brown eyes. I had dark black hair and light blue eyes. The only thing Marvin and I had in common was that the color of our skin happened to be white.

"Hopefully you'll be able to shed light on what's going on between you and Susanna... she wasn't very talkative with me."

He nodded and seemed like he expected me to say that. "Yeah, Susanna has some mental health issues. I'm her caretaker."

"Oh, you're a caretaker?"

"Yes, I am... I take care of her for free, though."

Marvin handed me a business card from his wallet. I glanced at it. It said that Marvin worked for the Confederated Tribes of Jericho Nation as an in-home caretaker.

"That can't be easy work," I said.

"Oh, it's nothing compared to what you guys go through... The world has been going crazy for the past couple of years. My brother is a cop, so I know how it goes."

Marvin, of course, was referring to the protests and riots that had been happening around the United States. Police weren't viewed by the general public in a positive light anymore. In fact, a lot of people didn't want the police around. Some groups started protests called "Defund the Police." The topic of being a police officer was cause for debate for most people. Both sides had valid concerns and feelings toward policing in the United States. The problem was, it was dividing our country.

In the social media age, every police shooting would be released to the public in a matter of hours from several news outlets. It seemed like there was a police shooting every day somewhere in the country. Some were justified; others not so much. It was getting harder and harder to gain the public's trust. Especially with some media groups painting a poor picture of police officers for the general public.

I dismissed his comment.

"Yeah, but I think most people support us and are smart enough to know the good cops from the bad ones. There are bad apples in every type of job."

"Couldn't agree with you more, Officer Lawson." He checked out my arms for a few seconds, and his eyes widened, "How often do you work out? That uniform can barely contain your arms! Nicely done."

The compliment was random. It seemed like he was trying to talk about anything except the reason I was called to the casino that night.

"Thank you, sir. Do you mind if I ask you some questions about what was going on with Susanna tonight?"

"Oh. yes, of course, officer."

"Did you and Susanna have a fight tonight?"

"Well, not a physical fight... more of an argument."

"OK, what was the argument about?"

"Like I said earlier, Susanna has some mental health issues. Susanna and I used to be married a couple of years back, but we got divorced. A few years later we decided to give it one more try...

She was living in tribal housing, and I was working for the tribe, so I decided to be her caretaker when the time came. Her health started to decline while we were together. I take care of her full-time now. However, she's my girlfriend, so that's why I do it for free and not as a work thing."

"Is it normal caretaker protocol to let a patient get drunk at the casino?"

"It's funny you should mention that... because that was what the argument was about."

"Really? Do explain."

"Susanna likes to come to the casino and play the slot machines... We've done it for years together. We usually take the bus to the casino and then take the bus back to tribal housing. Since she's tribal, we get to ride the bus for free... Anyway, I take her here and she gambles her tribal money and I get a few drinks... Tonight she was adamant about getting a drink with me. I told her no, and she got upset... She was angry for about thirty seconds and then moved on to the next slot machine."

"So you didn't let her drink any alcohol?"

"No, but I suspect she might have snuck some drinks when I wasn't looking."

"She doesn't seem like someone who could sneak around doing anything... No offense."

"You'd be surprised. Some days she's better than others, but when she drinks, it all goes downhill from there."

"Seems like you've had this issue before."

"Yes, several times... Usually, I get her home and she goes to bed."

"Is that what you're planning on doing tonight?"

"Yes, as soon as we're done here, sir."

"Did Susanna physically push you tonight?"

"Technically yes, but it wasn't her fault."

"Explain what happened, please."

"We were at the buffet getting some food. I knew she must have drunk some alcohol because of the way she was acting—and

I could smell it. Susanna's mental issue is that she has severe dementia. The alcohol doesn't help her dementia one bit."

"I can imagine. Does the alcohol help you take care of her? Because I can smell a strong odor coming off you as well."

Marvin snickered at the comment. "I must admit, I have had something of an alcohol problem myself. I promise I have it under control, though."

"I certainly hope so, if you're going to be taking care of your dementia-ridden ex-wife."

His smile and snicker stopped. "I can assure you that it is under control."

I nodded and said nothing.

"Is something wrong?" he asked.

"Still trying to figure that out. Tell me why she pushed you at the buffet."

"We sat at a table in the buffet with our food. A couple of Black gentlemen sat near us. And well, Susanna isn't a fan of black folk."

"What makes you say that?"

"For starters, she refers to them as nig—"

"I got it." I interrupted, "For future reference, you can just say African Americans or something like that to keep our conversation more appropriate."

"Ah, yes, sorry about that."

I read his body language as he sat in the chair. He didn't seem sorry.

I said, "So, back to the story about why she pushed you."

"Well, she was telling me that she didn't want to sit by any N-words and that she didn't want to be in the same area as an N-word. I, of course, didn't agree with that, so I begged her to be quiet before they heard her and got upset. Susanna stood up to leave the buffet, I tried to get her to stop walking and to sit down with her food. She decided to push me away and keep walking."

"Look, Mr. Bingham, just say Black men or African Americans. Nobody wants to hear that word or an abbreviation for that word. At least not here."

"Sorry, force of habit... I grew up in different times."

"So did my dad, but he knows how to be appropriate."

Marvin said nothing. I exhaled and kept my composure.

I asked, "Did you push her back?"

"Oh, heavens no."

"It didn't make you angry that she made such racist comments and then proceeded to push you?"

"Of course it did, but I wasn't going to lay my hands on a woman."

Yeah, I'm sure you're a real fucking saint, pal.

"Probably a good choice on your part," I said aloud. "Are you injured at all?"

"No."

"Do you wish to press charges?"

"No, sir."

I took a second to write down his answers in my notebook. It's important as a cop to keep good notes.

"Susanna didn't say much, but what she did say interested me." I said, "She kept repeating the words, 'bad man' over and over."

"That's weird. I wonder who she's talking about?"

"Has she said that about you before?"

"No, never."

"I'm gonna be honest. I think she was talking about you, Mr. Bingham."

"And I'm going to be just as honest with you, Officer Lawson. She wasn't talking about me."

"It's a random thing for a woman with severe dementia to say."

Marvin clapped his hands and pointed a single finger at me, "Oh, I know! She was talking about the N-words—sorry, African Americans—sitting next to us. She has a real racism problem. It's really bad. I've been trying to get her out of that type of thinking, but you know some of those older generations like myself were raised differently."

I said nothing.

"I'm really sorry. I know what I told you is disturbing, and I take no pleasure in telling you about how she feels about African Americans. I can assure you that she's just a confused old woman who I need to get home and take care of. She was wrong for saying that, and I completely take responsibility for her."

"I appreciate that, and so do the guests at the casino."

"Of course. Is there anything else I can do to help the situation?"

"Just one more thing. I'm going to need you to wait with security while I go review surveillance coverage to make sure everything you guys are telling me is the truth. I'm sure you're being honest, but I need to do my due diligence."

"Totally understandable."

"Do you think you could help keep her racial slurs down while I finish my investigation?"

He chuckled. "Yeah, I think I can do that."

I rose and left Marvin in the medical bay room. I had Susanna wait in the room with Marvin, accompanied by casino security. I walked to the surveillance review room to see what was seen on video coverage.

I watched the footage but saw nothing wrong with Marvin's behavior. Susanna repeating the words "bad man" made me think something more was going on. The video didn't have any audio so I couldn't hear what was being said. Marvin and Susanna were at the buffet having dinner. Susanna got up to leave; Marvin jumped up to try to stop her. Susanna pushed by him, it seemed like the push took everything she had out of her. The interesting thing is that I didn't see anybody else around them. There wasn't a single Black man near them in the buffet area, so why did he make up that story? What was I missing here? What was he hiding?

I returned to the medical room and asked Marvin to wait outside the room with security. I sat down with Susanna once again and attempted to speak with her. I decided to try to make the most of my contact with her and waste as little time as possible. I pulled up a picture on my cell phone of the famous NBA Player

LeBron James. I showed Susanna the picture. I wanted to see if she would get angry or make a racist comment about LeBron James being a Black man. I wanted to see if Marvin had made up that entire story.

Susanna gazed at my phone and smiled. I read her face and she wasn't angry in the slightest.

"Susanna... What do you think of this picture?"

"Cute, very cute," she gushed.

I searched for another African American male on my phone. I typed Denzel Washington and clicked the first photo of him. I showed Susanna the picture, "How does this picture make you feel?"

"Ooh, also cute."

"You think he's cute?"

"Mmm hmm." She nodded.

Interesting, I thought to myself. The argument wasn't about Susanna being racist. It was about Marvin. Susanna seemed to find Black men very attractive. Maybe Marvin got jealous of her looking at an attractive Black man at the casino.

I thanked Susanna for her time and had her step out of the room to wait with security. I asked Marvin to sit down with me.

"Are we free to go yet, officer?" he asked impatiently as he sat on the stool.

"Why'd you tell me a fake story?" I shot back.

"I don't know what you're talking about."

"You told me that Susanna was being racist, and that's what led to her pushing you. That wasn't the case, though. I just showed her multiple pictures of Black men and it seemed to excite her. One could say she prefers Black men."

"Of course, she's not going to sit there and tell a cop she's racist... Shit, she can't even remember what day it is right now, fella. Can we go? I really need to get her to bed."

I had no legal cause to keep him against his will. I wore a body camera on my police-issued bulletproof exterior vest that recorded everything. I wanted to keep him there and figure out why

Susanna was calling Marvin the bad man. Unfortunately, I would have been committing a crime by holding Marvin against his will without legal justification. I would have preferred to beat a confession out of him, but I digress.

I informed him, "Yes, you can go, but I still want to know why you lied."

"I didn't lie, Mr. Lawson... She's very confused and needs to go to bed. I hope you can understand. Thank you and have a nice night."

Marvin let himself out of the room and walked over to Susanna who was waiting with casino security. Marvin held his arm out for her and she grabbed onto it. I stepped out of the medical room and saw them leaving together. He assisted her out the doors of the casino as she limped alongside him. I knew in my heart that I would be seeing them again. It was only a matter of time.

I ended my shift that night and got some sleep during the morning hours. I woke up in the afternoon and did my normal routine of physical training. During my off time, I was a full-time CrossFit athlete and a CrossFit coach part-time.

I warmed up my body with some bodyweight moves. Often I'd be in the gym, upside down against a wall performing handstand pushups, lightly touching my head to the floor, then pressing back up. Then I would work on my heavy lifting.

My training days were long: three- to four-hour days. But if I had to work, I only had time to train for an hour: weight-lifting, cardio, and gymnastics. Then I added martial arts disciplines such as Krav Maga, boxing, Muay Thai, and Brazilian Jiu-Jitsu. On days when I rested my body from the martial arts, I did two hours of firearms training, focusing on my pistol and an AR-15 rifle. My goal was to turn my body into a human weapon that could save lives. Each training session helped.

I finished up and returned home in time to make myself a protein shake. I sat on my couch in the living room area of my house: three bedrooms, two bathrooms, one story. I lived in the peaceful small city of Dallas.

While I sat on my couch, I gazed at my cell phone and found Ashley's name in my contact list. I felt like texting her. I wondered if I was texting her too soon after meeting her. *No, just text her,* I thought.

No, no, you just met her yesterday, you creep.

I sat there for a couple more minutes and contemplated sending a text, yet I didn't know what to say. I usually didn't have a problem with sending a text to a woman, but I wanted to get off on the right foot with Ashley. If she gave me her number, why would she give it to me and expect me not to contact her? What the hell. Might as well give it a shot, right? I typed.

> Hey, it was really nice meeting you yesterday. Are you working tonight?

I pressed the send button and waited. A few minutes later she texted back.

> Hey! Yeah, it was great meeting you, too. Julio is feeling much better if you were wondering :)

I wasn't wondering. The fucker tried to kill me with a knife. I thought about a reply for a second and then typed.

> Oh, good. I figured he was in safe hands with you, but I appreciate you telling me. Are you working tonight? I might have someone for you to check on if you get the time.

Yeah, I'm working tonight. When are you on?

> I'll be on duty in an hour—meet you at the police department?

Sounds good, see you in a bit.

———

I let Ashley know when I arrived at the police station. She and Cardwell were driving to Jericho Nation but were fifteen minutes away. I thanked her for coming out to take on a new case.

The police department building was state-of-the-art and well-kept. When they arrived, I led Ashley and Cardwell across the brown linoleum flooring in the entryway, down the white-walled hallways, to the break room, which had a table large enough to seat twelve people. The table, built by the Native Elders of Jericho Nation, was wooden, neatly polished, and had the Jericho Nation Tribal Police logo carved in the middle.

We had several black cushioned seats that were built for comfort and reclined back and forth. I sat down in the break room with Ashley and Cardwell. I offered them food or drinks, but they'd just had lunch.

"So, what's this new case you got for us, War?" inquired Cardwell.

"I'm not sure if it's anything other than a gut feeling I got... But I had this weird contact with a couple of people last night. Do the names Marvin Bingham and Susanna Holt sound familiar?"

They shook their heads.

"Like I said, it might be nothing, but I get this feeling that there's something off about Marvin... Let me tell you the whole story."

I switched roles from the police officer taking the report to the witness passing on information. Cardwell, being the cop, wrote down what I was saying as Ashley asked me the questions. I described the domestic disturbance call. I informed them about the weird story Marvin told me and why I believed it was false. I told them about Susanna saying "bad man" over and over.

"I don't think Marvin will talk to me anymore, at least not right away. Last night he cut off the conversation as soon as I started making inquiries. Maybe you guys could do a welfare check? In the process of doing that, we might learn more about Susanna's mental state. I get the feeling that Marvin has Susanna against her will somehow, but I have no evidence to prove that. I can feel it in my stomach that something is wrong... Does that sound crazy?"

"No, not in the slightest," Ashley said in a genuine caring tone. "We'll see what we can do."

"Thank you."

"Anytime. We'll update you after we visit her. We got other patients to attend to tonight, but we'll come back tomorrow and check on Susanna."

"Perfect."

I gave Ashley and Cardwell the home address for Susanna and Marvin, which I'd gotten off their ID cards the night before. They wrote down the address and said their goodbyes. If I had known back then what I was getting Ashley into... I would have never asked her to check on Susanna.

CHAPTER
ELEVEN

The cold rain spattered the pavement of the streets in downtown Portland. Marvin Bingham sat in his old green Ford pickup watching a nearby bar. The city lights lit up the street, and people were strolling along the sidewalks. Portland was the biggest city in Oregon; people were out almost all hours of the night.

There were buildings surrounding the area. Some bars still had Halloween-themed decorations left from a few days prior. Traffic lights flashed from red to yellow to green. Vehicles drove in both directions on the street at a slow pace. Marvin's truck was full of empty beer cans, food wrappers, and dirty clothing. He'd started living out of his vehicle a week ago. He'd spent all the money he got from Diana on booze and any other vices he could get his hands on. Marvin was broke, yet again.

It was around eleven o'clock when he spotted the most beautiful woman. She was in her early twenties and stepped out of a limousine outside of the bar. She had dark-tanned skin, and bleached blond hair, and wore a shiny, skin-tight black dress with dark blue high heels that all served to show off how fit she was. Marvin thought to himself, *There's a girl with money.*

When Diana died, he'd left Jericho Nation for Portland. Marvin had lived pretty well for a few years, but, as it always did, the money evaporated in time. Six years later, Marvin, now in his forties, was hanging out in a part of the city that was for the younger generation. It was a nice part of town, but there were lots of dark alleys in Portland. Several homeless camps... plenty of crime. It was easy to be a victim in a bigger city.

He watched the beautiful woman enter the bar and noted all the men on the sidewalk following her with their eyes. The limousine drove away and a few of her friends came outside the bar and greeted her. She strode with such confidence. Such grace. She was way out of Marvin's league. There'd be no charming her into giving him money. Especially in the shape he was in. He hadn't showered for a week and the stench of dried sweat and stale alcohol filled his truck.

Marvin had to do something to change his situation, but he didn't know what... There wasn't going to be a cancer-riddled woman waiting for him to come along. As he sat there, his hands started to shake. He needed a drink, and he needed it badly.

He felt sick. He turned the heat up in his pickup and checked the gas gauge. He had plenty of gas to keep the engine idling. *Steal something from the liquor store... No, I'll get shot... but I need it, I need it to live... I need to kill. No, I'll get caught and go to prison. Be smart, Marv.*

Marvin rocked back and forth in his seat and rode out the wave of chills. He'd been experiencing alcohol withdrawal for a few weeks. Marvin wanted to buy more alcohol, *enough medicine to help him sleep... That's all.*

His heart rate spiked when he heard a loud clacking on the side of his window. A man was standing outside the driver's side window. An older guy, around his age, big, poorly dressed, probably homeless. Marvin rolled down his window with the manual crank inside his door.

"You got any change, man?" the guy asked.

Marvin responded, "No, I don't got anything but this pickup."

"How 'bout ya give me that then?"

"I can't—"

Before Marvin knew what hit him, the man reached through the open window and punched him square in the nose. Marvin's head snapped backward and his nose split. The man unlocked the door and then opened it up. Marvin was dazed from the blow, blood pouring down his face.

"Get the fuck out, mother fucker."

The large man grabbed Marvin by the front of his clothing and chucked him out onto the cold pavement. Marvin landed hard. He scraped up his elbows trying to break his fall. The keys were in the ignition. The man stepped into the pickup and sped away.

Marvin lay on the slimy wet pavement with the winter rain falling on him. People were sauntering around on the sidewalk, but none of them came to his aid. It seemed they were used to seeing that type of stuff. Marvin forced himself up, staggered to his feet, and began walking northbound. He knew of a homeless camp nearby. He hoped he could find shelter there. Marvin didn't own a cell phone, so calling 9-1-1 wasn't an option. Not that the cops would care; they probably had other things to attend to that night.

He made his way across the city, seeing all types of people. The farther into the city he walked, the darker it got. Fewer city lights, less traffic, fewer people on the sidewalk. He picked out some tents set up under an overpass and walked over to them.

The camp looked like a campground you'd see out in more rural areas: tents all over the place, random campfires set up in trash cans. The only difference was that it was in the middle of the city. Marvin was surprised the police hadn't made them move yet. At that moment he didn't care, he needed somewhere warm to sleep for the night.

He didn't make it far into the camp before three guys noticed. They surrounded him about twenty-five yards into the camp. They were young, probably in their midtwenties, with yellowing teeth, injection marks up their arms, pale skin, and skinny frames. They shined bright flashlights into his face.

"Who the hell are you?" one asked.

Marvin looked around, noticing them take positions around him. Marvin put his hands up to shield his eyes from the lights. "Just a guy who needs a place to sleep."

"You a fuckin' cop?" a guy behind Marvin questioned.

Marvin scoffed, "No, I ain't no fuckin' cop. I don't mean for any trouble."

"The fuck you don't. The more people we let in here, the more heat we have from the po-po," the one directly in front of him said.

"Guys, please. All I need is a place to sleep and I'll be gone in the morning."

"There's a fee... pay the fee and you're good."

"I don't have anything."

"Then get the fuck out of here."

"Please... Let me stay."

The one in front of Marvin punched him square in the stomach. Marvin crumbled down to his knees with a groan. They kicked him a few times on the ground for good measure.

"You don't belong here. Get the hell out."

Marvin struggled to his feet and stumbled out of the homeless camp.

"Fucking warm welcome here," he spat as he hobbled back out to the city streets.

———

Marvin found a large metal green trash can in an alleyway between two large buildings. The buildings towered over him; one was a fancy restaurant of some sort. Marvin lay down beside the trash can, with dried blood on his face, his gut wrecked, and cold rain coming down nonstop. He closed his eyes. The rain was unbearable.

"It doesn't get any fuckin' worse than this," Marvin muttered to himself.

He hopped into the trash can and closed the black-colored lid.

The smell was awful, but he was warmer and out of the rain. He closed his eyes and covered his nose... Oh, how the mighty have fallen.

Marvin's dreams cursed him. First Sharon, then Diana, sometimes both of them would come for him in the middle of the night. Sharon and Diana made a promise that they would kill him ten times over in the afterlife. Marvin believed it. He believed that he'd wanted to help them... but maybe that just wasn't his true nature. Deep down, he knew his true nature wasn't good.

He told both Sharon and Diana that he loved them and would have cured them if he could. Marvin tried justifying the murders to himself. *I put them out of their misery.* But he knew he wanted to do it.

One of his recurring dreams was Sharon and Diana dragging him underwater in the ocean. They incarcerated him underwater, suffocating him in the ocean until he woke up. The only sure way to stop the dreams was to drink enough to put himself in a liquor-induced coma.

———

The next thing he knew, he woke to thumping on the lid of the garbage can. The daylight brightness speared his eyes, as someone opened the lid. It was morning. A restaurant employee was taking out the trash. Marvin put his hands up as a natural reaction to defend himself.

"I mean no harm."

"OK. You gotta go, man, or I'm calling the cops," the guy replied.

"No problem. I'm gone."

Marvin scrambled out of the trash can and wiped off the random trash liquids and foods that managed to get on him as he slept. He noticed the restaurant employee was covering his nose.

Marvin scanned the area. No one else was there, so he headed back out to the streets.

He spent the day walking around, looking at people. The city was busier during the day. Marvin made a cardboard sign that said, "Not gonna lie. Just need money for a beer."

Marvin stood at a stoplight that had vehicles driving in all directions, eastbound, westbound, northbound, and southbound. College kids found the sign funny and stopped to give him a couple of bucks because they liked the sign. One kid stopped and rolled down his window. He mirrored a surfer guy with his backward hat on, with young healthy skin and blond hair curling around the hat from the bottom.

"Nice sign, broski. Party on, man!" the surfer said as he held a twenty-dollar bill out the window while making a hang-loose sign with his other hand. Marvin took the money.

"Thank you."

The college kid drove off, blaring some upbeat Jack Johnson song loud enough for Marvin to hear it. The melody had a laid-back tone to it, and Marvin liked the sound of it even though he didn't know the musician. He listened to the song as the kid drove off and then it faded away.

He had a few bucks, so he trekked to the nearby liquor store and bought two forty-ounce Olde English bottles. Marvin went back out to the streetlight and begged for the next few hours. He made a couple hundred dollars that day. Enough for a hotel room and plenty of alcohol for the night.

Marvin knew that he couldn't keep begging for money. He started thinking about ways to get more money to rent out a place to live somewhere. He needed a get-rich-quick scheme... Marvin pondered ideas... It wasn't just the money. He realized he wanted to feel the power he felt at the end of Diana's life... *Maybe that pretty woman in the limousine will go back to that bar soon.*

CHAPTER
TWELVE

arvin hurried to the bar where he'd been the night before. It was nightfall again, frigid, but this time no rain. Marvin caught a glimpse of his breath in the cold chilled air. He started strolling down the street and finding spots to watch the bar every night. Marvin came multiple nights but never spotted the woman returning.

He rented a cheap hotel room and bought a change of clothes at a thrift store. He was able to get by begging on a street corner daily. But he couldn't get enough alcohol to get intoxicated enough to forget his dreams.

About a week went by, but Marvin kept coming back to the bar. By this time, he had a plan to get rich again, and possibly take care of some other needs. He'd taken to "dumpster diving" to find items of interest. One day he found a rusted old waterline pipe that had broken off. The broken end had a sharp metal edge from the break. The pipe was about three feet long, and he could handle it with one hand.

Marvin began carrying the pipe around for self-defense. He'd figured out he wasn't in Jericho Nation anymore, people weren't so friendly in the city. Marvin roamed around Portland with his weapon. He slept with the pipe in his hands every night. Whether it was in a hotel room, a dark alley, or a dumpster, he had it.

———

One weeknight Marvin was wandering the streets and went too far to get back to his room in the boarded-up motel. Crowds were minimal, and it was getting late. He was thinking a nice private dark alley with some cover should do the trick.

He walked from alley to alley. Some alleys were full of people sleeping on the pavement so he would move on. While he was creeping around, he spotted a parked dark green 1980s model Ford pickup. The truck was idling outside a shady-looking 24/7 gas station. No one was inside. Marvin stalked his old ride. His long-lost truck, sitting right in front of him. Unattended. His for the taking. But that sonofabitch had beat him up and stolen his truck — caused every bit of misery since. The itch to kill again suddenly became intolerable. Here was a guy that needed killing.

Holding the pipe, Marvin jogged to the pickup and glanced around. Marvin's gaze caught a glimpse inside the convenience store attached to the gas station.

Through the glass, he could see the large dark man who stole his car. He was talking to the employee working at the cash register. They seemed to be having a good conversation. Marvin knew he couldn't take on a man that big in a fair fight. He'd have to catch him by surprise.

There was one other person under the awning at the gas station, pumping gas into a car. Marvin watched for a second, waiting for the person to leave. He glanced back at the store and saw the large man laughing it up with the cashier employee. The car under the awning had a full tank of gas and moved along. Marvin jumped into the bed of the pickup. He laid down to remain out of sight and waited...

———

He rode in the pickup bed for about twenty minutes without the driver being any the wiser. The man who'd stolen his pickup was driving along through downtown Portland. Marvin wanted to peek his head up to see where they were, but he knew he couldn't.

The boom of the loud engine started to putter as the vehicle came to a stop. It felt like the vehicle was parked up against a sidewalk on the passenger side of the vehicle. He heard the driver's side door open and then close. The doors were old and creaked every time they were moved. He heard footsteps of the large man stepping on the pavement.

Next, Marvin overheard the man's loud voice talking to someone nearby. Marvin inched his head up to see. The large man's back was to him as he talked to a homeless guy that was leaning up against an old brick building. Marvin saw his window of opportunity and leaped out from the bed of the truck. Marvin landed on the passenger side of the pickup and crouched down to remain hidden.

"You got what I want?" the large man said.

Marvin briefly looked again, and it appeared that they were making some sort of transaction. The large man waited and the homeless guy gave him whatever money he had left. The large man handed off a clear plastic baggy with a crystalline substance inside of it. The homeless guy thanked the large man. He didn't reply and turned around to walk back to the pickup.

Marvin was waiting in the street with his weapon. He swung like an MLB player swinging for a home run, hitting the guy square in the stomach. The strike recoiled, and as the thief staggered back, Marvin smashed a second blow to his shin. The bone broke. Blood gushed from the back of his calf where the shattered bone broke through.

The man collapsed, screaming. Nobody was around except the homeless guy. Marvin loomed over his prone victim, then glanced at the homeless guy.

"Leave," Marvin said, panting.

He didn't have to ask twice. The homeless guy grabbed whatever he could and hurried away. Marvin looked around again. An empty street, with several abandoned buildings. A crappy-looking apartment complex nearby, but most of the lights were off. No witnesses.

The thief was going into shock, clutching his leg and staring. A fragment of white bone looked like a miniature spear poking through his skin.

"Holy fucking shit! What the fuck! Ahhh—WHAT THE FUCK!" he howled.

Marvin swung like a logger with an ax. The rusted metal pipe smashed into the thief's forehead. Quiet. Like a switch had been flipped, and the light went out. The large man collapsed, his head flopping against the asphalt. Blood spewed from his head and trickled down the pavement. *Dead.*

Marvin rummaged through the man's pockets and took his keys back. He found around six hundred dollars cash in the guy's wallet. Marvin pocketed the cash and sprinted to the driver's seat. He wrapped up the pipe with his coat and tossed it into the passenger seat, turned the engine over, and drove away.

It felt good to have his truck back.

CHAPTER
THIRTEEN

Marvin had cash and his pickup back. Things were looking up. He'd killed a big guy in cold blood in the middle of a Portland street. Shortly after he killed the man who stole his pickup, Marvin tossed his weapon into the Willamette River. It made a small splash.

Days went by.

Nothing happened.

Marvin was growing increasingly paranoid.

Someday they'll find me. He kept moving. The only thing he wanted more than alcohol was a gun. His "itch" was starting to outweigh even his need for alcohol.

Marvin spent his days trying to buy a weapon from someone in the street. He spoke to the homeless population, trying to get the name of someone who'd sell him a gun. Some guys gave him good information, others thought he was a cop and wouldn't talk to him. Marvin finally got a name: "Gator."

A homeless guy on the street told Marvin where to find Gator. Marvin gave the guy a twenty and hoped the information was solid.

———

It was a quick drive to Gator's hangout. It was daylight, which was good because Marvin didn't want to do this at night. Gator's hangout was on a street corner at a laundromat building he owned. Marvin was advised that Gator's laundromat was a front for his "real business."

Marvin entered the laundromat. Nothing about it was fancy. It was an average run-of-the-mill laundromat. Marvin strolled around for a bit, asking if anyone knew Gator. A young guy in a ratty denim jacket said he knew him and exited through a door at the back. Marvin sat down on a bench to wait.

Moments later, a heavyset guy with a crewcut approached and commanded Marvin to wait outside the laundromat on the sidewalk.

"Gator will be out shortly to meet you."

Marvin nodded and walked outside to wait. After a few minutes of waiting, Marvin started to second-guess his decision. He wasn't used to this world. Maybe he was in over his head. Maybe the information he got was bad. The sunset looked pretty, though. The laundromat was on the east side of the Willamette. He could see the sun sinking beyond the river and a city bridge.

"Who the fuck are you, white boy?" *Gator*.

"I was told you were the guy to go to for a weapon," Marvin replied.

"You heard wrong. Get lost."

Gator was a small, sharply dressed black man with a spark of charisma when he spoke. He was short and lean; his suit had a green gator skin print on it. Gator resembled an over-the-top Bond villain... Behind him were two guys that towered over both Gator and Marvin. Marvin guessed they were bodyguards.

"Look... I need an untraceable gun. A .22-caliber pistol if you got it... you'll never see me again."

Gator examined him and scoffed. Then his hand rubbed his chin as if he was pondering a great deduction. Marvin couldn't have been a cop. A cop wouldn't ask for such a piece-of-shit gun... Or maybe they would, you can't trust anyone in that business.

"Check him," Gator said to his bodyguards.

"I ain't wearing a wire."

"Fuck you. You want a weapon, you play by my rules."

The two bodyguards manhandled Marvin like he was a small toy. Their pats made Marvin grunt.

"No weapon or wire," one of them told Gator.

"You wanted for anything?" Gator asked.

Marvin replied, "Not yet."

"You get caught, you never met me. Got it?"

"Got it."

"Seriously. You get caught and squeal to someone. There won't be a place my people can't find you. Ya dig?"

"I don't plan on getting caught."

"That's what they all say. A'ight... hook him up." Gator said as he peered up at his bodyguards.

"How much for a .22?"

"Two hundred dollars... cash for the gun and a box of ammo."

Marvin pondered the deal... he still had about two hundred fifty bucks left from the night he stole his pickup back. Fifty bucks would hold him over until his next move.

"Deal," agreed Marvin.

The two large bodyguards led Marvin through the laundromat and to the back alley behind the business. Marvin stepped into the back seat of a minivan with the two large men. One of the large men dug through a cardboard box and pulled out a rusty ole .22-caliber, six-shot pistol. The other bodyguard kept his eyes fixed on Marvin. They gave him the gun and the ammo.

"Get lost," one of them commanded.

Marvin tucked the gun into the waistband of his dirty jeans and walked westbound down the back alley, toward the sunset.

———

Marvin bought a couple more forty-ounce Olde English alcoholic beverages. Then he drove back to the bar where he'd seen the pretty girl in the limousine. Marvin parked and sat in his vehicle about a hundred yards from the bar entrance. He had a plan. No emotional connections this time.

Nightfall was upon him before he knew it. Marvin drank the Olde English to kill time. He was starting to catch a buzz, listening to music on the radio. He wore a brown Carhartt jacket and gripped his loaded .22-caliber six-shooter pistol in the right jacket pocket. Marvin's eyes went from the bar entrance to his rearview mirrors to make sure nobody surprised him. He wasn't going to be ambushed a second time.

Marvin finished both bottles of Olde English and started on a new bottle of whiskey. It was a cold Friday night, but it was the weekend and everyone had come out to enjoy the nightlife. But Marvin was waiting for one person. That's all he wanted.

He'd been sitting for an hour when a black limousine pulled up. The same pretty, wealthy woman got out of the back seat. She looked just as great as before, wearing a light blue dress this time. The sight of her aroused Marvin. His itch to kill aroused him even more.

She bent over and talked through the driver's side window of the limousine. Whatever the driver was saying seemed to make her happy because she was smiling quite a bit. She finished up her conversation and entered the bar alone.

Marvin waited, sipping on his whiskey. He drank about half of the bottle in ninety minutes. Two hours passed, and he was about three-quarters done with the bottle. He was feeling good.

The black limousine returned and parked near the front entrance of the bar. Marvin watched from a distance. The wealthy woman came out of the bar and climbed into the back seat of the limousine. The tail lights brightened and then dimmed. The vehicle started moving forward. Marvin scooted his pickup off the curb and followed.

Marvin drove behind the limousine the best he could, his nerves firing on all cylinders. The limousine left the city of Portland and took an on-ramp exit to I-5. The I-5 freeway was a five-lane highway that ran north and south along the West Coast of the United States.

Marvin wondered if the limo driver had seen him yet, but assured himself he was being paranoid. He had one hand on the steering wheel, and the other hand around his bottle of whiskey. The limo exited at the city of Sherwood.

Sherwood was one of the wealthiest cities in Oregon. When he entered the city behind the limousine, his old pickup stuck out like a sore thumb. The cheapest house in the city probably cost five times the most expensive one in Jericho Nation. Every house was made of perfect bricks, with stone-paved paths through the yard. Every vehicle was in pristine condition; every yard was perfectly trimmed and green as a golf course fairway. Marvin guessed that not much crime happened in Sherwood.

They were driving through a residential neighborhood at around twenty-five miles per hour. Marvin checked his gas gauge and noticed he was nearing empty.

"So you're gonna kill her like you killed me, huh, Marv?" Sharon's voice crept up in his head.

"I didn't kill you..." Marvin cried. Sharon's voice in his head was guaranteed to make him choke up, still.

"But you did kill me, you son of a bitch!" This time, Diana's voice was screaming in his head.

"Leave me alone."

"You enjoyed killing me, just like you enjoyed killing that fucker who stole your truck."

"Quiet, Diana!"

"All that power... I bet you get hard on that shit. You're a worthless coward, Marvin Bingham!"

Marvin chugged more of his whiskey. Almost done with the bottle. A few drinks left.

"You're not real," said Marvin.

"At least you're being more straight up with this girl. Planning on killing her and taking her shit is more honest than you did with me. Coward."

"I'm not gonna kill her! I'm not a killer... I put you out of your misery!"

"You're a pussy. Take ownership."

"Fuck you, Diana!"

His father's voice crept into his head next: *"Disappointment. Coward."*

Marvin slurped the rest of his whiskey bottle. He drove in silence. The voices stopped. Marvin pictured drowning Sharon, Diana, and his father in the whiskey so they couldn't talk anymore. It felt good shutting them up. He would never admit to them that they were right.

Her home was on a steep hillside, overlooking the neighborhood. The house had glass windows all over and a nice wooden foundation. Her driveway was paved with cement. It was a steep hike to get up the hill and to her front yard, but Marvin imagined the view would be worth it from inside.

Marvin's heart began to race as he watched the limousine pull into the driveway. He pitched the empty bottle of whiskey into the back seat and went for his gun. Marvin got out of his vehicle and sprinted to the limousine.

He banged on the window with the butt end of the gun and then positioned it at the driver.

"Gimme all the fuckin' money you got, you sons of bitches!" Marvin slurred. He may have been more intoxicated than he thought.

The driver glanced at him, confused for a second, then terrified when he saw the barrel of the pistol. Marvin heard the woman shouting in the back, "Drive, drive, drive!"

The driver shifted the gear of the limousine into reverse and slammed his foot down on the accelerator pedal. The limousine shot backward out of the driveway and onto the street once again. The driver spun the wheel and positioned the vehicle to face the way in which it came. The limousine driver sped off down the road in a hurry.

Marvin stood, amazed for a second, confused by what happened. He did not expect them to run away while he had a gun pointed at the driver's face. Marvin contemplated to himself that he could probably let them get away. Then it occurred to him that they'd seen his face.

"Fuck!"

He scurried to his pickup and tore off after the limousine. It was about 150 yards ahead and he was gaining. Its body was long and black with chrome wheels. The driver had to slow as they approached a sharp turn.

The limousine propelled up over the curb of a sidewalk. The limo smashed up and over the curb, and back onto the roadway. It wiped out a garbage can on the sidewalk. Random garbage soared everywhere.

Marvin, tunnel vision locked on the limousine, also ran over the curb, hitting the same garbage can. The garbage can spun into another parked vehicle in the driveway of a residence. The car alarm went off, loud, repeating horn-honking sounds that echoed throughout the neighborhood.

The limousine picked up speed on a straight stretch of road. Marvin was able to get close enough to ram the limousine. He was driving ninety miles per hour in a twenty-five-mile-per-hour zone. Marvin inched closer to the limousine...

The truck bumped the back end of the limo once. Again, harder. No effect, other than denting up the back end of the limo.

A lefthand turn approached; the limousine started to turn, just as Marvin rammed the back driver's side tail light. The limousine spun out of control, made a 360-degree rotation, and smashed into a telephone pole.

The impact of the crash warped the limousine into the shape of a C around the pole. Marvin thought the crash might have killed both occupants. But as he stopped in the middle of the street, the woman forced open the back door and crawled out. Marvin saw his window of opportunity.

He charged over, just as she stood up. Blood dripped down her forehead. Marvin lunged at her, grabbed her by the throat, and held his gun with his other hand. He thrust her back into the crashed limousine and pointed the gun at her forehead.

"Give me all your fucking money!" shouted Marvin.

"OK, OK... please don't kill me," she begged.

"Give me your money and I won't."

Marvin heard police sirens. They were nearby and would be there in minutes.

"My purse is right here... can I grab it?" She pointed at the inside of the vehicle. "You can have whatever you want. Just please don't kill me."

"Yeah, fuckin' grab it, lady."

Marvin released his grip on her throat and waited for her to grab the purse. She had another plan. She grabbed the barrel of the pistol and swung it so it pointed down at the ground. With her other hand, she used the heel of her palm and struck Marvin in his already broken nose. She twisted his wrist around and yanked the gun from his hand.

Marvin collapsed and fell straight to the ground, groaning and grabbing for his busted nose. The wealthy woman directed the gun at him and stood over him.

"Fuck you, motherfucker!" she hollered.

"The one woman I try to rob knows fuckin' karate... Typical," Marvin muttered to himself. She'd taken him down so quickly, he didn't know what happened.

The police sirens were getting louder. They would be there any second. They were bound to have a rapid response to a wealthy neighborhood like this one. Marvin considered that it might be less stressful for him to go to jail. He'd have a nice warm bed every night, and three good solid meals provided daily. Going to jail might not be so bad. Then Marvin remembered that he wouldn't be allowed to drink in jail. He realized he would have to go through withdrawal again. He thought about the nightmares. Marvin worried he'd commit suicide if he couldn't shut out his nightmares. He wasn't going to jail, not tonight, not ever.

Marvin recovered just enough to start thinking of a way out. His pickup was about twenty yards southwest of where he was laying. A short sprint to the pickup and he could get away. Marvin glanced up and saw the woman still pointing the gun at him. But as the handsome limousine driver climbed out of the vehicle, she turned and gazed into his eyes. Marvin wondered if the driver was her boyfriend. Maybe that was why she always entered and left the bar alone.

He jumped to his feet and started scampering toward his pickup. He didn't look back; he just ran. He could hear the driver yelling, "Shoot him, shoot him!" Marvin hoped she wouldn't have the courage to shoot.

A gunshot rang out, and Marvin felt it whiz over his head. The second shot fired and this time it seemed closer, and to the left of his head. A third shot came, and the window of his pickup shattered in front of him. Only ten more yards to go. A fourth shot came, and he felt it graze his right shoulder. It felt like a warm knife through butter, it sliced open his skin. Marvin reached the pickup, swung open the door, and belly-flopped in.

He'd left it idling, so he hunched down and hit the gas. More windows imploded as the woman kept shooting. He sped off, driving while hunkered down, and got to a safe distance to where he could sit upright and drive. Upright, he saw a swarm of police cars dead ahead.

Marvin saw a road to his left. His tires screeched as he swung the steering wheel over. By sheer luck, the road fed directly to the I-5 freeway exit. Marvin sped up, driving northbound toward Portland. There was little traffic. He floored it, hitting one hundred miles per hour. The whole truck was shaking like a rocket ship exiting the atmosphere. Marvin glanced at his rearview mirror. Three police cars, spread across three lanes, driving side by side.

He anxiously looked at his gas gauge again. Nearly empty. Marvin focused on finding an exit. He hit the city limits and took the first exit. Marvin found the city of Portland exit and slowed down enough to take the on-ramp up toward the city. The police cars lined up in a single file line and followed.

The cops were relentless, but Marvin was hellbent on escape. He remembered the homeless camp that he tried to go to after his truck was stolen. They seemed to not like anyone. *They wouldn't be helpful if a pack of cops came...*

Marvin took the police on a zigzag chase through the city. A couple of Portland officers joined in the pursuit. Marvin found the homeless camp—about two hundred tents set up under a large overpass in the darkest part of the city. He sped up to a nearby curb, smashed into it, and came to an abrupt stop. The crash dented the exterior of the truck.

Marvin wanted to say goodbye to his trusted pickup that he fought so hard to get back, but there was no time. He bailed out and scampered into the homeless camp. The police sirens woke up the campers and their emergency lights blinded them as they got out of their tents to see what was going on.

Marvin came racing through the camp with the red and blue lights flashing behind him. Multiple cops leaped out of their police vehicles and pursued him on foot. Homeless people came out of the woodwork and charged the cops. They started hollering at the police officers, "Get the fuck out of here! You don't belong here!"

"Get out of our way!" the cops yelled back. "Or we will tase all of you!"

Marvin's plan was working. He was blending in with the homeless crowd. On the far side of the homeless camp, he darted toward some nearby buildings and found an empty alley. Marvin jogged down the first alleyway and then the next, running in between several tall buildings.

At last—a large green dumpster. Marvin stopped, panting, and glanced around. He was in the clear. He climbed into the dumpster and dove in. He burrowed under several large black plastic bags full of garbage.

Cops galloped past moments later. One stopped and lifted the lid of the dumpster—and looked down at him.

Marvin had never been more still in his entire life. The officer looked down for about twenty seconds. Marvin held his breath. His body quivered. He didn't know how long he could stay silent. His heart was pounding so loud he was sure the cop would hear it. He needed to gasp for air, but he couldn't.

Just when he thought his lungs would explode, the officer dropped the lid and ran after the others.

Marvin let out a long, shaky exhalation. He stayed in the dumpster and waited until it was daylight. Cops hunted him for hours, but he stayed put. Marvin didn't dare sleep because he was worried he would have a nightmare and be found thrashing in his sleep.

At last, the sun rose. Marvin poked his head out of the dumpster. Nobody around. The air was cold again. Every breeze cut right through him. Marvin started hiking.

———

Marvin trudged back toward I-5. He was worried a cop would see him, but the cops never saw his face. Maybe he was going to get away clean.

The pickup wasn't registered to him. Marvin had driven it for years but never registered it. It had several owners before it came to Marvin; he'd bought it in a backwoods deal while drinking beers with some friends years ago. The plates would lead the cops nowhere near him.

Marvin made his way out to the freeway and left the city. He hitchhiked for twenty miles with his arm extended out and his thumb up. Eventually, as fate would have it, a group of like-minded people stopped to give him a ride. Marvin got in the car and never looked back.

CHAPTER
FIFTEEN

Ashley wasn't quite sure what she was getting into with Susanna Holt. The day after Warren Lawson contacted her and Cardwell, she promised him they would check on her. Something about Warren made her trust him. She'd seen about everything humanity had to offer through her work. Ashley was a trauma therapist and a licensed marriage and family counselor. She'd seen some of the greatest, most accomplished people in the world. Ashley had also seen the worst of the worst, and people who were just okay.

She got nothing but good vibes from Warren, and that excited her. Ashley thought he was cute, sure. But most of all, he was genuine. She had dated a couple of cops before; they were some of the best people she knew. Ashley wasn't easily impressed anymore, yet she couldn't stop thinking about Warren's piercing blue eyes.

Cardwell and Ashley worked the swing shift hours, noon to ten p.m. Ashley liked to stay up late, so it worked for her. Although it made it hard for her to see her son, Kanten. Kanten was nine years old and lived part of the week with his dad and the other part of the week with her. Ashley too often found herself FaceTiming her son while she was in a patrol vehicle.

Ashley met up with Cardwell at the Kirk County Sheriff's Office. They shared the same patrol vehicle every shift. Cardwell would drive, and she sat in the front passenger seat. Kirk County wasn't a big county: most of it was rural, with a few small cities. A lot of their time was spent driving down long straight stretches of highway. Luckily, Jericho Nation had a pretty view. Open fields surrounded the area, with a brightly lit casino in the center of town and snow on the higher elevated hills in the distance.

"What do you think of this Susanna Holt thing? Think it's a legit concern?" Cardwell asked as he drove.

"I think Warren is the type of guy who wouldn't ask us for a favor unless he absolutely needed it."

"I agree. But... Is someone getting a crush on Lawson?"

"Please... I don't get crushes. He wishes I had a crush."

"You're a shitty liar, Ash."

"He has a crush on me I'm pretty sure."

Cardwell chuckled, "Of course, you'd say that."

"Because I'm awesome and everyone loves me?"

"Uh-huh... Yeah...Just be careful with that one."

"Careful? Why do you say that?"

"I've heard stories about him..."

"Such as?"

"I hear he can be a bit of a man whore is all."

"I'm not looking to marry the guy, I just met him. Calm down, Dad."

"So you like him?"

"I didn't say that."

"But you think he's hot, and that's why we're doing this favor, huh?"

Ashley scoffed. "I might think he's a little cute... but that's not why I want to check on Susanna. I believe he brought up some valid concerns."

Cardwell conceded after a noticeable sigh. "Yes, he did. Let's hope we can get to the bottom of it."

———

They arrived at Susanna and Marvin's residence in the tribal housing area of the Jericho Nation Reservation. Jericho Nation was one of the wealthiest reservations in Oregon. The casino had always made the tribe a lot of cash; the housing complexes were nice single-story homes. The Confederated Tribes of Jericho Nation also employed people to do lawn maintenance for the tribal housing area.

Ashley and Cardwell went to the front door of the residence. The two-bedroom, one-bath house was painted white; the front door was red with white trim. Cardwell knocked; Ashley waited behind him. Ashley didn't carry a gun because she wasn't a police officer. All she had to defend herself was a pocket knife and the bulletproof vest the sheriff's office provided her.

Cardwell waited for about thirty seconds and then knocked three more times with the knuckles of his fist.

"Who the hell is it?" Marvin's voice hollered from inside.

"Kirk County MCRT, we're here to talk. Nobody is in trouble," Cardwell assured him.

Ashley and Cardwell heard footsteps coming to the door. They took a step back from the front door and waited. Marvin cracked the door open two inches. Ashley and Cardwell only spotted half of Marvin's face peeking out. Marvin locked eyes with Cardwell for a moment, then glanced at the badge and gun.

"I never heard of Kirk County MCRT, what kinda outfit are you guys? You look like cops." Marvin said. He reeked of alcohol. Ashley and Cardwell could smell it from outside the house.

"He's a cop, and I'm a therapist," Ashley added. "My name is Ashley Bradford and if you'd be so kind... We would like to speak with Susanna."

Marvin glanced over at Ashley. "Why do you need a cop here to talk to Susanna?"

"He's my partner. We work together on cases, both of our talents combined usually produce the best outcome."

"Ah, I see... Well, Susanna's sleepin' you'll have to come by another time to talk to her. Do you guys have a card or something? I'll ask if she'd like to talk to you."

"To my understanding... Susanna doesn't have the most capable mind to make decisions like that. That would be up to you, would it not?"

Marvin's eyes squinted for a second, "Not to be rude, because I don't like to be rude to a lady... but how do you know that?"

"We were requested to come out here and check on her. We do mental health evaluations."

"She's getting all the help she needs from me," Marvin shot back. "I think it's time for you guys to leave now. Have a good day."

"Okay, however—"

Marvin closed the door and turned the knobs, locking the door. Ashley and Cardwell heard the deadbolt.

"I guess he doesn't want our cards anymore," Cardwell said.

Ashley stepped past Cardwell and knocked on the door, louder than Cardwell had before. She obnoxiously pounded the side of her balled-up fist into the door.

"Go away!" shouted Marvin.

"Please, Mr. Bingham, if we could just have a few more minutes of your time." Ashley pleaded. "I wanted to give you my card."

"Leave it at the door. Have a good day."

Ashley and Cardwell fished out their business cards out of the pocket of the tactical pants they were wearing. They slid the cards between the door and the frame, then reluctantly walked away.

———

Marvin stalked them from the kitchen window. The window was about five feet away from the front door. Cardwell and Ashley drove away from the home and he let out a sigh of relief.

Marvin started to wonder why a therapist and a cop randomly showed up at his house, the night after the cops were called on him at the casino. Marvin realized that Officer Warren Lawson must have called them to come out to his residence. He got the feeling that someone was hunting him.

CHAPTER
SIXTEEN

A few days later, Ashley and I both had a day off. I texted her and asked if she wanted to go out on a date with me. We decided to go out for dinner on Sunday night. I worked the night prior, woke up, got ready, and drove to her house to pick her up.

She lived close by, so it wasn't much of a drive. Ashley was renting out a residence on the other side of the town I lived in. Dallas was a small city, and it only took five or ten minutes to get from one side to the other. It was a few days before Christmas, so the city was decorated for the holiday. Most of the houses had Christmas lights up, and reindeer props in the front yard. It looked like a Charlie Brown Christmas movie.

I picked her up around seven p.m. I parked along a sidewalk near her home and got out of my beloved gray 2014 Dodge Challenger, my civilian vehicle. I was dressed in gray slacks, a light blue polo shirt, nice black dress shoes, and a leather jacket. I knocked on her door and she answered wearing a rose-colored dress that went down to her ankles, a white sweater over-the-top with a golden necklace around her neck. Her blond hair was down to her shoulders, it had been straightened and looked great. Her brown dark eyes were easy to gaze into, but I did my best to stay composed.

"Hey, there... You look incredible," I said.

"You're looking pretty sharp yourself."

"Thanks, I spent two hundred bucks for this look. I figured gym clothes wouldn't impress you much."

"Wait, are you being serious?"

I chuckled. "No, I was trying to be funny... First dates can be so uncomfortable, you know?"

"Just to be clear... this is a date?"

"Damn right, it's a date. You're gonna wanna marry me by the time the night is over."

"We'll see about that."

I led the way to my car and opened the passenger side door for her.

We drove into Salem, the capital: a place called "Rudy's Steakhouse." The steaks there were fantastic, and the place was fancy and shiny to look at. I insisted on a table in the back corner of the restaurant with my back to a wall. I never liked having my back to a door. I preferred to be able to see who was coming and going. It's something that's drilled into cops from day one.

Ashley and I sat at a booth that had black cushioned seats and an immaculate black marble table. The table was immaculately clean. The waiter came by with some menus and asked us what we wanted to drink. I ordered water; she ordered a glass of wine. The waiter told us he would be back to get our order after a few minutes.

"This place is nice," Ashley said. "I haven't been here before."

"Yeah, I love the steaks here."

"I bet I cook a better steak than anyone in this place."

I noticed her smile. "I'd like to test that theory."

"If your theory about me wanting to marry you after tonight is correct... You'll have plenty of steak dinners in your future."

Now I was grinning. "That sounds like a good deal to me."

"Why is it that cops always have to sit in the back corner?

Always with their backs to the walls and their eyes on the exits and entrances."

"It seems you've experienced this a time or two."

"Well, I work with cops a lot... And I have a couple of exes who were cops. They did the same thing. It's like... programmed into you guys."

"I suppose it is... I think once you've experienced a case or two of things going horribly wrong, you search for any way to control the outcome or situation. So you find yourself taking any preventive measure you can. Like keeping an eye on who's coming and going, for example."

The waiter came by with red wine and water. We told him we weren't ready to order yet. The waiter nodded and walked away. Ashley took a sip of her wine.

"You know... I've asked several cops the question that I just asked you... I don't think any of them answered it so... efficiently and... delicately as you did."

"I speak what comes to mind." (Not really. If I spoke my mind most people would think I was unhinged.)

"I noticed that," she said.

"Trust me, sometimes it's embarrassing what's going on in my head. So don't give me too much credit yet."

Ashley laughed. At least that was more honest than my previous statement.

Anyway, we took note of our menu and decided on an order. I helped her pick a meal. I noticed she was a little indecisive, which was okay because I was good at making decisions. The waiter came back, and we ordered our food. The waiter jotted down our order and walked away. I noticed a married couple enter the restaurant and get led to a table. The restaurant wasn't very busy; it was Sunday night and most people who could afford to eat there had work the next day.

"So, I paid a visit to your friends Marvin Bingham and Susanna Holt," said Ashley.

"How'd it go?"

"We didn't get far."

Ashley explained to me what happened. She told me that Marvin smelled like a brewery, and added that Marvin looked like he could barely take care of himself, let alone another person. Ashley found it suspicious that he wouldn't let them talk to Susanna.

I bet if I kicked Marvin's door down and punched him in the mouth he'd cooperate more.

Instead, I asked, "What was suspicious about it?"

"He said that she was sleeping, yet he was hollering at us through the door. If she was sleeping and he was worried about waking her up... Why would he be yelling?"

"Because he wasn't worried about it."

"Exactly. Which begs the next question."

"What's he hiding?"

"Yes, that's what Cardwell and I were thinking, too."

"I rattled him when I spoke to him at the casino a few nights ago... When I started to put the pressure on him, he left as soon as he knew he could."

"Same thing with me. He tried brushing me aside by saying he'd ask Susanna if she wanted to talk to me when she woke up... I brought up the fact that she probably doesn't have the mental capacity to do so. Basically saying that it was his decision to make. I didn't think it was out of line for me to say that, but it made him angry and he shut the door on us."

"He's doing something to that woman. Something bad... I can feel it. He's afraid we're going to find out what it is by asking these questions."

"I don't think you're wrong. Did he mention anything about her mental health?"

I thought for a minute.

"He said she had dementia, but nothing other than that. He said she says weird things when she drinks."

"I know you told me this already, but what was it she was saying? Verbatim."

"She just kept saying 'bad man... bad man,' or she would just say, 'bad,' over and over."

"You asked him about that?"

"I did, and he brushed it off, saying it was about the black men who sat next to them at the buffet."

"That's right, I remember you saying that... Did you ask her about that? Maybe she *is* a racist?"

"I showed her pictures of several black guys to see what her reaction was. She was obviously attracted to them. I told you and Cardwell that part at the station."

"Oh yeah, that's right. Hmmm... and it's weird that Susanna and Marvin are exes. Why would you go take care of your ex-wife? I wouldn't go take care of any of my exes."

"My thoughts exactly. I think it's because Susanna is tribal. Tribal Elders usually have a large sum of money in their savings with the tribe."

"So he's looking for a payday?"

"That's my guess. I have no proof of that though."

"That only leaves us with one answer as to who the bad man is."

I answered, "The bad man is her caretaker—Marvin Bingham."

CHAPTER
SEVENTEEN

The food came and Ashley and I agreed to stop talking about work for the night. But the case intrigued us both. I liked bouncing ideas back and forth with her—but it was also important for us to enjoy the night without involving our jobs.

Our food was delicious. I ordered a large juicy sirloin steak with some mashed potatoes and vegetables. We enjoyed our food and spoke about where we were both from and what landed us in the professions we were in. Ashley was from Newport, a coastal city in Oregon. She told me she was thirty-four years old, and that surprised me because she looked like she was in her twenties. Her hair was so healthy and blond, she looked like she was born in Sweden.

"I know you said no more talking about work stuff, but I have to ask something," Ashley said, as she took the last bite of her steak.

"Yeah, sure, ask away."

"Why didn't you shoot Julio the other day? I mean, not that I wanted you to, but he came at you with a knife. You could have killed him and would have been completely justified... when I talked to Cardwell about it, he said he would have shot him too."

Trust me, Ashley, I wanted to jam him in the throat with his own knife.

Instead, I said, "I guess I didn't see the need."

"Really? Because it seems like a crazy guy coming at me with a knife would be a situation where I'd be likely to fire in self-defense."

"I do everything I can to prevent that."

"That's very admirable."

"I don't think so."

"Why's that?" Ashley asked.

Because if you knew the real reason, you wouldn't have agreed to go on a date with me.

"No reason," I said.

"No, finish that thought. I wanna hear it."

Shit.

"Well, I get the feeling that you admire me for not shooting him because, in the end, it saved his life."

"Yeah, that's exactly how I feel. You saved that man's life when nine out of ten cops would have shot him in the head without a second thought."

"I didn't do it for him, Ashley... I did it for me. I did it for my family."

"What do you mean by that?"

I exhaled a deep breath and took a quick sip of water.

"Killing someone takes a toll on a person, but most of all it takes a toll on the people around you... I can't do that to my family. I already put them through enough by doing this damn job as long as I have. They shouldn't have to endure more."

Good save... Hey, the family part was true.

"So, killing someone doesn't sit right with you because you worry about what it will do to your loved ones?"

"Killing someone is much more than what they show in the movies or TV shows. It's about as high-stakes a decision as you can make in this lifetime. It will stick with you until the day you die. I train myself intensely, every day, to make sure I've done everything I can to prevent myself from ever having to take a life. It's never just the shooter and the victim who are involved in an officer-involved shooting. It's the families on both sides of it too."

Control your rage or it will end you, my dad once said.

"You really believe that, don't you? That's not some line you practice to get laid is it?" Ashley inquired.

"Cops have to have honor. If this job is done right, there is nothing more honorable."

I'm still working on the honor part, but none of us are perfect, right?

"Except for being a therapist. That's probably more honorable and heroic."

I laughed. "Definitely. Cops are overrated."

"I've been known to be very strong and brave. That's what they say about me at work."

"I'm sure they do."

The waiter came back. I got the check, and we headed to the car.

"Do you have to be up early tomorrow?" wondered Ashley.

"No, I don't. You?" I replied.

"Nope. Mind if I come over to your house? I need a little more convincing on the whole marriage thing."

"By all means, allow me to continue making my case."

———

I drove us back to my house and showed her around. I wasn't in love with this girl by any means, but I was definitely intrigued. My house was a classic bachelor pad. I had posters of Jessica Simpson as Daisy Duke from the "Dukes of Hazzard" movie on my living room wall.

"Good ole Jessica, looking good as always," Ashley quipped.

Ashley walked around the house, and my cat, Rocket, greeted her in the living room. Rocket rubbed up against her legs, and Ashley knelt to pet her. Rocket let Ashley scratch her ears and started purring.

"Your cat seems to love me," she said.

"She's a sweet cat."

"I gotta say, I would have pegged you for a dog person."

"If I had more time in a day, I'd probably have a dog instead of a cat."

"Cats are easier to take care of."

We played Jenga for a while. I set up the pieces on a coffee table in my living room. We sat on opposite sides of the table, anxiously pulling a piece off the tower, hoping we wouldn't be the ones that lost. We played a few games of that, she won a few, I won a few—an even split.

We grew tired of that and decided to start playing songs on the speaker of my flat-screen fifty-inch TV. She picked a song called "Shelter" by Ben Nichols. The song had a pleasant melody to it, and I asked her to dance. She accepted the offer.

Ashley and I slow-danced in my living room to the slow beat. Her head rested on my chest. My hand gently held hers, my other hand rested on her lower back. Her hands were soft. We stepped side to side as I listened to the lyrics. All I wanted to do was keep her close.

Romance has never been my thing. This moment was so romantic, I should have puked like a teenage girl suffering an exorcism. Yet, that didn't happen. That's a good thing, right?

The song neared the end, and we stared each other in the eye. It was the moment we both knew we were screwed. This was much more than a one-night stand. I leaned in and kissed her on the lips. She grabbed the back of my head and kissed me back.

———

Ashley stayed the night, and we fell asleep cuddling. We woke up around nine the next morning. Ashley had to go see her kid, Kanten, who was in Newport with his dad. She had high praise for her kid, her pride and joy. The excitement in her voice showed she meant it. I put some clothes on and gave her a ride back to her house in Dallas. When I dropped her off, she leaned across the passenger seat and gave me a goodbye kiss.

"Have a good rest of your days off," Ashley said.

"Have a great time with your kid, he sounds awesome."

"He is... See you around."

"See you."

I was not used to being up at that hour; I usually slept till the early afternoon. I drove home, went back to bed, and fell asleep.

CHAPTER
EIGHTEEN

"*A*unt *Susanna isn't doing very well.*" Camille would never forget that phone call from her sister years ago.

Camille Sherwood, the thirty-year-old niece of Susanna Holt, was Native American and proud of it. Her Aunt Susanna had babysat her when she was young. Camille had light brown skin, black hair, and brown eyes. She was a recovering alcoholic and drug addict. Camille had learned in her twenties that her addiction was taking years off her life, so she decided to get clean.

She lived on the Indian Reservation in the town of Siletz, Oregon. The Siletz Indian Reservation was different from the Jericho Nation Reservation. Some people believed Siletz was crime-ridden, others loved it there. Camille didn't think much of Siletz, but the cost of housing was cheap. Her family had suffered a lot of harsh times there, but it was home. For better or for worse.

Camille traveled to Jericho Nation to see Susanna. Her cousin informed Camille that her Aunt Susanna was not feeling well. Camille's cousin told her that Susanna's caretaker, Marvin, was not allowing people to see Susanna.

This raised questions for Camille: what gave Marvin the right to shut out Susanna's family? Camille had the same problem the last time she tried to visit Susanna. She decided to pay her Aunt Susanna a visit—no matter what this Marvin guy said.

Camille strolled up to Marvin and Susanna's residence and knocked on the front door. It was early afternoon; yet another cold December day. Camille felt a shiver down her spine as she waited for Marvin to answer the door. She had a perfectly wrapped Christmas gift.

Marvin answered the door. Camille heard the latch unlock and spied the doorknob twist. Marvin swung the door open.

"Help you?" Marvin muttered in a tone that did not suggest he wanted to help anyone.

"Hey... I have a gift for my aunt that I would like to give to her."

Marvin snatched the gift and examined it for a few seconds. "What'd ya get her?"

"It's a Christmas ornament I made... She made me one when I was ten, and ever since we try to make each other an ornament every Christmas. It's sorta our little tradition."

"Ah, how sweet," Marvin said blandly. "I wish you woulda called before you came. Susanna's sleeping right now and I don't want to wake her. She needs her sleep."

"This will only take a second."

"Sorry, no can do."

"I don't think you understand. I'm only here for the day to see her."

"Sorry about your luck."

Camille tried to keep her expression neutral, but her teeth started to grind.

"Look, Marvin. Let me see if she's okay."

"'If she's okay?' What do you mean by that? Of course, she's okay."

"If she's okay, why couldn't my cousin come to see her yesterday?"

"Because I had to take Susanna to the doctor for a checkup."

"Uh-huh, and how about after that? When you got back and my cousin asked again?"

"I don't got time for this. Please leave before I call the cops."

"Call the cops? On me? For what? Trying to check on my aunt who you have been hiding from our family?"

"I'm not hiding her, Camille, I'm taking care of her."

"Yeah, how so?"

Marvin ignored Camille and started to shut the door. Camille stuck her hand out and impeded the door from shutting with the palm of her hand. Camille wasn't a big lady, but she wasn't small either. She was short and round, like a human bowling ball.

"Let go of my door," Marvin said.

"Not till you let me see my aunt."

Marvin cowered behind the door and started to push against Camille. Camille put both of her palms on the door and stood her ground. They were at a standstill as a game of tug of war with the door ensued.

Suddenly, Camille was falling face-first into the house onto the wooden floor. Marvin stepped back and let the momentum take her into a fall, as he opened a door to a nearby closet and grabbed a shotgun. Marvin cocked the hammer back, loading a round into the chamber.

Camille glanced up at him from the floor. Her face turned pale as she saw the shotgun sighted on her. One squeeze of the trigger and her head would be completely removed from her torso.

"If you don't leave, I'm within my rights to shoot you here and now. This is your last fucking chance."

Camille pushed herself off the floor and slowly backed out. She felt her feet touch down on the asphalt walkway outside the house.

"I don't know why she ever trusted you. I always knew there was something wrong with you... We know you aren't here as a good Samaritan taking care of your ex-wife. We remember how you treated Aunt Susanna when you were married to her," Camille said as she backed away. "This isn't over."

"Well, if you send any more family down here, you can tell them they can talk to the barrel of my shotgun. Get lost, bitch."

"I'll be sure to let my brothers know you said that."

Marvin's face turned ashen. Camille deduced he hadn't realized they had been released from prison. He lowered his shotgun. Camille spotted her gift lying in the hallway, about five feet behind Marvin.

"Be sure to get the gift to her," she said, glaring at him before she walked away.

Marvin shut the door and watched her leave from the kitchen window.

———

Camille halted at the nearest stop sign and made a call on her cell phone. She could still see Susanna and Marvin's house in her rearview mirror. The phone rang once. Anakin, her brother, answered.

"What's up, sis?" Loud rap music was playing in the background.

"I need you and Mato to come to Jericho Nation. Aunt Susanna is in trouble."

"We'll be there ASAP."

SILETZ, OREGON

Anakin and Mato were having a daytime house party when Camille called. After Camille told Anakin that their Aunt Susanna might be in trouble, the needs of the gang took a back seat. Anakin had his girlfriend sitting on his lap when he took the call; he told her to get up so he could locate his brother.

Mato was smoking a cigar with a friend in the backyard. It was a frosty, sleet-filled, rainy day—thirty degrees, but for some reason, the rain would not turn into snow. The cold wet air made it seem even colder than it was.

"What's up, bro?" Mato asked in his usual deep, monotone voice.

"We need to make a trip to Jericho Nation."

"Camille found trouble down there today?"

"Yeah, that white man we never liked is taking care of Aunt Susanna. Camille says something is wrong."

"What's wrong?"

"Don't know yet, but she wouldn't ask us to come out if there was no issue."

"True."

"When was the last time you saw Aunt Susanna? Seems like she fell off the face of the earth about three years ago. We used to see her all the time."

"Yeah, she started having those health issues..."

"We owe it to her to find out what that piece-of-shit white man is doing to her."

"I agree. I'll pack a bag tonight."

Anakin nodded to his brother. Their friend, dressed in the same red-colored clothing as Mato and Anakin, added, "We got your back on this one, cuz. Any white man messing with family gets fucked up!"

"Hell yeah, they do," answered Anakin.

CHAPTER
TWENTY

After my night with Ashley, I decided to call the Tribal In-Home Nursing Department. Susanna was trying to tell me something was wrong but didn't have the mental capacity to do so. The way I saw it, it was my duty to find out what exactly she was trying to inform me.

I was in the parking lot of a Walmart, about ready to do some last-minute Christmas shopping. It was two days before Christmas and I needed to get my newest niece, Laurel, a gift. I sat in the driver's seat of my Dodge Challenger with the engine off, listening to rain pound against the hood of the car. I noticed people jogging through the parking lot with shopping carts and then quickly unloading bags into their cars.

A few rings later and the in-home nursing office answered.

"Hello?" a lady's voice answered.

"Hi, this is Officer Lawson with the Jericho Nation Tribal Police Department. How are you today?"

"Oh, hey there, what can I do for you, Officer?"

I explained to the lady that I was inquiring about a caretaker at the tribe named Marvin Bingham, who was taking care of Susanna Holt. They advised me that there were no records of Marvin taking care of Susanna in any official capacity. I asked if Susanna had a listed caretaker. The woman on the phone then advised me that Marvin had signed himself off as her caretaker. Marvin did that because Susanna didn't have the mental capacity to request one.

"Wait, how does that work? He can just make himself her listed caretaker? Just like that?" I questioned.

"Well, yes. You see, Susanna has a serious case of dementia... To the point where she can't remember much of anything. She remembers things from when she was younger, but the past five or so years are a blur. Marvin, being her spouse, answered our questions, and led to us not having any major concerns with him being her caretaker. Marvin also works here at the tribe and we all trust him."

"Ex-Spouse. Marvin is Susanna's ex-spouse," I said.

"Yeah, but they had gotten back together just before Susanna had a mental breakdown... It's very sad."

I asked the in-home nurse when Susanna had the mental breakdown. Around a year ago. I suggested that they should check on Susanna. The nurse insisted they had no concerns that required an in-home visit from their department. I inquired if Susanna was a patient of their in-home nursing program.

"No, we have no records of Susanna being a part of our program."

They seemed to know a lot about her and Marvin, I noted. I moved on. "What if an officer was requesting that you go there and physically check Susanna's health? Would that help?"

"Yes, I suppose it would, but you would have to come here and fill out our forms first."

"Okay, the only problem is that I'm not on duty until tomorrow. I'd like this done as soon as possible."

"I see... Is there a specific reason you're concerned? If so, why is it that you can't handle this yourself?"

"Well, I have to have a thing called probable cause to enter a house without permission of the homeowner. Let's just say I had contact with Marvin recently and he was less than helpful.

Susanna said some things that raised my suspicions and I want to make sure I'm following up on that."

"I understand, but you have to know that Susanna does say things that don't make sense. Most of us take what she says with a grain of salt."

"I'm sure you do. However, if you could do this, it would be incredibly helpful in closing my investigation."

"Okay, come on over and we'll get this started. We'll be off for the holiday until New Year's, so you'll have to come today."

Shit. There *was* no way I could skip getting my niece her Christmas gift. Olivia would have my balls in a vice.

I said, "What if I send an officer over there to do it on my behalf?"

"That should work."

"Great, thank you."

I hung up, scrolled through the contact list, and tapped Takoda Tehama. I hit the call button for my best friend and partner and listened to it ring. No answer.

I waited for a little bit longer, listening to the rain hit the rooftop of my car. The sound reminded me of the times I spent with my father. We'd listen to the rain hit the tin roof of our barn when I was ten. We'd feed our cows and then listen to the calming sound of the rain and drink soda.

My phone's ringtone sounded, interrupting my memory. It should be noted that I had the best ringtone ever. The lyrics of AC/DC's "Thunderstruck" started blaring out of my phone. I listened to the sweet guitar solo for a few seconds and then answered, "What's up, my brother from another mother?"

"Oh, just staying busy, training up the new guys," Takoda replied.

"Saving the community, I assume."

"Most definitely."

"That's good, I think I'll take another day off since the community is saved and no longer needs me," I quipped. "How's the new guy doing?"

Takoda was training a brand new officer for our department. His name was Clinton Horner. We called him Clint for short, and he was eager to learn how to become a better cop. Takoda spent most of his time with Clint. Takoda was aiming to train Clint to be ready to be a solo police officer by next month.

"New guy is doing all right, still has lots to learn," Takoda answered. "So what do I owe the pleasure of a phone call from the legendary Warren Lawson?"

"Legendary?"

"Yeah, I was just telling Clint the legend of Captain America. A.K.A.-Warren Lawson."

I dismissed his smart-ass remark with an eye roll. "Whatever... I need a favor."

"Sure, what is it?"

I explained to Takoda that I needed him to go to the in-home nursing department and request them to go check on Susanna Holt. I filled Takoda in, especially about how weird it was that Marvin wouldn't let Ashley see Susanna.

"Yeah, that's weird. What do you think he's doing to her?"

"I don't know, but according to Susanna, it's bad."

"I'll see what we can do and keep you updated."

"If you get the time, can you do some research on this Marvin Bingham guy? See if you can find some dirt."

"Will do."

"Thanks, man, be safe."

I clicked off and glanced outside once more. It would be nice if it didn't rain every day in Oregon. A bit of snow would be a change of pace. I was wearing a light hoodie with a leather jacket over-the-top and some jeans. I flung the hood over my head, got out of my car, and headed into the Walmart along with the rest of the crowd of Christmas shoppers.

———

They sent three in-home nurses to the Marvin Bingham/Susanna Holt residence, including a supervisor named Monica Hawke. Monica had worked for fifteen years and was in her midfifties. The second was another woman the same age as Monica, and her name was Lydia Bishop. She just happened to be one of Warren Lawson's cousins. The third was a young woman who had recently graduated from college and was a new employee. Her name was Justine King. Monica led them to the door and knocked as politely as she could. The knocks were soundless; Lydia and Justine barely heard them, standing right next to Monica.

"Looks like nobody is home. Our job is done here," said Monica.

Lydia and Justine exchanged a look.

"Are you sure? Maybe we should knock louder," Justine offered.

"We got other patients to take care of. This was just a wild goose chase for the police department anyway."

Monica trotted back to their government vehicle. Justine shook her head and then reluctantly followed Monica. Lydia stood there and stared at the door long enough for it to be noticeable.

"Lydia! Let's go. Other patients need us now," Monica hollered from the car.

It didn't sit right with Lydia, but it wasn't her job to figure that out. Lydia went back to the car, and they drove off to the next patient of the day. But she didn't forget about Susanna Holt.

It was three o'clock in the afternoon when the nurses came to Marvin's door. Marvin did not like the nonstop attention the house was getting. He usually hadn't had to deal with this issue before. Marvin believed he had a handle on his needs, *his itch*. Marvin's weakness was the get-rich-quick schemes. He usually picked targets who had money. He saw people as an investment. People in declining health.

He waited for the in-home nurses to leave. Marvin strode down the wooden flooring of the house, with the white-painted walls. On the walls of the hallway were framed moments frozen in time. There was a photo of Marvin and Susanna together in the year 2005. The year that Marvin decided to momentarily quit his old ways. After his close call in Portland a few years before, he'd been looking for a different type of life.

Marvin sauntered down the hallway of the house, savoring the moment as he came to a half-open bedroom door. Marvin winced at the overwhelming odor of urine, feces, and rotting flesh. He looked in and caught sight of Susanna laying on her back, staring at him. She groaned, trying to get his attention.

The bed was stained, and her clothes hadn't been washed for weeks. The stench was worse than a dumpsite.

Marvin intently gazed at Susanna. "Close your eyes and get some sleep... Sweet dreams, darling."

Susanna squirmed under the sheets of her bed, trying to get up. Marvin grinned, closed the door, and strolled back to the living room.

Takoda called me with important information at the end of his shift, at around six p.m. I was at home wrapping gifts like a champ. Actually, I never wrapped gifts, I always bought gift bags. My family knew which gifts were from me because they would never be wrapped.

Takoda notified me that the in-home nurses went to the house to check on Susanna, but nobody was home.

"Bullshit," I blurted. "Where the hell is he taking Susanna around three p.m.?"

"Definitely not to the doctor. I checked with some local hospitals in the area. After you described the mental health issues she was having at the casino, I figured she saw a doctor regularly. Or at least should be. I learned that Susanna goes to McMinnville County Hospital, but has missed her last two appointments."

"Hmm, interesting. He can go out gambling at the casino with her, but not for a hospital checkup? I saw Susanna at the casino a few days ago, and now Marvin hasn't let anyone in the house and hasn't gone anywhere since then. He's hiding her."

"Correct, my friend. I did some more research on my handy dandy computer for you."

Takoda was a wizard on a computer. The guy could find any piece of information on the internet. I was never into technology or computers, so other than using Microsoft Word for the occasional police report, I was useless when it came to technology.

"Why am I not surprised that you found dirt on this guy? What'd you find?"

"Well, he has a very suspicious history when it comes to his former lovers," replied Takoda.

Takoda proceeded to tell me the history of Marvin Bingham and the former loves of his life. Takoda advised me how there were two cases in Jericho Nation where one of his girlfriends died by falling on a rock. The other girlfriend drowned in a bathtub. Both cases were cleared by the Kirk County Medical Examiner as accidental deaths.

"How much do you wanna bet that Marvin profited from their deaths somehow," I commented.

"That, or he's a serial killer. Maybe he kills these women and stages them to look different. About 90 percent of homicide cases are related to domestic violence."

"A serial killer, Takoda? This isn't L.A. Marvin is no serial killer. I looked him in the eye. He's a pussy."

"Your point being what exactly? Most serial killers are exactly what you just described. They're little weasels who prey on the weak to feel powerful."

"True, but if he was a serial killer, we'd have had a lot more suspicious death cases than what you dug up on the internet."

"Yeah, I would have found more, that's for sure. So you think the motive was money-related?"

"Has to be. The fact that he's back with Susanna after she divorced him years ago makes me think it's related to money. Susanna is tribal and we all know how much money tribal elders get from their trust funds in Jericho Nation. I think he's getting in her good graces so he can get that money when she dies."

"Good point. I'll do some research from home and see if I can find anything that connects with Marvin getting money from his ex-girlfriends."

"Thanks, brother."

"Anytime."

———

Meanwhile, Anakin and Mato were entering Jericho Nation on the state highway. They glanced over and saw the bright lights of the casino to their right. To their left were trees and green grass as far as the eye could see, the sunset was straight ahead of them as they were driving west toward the coast. Behind them was a van full of Indian Power Organization members, ready to pay Marvin a visit.

The next day, I drove to the McMinnville County Hospital first thing. Takoda had learned Susanna's doctor's name: Henry Perez. I wanted to see what the doctor thought of Susanna's health.

The hospital was small, which made sense because McMinnville was a city of around thirty-two thousand people. I went to the reception desk and talked to a woman in green scrubs. She saw my police uniform and took notice.

"What brings you here, officer?"

"I'm looking for Dr. Henry Perez; is he here?"

"He certainly is; he might be busy at the moment. Would you like to speak with him?"

"I would, as soon as he can, please. And thank you."

"Of course. I'll go let him know."

The lady sauntered off to find the good doctor. I bided my time and observed pictures on the wall of the staff working with children and pictures of employees with kids on a field trip to the hospital. The kids were no older than nine or ten years old. I noticed some pictures of kids dressed in Halloween costumes and doctors giving them candy. This hospital seemed more relaxed than most.

A few minutes later, a fit, youngish man with dark brown skin came to the desk and extended his hand. "Hi, I'm Dr. Perez. What can I do for you?"

"I was wondering if I could have a moment of your time. I need to ask some questions about a case I'm working on. Is there a place we could talk?"

"Yes, of course. Let's go to my office."

Perez was a handsome guy a couple of inches shorter than me. He had black hair with some expensive hair products in it. His teeth were immaculate; it was like they shone when he smiled.

I followed him down a hallway and toward a brown door with a silver metal doorknob on it. The door had a plaque that said, HENRY PEREZ, M.D.

Perez swiped a scan card on a black device near the door. Its solid red light turned green after he scanned the card.

Perez shut the door behind us. I glanced around the room. He had pictures of himself all over, as well as several diplomas and academic accomplishments framed and hung on the walls. There were photos of him on the Las Vegas strip with a few big-breasted, barely dressed women. There were some pictures of him on the University of Oregon swim team. I also noticed some trophies he won while on the swim team.

He walked around his large, gray, U-shaped desk that had three levels of file drawers. In the center of the desk was a black padded chair with wheels on the bottom and armrests on both sides.

I sat in the less comfortable chair on the outside of the desk, closest to the door. The chair was a metal folding chair. Apparently, this guy didn't care about people being comfortable while visiting his office.

"All right, Officer, you have my undivided attention. Ask your questions."

"I'll be quick. I'm here about one of your patients: Susanna Holt. She had an appointment scheduled with you earlier this week, but she missed it. Her caretaker is Marvin Bingham."

"Ah, yes! Marvin... He's a great guy, I really enjoy him. Is everything all right? I hope Susanna is doing okay."

"Yeah, Susanna is fine. I was wondering what your thoughts are on her health."

"Hmm... Well, nothing sticks out off the top of my head."

"Is there any way you could check her files? I can't discuss details of the case, but I think Susanna's life may be in danger."

"Uh, yeah, sure. Let me get them."

Perez opened one of the drawers to his desk and skimmed over several documents. He found the one he was looking for and dug out a manila folder with several stacks of paper inside. Doctor Perez flopped the item on his desk and opened it up. He rifled through the paperwork and eventually fished out the Susanna Holt documentation.

"Oh! Here it is... Looks like she has diabetes, and Marvin has been managing her insulin for her. The main issue it looks like is that she has severe dementia and years of alcoholism. Her liver appears to be in a state of disrepair, but still manageable. Overall, she is managing with the help of Marvin."

"Would you mind if I took a look at those?" I asked as I pointed at the paperwork.

"Usually we would need a subpoena for that..."

"Come on, Doc. I don't need to seize anything, I just need to look at a few things, to see if anything might be evidentiary. If I see anything like that, I'll stop reading and hand them back. Then I will come back with your subpoena."

"I don't know... I could get in big trouble for releasing patient information."

"I know, and I promise you I will not betray your trust. You have my word."

Perez contemplated it for a second. He scratched his short black beard.

"Well, if you were to look at them as I went to the bathroom, I suppose there would be nothing I could do to stop you. Legally speaking, that is."

"You feel a bathroom break coming on, Doctor?"

"I certainly am... I'll be back in, uh... Let's say fifteen minutes. Then we can continue this discussion."

"Sounds good to me."

Doctor Perez excused himself from the office. As he opened the door to the hallway, I could hear the indistinct chatter of people in several hospital beds. The door closed, and the room went quiet again.

CHAPTER

TWENTY-THREE

There were pages and pages of key documentation to sort through. Half of it I didn't quite understand due to my lack of knowledge in the medical field. I snapped some quick photographs of the documents on my phone. If I had photos of the documents, I could show a medical professional and see what they thought of Susanna's health evaluations.

I found a section that showed Susanna's weigh-ins. They weighed her each time she made an appointment. I noticed that Susanna had lost about ten pounds since September 2019. I was no doctor, but I knew that a person with diabetes shouldn't be losing weight. Although the doctor's notes stated that he was not yet concerned about it.

The last weight he had documented for her was about two months prior: Susanna was five foot two and weighed 140 pounds.

I recalled seeing Susanna at the casino only a few days before my visit with Dr. Perez. She was not weighing 140 pounds. I couldn't know for sure what her exact weight was, but she had to have been under 120. Which means she would have lost twenty pounds in a two-month time frame. I made sure to write that down in my notebook so I'd remember to ask about it with a medical professional later.

The documents said Susanna was a patient for the Jericho Nation Tribal In-Home Nursing Program. *Wait a minute... that lady on the phone told me that Susanna was never in the Tribal In-Home Nursing Program.*

Perez didn't have all the notes on what the in-home nursing program did for Susanna. However, it did mention that Perez was in constant contact with the shift supervisor, Monica Hawke. Perez had noted that he contacted Hawke, and she said Susanna did not need any medical care from a doctor. Monica had formed the opinion that Marvin was doing a good job taking care of Susanna. It also stated that Marvin was going above and beyond by taking Susanna to her nurse's appointments at the tribe and then going to her doctor in McMinnville.

The document I was looking at made it seem like Marvin was the caretaker of the year. Another annoying thought I had was the fact that everyone I talked to in the medical field seemed to love Marvin. There was something not right about the guy, yet all these nurses and doctors seemed to love him. He wouldn't impress them much if they saw him getting drunk at the casino with the woman he claims to be taking care of.

I glanced over the documents regarding Monica Hawke. She was working with Dr. Caroline Wilson, who worked for the medical clinic of the Confederated Tribes of Jericho Nation. It seemed that Wilson was telling Hawke to contact and inform Doctor Perez of the information on Susanna's health. Wilson was clearly the one calling the shots in Jericho Nation. I took more photographs and continued flipping through the pages.

While I read the documents, I wondered if I was being a paranoid police officer. Or was I right? If I was right... *Why does it seem like none of these doctors or nurses cared to check Susanna's health? Why was it like pulling teeth to get some cooperation from the nurses in Jericho Nation?*

A knock at the door interrupted my thoughts. Perez. I heard the scan card at the door with the sound of beeping approval. I relocated away from the documents and sat back on the metal folding chair across from the desk.

He entered the room with a cup of steaming coffee in a white paper cup. He blew on the coffee, sat at his desk, and saw the documents spread out.

"Oh, I must have forgotten I left these out... It's crazy how forgetful I get during these busy times," Perez said as he put the Susanna Holt files back.

I grinned and said nothing.

"Do you have any more questions for me?"

"Actually, I do... One more, if you have the time."

"Of course. What is it?"

"Is it not troubling to you for patients to miss appointments without explanation?"

"No, I wouldn't say that it is. It happens quite often. If the patient has more severe health issues, we will contact them to see if they're okay. Susanna wasn't in what we call the 'critical risk' category."

"What category would you say she was in?"

"The low-risk category."

"And if a diabetic patient was to lose twenty pounds over the course of three months. Would that put her in a critical risk category?"

"I'm not sure, I would have to assess the patient first. I will say that it's very concerning when a diabetic patient loses ten or more pounds."

"I had contact with Susanna recently. She looks like she has lost a considerable amount of weight. I would say she looked around a hundred and twenty, maybe a hundred and twenty-five pounds."

"If that's the case, I'll be sure to call and check in with Marvin. I'll be insistent about an appointment."

"Thank you, Doctor. I'll see myself out. Have a good rest of your shift."

"You as well."

CHAPTER
TWENTY-FOUR

As I arrived to start my shift, Takoda was finishing his watch. I drove up in my personal vehicle and pressed a button on the remote that opened the gates to our private employee parking lot.

The lot was sealed off by an eight-foot chain-link fence reinforced with dark brown tiles to block people's view into the parking area. The fence encompassed a forty-yard radius. I moved through the slowly opening gate and parked next to Takoda's minivan. I noticed him talking to Clint in the parking lot, most likely giving him a pep talk of some sort.

Getting out, I saw Clint walking away from Takoda. We waved to each other as Takoda meandered over. His five-foot-nine, lean, wiry frame always made me feel like a giant next to him. It was already getting frigid outside, but dry. I felt the asphalt under my feet starting to build ice. The sun had just gone down; light gray clouds covered the sky. Takoda was wearing a coat and a beanie.

"Did you follow up on that info I gave you on the McMinnville doctor?" He inquired.

"Yeah, got time to talk for a few?"

"Sure."

"Let's go inside. It's colder than a witch's titty out here."

We walked into a warm police department. Takoda and I always agreed on pretty much anything. I think we always got along so well because we were so similar in how we thought. We looked somewhat similar, in the face, and like me, Takoda was a Native American with white skin.

The white skin always confused the full-blooded Native Americans on the reservation. Takoda had a trimmed black beard to go along with his dark black hair and brown eyes. That was another difference: mine are blue. He always told me I should grow a beard, but I refused to. He said his beard kept his face warm on cold winter nights.

Takoda and I plopped down in the patrol room office at our assigned desks. The patrol room office had desks on the outer portion of the room, with brown marble flooring, Dell computer systems, and a large whiteboard with our names on it. The whiteboard was for us to write down reminders for our cases that we needed to follow up on.

On each desk? Piles of paperwork, neatly separated for officers to get back to when they got back on duty. Our chairs were black cushioned computer chairs without armrests. The armrests always got in the way of our handguns on our hips whenever we'd sit down.

"So, what do you got?" Takoda asked with excitement.

I handed him my cell phone. "I looked over the medical records."

"How the hell did you pull that off without a subpoena?"

"I pulled a page out of your book. I gave him a blow job and he let me do whatever I wanted."

"See, I told you that works! Just got to cradle the balls from time to time."

We laughed and then Takoda turned his focus to the pictures on my phone, scrolling left as he scanned each photo.

"What am I looking at here?"

"Look at picture eleven. Zoom in at the bottom of the page:

Tribal In-Home Nursing Program."

"I thought there was no record of medical care for Susanna from the tribe?"

"I thought that too."

Takoda read the photo and handed the phone back to me.

"What in the fuck is going on?" he asked.

"I don't know, but I will find out."

"**W**hy would the in-home nursing staff department lie to us?" Takoda wondered.

"Because they're hiding something from us?"

"Maybe negligence... They could have missed something huge in regard to Susanna's health and then covered it up."

"I could see that happening. The doctor in McMinnville didn't need to cooperate with me, but he did, which makes me think he doesn't know."

"I agree. It seemed like the doctors and nurses from our medical clinic were saying that Susanna was fine and hardly required care."

"Perez had to have known that the reports they made were wrong, right? I mean, he'd have to miss something too. You'd think he'd catch something in the past year he'd been seeing Susanna."

"Maybe, or maybe not. Not if you're not looking for it. Perez could have gone into this thing thinking it was an easy patient. Saving his energy for the patients that were in critical condition."

"That's plausible." I answered, then added, "The fact that he didn't erase any files regarding Susanna, and he helped me makes me think he's all right... But he was probably negligent."

"Inexperience could lead to missing key details... I did more research on Marvin... It looks like he fell off the face of the planet in 2002. He had a trespass charge in Eugene, but that's the last police report with him in it."

"This doesn't make sense... If he killed those women, why would he have just stopped for over twenty years? Could he have been that unlucky?"

"Do you believe in coincidences? I sure as hell don't."

"Yeah, me neither. Maybe someone helped him along the way. He doesn't strike me as someone intelligent enough to hide it that well."

We both pondered this for a minute.

"Did you check the family ties? Maybe a dad, sister, mom, or brother would know more," I said.

"He had parents when he was young. They died when he was a teen, and he went to foster care. There is a listed name for a younger brother... But when I check the name of the brother, there's nothing on file."

"Someone out there has to know more about this guy."

Another lead to follow up on...

Takoda let out a stressed sigh and said, "We have to let Chief McCarthy and Lieutenant Fernandez know. This is gonna be a shit storm."

"Don't I know it, brother. And we're just getting started."

***

At the front door of the police department, a woman was ringing the doorbell. Takoda logged onto his computer and pulled up outdoor security cameras. He zoomed in and saw a white minivan and an incredibly large Native American with tattoos standing outside the van. Next to the large man was a smaller, leaner Native American. They looked like twin brothers, but different in mass.

Takoda and I glanced at each other. "You know who they are?"

"No idea. Let's see what other kind of shit you can stir up on Christmas Eve," Takoda quipped.

"You can go, man. I know you want to be with your family," I said.

"With that tank of a man outside the police department? Not gonna happen, partner. Let's go see what the lady wants."

There was no sense in arguing with Takoda. I opened our glass door with a metal push-open handle. Camille Sherwood stood under an awning that had a symbol of the Confederated Tribes of Jericho Nation at the top of it.

The symbol was brown, in the shape of a circle, and inside the circle were the words written "The Confederated Tribes of Jericho Nation." Attached to the brown circle were five feathers, signifying the five different Native American tribes that came together to form what is known as the Confederated Tribes of Jericho Nation. Beside the logo of the Jericho Nation Tribe was a star colored black, and on the inside of the star were the words Jericho Nation Police Department.

Takoda and I stepped out onto the cement sidewalk that bordered our building. Camille was wearing a sweatshirt and some jeans. She hugged herself, rubbing her arms with her hands.

It had been a while since I had seen Camille. I had arrested her for a DUII years ago, but other than that, she had not gotten into trouble. She always seemed like a sweet girl in a rough environment.

"What can I do for you?" I asked.

"Officer Lawson, do you have a minute?" Camille replied.

"Of course. Come on in."

"If you don't mind waiting, my grandma and grandpa came to talk to you as well. Also my cousin, Emily."

"Yeah, no problem."

Camille looked over at the huge Native man and his smaller look-alike.

"Hey, Mato! Could you help Emily with Grandma and Grandpa please?"

The massive human nodded and went over to the minivan and unlatched the back sliding door. The smaller guy went and helped as well. A white woman got out of the backseat area. She was young, around Camille's age, with dark hair, and a large body frame. Presumably Camille's cousin, Emily.

Emily helped a frail elderly Native American female with dark brown skin out of the backseat. The grandma had to be at least eighty years old. Her hair was white, but still somewhat healthy and she was skinny. Emily and the one Camille called Mato helped her step down from the minivan to the asphalt of the parking lot. Emily walked the grandma over to the sidewalk. They had to take a small step up onto the cement to approach us. It was as much as the grandma could muster to take the step.

The big tattooed Native guy and his twin brother caught my eye. These guys looked like Native Warriors. They must have been from out of town for me not to know them.

The grandma and Emily made their way to me, walking like the grandma was made of glass. Emily was wearing a pair of blue jeans and a red-and-green Christmas sweater. The grandma seemed sweet; she was very appreciative of Emily and the two males who were helping her. She wore a pair of black sweatpants and a blue sweater.

The grandpa appeared to be the exact opposite of the grandma in personality. He was wearing a pair of muddied-up blue jeans and a long-sleeved red-and-black plaid flannel shirt with the sleeves rolled to his elbows. He looked about eighty-five years old, with light skin. And lean, and appeared to be active on a daily basis. The big guy and the small lean guy went to help him out of the van, but the old man hollered, "Get your goddamn hands off me. I don't need no help getting out of this van... I survived the Korean War, Goddammit!"

The grandpa slowly made his way out of the minivan and fixed his gaze on the big guy. "Did you make it through the Korean War?"

"No, Grandpa, I did not." Mato had a noticeably deep voice. He rolled his eyes as if he knew what his grandpa was going to say next.

"Yeah, that's right! Neither one of you did! I did, though... I can still kick your asses, you know?"

"We know, Grandpa," the smaller guy said.

Grandpa nodded as if to say, *Damn right you know.* Then he made the walk over to the group of us waiting on the sidewalk under his own power, grunting as if he was climbing Mount Everest.

"My name is Robert Holt. My friends call me Bobby," the elder said as he shook my hand with a surprisingly strong grip.

"Hello, I'm Officer Warren Lawson and my partner here is Takoda Tehama. It's nice to meet you."

The grandma did a curtsy toward Takoda and me.

"My name is Halona Holt. We all respect you quite a bit, Officer Lawson. That's why we're here to ask for your help."

As we made our way back to our office, I could tell Takoda was reconsidering staying past his required work hours as he realized he was going to work an hour of overtime just helping the grandma walk the thirty feet from her car to the break room.

Takoda and I decided that we should all talk in the break room area because it would comfortably seat everyone. Grandma Halona Holt was proud of the table in the center of the big room. She was one of the elders who had helped build it for the department.

It was handmade, carved with the best tools, and could seat up to twenty people. On the walls of the break room were frames that contained tribal patches from other tribal police departments around the United States.

Takoda and I sat on one side of the table and the family gathered on the other, facing us. Takoda offered them drinks or snacks, but they respectfully declined.

"So... what can I do to help you?" I asked.

"You could start by ridding the earth of Marvin Bingham. That would be a good start," Robert Holt blurted out.

"As you know, sir, police officers aren't executioners, so I'm afraid that won't be something I could help with."

"The dang-gum news always paints y'all to be executioners, anyway. Might as well go put a round or two in that sum bitch."

"Robert Perry Holt! You quit that right now," Grandma Holt hissed. "I can't believe I've stayed married to you for upward of fifty years.," she said to me. "We're all very frustrated, I apologize."

"Frustrated is an understatement. Pissed off would be a better way of putting it." Camille added.

"Okay, so tell us why you'd want someone to kill Marvin Bingham?"

Robert leaned forward. "You got any beer son? It will take us all night to list all the reasons."

Takoda let out a chuckle, but then quickly regained his composure.

"How about you list a few?"

Robert slapped his hand on the table. I could practically see his blood pressure rising. "By golly, that motherfucker…"

"Grandpa! Take a breath… Please, let me explain," Camille interrupted.

Robert calmed down and let out a long whoosh of air.

"We're here because of my aunt, Susanna Holt," Camille explained.

"My only remaining daughter," Grandma Holt said in a quavering voice. "My elder girl, Halona, was named after me."

I waited to reply and let the words resonate. I wondered what happened to her other daughter, but that would be a story for another time. Emily, who was seated by Camille, leaned forward.

"I heard you had contact with our Aunt Susanna and Marvin a few days ago," she said. "Is that true?"

Her tone was angry, and for a second I felt like I was on trial.

"I did. Why do you ask?"

"I'm wondering why nothing was done," she asked as she crossed her arms across her chest and leaned back in her chair.

"Emily, stop it… Officer Lawson is a good person. He's helped our families on numerous occasions," Grandma Holt reminded her.

"I know, Grandma, but it's weird to me that he had contact with Marvin and Aunt Susanna and didn't do a damn thing."

"Where did you learn that I spoke to your Aunt Susanna and Marvin?"

"I work at the casino in the table games area. I saw you talking to them on the gaming floor. Before you talked to them, I'd just got done yelling at Marvin for bringing my incredibly sick aunt to the casino. As I walked away to go back to work, I saw you talking to them. I thought it may have been because of me, but you guys never came to talk. So I figured it was something else."

"It was... and I can't specify why nothing was done. I can only tell you that I had no legal cause to arrest anyone at that point in time."

"Are you blind? How'd you not see that Marvin is completely neglecting Susanna? He's supposed to be taking care of her!" Emily's voice rose.

Sometimes in police work, it's hard to explain what police officers can and can't do. I wanted to come out and say that I knew something was wrong. If it were up to me, I would have knocked Marvin's teeth out. However, I couldn't go on record saying that, no matter how badly I wanted to.

"Look, Emily," Takoda interjected. "These situations are very delicate and I think what Officer Lawson is trying to explain is that we're working within the confines of the law. We both want to hear what you guys have to say, but for that to happen we all need to remain calm and listen to one another. Is that fair?"

They all nodded.

"Okay, good."

"What proof do you need? We'll get you plenty," Camille said.

"We just want to hear your side of the story," responded Takoda.

When you're investigating a case, an important thing about police work is to search for the facts, not who the "bad guy" is.

Some cops tend to get it in their mind that one individual did it and they get stuck focusing on that one person. Whenever I investigated a case, I always told myself, *I'm a fact collector. Find the facts and then act.* With that said, it was hard not to want to focus all my energy on arresting a scum like Marvin Bingham.

Takoda and I listened as Halona and Robert Holt, Emily, and Camille told us the problems they'd been having with Marvin. Emily and Camille used to see Susanna on a daily basis, dating back to 2016. Halona and Robert would have lunch dates at Susanna's house weekly.

One day, Marvin made his return to Susanna's life. Susanna had been in an on-again, off-again battle with alcoholism throughout her life. When she was single, it seemed like she could stay sober. When she would start dating again, she seemed to attract alcoholics like Marvin.

They all knew that Susanna was back to getting drunk every day, but they still tried to visit her as much as possible. All four had disliked Marvin years ago when he and Susanna were married, briefly, in 2005. When they divorced the next year, her family rejoiced.

"So why would Susanna get back together with Marvin?" I asked. None of them knew for sure, but they speculated that she was lonely and he was the closest available male. She was in her midfifties and had not much to show for her life. Perhaps she had called her ex to keep her company.

Sometime in 2017, several months after Marvin moved in with her, Susanna started to have dementia problems, Camille said. She once found Susanna walking in the middle of the tribal housing area. Camille asked Susanna what she was doing walking around alone on a cold winter night. Susanna blankly gazed at Camille and was confused. Camille took her back to her residence, where Marvin was chugging beers like his life depended on it.

Emily chimed in and said that back in 2018, they called APS, or the Adult Protective Service, and requested they investigate Marvin. Emily said that she and Camille voiced their concern to

APS about Marvin becoming Susanna's new caretaker. A brief investigation was conducted, but nothing was done.

I gave Takoda a look. His expression told me he was thinking the same thing: *How could APS start and close an investigation without notifying the local police department?* APS usually worked closely with the local police department on elder-neglect cases. I had never heard of a case where they worked without assistance from the police.

They all took turns telling a few stories that led them to believe Marvin was neglecting his duties as a caretaker. Camille was the first to say she believed Marvin was trying to kill Susanna, so he could have access to her savings account. Most of the money in her savings came from the Confederated Tribes of Jericho Nation. The other family members at the table agreed.

Camille said it was several months ago—around August—when Marvin started denying the family access to Susanna. Camille and Emily said they'd both tried to play nice with Marvin. However, Camille was done being nice after Marvin shoved a shotgun in her face.

I asked Camille to explain the shotgun incident, and she did. I believed her, but I had no proof to charge Marvin for the crime, which is a common problem for cops. *Not enough evidence.*

"Please help us, Officer Lawson... I lost one daughter already. I can't outlive another." Grandma Holt said.

I reached across the table and took her hand. "I'm going to do everything in my power to help."

"Thank you."

Grandma Holt's eyes were sorrowful—the eyes of a woman who had seen enough tragedy throughout her long life. I leaned back in my chair and wrote down in my notebook that I needed to talk with APS about their investigation.

"When did you call APS to investigate Marvin?" I asked Emily.

"I don't know, sometime in 2018."

"If you had to guess, what month?"

"Ummm, probably summer? Like June or July."

I wrote down that information in my notebook.

The conversation seemed productive until Robert felt the need to chime in. Robert wasn't sad, he was angry. He expressed his grief and anxiety differently than the women around him. Robert stared at me and Takoda with great intensity.

"I want you two to look at me for a second," he ordered.

We did as he asked and gazed at him.

"You see those two boys out there? Anakin and Mato are their names. Those boys are my grandkids." Robert pointed toward Mato and Anakin standing in the parking lot, talking. We could see them through a large ten-foot window that faced the front entrance of the police department.

I noticed that they both had tattoos on their necks that I wasn't familiar with. They looked about seven to ten years older than me. They took after the ancient Native soldiers of the past. They were from somewhere else that was for sure. Another tribal reservation. A harsher reservation.

"Yeah, we saw the two gentlemen out there... It's hard to miss the big one." I said.

Robert chuckled. "Well, his size comes in handy if you know what I mean."

"Robert, stop it." Grandma Holt hissed at him again.

"No Grandma, he's right," Camille put in. "I don't want to lie to you, Officer Lawson and Officer Tehama. I want us all to be as honest as possible."

"We'd prefer that too," I replied.

"We're coming to you with this issue because we trust you guys. We know you care about us and the community. If it wasn't you or Tehama doing this investigation, we wouldn't be reporting it. Mato and Anakin would be handling it."

"What is it you're trying to say?"

"We're giving you guys a shot to do this the right way. Otherwise, I'll have my brothers handle it. Like they did to my mother's killer."

It didn't take a genius to figure out that someone brutally murdered Grandma Holt's daughter. I understood what this family had gone through. Takoda and I thanked them for coming to us and showing restraint. It was a huge step for the tribal community, which was never known for exercising prudence or going through regular channels. They were known for handling issues themselves. Calling the police was usually the last thing people in Jericho Nation did.

I helped Grandma Holt back to the minivan. Mato and Anakin stared at me like I was an outsider who didn't belong, but Grandma Holt thanked me again for my time. Robert shook my hand and reminded me that his outbursts weren't directed at me, they were directed at the situation Marvin had caused.

Robert got into the back seat with his wife of fifty-plus years. Camille and Emily climbed into the back seat of the van and told me to have a good night of work. Camille closed the back sliding door, and I turned to walk back to the police department. I had to pass Anakin and Mato, who had ominous expressions on their faces. I gave them a polite nod as I passed.

"You better take care of this, Officer," Anakin said.

I turned around. They were standing about five feet away, with their eyes fixed on me. Like I was their next lunch. These guys were predators in the animal kingdom. Men like that had a unique feel to them. A certain aura.

"Excuse me?" I replied.

"My brother said, 'You better take care of this.'" Mato reiterated.

"Or you will, right? Yeah, your sister already told me. I'm not gonna let that happen."

"We know how white man law works, Lawson. Make sure the charges stick," Anakin said.

At first, I was surprised they knew my name. Then again, it's a small town, plus the name tag on my chest said, Lawson.

"I'll do my best... but for now, you two need to stay out of it."

"Or what?"

"I rather not do this. We're on the same side here."

Mato questioned, "Are we? Because we want justice. White man's law doesn't know what justice is."

"No, from the sounds of it, you want vengeance. There's a difference."

"Not where we come from," Anakin said.

"I know you don't know me, but I'm asking you to trust me to do this the right way."

"You have a strong reputation, Lawson. If it wasn't for that, we wouldn't give you the benefit of the doubt. We're giving you a chance. One chance. If it doesn't work, we are going to handle it our way."

———

There wasn't much to say to Anakin's demands. I acknowledged what he said with a nod and walked away.

Now I have those two to worry about. I made a mental note to look up Anakin and Mato's history when I got the chance.

As soon as I set foot into the police department, I found Takoda had changed out of his uniform and into his civilian clothes. He was wearing a brown Columbia jacket with a long-sleeved black shirt and blue jeans. Takoda was reclined back in the break room with his feet on the table.

"If it wasn't enough that the doctors and nurses weren't doing their jobs... now it looks like we have to investigate APS most likely didn't do their jobs either," he remarked.

"We need to find out what Susanna's will says," I replied.

"Can't do that without the help of her caretaker."

"And you know we aren't getting cooperation from that slime."

"So we follow up on the APS thing. See what their investigation turned up. Maybe there isn't a case here. Maybe we're all jumping to conclusions."

"No, there's a case here. There's too much going on for this to be nothing. Something isn't adding up."

"All right, just sayin', if we go down this road, we not only have to charge Marvin. We might end up charging several medical professionals and APS employees in the process. We don't know who else neglected to report this to law enforcement."

"Fuck them. I don't care if the president is in on this. Negligence in this case is criminal. And when I prove it, I'll take down whoever gets in my way."

"Thought you would say that," said Takoda with a wry grin.

"When have I ever backed down from a good fight?"

"And when have I not backed you up?"

"Good point."

"I won't leave you hanging no matter what. Never."

"I know. Thanks, brother."

Takoda nodded.

"So... Do you want to tell Chief McCarthy or Lieutenant Fernandez about this? Because I'm not telling them both."

"Let me do some digging on these hospital records. Then, we'll tell them together."

Who the fuck did Anakin and Mato think they were? Telling me they were gonna do it their way. Like there wasn't any way I could stop them. It piqued my interest, though. Just who were these two men? Why were they in Jericho Nation? And would they become a problem for me later?

Takoda was also interested—and convinced Mato and Anakin weren't from Jericho Nation. When I informed him of my conversation with them outside the police department, he was even more intrigued.

The two brothers looked like athletes. Mato had the build of an NFL Defensive Lineman, and Anakin was lean, tall, and with very little body fat. He probably was a boxer. Upon reflection, I remember seeing Anakin's knuckles had an old break on the middle finger area of his right hand. The two would be a physical problem for me, should it come to it. The perfect combination of brute strength and speed.

Takoda logged onto his computer in the patrol room and started researching the police database. I watched over his shoulder as the screen popped up. There was no point in me searching at the same time. It was no contest that Takoda would find the information before me.

As the report system was firing up, Takoda said, "I don't know many guys who have the balls to threaten you."

"Talk is cheap."

"Maybe it's not all talk with them. Camille said they murdered their father? That's pretty hardcore."

I didn't respond. Takoda was right on two counts. Generally speaking, nobody threatened me. Whether I was on duty or off duty. People knew my reputation. My work ethic, my training habits. The second thing he was right about was them being hardened criminals. Killing your father is some biblical type shit.

"Here, I got something," Takoda said.

The report loaded up on the screen. It was an old report, dated back in June 2003: a homicide investigation in Siletz, Oregon—another tribal reservation.

There were numerous reports on the incident. Two murders happened that night. First was the victim, Halona Holt, the mother of Anakin and Mato. The suspected murderer was their father, Pillan.

"Holy shit," Takoda muttered as we read on.

I knew the Siletz reservation well. It was a known base of operations for a well-known Native American gang known as "IPO," the Indian Power Organization. The report documented that Pillan was a prominent member of the IPO. There was a history of abuse with the family. Pillan had beaten Halona several times and when Mato and Anakin were children, they were subject to his abuse as well.

The report was getting pretty lengthy and my stomach was growling so I decided to go to the break room and get some food. Takoda decided to print out the report and read it to me as I stuffed my face full of a juicy chicken breast.

He walked into the break room with a stack of papers and said, "This is probably one of the craziest police reports I've ever read."

Between bites, I replied, "Why?"

"On the night that the twin brothers murdered their father, their mother was killed only an hour before. A Lincoln County deputy recounts the story of Mato and Anakin tracking their father's blood and finding him at the residence. Where they would eventually kill him."

"So they're hunters."

"Yeah, and get this. The father, Pillan, was found in the home with an arrow shot through his eye and blood all over the carpets. Detective's accounts of the scene say that it looked like a fight took place between Anakin, Mato, and Pillan. Pillan lost in a gruesome fashion. The autopsy report says that before he got the arrow in the eye, and through the skull, he had broken bones all over his entire body."

"So they tortured him?"

"Sounds like Pillan tried to fight back. He was listed as a pretty big guy: six-foot, 225 pounds. And he did prison time so I imagine he was built pretty bulky."

"How old were they when this took place?"

Takoda scanned through the report some more, "They were seventeen. Both Anakin and Mato graduated from high school earlier that day."

I shook my head in dismay. "That's rough."

"That's an understatement."

"What were their records like before this incident?"

"Clean as a whistle."

"What? That can't be. Let me see that," I said, as I extended my hand.

Takoda handed me the stack of paper and I started to read through it. As I read, Takoda went back to his computer to research news stories about the case.

Takoda was right: both Anakin and Mato seemed to have had clean records and no prior history.

I hollered from the break room, "Can you check the reports from their parole officers while you're at it?"

"Already on it."

I grinned. Takoda was thorough in his research and I appreciated that about him. I was too impatient to sit at a computer all night to do it myself. He could also bypass any security blocks on certain reports because he knew how to hack computers. He tried teaching me how to hack computers, but I told him I didn't want to add professional nerd to my resume.

Anyway, the story went on and I kept reading like it was a Stephen King novel that I couldn't put down. I started to picture it happening in my head as I read all the different points of view. There were detectives, patrol officers, and a SWAT team all involved in the case.

I imagined Mato and Anakin were trained in their Native way of how to hunt prey. Which was a reason they tracked him down so fast. Another reason was that they knew their enemy well. So they could predict where he was going and find him.

Mato's bulk with Anakin's lean frame of a boxer was a potent combination. The ying to the yang, some would say. I pictured them breaking into Pillan's house and blending Mato's strength and Anakin's speed to take down their father. Then, they proceeded to have a verbal stand-off with the Oregon State SWAT team.

The autopsy report stated Pillan's time of death was anywhere between fifteen to twenty minutes before the SWAT team found them at the home. Which told me that they had the opportunity to run, but chose to stay.

I also ascertained that Mato and Anakin had not hurt any law enforcement during the incident. They showed honor and respect toward the police. Which was rare for a pair of individuals who'd just committed a violent act such as shooting an arrow through their father's eye.

Anakin and Mato provided statements to the detectives later on, after they were arrested. That's where I learned more about their upbringing.

All these two had was their mother, Halona. Pillan was off doing drugs and doing whatever gangbanger shit the IPO wanted him to do. Meanwhile, Anakin and Mato probably suffered night after night from his drunken rampages. After Pillan brutally beat and murdered their mother, they no longer cared what happened to them. Seeing their mother battered, lifeless, and unrecognizable changed them forever.

There were photos of the aftermath. Halona had stab wounds in her abdomen, and her entire face was swollen. Her lips protruded out, and a laceration cut across her broken nose. The eyes were bloodshot red and showed hemorrhaging had occurred. Her throat had ligature marks that looked like fingerprints.

"Jesus…"

Needless to say, I lost my appetite. Anyway, I moved on to the next photo which was of Pillan's dead body. It wasn't much better. Blood pooled from his head and all over the carpet under his body. He had several teeth missing. His jaw was detached and dangling to the side like a piece of rubber. The arrow was shot at point-blank range by someone with immense bow pull strength. I assumed Mato took the shot after Pillan got the shit kicked out of him.

The picture of Halona moved me, but the picture of Pillan made me feel a strong sense of vengeance. If someone killed my mother like that, I would kill them too. No qualms about it. Hell, I'd probably shit in their mouth after the fact for good measure. So in my opinion, Mato and Anakin had held back a bit.

Takoda walked in with more documentation, "Take a look at this."

More papers plopped on the break room table. I was done eating anyway. I opened the file folders and started skimming more interviews with the brothers.

"I'll save you some time and just tell you what these say," said Takoda.

"I appreciate it. Go on."

"After these two were arrested, they went to prison. They got out for good behavior. Mato and Anakin were boxers. They did prison-sanctioned tournaments and won several events. Mato was in the heavyweight division, Anakin in middleweight."

"Yeah, I could've guessed that by looking at them. Sounds like they were good. Why not try a career in boxing when they got out?"

"They got out of prison in 2015. It seems that while they were in prison, they became radicalized in the IPO culture."

"The apple doesn't fall too far from the tree then. So they became IPO just like their father."

"Yep. You know how it is in prison. You have to join a gang if you want to survive. That's the way it goes."

"All right, so it's safe to say that they're still IPO?"

"Definitely."

"What else do you got?"

"Interviews with their parole officers say that Susanna Holt was like a mother to Camille, Mato, and Anakin. Even when Halona was alive, Susanna was close to the family. While the guys were in prison, Susanna was their main visitor. She visited them once a day, every day for years."

"She loved them as if they were her own."

"Seems that way."

"Anakin even disclosed to his PO that he contemplated suicide while in prison. But Susanna visiting him helped him through dark times. Anakin also speaks highly of a woman named Hilary. It seems the two are high school sweethearts."

"Puke."

Takoda rolled his eyes and continued, "Anyway, I did a quick Facebook search to see if they're still together. It seems that they are. She's a pretty, blond, white gal, which surprised me."

"Well, if Anakin is ever on the run from us, at least we know where he'll be going to lay his head down. What about Mato? The big guy. Does he have any special somebodies?"

"The jolly green giant appears to have no significant others. He seems to love his family dearly, and that's about it."

"A sorta lone wolf type of guy. I like him already."

"You won't like him if we find ourselves on the wrong side of this guy."

"Yeah, we'll see about that."

Takoda checked his wristwatch and realized he needed to get going if he wanted any chance of seeing his wife before she went to bed. He left me with the documents and rushed out.

I examined more pictures that detectives took after Pillan died. Mato and Anakin had red puffy marks on their knuckles. There were pictures of their faces after the fight; they seemed unscathed.

I eyed the pictures in deep thought. Mato and Anakin could have easily been me. But I was raised in a healthy, safe environment with a loving father and mother. They weren't. They had to fight every day to survive.

My mind wandered into my childhood. I realized how lucky I was that my dad moved me and my family off the reservation when I was five. Or maybe another cop would be looking at a mug shot of me from years ago.

So, what did I learn about these guys? Well, they weren't cop killers, which was a plus. Yet that could change if I failed to protect their Aunt Susanna. Mato and Anakin were tough sons of bitches and survived prison. Not only survived but came out at the top of the food chain. They killed their own father. They would have no problem killing anyone who got on their bad side.

Which included me if I failed to protect their mother figure, Susanna. I did my best to find some version of justice that didn't require my dark side. I could hear my father's voice telling me, "Don't let the violence end you."

Vigilante or cop? Vengeance or justice? Which was most honorable? Although my heart desired vengeance, my soul knew justice was the better route. The more sustainable choice. And they sounded ready to whack Marvin because of their love for Susanna. I couldn't let that happen. That was the job. That's the oath I took. Whether I agree with it or not, is another question entirely.

As much as I would love to see Marvin's smeared brains up on a wall after Mato smashed him, it wasn't right. It wasn't honorable. Or just. A man has to have a code. My code was about keeping people alive. All people. Even cocksuckers like Marvin

Bingham, who I'd like to burn to death. Then, perhaps, piss on his ashes.

Bottom line. Mato and Anakin—for as scary as they were—had a good-ish side. They weren't the Marvin Binghams of the world. If I could get to Marvin, gain probable cause to arrest him, and then put him away in a prison cell, maybe I could prevent Mato and Anakin from making a decision that could land them in prison. Or at least stop them from becoming an enemy of mine.

Because when it came down to it. I would stick to my code, and they would stick to theirs. And our ideologies would clash. I had no doubt that if that happened, there would be an extremely violent outcome. Either for me or for them. Only time would tell.

I thought about Ashley. I should make an effort to show I was interested. I wondered if our date was going to be a one-night thing. So I texted her a Merry Christmas Eve. In a few seconds, she wished me the same. She had the night off for the holiday.

As we texted, I sat in my office alone. It was a few hours after Takoda had gone home. Things were quiet, so I texted Ashley about Susanna Holt. She seemed as invested in the case as I was. I asked if she knew any doctors or medical professionals that could review the medical records and answer my questions privately. I explained that Perez had done me a favor, and I needed to keep it quiet because technically I acquired the medical files without legal cause. Ashley understood and advised me she knew a doctor who owed her a favor. We set a date to go to Salem County Hospital the day after Christmas to visit the doctor together.

I finished my shift on Christmas morning. I drove out to my parent's house, where my older brother and sister had stayed overnight for the holiday. Keith had driven down from Washington with his wife, Kelsi, and her beautiful two-year-old daughter, Kaylee. Olivia, her husband Dean, and their six-month-old child, Laurel, were also there. The house was full. It was around seven in the morning, so I had to be stealthy letting myself in.

I tried to move silently up the stairs to the top story of the house. I slid my work boots off and snuck around on my tiptoes. As I got to the top of the stairs and turned into the hallway to my old bedroom, I practically ran into Dean, standing there with a cup of coffee in one hand and a Karambit knife in the other.

"Hey, brother," Dean whispered as he put the knife away.

"Fucking scared the shit out of me, Goddammit," I replied in a low voice.

Dean chuckled and took a drink of his coffee. Dean was a close friend. When I went to community college, Dean went to Marine Special Forces school. He was a marine recon operator. No intruder was going to get the jump on him. An expert in weaponry, he stood six-foot-three and was 225 pounds of lean muscle. Dean and I trained together often. We did CrossFit workouts together, martial arts, and firearms training.

"Growing your hair and beard out, I see," I said softly.

"Yep. I told your sister I was going to grow this beautiful long blond hair and look like the mighty Thor one day," he quipped.

He did look similar to the actor Chris Hemsworth, who played Thor, the god of thunder, in all the Marvel films: blue eyes with blond hair and a beard to match. We embraced each other, and I went to my old bedroom.

My mom kept my room exactly how I left it when I was a high schooler, except she'd added photos of me on the wall from my high school days. There were also framed awards and a couple of trophies that said PLAYER OF THE YEAR 2009 (football) and 2010 (basketball).

There were photos of me standing with my mom and dad after a football game. My dad, the spitting image of Tom Selleck, with a thick brown mustache, tall lean farmer's build, and brown hair. My mom. The ageless wonder, we called her. Her smile was wide and contagious. Her blue eyes sparkled in the photo and her black hair was flawless. After gazing at the fond memories, I got into bed and fell asleep.

A few hours later, it was time to head to my grandma's house for Christmas breakfast at ten thirty. I got about three hours of sleep: not much, but it was a solid rest. My dad came into my room to wake me up with Kaylee.

"Hey, son, time to wake up," Dad said as he put his hand on my shoulder.

"Time to wake up Unk War-War!" Kaylee announced. She still had trouble pronouncing the word Uncle, but she was getting better every time I saw her.

I smiled. I was lying on my stomach, so I opened my eyes and rolled over. I grinned at Kaylee and she started to reach out to me.

"Give Unk War-War some love to wake him up. We got gifts to get to, don't we, Kaylee Grace?" my dad said.

"Yaaaas!" Kaylee couldn't contain her excitement.

She crawled on the bed to me and gave me a big hug. I sat upright so she could crawl onto my lap and nuzzle her little head on my chest.

As I held Kaylee, my dad asked, "How'd you sleep?"

"Not long, but I slept well."

"Come on Unk War-War! It's time to go see Gam-gam!" Kaylee said as she raised her hands in the air like a performer in a stage play.

"All right, sweetheart, I'm coming."

"I wuvs you, Unk War-War."

"I wuvs you too, honey."

It took me about fifteen minutes to roll out of bed. I could have hung out with Kaylee all day and would have been perfectly content. However, I was blessed with a family whom I loved and I wanted to see all of them.

Grandma's house was our family tradition for Christmas morning. We would go to her house in Willamina and have breakfast with the whole family. I had tons of cousins, and we were all bonded. My grandma's house wasn't very big, but we didn't mind the cramped space.

Everyone's favorite uncle, Uncle Tom, his full name, Thomas Lawson, cooked a mess of eggs, bacon, ham, potatoes, and pancakes. He cooked piles of food and had it laid out on multiple tables for us to dish up ourselves.

After breakfast, we'd all sit in the living room area and exchange gifts. While we were sitting down, my sister Olivia brought her daughter Laurel over to me.

"Can you hold her for a bit? Dean and I are passing out gifts." Laurel was cuter than a button. Her eyes were wide, like an adorable bug.

"My pleasure."

I cradled Laurel in my arms. She couldn't speak yet, but she had the biggest, prettiest blue eyes I'd ever seen. Laurel looked up at me and smiled. Her little grin warmed my heart, and I kissed her forehead. She started kicking her feet like she was pedaling an invisible bicycle, then grabbed my face and stuck her finger in my mouth.

While Dean was handing out gifts, he came over to us. "Yeah, she does that. She likes to grab and tug on my beard all the time. Since you don't have a beard, I guess she's just gonna latch onto your mouth."

We both laughed.

"Well, all righty then!" I announced as I did my best Jim Carrey impersonation.

Laurel laughed and kept tugging on my bottom lip as I contorted my face and widened my eyes to make my face look even more like a cartoon. Laurel's laugh was infectious and instantly put people in a good mood.

———

After the gift exchange, I offered to carry everyone's gifts out to the vehicles. I had a large handful of gifts and Dean carried some out as well. We put them in the back seat of my dad's SUV and Dean's Ford pickup. As Dean and I were walking back to the house, my cousin Lydia Bishop was smoking a cigarette outside in the front yard. She blew a smoke cloud and glanced at me.

"Warren, do you have a minute? I have to tell you something."

Dean looked at me, and I gave him an approving nod. Dean strolled off toward the house and I went over to the front yard area where Lydia was smoking. It was a sunny, frosty morning, but cold. My grandma's green yard was silvered with frost.

"What's wrong? Is everything okay?"

Lydia said, "I'm not sure... It's about Susanna Holt and Marvin Bingham."

CHAPTER
THIRTY

I wondered how the hell Lydia knew about Marvin Bingham. Then I recollected that she worked for the in-home nursing department at the Jericho Nation medical clinic.

"I'm sorry to bring this up on Christmas... I just feel I should tell you." Lydia explained.

"It's okay, I have to go back to work tonight anyway, so it doesn't feel like a day off to me," I said. "What is it that you want to tell me?"

Lydia sighed and shivered due to the icy, numbing air. She took a puff of her cigarette, looked away from me, and blew the smoke out away from my face. The smoke cloud drifted away and then dissipated in the air.

"I think my boss is hiding something from the police department."

"Hiding what exactly?"

"I'm not sure. The other day, Officer Tehama came to our office to fill out paperwork for a request... Usually, she has no problem with that, especially with law enforcement, but this time was different."

"Which one is your boss again?"

"Monica Hawke."

"Okay, go on."

Lydia told me what happened when they went to Marvin Bingham and Susanna Holt's residence to do a welfare check. Lydia informed me of the uncomfortableness she felt afterward.

"It seemed like Monica didn't want anyone to answer the door. It was the weirdest thing. I've never seen her act that way."

"What way?"

"Like she was hiding something. She knocked so quietly on the door that a person with supernatural hearing couldn't have heard it."

"Did you confront Monica about this?"

"Well, I was visibly upset by the lack of care she displayed. Monica dismissed it, saying that it was a wild goose chase for the police department. She said other patients needed us more than Susanna Holt."

"Do you believe her?"

"No. If I did, I wouldn't be standing here talking to you."

"Now that you're bringing this up," I said, "would you mind if I asked you a question?"

"Shoot."

"Was Susanna Holt ever a patient at the in-home nursing department at the tribe?"

"Susanna? Oh yeah, she still is, I'm pretty sure. She sees Dr. Wilson at the medical clinic. Why?"

"Just curious."

That confirmed what I was thinking before. The in-home nursing and medical department for the tribe was in on this. In what shape or form, I did not know. However, they must have done something to Susanna Holt and were trying to cover it up. That was the only reason I could imagine I was told they never had Susanna Holt as a patient when I called before.

"Lydia, I need you to do me a favor."

"What do you need?"

"I have a plan to get you into Marvin Bingham's house."

L ydia fixed her confused gaze on me. She was clearly uncomfortable with the idea as I said it, but I thought I could change her mind.

"How do you plan on doing that?" questioned Lydia.

"From what I hear, Marvin likes his alcohol."

"Yeah, so?"

"If you can go back to visit Susanna again, maybe you could talk him into letting you give Susanna a bath or something. Make an offer to help him take care of Susanna and see what he says. He'll probably say no, but then you can tell him if he refuses your help—that you'll call the cops for a welfare check."

"I don't think that'll work."

"It'll work if you tell him that you don't want to call the cops. If you make it seem like the cops are your common enemy. He might let you check on Susanna and render aid to save his own bacon. With all the attention on his house lately, I think he'll see it as a chance to escape an investigation."

"Let's say it works. What do I do once I am in the house?"

"Have your cell phone ready and take as many photographs of Susanna as you can. Susanna won't tell you much, so don't try to get information out of her. You'll have to collect photographs, without Marvin noticing."

"Monica will fire me if she finds out. Dr. Wilson will go apeshit."

"Is there anyone you work with who you trust?"

Lydia pondered this for a moment. I watched her finish off the last of her cigarette and toss it to the ground. She put her foot on the smoldering butt end of the cigarette.

"Justine is a good one. I could bring her."

"Make sure she keeps it to herself. You carry a gun at all?"

Lydia had a purse strapped around her left shoulder. The bag hung behind her, near her lower back. She flung it over to the front of her body. The purse was black, nothing fancy. Lydia unzipped the purse and displayed a .32-caliber pistol.

"Don't go anywhere on the res without it," Lydia said.

"Good. If Marvin starts to worry you, text me right away and get out of there. Got it?"

"Got it."

I explained more to Lydia how I wanted her to approach the situation with Marvin and gave her pointers on what to say to avoid suspicion. Before I knew it, we had been talking for thirty minutes. I thanked her for the information and we went our separate ways.

———

Christmas time is always a great time of year for my family and me. I drove back out to my parents' house after spending time at my grandma's. I rotated my car onto Lawson Lane, the street my parents lived on, where I had grown up. Lawson Lane was named after my great, great-grandfather, who was a hero in World War II. I never met the man, but my grandma tells me he was an amazing individual.

It was afternoon, still cold out, but the sun was shining. I was wearing a leather jacket over my Under Armour long-sleeved shirt to stay warm. As I entered my parents' house and overheard the chatter of everyone who beat me home.

I walked to the living room area and saw Kaylee and Laurel playing on the carpet together. Kaylee seemed intrigued as to why Laurel couldn't crawl so well yet. Both were having a good time. I hugged my mom, and she told me how happy she was that I could join them for Christmas.

I clutched my mom a little bit tighter, thinking that she was three years older than Susanna Holt, and looked twenty years younger. I had this sick feeling in my stomach that I should have arrested Marvin on the spot that night at the casino.

I pictured how I would feel if my mom was Susanna Holt. Was I as negligent as the medical staff for the Confederated Tribes of Jericho Nation? I hoped not.

I realized what it must feel like for the family of Susanna Holt. Heartbreaking.

CHAPTER
THIRTY-TWO

Anakin spent his Christmas with his family in Jericho Nation, along with his girlfriend, Hilary. At nightfall, Anakin decided to take a walk with Hilary. Anakin wanted to hike away all the holiday meals he'd eaten. He joked to Hilary that he was going to have a food baby later in the night.

"That's gross," Hilary replied.

"Yes, my love, I suppose it is. Still funny though, right?"

"Only a little. Mostly gross." They both chuckled.

Hilary and Anakin strolled down the sidewalk of Jericho Nation Road, a narrow, two-lane roadway, flanked by cement sidewalks. It got skin-piercingly chilly as the sun went down, but the stars were bright and easy to see.

Anakin thought, as he had many times before, that Hilary looked too innocent to be with a man like him—a gang member with a criminal record. She was a tall strawberry blonde, lean, with brown eyes. Her skin was pale white—so white that she almost looked like a ghost at night and she was nearly as tall as he was.

"Something's been on your mind. I can tell," said Hilary.

"Oh, I'm fine, babe. Don't worry about it."

"It's your Aunt Susanna, huh?"

Anakin nodded.

"You want to handle the issue yourself, don't you?"

"I do."

"You're doing it the right way for our relationship."

Anakin sighed. "I can't help but think about what happened to my mom on holidays like Christmas." Anakin stopped to get his voice under control, then continued.

"And when that happened, Aunt Susanna was there for me. She was always there for me. I really missed them both today... I don't want to be too late for my aunt like I was for my mother."

Hilary grasped Anakin's hand and held it gently as they walked.

"I know, Anakin. But if you do something that gets you arrested, I'll lose you again for another twelve years, if not more. I can't do that again. Your parole officer will make sure to lock you up for good."

"I know. But I'm a soldier. I'm a protector. The longer I wait, the more likely I am to lose my aunt. My second mother. I don't know if I can take that kind of loss again."

Hilary stopped walking and stared at Anakin. He stopped, too, and saw the look on her face.

She pointed at her belly. "This baby can't afford to grow up without a father," she said, her voice trembling. "I told you I'd wait for you when you got arrested. We were on the beach celebrating graduation and then, poof, you just ran off. The next time I saw you, you were in a prison. I was a high school girl with a crush then, but I kept my word, Anakin. I waited. I stuck it out for you because I love you. Now I need you to let the police do their job so we can have a life together. I can't lose you again. I won't go through it a second time."

Anakin nodded, but his guts were twisted. He dropped his chin to his chest and stared at the ground, then looked back up at Hilary and said, "Come here."

He wrapped his arms around her. Hilary buried her head in his shoulder.

"I'm not going anywhere," he assured her.

Anakin knelt to one knee and kissed Hilary's stomach. Anakin rubbed her belly some more, hoping to feel his unborn child inside her, but it was too early for kicking.

Hilary glanced to her right and saw headlights in the distance. The 1985 Ford Bronco rolled up beside them and stopped. It was Mato in the driver's seat with the window down. Anakin stood up, turned, and faced the vehicle.

"Anakin, the boys want to talk about what we're doing here. Should I tell them to meet up at the Agency Creek woods to talk?" Mato said

"Yeah. Can you give Hilary a ride back home first?" Anakin asked.

"Of course, brother."

Hilary gave Anakin a concerned look as if he just ignored everything she just said. Anakin walked her to the passenger side seat. Mato drove them back home. Once back at the house, Anakin escorted her to the door.

"What are you and the gang discussing tonight?" Hilary inquired with a touch of annoyance in her voice.

"You know what we'll be discussing. If they're needed or not."

"And are they?"

"Well, if I can't risk my freedom, then they can on my behalf. That way I can be a father and future husband to you." Anakin charmed her.

"Your hands will be clean of it that way?"

"Yes."

"Then do it. Have them kill the bastard."

Ashley and I decided to take a trip to the Salem County Hospital the day after Christmas. I greeted her in the hospital parking lot. Both of us were out of uniform. I was sporting a pair of black slacks, black dress shoes, and a black button-up dress shirt with a gray pressed coat over-the-top. I had my badge visible, as it hung from a necklace around my neck. And I had my personal .45-caliber 1911 Colt on my hip, concealed by my jacket.

Ashley was wearing a white beanie, a teal fleece jacket, and a pair of jeans. She looked great. Her dark brown eyes popped with the light-colored clothing.

We started our trot in the parking lot area, the frosty air cutting through our clothes. I let her lead the way. She used to work there, and she knew the doctor we were seeing. The Salem County Hospital was much busier than the McMinnville County Hospital. The hospital was about five stories tall and had multiple buildings all over the property, resembling a college campus.

"So, uh... How do you know this doctor, anyway?"

She looked fixedly at me and smiled. "I used to work here."

"Hmm, okay."

She broke the silence.

"Okay, we used to hook up from time to time."

"'Oh, I see,' said the blind man."

"Is that a hint of jealousy in your voice?"

I scoffed, "Me, jealous? HA!"

I may have exaggerated the fake laugh.

"Men. You guys always have to act so tough."

"I swear I'm not the jealous type. I bet he isn't even that attractive."

———

Dr. Jeremy Powley was very attractive. I was starting to wonder if I was on the set of a medical drama TV show. Every doctor I met seemed to be a strapping handsome fellow. Powley was around forty years old, bald head, fit, trimmed facial hair, and Asian American. He had the bearing of an ex-military man turned doctor.

Ashley and I sat in his office. I resisted the temptation to bump knuckles with Powley and advise him that we were tunnel buddies with the woman who sat in the room with us. That would have made things awkward, so I kept my mouth shut.

Powley's office was nicer than Perez's had been, and a little more professional. The seating arrangements were similar, but the chairs were very comfortable.

"It's nice to see you again, Ashley." Powley grinned from ear to ear at Ashley, obviously wallowing in fond memories of inter-course with Ashley. *What a pig.*

"This is my boyfriend, Warren Lawson," she replied.

I was shocked. We hadn't made anything official after the night we shared together. But I didn't hate the label, so I went with it.

Powley exchanged pleasantries, then got down to the task at hand. He asked me about the medical records. Ashley and I stressed to him that he could never go on record stating he'd seen these records. However, it would be helpful if he could give me his expert opinion. Powley was skeptical, but Ashley and I explained how serious this case was, and he decided to help us out.

I handed him my phone with all the pictures of the medical records. Powley looked at each photo and read the records very thoroughly, which I appreciated. It made it easier to forget that he was picturing my girlfriend naked half of the time I was there, and therefore easier for me not to knock him the fuck out.

He jotted some notes on a sticky notepad as he read. It looked like he was finding several problems. Finally, he finished reading and glanced over at me.

"Do I want to know how you got photos of these records?"

"No, you don't."

"Fair enough. All right, I got a few things you might want to check out."

"Whaddya got?"

"The main thing I'm not seeing is actually a pretty simple task. None of these evaluations mentions that Susanna Holt's feet were checked. Checking the feet of a diabetic patient is extremely important and also very routine. I'm not sure why they didn't document that."

"Good to know. Go on."

"Weight loss is concerning as well. The fact that they have her in a low-risk category is strange... Also, there is an IQ test that they did with Susanna about a year ago."

"Yeah, I saw that. It said she scored a zero out of thirty. How bad is that?"

"Very bad. That test is a very basic knowledge test. Questions on the test are usually as simple as, Who's the current president? What day is it? What state are you in? So on and so forth."

"And she scored a zero on that? Wouldn't that basically make her mentally retarded? Medically speaking?"

"Medically speaking, yes. In fact, if we have a patient that scores a zero on that test, we require them to have a higher level of medical care. Dementia patients that are so far gone like that require 24/7 nursing care."

"So if her caretaker was taking her to the casino and getting drunk... You wouldn't recommend that?"

"Not a chance in hell. Susanna should be in a hospital bed. I don't get why the tribe didn't forward their reports to us or a bigger hospital to assist. Instead, they went through McMinnville County Hospital, which doesn't have the resources to help Susanna like we would. Then they lie on the report and say that Susanna is okay in the care of this Marvin guy."

"You don't think it's possible for Marvin to take care of her alone?"

"No. He could be doing everything in his power to help her, and it wouldn't be enough. Based on this information, she should have nurses working with her around the clock."

I wrote down several helpful notes from Powley. I guess he ended up being okay after all. Who knew I was the jealous type? I couldn't remember the last time I got jealous because a girl was getting attention from another man. I guess I'd never liked anyone enough to care.

After the conversation with Doctor Powley, Ashley and I walked back to our cars. I thanked her for setting up the appointment and she said she was happy to help. We stopped at the driver's side door of a gunmetal gray Toyota 4Runner with a noticeable pink trim around the license plates.

"I couldn't help but notice you calling me your boyfriend in there."

"Oh, yeah. Sorry, I didn't want it to get weird with him being all flirty. I'm sure a guy like you has a million girls to call any given night," she said, looking nervous.

"Yeah, I could call a few. But I only want one."

"Really? You don't have a wife or a girlfriend?"

"Nope. I just got out of a relationship with a girl named Julia before I met you. Other than that, I usually keep to myself. What about you?"

"Same... Single as can be." She paused. "What happened with your relationship with Julia?"

"She was a great girl, but the job I do was hard on her. She had a history of family members being hurt in law enforcement. The stress was getting to her, so we called it quits."

"How long did you date?"

"Not long, just a few months."

"'I see,' said the blind man," Ashley said mockingly.

I smiled.

"This is kind of out of left field, and maybe a bit rushed, but I don't care at the moment."

"Umm, okay."

"Let's give this thing a shot. Let's date."

She smiled. "Really? You want me to be your girlfriend?"

"I do."

"Well, I think that's a wonderful idea."

I grinned, and she smiled back. I leaned in and kissed her on the lips. Hot. Oh, how fun the honeymoon phase can be.

CHAPTER
THIRTY-FOUR

It was the first week of January. The holiday season had passed, and it was time for everyone to go back to work. Lydia Bishop was in the medical clinic parking lot, pondering how to approach Justine about Susanna Holt. She had written down the tips that Warren gave her.

Lydia caught up with Justine in the parking lot as they were both heading toward the clinic. As she predicted, Justine did want to go back and check on Susanna. Lydia reminded her that she was to keep this quiet and not to alert Monica or Caroline Wilson. They devised a plan to stop by Susanna Holt's residence during their routine daily stops through Tribal Housing. Monica approved their departure and Lydia drove the minivan straight to the Bingham/Holt residence.

Lydia and Justine trudged to the door nervously. Lydia knocked on the door, much louder than her boss Monica had done.

No answer.

Lydia knocked a second time and then a third.

"What do you want?" Marvin hollered, sounding annoyed.

"Medical in-home nursing, here to assist," Lydia replied.

"We don't need help. Go away!"

"We aren't leaving until we see Susanna!" Justine fired back.

After a few seconds of silence, Marvin swung the door open. The odor of whiskey hit their noses as soon as he opened the door. His hair was a mess. He was wearing a pair of pajama bottoms with a white tank top.

"Do I need to call the cops for trespassing?" threatened Marvin.

"No, we're here to avoid the cops being called, sir. Officer Lawson has been very insistent about checking on Susanna. Now, if we don't give him a report, he will have to come himself. Dr. Wilson and Monica have informed me that they don't want police involved when it comes to Susanna," said Lydia.

"Dr. Wilson said that to you?"

"Yes, and Nurse Monica Hawke, who you might know? She agreed that Susanna is not a case that the police need to be involved in. We both know that."

"Of course. So... what can I do to avoid that?"

"We need to check on Susanna. Let us give her a bath, give her some medications, and we'll be on our merry way. Then we can inform the officer he has nothing to worry about."

Marvin pondered a minute. "This isn't some trick, is it?"

"Of course not. Has Dr. Wilson or Monica let you down?"

He smiled. "No, they haven't."

"Exactly. So may we come in? It will only take a few minutes."

"Fine, come in."

Marvin begrudgingly allowed Lydia and Justine in the house. As soon as they set foot into the home, their shoes stuck to something sticky on the floor. The smell of woman's perfume mingled with the odors of stale alcohol and cigarette smoke.

They walked down the hallway and to Susanna's room—a ten-by-fifteen-foot, probably the smallest in the house. It smelled like a sewage tunnel in the bedroom. Lydia and Justine did their best to keep a straight face, but the shock of Susanna's physical state was alarming.

Marvin stared at Lydia and stepped into her personal space. "No cops, got it?"

Lydia went cross-eyed looking at Marvin's finger in her face.

"Of course, Mr. Bingham. We'll take care of this."

Justine rolled her eyes at Lydia behind Marvin's back. Lydia kept a straight face, mindful of Warren's meticulous instructions to keep Bingham pacified.

Lydia and Justine went into the room with the unbearable smell.

"Hi, Susanna, it's Nurse Bishop... I'm here to help you today. Would you like a bath?"

Susanna grunted and nodded her head.

"All right, honey, let's get you out of bed.

"Marvin, could you direct us to the bathroom?"

Lydia and Justine helped Susanna out of bed and noticed a urine and feces stain that covered the entirety of the bed and her gown. Susanna needed a wheelchair.

"Yeah, she recently stopped being able to walk," Marvin said as he rolled it in.

They wheeled her down the hallway and to the bathroom. The odor followed Susanna wherever she went. Once they got to the bathroom, Marvin attempted to stand in and watch their every move.

"I'm sorry Marvin, but we're going to need privacy to do our jobs," Lydia told him.

"If you take any pictures, I'll tell Dr. Wilson."

"I know, and we won't. We want to avoid any police involvement. Just like you."

Marvin left, calling back over his shoulder, "Try to get that stench off her. It fuckin' stinks up the place!"

Lydia swallowed her irritation, stuffing the strong temptation to use her pistol on Marvin. Instead, she shut the door. Lydia couldn't help but shed a tear when she saw a hopeless, vulnerable elderly woman so badly battered. Occasionally, they'd see Susanna jerk away from them in fear. Like she was expecting to be struck.

Justine started taking Susanna's clothing off. She had been in the same clothing for a long time. Each item of clothing was stiff with dried-up sweat, urine, blood, and feces. They slid off the socks on Susanna's feet, and what they saw next would haunt them forever.

T he landline in my office rang. The caller ID showed the medical clinic. I'd just started my shift at six p.m., and I knew that the medical clinic closed at five. It could only mean one thing.

"This is Officer Lawson. How can I help you?"

A female whose voice I didn't recognize responded, "Hello, Officer Lawson. This is RN Nichole Elkins. I'm calling to report elder abuse."

"Susanna Holt?"

Takoda walked into the patrol room as I was talking to Elkins. He looked at the digital caller ID screen and raised his eyebrows. I pressed the speakerphone button so he could hear.

"Yes, Susanna Holt. How'd you know?" Elkins responded.

"Lucky guess. What do you have?"

"I can't quite describe it, but it's really bad. We have pictures for you to see."

"I'll be right down."

The call ended, and I shot Takoda a nervous look. He again realized he was definitely not going to go home to his family on time that night.

"I guess you forgot to cue me in on this part of the plan?" Takoda said.

"Sorry, it was a kind of hail Mary. I didn't think it'd work."

"What'd you do?"

I explained to Takoda the plan I'd hatched with Lydia on Christmas day.

"And you failed to mention this? We still need to advise our superiors."

"I know, but I have to get Susanna out of that house. You know something is going on there. Looks like we're finally going to find out."

"All right, I'm going with you."

"Copy that. I'm gonna call MCRT and have them come out as well. I have a feeling that in this small town, someone, somewhere, will tell the family about what's going on. We'll need someone to talk them down for us."

"Good idea. Plus you get to see your pretty new girlfriend." Takoda grinned.

"Yeah, there's that too."

———

I contacted Ashley and Cardwell and told them what was going on with the case. Cardwell said that they would be en route to our location. They were in the city of Salem, about thirty minutes away.

Takoda and I made our way to the medical clinic and parked our patrol vehicles near the emergency entrance. As we climbed out of the police cruisers, a few flakes of snow started to fall. I examined the ground but didn't see any snow sticking. But it was dark outside, and my head was freezing as soon as I stepped out. I put a beanie on and headed into the clinic.

We entered through a couple of glass doors with green wooden trim. The handles were gold. The warm indoor air hit our faces. The clinic was two stories tall, with several departments inside the building. We saw the dental department, in-home nursing, behavioral health division, optometry, pharmacy, and other medical fields. It was like being in a food court with a bunch of different vendors, only all medical professionals.

I led the way as we stepped on the green and red tribal rugs, with a wolf symbol on them. Under the rugs were gray tile floors. Multiple waiting areas were furnished with couches and TVs, empty now since it was after closing time.

I'd received the call from the in-home nursing department so we went to their area. The metal shed door was pulled down across the reception window. Above the glass window was written in big bold letters, **IN-HOME NURSING MEDICAL DEPARTMENT.**

There was a brown door to the right of the window. I knocked and a blond nurse answered the door. Her ID badge said, "RN Elkins."

We followed her to an office where Lydia, Justine, and an unknown doctor were waiting for us sitting around a table in the center of the room.

Before I entered I already knew something dark had happened. It felt like the lights around me went off, and I was walking in a murky tunnel toward the table.

On the table was a manila envelope that had been labeled with the word PHOTOS. I set foot into the office and saw Lydia huddled in a chair to my left. Her eyes were red and swollen. A nurse I knew as Justine was sitting next to her, with the same demeanor. The doctor was holding a tissue.

Nurse Elkins grabbed the manila envelope and handed it to me.

"I should warn you. These photos are very gruesome."

"I think we can handle it."

I opened the envelope and fished out a stack of digitally printed photographs as large as a piece of notebook paper. Takoda stood next to my right shoulder, and I held the photos in a position so we could both see them. Takoda and I glanced at each other in disgust after viewing the first of many photos. We were looking at a victim of pure evil.

JERICHO NATION MEDICAL CLINIC

The first photo showed a gruesome infection on Susanna Holt's foot. Her foot was swollen so badly that the bulge in the foot looked about to pop. The heel of her foot had completely rotted off, and I observed white insects crawling around her flesh. The second photo was of her other foot, which was just as bad. Both of her feet had grim-looking maggots living inside the rotted brown holes of her heels.

A third photo revealed that the infection continued up Susanna's body. Most of the skin on Susanna's legs had peeled off. Susanna's rear end was grotesque and covered in blood. Mixed among the blood of Susanna's butt cheeks were yellow urine and brown feces stains. I imagined that she couldn't even sit down without being in excruciating pain.

There was bruising of different coloration on her torso. The bruising coloring went from yellow to blue to dark black throughout her body. Some bruises had almost healed; others were fresh. One horrific bruise mark was the shape of a pole or a bat, that marked right along her ribcage.

I rubbed my tired eyes and kept flipping through the photos.

Takoda snapped a photo after I was done reviewing a photo and moved on to the next. In one of the photos, Susanna had a collarbone that was protruding nearly out of her skin. Her right collarbone looked deformed; her left collarbone wasn't visible. She suffered a broken collarbone injury at an unknown time, long ago, and it had healed incorrectly. I wondered what sickening story led to her fracturing her collarbone in Marvin's care.

The skin on Susanna's back was torn off in random areas. The skin that she did have looked like it was about to rot off. Her arms had light bruising on them in the shape of fingerprints. Like someone had held her down.

There was one photo of Susanna's face. Her face, somehow, was not damaged. I recalled Susanna wearing clothing that covered her from head to toe on the night I saw her at the casino.

Susanna's fearful eyes spoke to me. I stared at that picture the longest. I couldn't help but imagine the monstrous pain she must have been in. People don't get infections like she had in a few weeks. Those types of infections are created from months, maybe even years of neglect. I was not looking at an elder-neglect victim. I was looking at a victim of torture. The torture that nobody had done anything about.

"She was trying to get my attention that night at the casino," I whispered to Takoda.

"Don't. Don't do that to yourself."

After reviewing the photos, I realized that there was no saving Susanna. I had a naïve thought when the investigation started. I pictured myself solving the case and getting Susanna the help she needed before it was too late. This was a homicide case, no doubt about it. I wasn't a medical professional, but if I had to guess, Susanna only had days, maybe a few weeks to live before the infections and injuries finally killed her.

The feeling of guilt washed over me. I felt my lips tremble.

I let her down...

I exhaled sharply and kept my composure. This wasn't about

me. It was about getting justice for the family. That's how I had to start viewing it. I wondered if I should have let Mato and Anakin handle the issue. Marvin had it coming.

Takoda helped out by talking to Justine and Lydia. Both of them were understandably hysterical. Lydia asked me several times, "Is my boss a criminal? Was she doing this with Marvin? What the hell is going on?"

We didn't have all the answers yet, but someone in the medical field was letting Marvin do this and covering it up, that much was clear. It was Caroline Wilson, Monica Hawke, or both.

Ashley and Cardwell arrived and Takoda led them into the office. Once they were with us, I asked Takoda to call our superiors and inform them of the case. Takoda stepped out of the room to do so.

"What do we got?" Cardwell asked.

I handed him the photos.

"See for yourself."

Cardwell's gaze went down, and Ashley looked, standing by his shoulder. I watched their repulsed reactions as they stared at the photos in horror. Ashley stepped away for a few seconds, her face pale, her hand over her mouth. For a second, I thought she was going to throw up, but she was able to recollect herself.

Cardwell looked up from the photos

"This is one of the worst things I've seen in thirty years," he said hoarsely. I knew him to be a man who experienced some pretty bad things.

Ashley had told me earlier how Cardwell used to be on the Oregon State Police SWAT team. He'd seen his fair share of officer-involved shootings, which are the worst days in an officer's life. Of all those years of trauma, this ranked among the worst of his experiences.

I confirmed with Lydia that the pictures were taken that day. Cardwell and Ashley stayed with Lydia and the others.

I marched out to my patrol vehicle. Takoda was on the phone with Sergeant Rod Mollahan.

Takoda put his hand over the speaker.

"Are you heading over to contact Bingham?"

"You're goddamn right I am."

THE BINGHAM RESIDENCE

Takoda swiftly ended his phone call, and I floored it, heading to Bingham's—Susanna's—house.

I was too late before, Susanna, but I'm gonna do what I can now.

As we approached the driveway, I cut the engine loose and let it drift to a stop. There were lights on inside. The snow was falling harder and sticking to the roof.

The snow-filled ground crunched as my boot touched down from my vehicle. Takoda walked up behind me.

"Remember, keep your cool. Don't let him get in your head."

I nodded and said nothing.

Snow fell on our black uniforms, making us more visible in the darkness.

We knocked loudly.

"Police. Open up!"

Sometimes I wish knocking and announcing weren't a required thing for police officers. But I had to build a case. A case this important you can't rush it. You need statements, confessions, and more evidence for the district attorney to convict the shithead. The pictures alone weren't enough. I needed to verify the injuries in person before I could arrest him. I needed to play the long game.

Marvin answered the door in nothing but a pair of jeans. He was buckling his belt, then scratched his groin.

"Officer Lawson!" Marvin slurred his speech and leaned up against a wall. "What do I owe the pleasure?"

Stay calm, stay calm, stay calm. Don't kill him. Don't let your rage end you.

I responded, "We need to talk to you about Susanna. May we come in?"

"That fuckin' bitch." Marvin mumbled to himself.

"What was that?" Takoda asked.

"Uh..." Marvin regathered himself. "No, you can't come in. Please leave. We're fine."

Marvin attempted to close the door in my face. I stuck my hand out and stopped the door from shutting. Marvin was trying to push the door shut by leaning his unimpressive body weight into the door.

"I'm afraid we're going to have to insist," I snarled.

Marvin stopped pushing on the door and took a step back.

"Am I going to jail?"

"We need to check on Susanna, now."

"And if I continue to tell you no?"

"Then I'll kick the fucking door off the hinges and force my way in." I gritted my teeth.

Takoda added, "And he'll knock out anyone who gets in his way. Trust me, I've seen it. It's not pretty. We'd prefer you to cooperate."

"Do you have a search warrant?" Marvin inquired.

"Exigent circumstances. We don't need a search warrant." I answered.

Marvin stood there, drunk as a skunk, wondering what his next move would be. I remembered Camille telling me about a shotgun.

I added, "If you reach for anything, we'll assume it's a weapon, and I'll scatter your brains all over that wall. Got it?"

Marvin fixed his gaze on me.

"I wasn't gonna reach for anything."

"Sure, you weren't. Get out of my way."

Marvin stepped back, and I shoved the door open. I trampled past Marvin, brushing my shoulder against his. I made my way through the house and recognized the smell—like the odor of a rotting animal that I smelled at the casino when I first met Susanna. But ten times worse.

I followed the smell. Takoda waited with Marvin near the front door.

The hallway looked like it belonged in a Stephen King novel.

I found a door and opened it. As I swung the door open, the odor overwhelmed me and I nearly vomited on the wooden floor. Susanna was lying on her side, facing the door.

Susanna's breath was loud and labored. She was making a horrible moaning noise. She was barely alive. I checked her body for the infections I saw in the photos. The infections were all there, proving the photos were reliable evidence. The infections were even worse in person. It looked the same, but the scent was unbearable. The maggots were crawling all over her body, eating Susanna's flesh.

My teeth ground together. Dementia had stopped almost all brain functions for Susanna. The only thing she understood was that she was suffering.

I tried talking to Susanna and attempted to move her body so she would stop being in such pain. But when I shifted her body a little, her agonized cry shook me to my core. Eventually, she stopped making noise, and I determined she was more comfortable.

I stepped out of the room for a second, gathered myself, and contacted my dispatch via radio. I advised them to get medics out to our location as soon as possible. I went back to the doorway where Marvin and Takoda were standing.

"Where would you like to talk?" I asked Marvin.

"Am I going to jail?"

"Let's talk first. I'm sure you have an explanation for all this."

Marvin led the way and we followed him to the living room. The wooden flooring hallway from the doorway led to another hallway which led to the bedrooms of the house. To the left was the carpeted living room area. There was a brown couch and a cushioned green reclining chair. The couch and chair were facing a forty-two-inch, flat screen, wall-mounted TV. A bookshelf was stacked with several James Patterson novels and a pile of John Grisham books that took up most of the shelf. One book stuck out to me: it was about Ted Bundy. *The Stranger Beside Me*.

Marvin flopped down on the edge of the reclining chair. I sat on the couch, and Takoda remained standing.

A few minutes later, Takoda went back to the front door and saw red-and-white lights flashing from a distance. The ambulance soon arrived at the house and Takoda met with them in the driveway. Takoda began explaining the situation to the medics, and I started my interrogation with Marvin.

M arvin looked at me nervously. I couldn't help but have the aura of someone who wanted to kill. I shuffled my body forward and leaned my torso toward Marvin.

"All right, Marvin, Susanna is in pretty bad shape. I have to read you your Miranda Rights before I ask you any questions. Do you understand?" I asked.

"Yeah."

I told Marvin the Miranda Rights verbatim from memory. The verbiage was imprinted in my brain. For those of you that don't know what the Miranda Rights are. It's the whole "you have the right to remain silent" spiel you see on pretty much every law and order episode.

If I got statements before making him aware of his rights, the statements could be disregarded as evidence. If confessions are disregarded as evidence, it can really hurt the case. I asked him if he understood, then if he was willing to speak with me. To my surprise, he continued to speak to me. He was so inebriated, I had to wonder if he knew what was happening.

"This whole situation is a bit messy, Marvin, I'm not gonna lie to you." I explained, "Susanna is in bad shape, and you're her caretaker. However, there are two sides to every story and it's my job to know your side of things. How'd Susanna manage to get to this level of unhealthiness?"

"I'm not sure, Officer Lawson... I'd been taking her to the hospital and seeing the doctors weekly. They all said she was fine, but her health keeps decreasing. I don't want anything to happen to my Susanna! I love her!"

You piece of shit. I should cave your face in with my boot.

"When was the last doctor's appointment?" I inquired.

"Last week."

"Where at?"

"McMinnville County Hospital."

"Wrong. Try again, Marvin."

"What do you mean?"

"I paid Dr. Perez a visit. You missed your last two appointments. Why's that?"

"Uh, uh...," he stuttered. "I think Susanna had family come over or we had the in-home nurses come instead. Because her health was too bad to travel."

"She wasn't too unhealthy to go to the casino a few weeks ago while you got drunk."

Marvin didn't have a quick reply to this question. He rubbed his eyes and exhaled loudly. I smelled bourbon.

"That was the last week she could move around. She stopped walking the day after that." His speech was still slurred, but for once he'd told the truth. The infections in her feet must have made it impossible for her to walk.

"Explain to me what happened when you realized Susanna couldn't walk."

Marvin paused again and acted as if I was asking him to solve a trigonometry question. "One day she was walking in the living room and she fell, out of the blue."

"Where were you when she was walking around the house?"

Marvin started to realize he was talking himself into a confession and changed the topic, "I thought you were here to get my side of things?"

Takoda and the medics came in and walked down the hallway. Takoda led the medics to Susanna. Takoda went around the wall that separated the living room from the bedrooms and joined me with Marvin.

Marvin added, "I'm starting to think I'm going to jail no matter what."

"No, no... Why would you be going to jail, Marv? I mean it's all about you, is it not? It's really hard to be a caretaker... Let's hear what you have to say. Please explain this."

I asked Takoda to hand me the envelope that contained the photos that Lydia took. I rose and grabbed the envelope from his hand and dug out the photos. I stood over Marvin as he remained seated. I flung the first of many appalling photos to Marvin. The photo bounced off his chest and landed on his lap. Marvin glanced down at the photo and I repeated my question, "Explain that. Explain how the hell someone gets to that point and nobody does anything about it."

Marvin stared at the photo and said nothing. I tossed a second photo like I was throwing a frisbee. The photo bounced off his head, "Explain that one too."

Marvin said nothing.

"What was it, Marvin? Was it her tribal fund? Is that what you wanted?" My hand was shaking.

He didn't so much as shed a tear. He simply grabbed one photo off his lap and then picked up the second one off the ground.

Marvin rose with the two photos and said, "You dropped these."

His voice was joyful, and he flashed me a smile with his yellow teeth. I could have punched him right there. I grabbed the photos from him and told Marvin to sit back down like he was a dog.

Just then, Cardwell and Ashley stepped through the door. Takoda pointed them to the back bedroom where medics were working on Susanna. I regrouped and sat beside Marvin on the couch. I noticed Marvin's eyes locked in on Cardwell's massive body when he entered the home.

"You seem impressed by the photos," I said.

Marvin's eyes went back to me, "Me? No, I wasn't. Why would you say that?"

"Because you were smiling. It's funny, the human body can't hide its true emotions. If you pay attention long enough, you'll see their little tells. The smile was brief, but I saw it, Marvin."

"I'm afraid you're mistaken, Officer Lawson."

"I'm not mistaken at all. Stand up, turn around, and place your hands behind your back. You're under arrest."

Marvin froze his gaze on me for a second and remained seated. I stood and was about to grab him myself. Marvin shot upright and raised his hands, "All right, all right, I'm cooperating."

I put the handcuffs around his wrists and put him in my squad car.

Before medics transported Susanna to the Salem County Hospital, I directed them not to take Susanna to McMinnville County Hospital under any circumstances.

Then I transported Marvin to the Kirk County Jail, and he was locked up for several felony charges.

CHAPTER
THIRTY-NINE

Anakin, Mato, and other family members got a call from the hospital soon after she arrived there. Doctors and nurses had done several scans of Susanna's body and found internal injuries, in addition to the deplorable and life-threatening ulceration of her skin. Susanna had a broken collarbone and a few punctured ribs to go along with it. She was on life support.

Mato and Anakin went to the hospital together to see their aunt.

As they entered her fourth-floor hospital room, they could hear the heart monitor beeping near Susanna's still body. Susanna had an IV to combat dehydration. There was a feeding tube inserted in the corner of her mouth. She was so dehydrated it was as if she'd been living in the Sahara desert for years without water. There were all kinds of equipment attached to her body. Mato and Anakin realized these machines were the only things keeping her alive.

The doctor paid his condolences and left them to be alone with Susanna. From Susanna's hospital room, the streetlights of the city of Salem were visible. Cars stopped at stoplights in the distance. The city lights were beautiful at night.

Anakin and Mato stood on either side of the bed and eyed Susanna in sorrow.

Anakin felt a lump in his throat as he gazed at her. After a few seconds, he had to look away. Visions of his mother dead in his arms crept into his mind.

She was dressed in a white hospital gown and had green blanket sheets covering her. Susanna's hospital bed was inclined slightly upward, to make it easier for her to breathe. Mato reached past the tubes and machinery to find Susanna's soft, supple hand. Susanna's eyes were shut, but the doctor said she could still hear them.

"I love you, Aunt Susanna," Mato sobbed. He knelt beside the bed, still holding her hand. "We're going to help you through this."

Anakin built up the courage to face Susanna and echoed his brother's movements, kneeling and taking her hand.

Mato glanced at Anakin, his eyes still wet. "We were too late."

"We didn't know this was going to happen," responded Anakin.

He focused on Susanna, and spoke to her.

"You're the mother I never got to have after high school. Without you, I don't think I would have made it out of prison."

"You're our rock, Aunt Susanna, and if you can hear us... Squeeze our hands. Let us know you're still in there fighting to survive," said Mato.

The faintest squeeze came from each hand. Susanna was in there somewhere, still fighting. The squeeze was weak, but it was proof that she was semiconscious.

"We're going to make this right. Marvin won't see another day alive if he's ever released from jail," Anakin added grimly.

Mato nodded. "If it's the last thing we do... We'll do it. You say the word, and we'll kill the white man they call Marvin."

Anakin felt another squeeze. His eyes met Mato's, and he knew his brother had felt the same.

CHAPTER
FORTY

The next morning I finished my shift and was ready for a long slumber. When I pulled into my driveway, I saw Ashley's car in the free space of the cement. It was 07:00 and the neighbor's dogs were barking. It was still dark, but the two inches of snow on the ground made it easier to see.

After I parked and got out, I saw Ashley reclined in the front seat of her Toyota 4Runner, sleeping. I exited my civilian vehicle, the Dodge Challenger, and heard her engine idling.

I knocked on the window.

"Ashley? What are you doing here?"

She woke up startled, flailing her hands in the air and then clenching her fist like she was about to throw a wild punch into her own window. Then she saw it was me and calmed down. She turned her key in the ignition and shut off the vehicle. Ashley opened her door to talk to me.

"Hey. I wanted to see how you were."

"How long have you been here waiting for me?" I asked.

"Since I got off work... I forgot when your shift ended, so I figured if I waited until you got home, I'd catch you before you fell asleep."

"Do you realize how stalker-ish that sounds?"

She pondered this for a second. "Yeah, it does, huh? I promise I'm not stalking you. Just trying to be a supportive girlfriend."

I smiled.

"Thank you, but I'm all right. Are you okay? That stuff probably isn't easy for you to see... It's a normal occurrence for me, unfortunately."

"Nothing about that was normal... Cardwell was even shaken up. He had to go home and vent to his fiancé about it. I've never seen him upset like that... It's okay to be sad, Warren."

"I suppose you're right. It was pretty bad," I agreed. "Do you want to talk inside? It's really chilly out here."

"That sounds nice."

————

We lay in bed together with her head on my chest, arms wrapped around my waist. I lay on my back, looking up at the ceiling in deep thought, both of us in the nude, covered by my blankets.

"What was the hardest part about this case?" Ashley asked softly.

I let out a noticeably long exhalation. Lord knew I didn't want to talk about it. I allowed my thoughts to percolate.

"I promise it won't kill you to open up to me about your work," she said. "It's healthy and I am a good listener. It's my job, after all."

"I know. But it's hard for me. I never opened up to anyone about the work I do."

"And you've been a cop for how long?"

"Six years."

"That's a lonely island you put yourself on for that long."

"I don't see the sense in reliving trauma. It just makes you unbearably emotional. Can't we enjoy each other's company and get some rest?"

"We can... And I will never try to force you to talk to me if you don't want to. However, I can tell Susanna Holt is weighing heavy on your heart. I think if you spoke about it before you fell asleep, you might find that it helps."

"Is this what you do with your therapy patients?"

"Yes, in fact, I do."

"Does it work for them?"

"If it didn't, I wouldn't use that technique."

"Good point."

She rubbed her finger along the abs of my stomach, up to my chest, then to my face. Her head tilted up, and she looked at me with her brown doe eyes.

"The hardest part was hearing how much pain she was in when I found her..."

CHAPTER
FORTY-ONE

Later that afternoon, Marvin Bingham awaited his attorney in an interview room at the jail. The room was the blandest ten-by-ten room the jail could find. It had cement brick walls, a large mirror, a table, and two chairs on each side of the metal table. In the top far corner of the room, attached to the ceiling, was a black camera with a blinking red light.

Marvin was wearing his bright orange jumpsuit. The room was freezing, so he rubbed the palms of his hands on his arms trying to get warm. A couple of corrections deputies were standing on either side of Marvin until his lawyer arrived.

The sharply dressed man entered, looking like Marvin's savior. He was in his fifties with a full, groomed beard, black hair, and a belly that hung past his groin. He was wearing an all-black dress suit, with a salmon-colored dress shirt and blue tie. He wore a pair of reading glasses and carried with him a bulging black briefcase. He had a large brown mole on his cheekbone that Marvin stared at without meaning to.

The lawyer was relaxed and thanked the two correction deputies for waiting. He banged his briefcase on the table and sat back in his chair. He slid his reading glasses off for a second, rubbed the lenses with the sleeve of his jacket, and put the glasses back on. He took his jacket off and wrapped it around the chair.

"Howdy, Mr. Bingham, I'll be your attorney. My name is Neil Marshall. It's nice to meet you."

They shook hands, and Neil laid a notepad on the table.

"All right, tell me everything. Don't spare any details. What we say stays between us. I could give a shit whether you did it or didn't do it. Tell me everything and I'll be able to be the most effective in helping you through this."

Marvin pondered, "What about the camera? It'll catch what I say."

"Not anymore." Neil pointed out that the red light on the camera was no longer blinking.

"Sorry, I don't know who to trust. The people I trusted, kind of stabbed me in the back. Which landed me here," said Marvin.

"What do you mean?"

"Well, do you want to hear the full story or should I just explain what I just mentioned?"

"Give me the full story."

Marvin leaned forward in his chair and told Neil everything. Well, almost everything. Actually, just the parts Marvin wanted him to know. The start of rekindling his relationship with Susanna, to him being her caretaker, to the health decline. He left out the parts where he neglected Susanna or anything that made him seem like the bad guy. Neil listened intently and took meticulous notes and made Marvin feel like he was the center of his universe.

"And now I get to the part in the story about the person who betrayed me," Marvin said. "I was friends with this doctor who worked for the tribe. You see, she ran the entire medical department. She was the head honcho. Anyway, she was the one in charge of all the checkups on Susanna. Then one day she realized that she hadn't been checking Susanna's feet like she was supposed to with diabetic patients..."

"What was the name of this doctor?"

"Caroline Wilson. She worked closely with the in-home nurse

manager, Monica Hawke. Monica answered Caroline's every beck and call, you see... Anyway, they knew about Susanna's health and didn't say shit about it. Aren't they medical professionals? Shouldn't they be more knowledgeable than me on what to do with her?"

"Yes, they are. How were you supposed to know that Susanna's health was declining if they checked on her two weeks ago and said she was okay? It's the doctor that should be arrested, not you."

"Thank you! Finally, someone who sees my side of things. Officer Lawson didn't even give me a chance to explain. He couldn't wait to haul my ass to jail."

"Do you think the officer had a prejudice against you?"

"Fuck, yeah, he did. He was out to get me the moment he met me."

Neil wrote down some more notes.

"We'll have you out of here in no time, Mr. Bingham. In the meantime, you might want to find new friends."

Marvin laughed. "Ain't that the truth."

They both chuckled. "Are there any other people involved that you want to tell me about?" Neil asked.

Marvin thought long and hard about that question. Neil could sense there was something else that Marvin was hiding, but for some reason wasn't telling him.

"Nope, just that Dr. Caroline Wilson should be sitting here and not me."

"Are you sure?"

"Positive."

Neil grabbed his briefcase and notepad. He stuffed his notepad with several files in his briefcase. "Based on what you're telling me I believe I can get the charges dropped to misdemeanors at the very least. After that, I'll work on getting them dropped entirely. I'll shift the attention of this case to the medical employees who neglected to do their job. Then, hire a private investigator, and you'll be free of this in no time. Once I plead the charges down to misdemeanors tomorrow, you'll have a release hearing and will be free to leave the jail until our court date."

"Thank you, thank you!" Marvin praised Neil like he was a god.

"Just doing my job. You'll have to stay another night at the jail, though. Come tomorrow, after I plead your case to the judge at the morning's release hearing. You'll be a free man, Mr. Bingham."

Marvin rested soundly in his jail cell that night, knowing it would be over the next day. He awoke early and was escorted to his release hearing where Neil would present their case. Marvin trudged into the uncomfortable tension of what a courtroom naturally brings. The courtroom had old wooden chairs and rows from front to back of wooden sitting arrangements. The black-robed judge sat above everyone on his perch.

Two tables faced straight across from the judge, and next to the judge was a spot just below his elevated bench: the "witness stand." Marvin walked to a table where Neil sat waiting for him. The release hearing did not require a grand jury or allow many spectators; it was more of a private arrangement. The only other people in the courtroom were Corrections Deputies.

Neil faced Marvin while seated in his chair and motioned him to move his head closer to his.

"Let me do the talking, all right? If the judge asks you about your plea, you say 'not guilty.' Got it?" Neil whispered. "That is all you're required to say."

Marvin nodded, as he noticed the echoing silence in the room. It was hard to let yourself relax in that type of setting. Marvin started to feel withdrawal from not drinking for more than twenty-four hours. His body started trickling sweat for no reason.

When he felt the sweat streaming down his face, Marvin was considering running to the nearest liquor store and drinking a beer. He had to remind himself, *not guilty, plead not guilty.* Remembering two words had never been so hard.

The next thought he had was if he was still going to be able to get money from Susanna. She was in the hospital, and most likely still alive. He'd been surviving on her per capita tribal checks the past year. It also occurred to him that the longer she was alive, the less likely it was that he would inherit anything.

Two jobs. Get a drink, and make sure Susanna dies. How would he pull off Susanna's death without being caught? Marvin believed that nobody could change the will except Susanna, so if she wasn't able to, he would get the money he deserved. Another question for the outstanding Defense Attorney, Neil Marshall, to answer later.

The judge left the courtroom and let the prosecuting lawyers and defense attorneys get ready to make their arguments. A few minutes later the judge returned. Everyone in the courtroom stood up for the judge. As the judge sat down, he said, "Please be seated."

Everyone sat down and the argument to release Marvin began. Marvin was asked at the beginning what his plea was and Marvin did as he was told, "Not guilty, Your Honor."

The hearing continued for another hour. Marvin tuned out most of the conversation; he was nodding off, due to complete boredom, but he managed to keep himself awake until the end.

At the end of the hearing, the judge granted Marvin his release. The judge noted that Marvin's criminal background was minimal and that he was not a danger to the public. Neil argued that the crime he was charged with was the doctor's and nurse's fault, not Marvin's. The judge advised them that they would make that determination another day. Marvin was ordered to come back at a later date for court. And then he was released into the free world.

———

Ashley and I were playing mini-golf when I got the call later that night. I was standing there on the putting green, watching Ashley sink a near-impossible hole-in-one shot when I heard "Thunderstruck" from my phone. As Ashley broke into a victory dance, I saw Takoda was calling.

"Hey, what's up?"

"I just received a call from the DA's office."

"They called me earlier, but I ignored it because I'm on a date with Ashley. What'd they say?"

"Marvin Bingham got released from jail today."

CHAPTER
FORTY-THREE

Susanna's family had stayed at the hospital with her every day since Warren and Takoda found her. They took turns staying in the hospital room with her. Mato and Anakin camped outside her hospital room, sleeping in uncomfortable chairs most of the time. Camille came; Grandma Holt and Robert were there. Emily and her kids came.

The family struggled to deal with the aftermath. On one end of the spectrum, they were happy to finally see her again. Marvin had successfully kept them away from her for a year and a half. The other end of the spectrum was seeing the physical state that Susanna was in.

Hilary came by and she and Anakin strolled around the hospital a couple of times to get some fresh air. She was concerned about him and knew Anakin well enough to know where his mind was wandering off to. Anakin wanted revenge. His eyes said it all. Hilary convinced him that Marvin would pay his debt in prison and that was good enough. Anakin thought no amount of prison time was punishment enough for Marvin, but he didn't want to go back to prison himself, either.

When Anakin and Hilary came back from their second walk,

they went to Susanna's hospital room to wait in their chairs. Mato was standing when they returned, and Anakin saw him pacing back and forth in the hallway outside the room. Anakin imagined the worst and rushed over.

"Is everything okay, Mato?"

Mato glanced at Anakin. "No... The white men fucked us again."

"What do you mean?"

"Marvin Bingham has been released from jail already."

"No. That can't be. They just arrested him yesterday."

"Look."

Mato handed Anakin his cell phone, which displayed the Kirk County Jail inmate roster sheet. Anakin placed his fingers on the screen and scrolled down, frantically looking for Marvin's name. It wasn't there.

"Scroll to the release hearing page," said Mato.

Anakin flipped past the inmate roster page and located Marvin's name on the release hearing page. He found Marvin Bingham's information and clicked on it. It read:

MARVIN BINGHAM

CHARGES: ELDER NEGLECT, ASSAULT I, CRIMINAL MISTREATMENT I

BAIL: $150,000

RELEASE HEARING: 1/4/20

RELEASE STATUS: GRANTED

Anakin shook his head in disbelief as he returned Mato's phone to him. Mato tucked the phone in his pocket.

"I can't believe they released him already," Hilary said.

She rubbed Anakin's back in an attempt to keep him calm.

"I can. I can fucking believe it," he commented grimly. "We killed our mother's killer, and we were held without bail. This fucking white man tortures our aunt for god knows how long and gets out the next day. We should have done it our way in the first place. We were stupid to think Lawson could handle this."

Hilary disagreed. "This isn't Officer Lawson's fault. He made the arrest. He got us more days with Susanna... He tried to get justice for us, Anakin."

"He tried and he failed," Mato interrupted.

Hilary sighed, knowing where this conversation was heading.

"OK, but whatever you do. Anakin can't be involved."

"I'm sorry, my love, but I have to be," replied Anakin. "Soldiers don't hire other soldiers to do their work. Soldiers do their own work."

"The cops will arrest you... You won't meet your baby."

"Then you should tell our child that his father was an honorable man, who was locked up for standing up against the white man's injustice."

Mato wanted to grow old helping raise Anakin's new baby and be an uncle. Yet he knew what had to be done. If Susanna and the brothers traded places, she would have found a way to avenge them.

"I won't let the cops take him in, Hilary. You have my word." Mato promised.

"Thanks, Mato... but I don't want you guys to get in trouble. I need you both..."

"And Aunt Susanna needs us to avenge her. You know in your heart this is what has to be done."

Hilary's eyes filled, and she whirled and rushed away. Anakin hollered for Hilary to stay, but she ignored him. He started to follow her, but she screamed, "Don't you fucking follow me!"

Anakin defensively put his hands up and apologized He never meant to harm Hilary. She was his princess. There were doctors, nurses, patients, and all types of people walking around the hallway and they started to stare. Anakin's look, with tattoos all over his arms and neck, didn't help his case when Hilary screamed.

A security officer walked up to Anakin.

"Is everything okay here, sir?"

"We're fine; piss off." Mato butted in.

The security officer looked up about a foot at Mato's angry face and decided that he was picking the wrong battle. He walked briskly away.

Anakin watched as Hilary entered an elevator and vanished from sight.

Mato wrapped his arm around his brother. "She'll get over it. In time she will come to understand."

"I can only hope," Anakin responded. "Do we still have our boys in town or have they left?"

"They are here for as long as we need."

"Let's tell them to get ready."

"For what? We can handle Marvin alone."

"Yes, but we may have to deal with cops. If that's the case I would like our guys to be the ones taking the fall. Not us."

"We won't need them. I won't let them take you in, brother. No matter what."

"I know. I won't let them arrest you either."

CHAPTER
FORTY-FOUR

I marched into the Kirk County Courthouse and headed straight to the district attorney's office. Several people were plodding around the building who knew me from years of court testimonies. I ignored them, as I was way too pissed off to make conversation.

I heard murmurs behind me, people saying, "What's with him?"

The county clerk's desk stood in my way as I approached the entrance to the private offices of the prosecutors. The county clerk spoke to me through a sheet of glass, using a speakerphone.

"How may I help you?"

"I'm here for a meeting with the prosecutor's office. Officer Lawson, Jericho Nation Tribal PD." I said as I smacked my badge to the window. The loud clunk made the clerk jump in her seat. When she let me in, she noticed I wasn't wearing the most professional of clothing for the setting. I had on a pair of work boots, some blue jeans, and a black flannel, long-sleeved, button-up shirt. I bore a resemblance to an extremely pissed-off logger.

I heard a lot of laughing coming from the break room area, so I followed the sound.

I saw a group of DAs laughing like a group of wild hyenas and asked, "Who's working the Susanna Holt case?"

They stopped laughing. One of them said, "Well, nice to see you, too, Lawson."

"Whose working the fucking Susanna Holt case?"

I glared at them like a serial killer. They probably picked up that I was not in a mood to laugh.

"Andrew Ketelson," one said. "New guy. Other end of the hall."

I headed back the way I had come. As I left, I heard more people frightened by the way I was acting, but I did not care. No more facade, no more act. Time for the real me.

The floors were black; the walls were gray. A tan-colored door had a black-on-white nameplate that said KIRK COUNTY DISTRICT ATTORNEY ANDREW KETELSON.

On the other side of the door, I overheard his voice. On the phone talking to someone about something super important, I'm sure.

I barged in. "Got a minute?"

He held a finger up without so much as a look in my direction. He continued to talk on the phone.

"I need to talk now."

DA Ketelson continued to ignore my wishes. I walked over to his desk and ripped the phone from his hand.

"He's gonna have to call you back."

I hung up the phone so hard that I nearly broke his phone monitor machine.

"I. Said. I. Need to fucking talk." I slammed my hands on his neatly polished desk and stared him straight in the eyes. Andrew leaned way back in his chair and frantically looked at the doorway to his office, hoping someone would come to save him.

"I'm Officer Lawson. Nice to meet you."

Andrew looked like a model with his perfectly symmetrical face, and hands that showed no sign of callus. The hardest work he probably did was talk in a courtroom. Which he didn't seem to be good at, considering the reason I was at his desk. I wanted to throttle his little hobbit-size neck, but I took the mature approach.

"How the fuck do you allow a guy like Marvin Bingham to be released? Do you even know how to do your job? You lawyers are worthless."

"Officer Lawson, I don't appreciate your tone," Andrew replied, licking his lips and trying to recapture his cool.

"And I don't appreciate you letting killers walk free, you cocksucker."

My fist slammed into the table. If it had been his face, he'd have been down for the count.

Andrew put his hands up defensively.

"Please, Officer Lawson, that tone is not needed here. One more outburst and I'll have you fired. Can you please calm down so we can discuss this like mature adults?"

"Yeah, I'll put that on my to-do list. Right after inserting used needles into my dick. Now, tell me why the fuck Marvin Bingham has been released already?"

Andrew sighed and extended his hand to motion me to the chair across from his desk, "Take a seat. I'll explain."

"This I gotta hear." I sat down.

"Mr. Bingham's defense attorney is a very skilled lawyer. In fact, he is pretty spendy so I'm not sure how Mr. Bingham affords him. It was like he knew that Neil Marshall was the only lawyer that could get him out of the mess he was in."

"Neil Marshall is the defense on this?"

"Yes. Anyway, Mr. Marshall presented a case stating that the people at fault for Ms. Holt's predicament were the doctors, and not Mr. Bingham, who also does not have a significant criminal record."

"How does he figure that?"

"They're the medical professionals, for one. For two, Mr. Bingham fulfilled his duties by taking her to the medical clinic. It's not his fault that the doctors were negligent."

"Ray Charles could have seen that Susanna Holt needed more

medical attention than what was being given to her. Come on! Is this your first rodeo? Are you really that fucking stupid to think that Marvin had no idea what was going on with Susanna? There were shit stains on the walls of her bedroom, for crying out loud! And that's just the bare minimum of our findings!"

"I know, but I don't write the laws, and neither do you. I will be dropping this case. Otherwise, we'll get ripped apart during the trial."

"Let the defense question my investigation. Show those photos to any jury and they'll convict the bastard. Don't drop this case! Charge him with the felonies. We can win this in court."

"My hands are tied. I'm sorry... I truly am. I believe you did a good thing by arresting Mr. Bingham. Unfortunately, this case is not as cut and dry as we may have hoped."

I shook my head. "Can I arrest the doctors?"

"You could, but you need more evidence. A confession that they neglected to check Susanna's feet and covered it up."

"They aren't going to just tell me they did that."

"Then they can be sued civilly by the family... For us to get a conviction on Mr. Bingham, you would have needed to do about five more weeks of investigating and building your case. Instead, you went right to arrest him. We need more evidence. As it stands right now. The defense will get some expert to testify and say that it's possible for Marvin not to have known the extent of her injuries. Then we won't have a leg to stand on in court."

"If I didn't arrest him when I did, Susanna would be lying in her piss-stained bed dying a slow, miserable death."

"I understand that, but you didn't get a confession from Marvin, and you didn't question him about the hospital staff. You just went ahead and arrested him."

"Because he fucking did it. You know it and I know it. Who gives a shit about the so-called expert the defense will call in to testify? Why is everything so fucking complicated when it comes to prosecuting?"

Andrew let out another audible exhale; he was clearly uncomfortable.

"I don't know, Officer Lawson. I'm sorry my work is not up to your standard."

"Me too."

I stood and started to leave. I stopped at the doorway and looked at him.

"I can't let this go."

CHAPTER
FORTY-FIVE

arvin Bingham strolled the streets of Dallas after being released. He went to the nearest liquor store and bought a bottle with most of the remaining cash in his wallet. Next, he walked around town drinking out of the bottle wrapped in a brown paper bag.

The drink had never tasted so good. During his trip to the liquor store, it felt as if he was running a triathlon. His energy level was low, as his body was primarily focused on the early stages of withdrawal.

As he left the liquor store, Marvin encountered a wet, skinny dog that was wandering around the parking lot alone. Marvin watched the wet, homeless dog roam around the parking lot, sticking its nose in every nearby trash can, looking for a snack. The dog was begging for food as people passed by, but without much luck, because he was dirty, smelly, and not attractive to small children.

Marvin glanced around and saw a market in the same parking lot area as the liquor store. He made his way to the market and bought a package of hot dogs. He walked back out with a bag of food and sauntered over to the homeless dog.

He knelt. "Hey there, boy."

Marvin petted the dog, whose tongue hung out of its mouth to the side, as it was panting. He put the food on the ground, and the dog started scarfing it down instantly.

"There ya go, boy."

With the dog taken care of, he started to head due north out of town. Marvin wished he could take the dog with him, but he was on his way to meet someone.

The city was small and quaint. There were only three or four stoplights in the city from what Marvin could tell. The roads were icy, so there weren't very many cars out. The city seemed peaceful, and he felt safe.

It was about a six-mile hike out of town. About halfway through the walk, he had finished a fifth of alcohol. The alcohol warmed up his blood so he couldn't feel the winter wind. He was wearing a pair of jeans and a sweatshirt. Had he not been so drunk, he'd probably be freezing, but he was numb to it.

Marvin approached Highway 22. The roadway was an east-west, two-lane blacktop. Marvin found a nice park-and-ride gravel lot on the eastbound shoulder and waited. He wished he bought two bottles of alcohol, but he was never known for thinking ahead.

A few minutes later, the sound of tires crackling on the loose gravel rock caught Marvin's attention. A dark blue 2019 model Jeep Cherokee drove into the park-and-ride. Marvin saw the Jeep drive up next to him. The passenger side of the vehicle was closest to where Marvin was standing. The front passenger window buzzed down.

"Get in the car," the driver snapped.

Marvin didn't argue and crawled in. He sat in the front passenger seat. They turned eastbound onto Highway 22. The driver was MCRT Deputy Brent Cardwell.

Brent Cardwell was off duty when he contacted Marvin. Cardwell glanced at Marvin with disgust as he drove along the highway. His vehicle handled the ice nicely as they drove at higher speeds than other vehicles on the road.

"How fucking stupid do you have to be?" Cardwell blurted. "How many times have I told you to be careful when it comes to your stupid shit?"

Marvin replied, "Nobody knew! Then I get called in at the casino one night... and it all goes to hell."

"I'm not going to be able to cover up this one for you."

"If you could have told me Jericho Nation Tribal PD had a detective, that would've been useful information."

"They don't. Just a couple of very dedicated patrol cops."

"How good are they?"

"Lawson is good, really good. He has one of the highest arrest and conviction rates in the state. His partner Tehama is right there with him."

"Fuck... How was I supposed to know this was gonna happen? We had such a good setup, Brent... Your woman sold me out."

"She wouldn't do that to me."

"I'm not trying to cause a domestic disturbance between y'all, but the leak came from her. I know it, that's why those nurses tricked me... and she is gonna go down for it."

"You shut your mouth. Nobody is going down for shit. Got it?"

"All right, all right."

———

Brent and Marvin were about as close as often-estranged brothers could be. Marvin was the older, but Cardwell was the one who had his life together. Growing up, their father abused them and their mother abused drugs. They grew up in Portland, living in an area that was controlled by a homeless population.

One night, Brent and Marvin lost their mother and father in a traffic accident. Marvin was sixteen; Brent was ten. They had no family who could take care of them after their parents died. Foster care had more promise than their own family members did.

Marvin went to one family and Brent to another. Cardwell ended up legally changing his name at twelve, thanks to his single foster dad. Marvin kept the last name, Bingham. Cardwell had a foster father who was a stable, emotionally healthy law enforcement officer. Marvin, unfortunately, got more of the same parenting as he'd gotten in their family of origin.

The brothers sometimes reconnected from time to time. The older they got, the more Cardwell saw a mix of his mother and father in Marvin. Cardwell tried everything to keep Marvin from becoming their parents, but he was busy in the early stages of police work and fell out of contact with Marvin. Cardwell fell in love with climbing the ranks of the police world. Nobody seemed to know his past, which came as a relief to him.

Ten or more years into his career, in 2002, Cardwell looked for his older brother and found Marvin living in a homeless camp on the southern border of Oregon. Cardwell helped his brother get back on his feet. A part of him felt guilty for losing track of him.

When they were younger, Marvin had taken the worst of their dad's abuse. Marvin was the older one and always took responsibility for Brent. Cardwell would never forget Marvin taking torturous abuse from their father night after night. Marvin never turned his back on Brent when they were kids. Cardwell couldn't abandon Marvin now.

Cardwell was living in Salem. He let Marvin move into his guest bedroom. He was there for all Marvin's withdrawals—and his relapses. Cardwell worked twelve-hour graveyard shifts. When he got off work, he'd come home to his brother hugging the toilet.

Once Marvin finally started to get better, confessions started to spill out of him. Marvin told his brother about a new addiction that is worse than anything he'd ever experienced. Marvin confessed to Cardwell that he was addicted to death—to the power of taking a life.

With this newfound information, Cardwell felt he had to conjure up a plan to keep his brother from prison. When Marvin told the story of Diana's murder, it was like it was a wet dream. Cardwell felt like vomiting, but he kept his composure for his brother's sake. He told himself that his brother was so drunk, that he might've been confused about what happened. Maybe he didn't actually kill this woman. The cops who'd investigated called it an accidental death. Maybe Marvin was just making this shit up to make himself feel powerful. Cardwell couldn't believe the worst. Not then. Eventually, though, he stopped lying to himself and that's when he had to come up with something to keep his brother from ending up in prison.

Then Cardwell came up with an idea—a way to turn Marvin's morbid obsession into something good. Cardwell explained to Marvin that he was not to kill anyone outside the walls of his job. But he could work at a hospice where death was always around the corner.

Marvin landed a job at the hospice center and while he was there, he silently killed elderly people in their sleep. Marvin's addiction was sated for the time being. Cardwell's plan was working.

Cardwell justified it in his head: the victims were dying

anyway, so these were, at worst, mercy killings. To keep Marvin interested, Cardwell talked to him about the dos and don'ts regarding leaving evidence at a crime scene. Sometimes Marvin would mess things up, but Cardwell was quick to cover his brother's tracks. It was better that Marvin fed his need on victims who were on their death bed instead of innocent people out in the world with a long life ahead of them.

The hospice center job kept Marvin sober as well. Marvin started to get healthier. After a year of living together, Cardwell was seeing Marvin in a new light. Despite everything, Marvin was Cardwell's brother, and he still loved him. Then Marvin decided to venture into the world on his own as a sober man.

———

Cardwell continued to drive eastbound on an empty highway. The sun was going down. The temperature sensor near his steering wheel read thirty-two degrees.

"Do you have anywhere you can go?" Cardwell asked.

Marvin replied, "Susanna's house."

"That's the only place you can go?"

"Yeah."

"Doesn't seem like the best spot for you right now, but all right."

"So what are you going to do about Caroline?"

"Let me handle that. You worry about staying out of trouble for the next few months... What is it with you and this Susanna woman? I told you not to drag this out any longer once she got sick. Put her out of her misery, remember?"

"She's the one that got away."

"So what? You're torturing her?"

"No, not like that... I mean, I actually liked her. Loved her, even. That's why I married her. She reminded me of Sharon. For a little bit, I didn't want to kill anybody when I was with her. They say love can beat anything. I think that's true for everyone except me."

"I believe you... Were there any other things that were special to you about Susanna?"

"No... not at all."

"Her tribal savings account had nothing to do with your attraction to her?"

"Sure, that may have helped a little... But I did love her. That's why I married her. I was devastated when she divorced me."

"I remember... Now explain to me why this happened?"

"We got back together, and I thought it was great... Then, she started to get sick. I should have gotten someone to take care of her."

Marvin stared out the window of the Jeep, looking ashamed.

"But my need for death took control of my body. I couldn't help it. As soon as she pissed me off during a few arguments, *I wanted to kill her.* It was all I wanted. My love for her didn't matter anymore. Like one side of me was begging to keep her alive and the other side of me wanted to kill her. And, well, I guess this was the result."

Cardwell kept his gaze on the road. He didn't say a word. Marvin looked over at him and asked somberly, "Do you still love me?"

There was a long pause before Cardwell replied.

"I still love you, Marv."

"Oh, cool." Marvin smiled and went back to his day as normal.

Cardwell's eyes started to water, but he forced back his tears.

JERICHO NATION, OREGON

Cardwell dropped Marvin off near the casino so he could catch a bus home. After watching Marvin get on a bus, Cardwell spun the wheel and headed for the western edge of Jericho Nation.

Upon arrival, he made a lefthand turn into a 500-yard-long, steep gravel driveway, bouncing around in the potholes as he drove deeper into the woods. All around him were trees larger than buildings in a big city—some of the biggest Douglas fir trees in the state. The forest looked like an ocean of green and brown.

The tires of Cardwell's Jeep spun on the ice for a brief second but were able to regain traction as it climbed the hill. In the distance was a beautiful log cabin home, sitting on a hill in the center of the forest.

As Cardwell got closer, the house started to look bigger. The log cabin had two floors. The foundation at the bottom of the house was built of stones. There was a deck built along the house with a fence about three feet high around the deck. The corners of the fence were made of mini logs.

The windows were so shiny, you could see the reflection for miles. The stone-paved walkways around the house were multicolored, ranging from light blue, light gray, to dark gray. The brown color of the log cabin ranged from lighter brown to darker brown areas around the house. It was a castle of a log cabin.

At the entrance was a black steel gate. Cardwell stopped. There was a camera near the top of the metal gate. There were large stone pillars on each side. A voice came on over the intercom near the panel area on the nearest pillar.

"I guess I can let you in." The female voice sarcastically sounded.

Cardwell wasn't in the mood to make jokes. The gate leisurely opened, and he drove up the hill to the home's driveway area. He parked his vehicle by his friend's pink Toyota Tacoma pickup and hiked up the stone-paved walkway to the steps of the deck.

She was waiting on the deck—the love of his life. She wore a pair of jeans with a black blouse, cowboy boots, and a brown Carhartt jacket. She had dark black hair and bright blue eyes. She was about ten years younger than Cardwell, in her forties, but looked prettier than most thirty-year-old women. Cardwell knew he had hit the jackpot when he began dating her.

Her name was Caroline Wilson—the Caroline Wilson who happened to be a doctor at the Jericho Nation Tribal Medical Clinic.

"What's wrong?" she asked.

"We need to talk."

"About what?"

"Marvin's been arrested."

"Brent Cardwell," she said as if she were his mother, "I'm not in the mood for games."

Brent inched closer and took Caroline's hands. He looked down at her ring finger and saw a wedding band on it—one he'd given her. Brent smiled at the memory.

"You are kidding, right?" Caroline said again, trying to reassure herself.

Brent shook his head. "I wish I was."

"Did he get arrested for what I think he got arrested for?"

Brent nodded.

"Shit!" she shouted as she let go of his hand and stormed away. "I should have never listened to you when we decided to not report Marvin's fuckup!"

"I'm sorry... and now we're both on the hook for it."

"Do they know about me?"

Brent sighed, "Yes, they know. Marvin thinks," he broke off, struggling for the right words. "He thinks you sent the cops after him. He said an in-home nurse tricked him into letting them take care of Susanna. That's how the cops found out."

"Not a chance. Monica does anything I say, or her life will be a living hell and she knows it. There's no way she betrayed me."

"Is it possible that you pushed too hard?"

"No, it's not fucking possible, Brent."

"Let's go inside and figure this out."

Inside the log cabin were leather reclining chairs, a luxurious brown La-Z-Boy couch, a coffee table area, and a sixty-inch flatscreen TV mounted on the wall. A single carpet lay under the coffee table in the living room. The living room-dining area was open to the kitchen, and the first thing to be seen when entering the house. A hallway led to a stairway and the back door of the house.

Above them were wooden polished stairs with black metal railings. The stairs led to four bedrooms and a bathroom. There was another bathroom downstairs.

The dining area had a delightful metal round table that could seat six people. The fully equipped kitchen had light colors, enhancing the country-style ambiance. Caroline stomped to the kitchen, grabbed a couple of glasses, and poured the bourbon as Brent sat down on a recliner. She strode over to their sumptuous fridge and hit the ice-maker machine, nearly punching it. The machine popped some ice cubes into their drinks.

Caroline joined Brent in the living room and sat on the La-Z-boy couch. Under the TV was a fireplace, where Caroline had a moderate-size fire going.

"Thank you," Brent said as he took a drink.

Caroline chugged a glass full of bourbon and made a sour face in the process.

"How much do the cops know about me?"

"Marvin said he used you guys as an excuse to get released today. Seemed like the judge thought it was a reasonable argument that it was up to the medical professionals to see Susanna's health issues and let him walk. He'll have court on a later date, but this thing isn't over."

"Fuck. I'm screwed, Brent! They'll see that we erased all the files for Susanna. Marvin, that selfish prick. I should have never trusted you with this whole thing! I'm gonna lose everything!"

"No, you're not."

"Really? How do you figure that?"

"I have a plan."

Caroline glared at Brent as if he was mentally deficient. "You have a plan, huh? What is it? Run to Mexico? Because that's the only plan I have!"

"We could go to Brazil. I hear it's beautiful this time of year," Brent quipped.

"I am not in the mood."

Brent rose and strolled over to a window and looked out at the clear sky. The stars and a full moon lit up the entire property. He gazed at the sturdy fence around the property proudly; he'd personally built it. The night was growing colder by the second, but they had the best view in the county. Caroline stayed seated, still upset but not so angry that she didn't notice the stress Brent was under.

"Damn it, Marvin, why couldn't you listen?" Brent mumbled to himself.

Caroline changed her tone.

"I'm sorry honey... I didn't even take a second to realize how hard this must be for you."

"We're so damn close... Both of us are so close to a perfect retirement," Brent responded, shaking his head. "If he just did what I told him... but Marvin had to go to the casino and attract attention."

Caroline stepped over to the window next to Brent. Brent finished off the rest of his bourbon. Caroline looked up at Brent's abnormally tall frame.

"I know you'll find a way for us to get out of this."

Brent faced her.

"Did you know Marvin was born without the normal amount of chromosomes? Since birth, he's been unable to understand the social norms of a human being. Yet he somehow always cared for me. It could have easily been me that was born that way instead of him."

"I know, Brent... I would have done the same for any of my family if I were in your shoes. That's why I agreed to help you. Because I love you and I know you're a good man."

"And I'm so goddamn sorry about involving you. They'll come for you, eventually. It's only a matter of time. If we get caught, you'll need to hire an attorney. Neil Marshall is his name. He's the best in the business. He'll be able to help."

"I'd rather not get caught at all or need to hire an attorney."

"Me neither... If worse comes to worst, we'll run to the beaches of Brazil and ride it out there."

"Sipping on margaritas while lying on a beach with you sounds pretty great."

"We'll make it through this. You just gotta trust me. No matter what, I will not let them put you in a prison cell."

"I trust you, but..." Caroline began. "Someone will have to take the fall. It'll be either your brother or me."

"It won't be either of you... Monica Hawke will be the one who takes the fall for this."

———

THE BINGHAM RESIDENCE

Anakin and Mato parked on a street over from Marvin Bingham's residence. Marvin lived in a cul-de-sac with five houses that all mirrored each other. They sat there with the engine idling, pumping as much heat as it could muster. Anakin and Mato wanted to attack as soon as possible, but they knew that these things needed to be planned. In the rearview mirror, they could see the smoke of the exhaust filling the air around them. Next, a white bus drove by them and halted in front of the house. Marvin Bingham got out of the bus and walked in.

I sat in Chief McCarthy's office getting an earful from him and Lieutenant Fernandez regarding my recent behavior. Fernandez stood behind the chief, who was seated in a chair with his computer set up to his right. I sat in the chief's direct line of sight.

"Did you really tell a district attorney that you would calm down, right after you inserted used needles in your dick?" McCarthy hollered, spraying spit.

I chuckled when he said it. Hearing someone else say it made me laugh harder than I thought it would. McCarthy pointed a single finger at me and slammed the table with his other hand.

"Don't you fucking laugh, Lawson! This is not the appropriate time."

I gathered myself. "Yeah, I said that, Chief. I'm sorry."

"How many times do I have to tell you? You call me and let me handle the DA's office and their bullshit. DO NOT INVOLVE YOURSELF!"

"Well, if they could do their jobs right..."

"Zip it!"

I stopped talking and remained silent as a church mouse. Lieutenant Fernandez said calmly, "You know we love you, Warren. We love that you're fighting for your victims. But let us do that for you. We don't need the DA's office breathing down our necks, making our things harder."

McCarthy took a couple of deep breaths.

"Lieutenant Fernandez is right... You let *us* tell the DA that *we'll* calm down right after shoving needles in our cocks," he quipped. "I can't believe you said that."

"I was mad. I'm sorry, Chief. It won't happen again."

"It better not. Our hands are tied. We have to write a letter of reprimand and put it in your file. It'll make the DA's office happy that we enforced the issue," Fernandez informed me.

"Understood. You won't hear any complaints from me."

"Good. You're dismissed," said McCarthy.

I stood and started to walk out of the office. I heard Chief McCarthy's voice behind me.

"And Lawson... Just so you know, the DA won't be dropping your case. Although your actions were wrong, they were executed in good faith. Your argument is valid. We're going to fight tooth and nail to make sure the DA prosecutes on behalf of the family of Susanna Holt."

"Thanks, Chief."

"Anytime. Keep up the good work."

I nodded and left the office.

———

Takoda was waiting in the patrol office of the police department. He glanced up at me from his chair as I entered.

"How bad did you get your ass chewed?" Takoda asked cheerfully.

"Not as bad as I thought I would. How are you doing after everything?" I replied as I sat down at my desk, next to Takoda.

"I'm doing all right, man... It's a nasty world. How about you?"

"I think my visit to the DA says it all."

"Did they head home?" he asked, referring to McCarthy and Fernandez.

"Yeah, they left."

"Are you getting suspended?"

"Nope... They're writing a letter to put in my file saying I acted unprofessional."

"Then they don't care. I'm sure they wanted to say the same thing when Marvin was released."

"I can't understand how one person could do that to another... He let her rot for god knows how long."

"I had the same thought." Takoda rubbed his fingers through his hair.

"His smile said it all. Did you see it? When he handed me back the photos?"

"It was hard not to notice."

"The family will want retribution. Once they find out Marvin was released. They'll kill him."

"And with everything on the internet now... They might already know about it."

"We can't let Marvin Bingham die."

"Screw him. He needs to go... Some men you save, others you let die. We aren't executioners... but we don't have to save him. You saw what he did, Warren. He's a waste of space."

"No, fuck that," I sternly countered. "If his life doesn't matter, then nobody's life matters. Either they all matter or they don't. That's the job."

Takoda inhaled deeply.

"Warren... I need you to consider what you're saying. Those two Native brothers are killers. If they show up to kill Marvin, you'll have to kill them to defend that piece of shit. You need to consider all your choices here."

"There is only one option, Takoda. We stop people from dying. No matter who they are."

"I just want you to consider all your options... Because people who end up trying to kill you, end up trying to kill me, too."

"You'll be going home to your wife and kid. I got this handled... You've worked for twelve hours already."

"My money is on the brothers showing up tonight, and if they do, you'll be all on your own out here. No cops will be able to get here for at least an hour with all the ice out. I'm staying with you, brother. I can't let you do this alone."

I rose from my chair, and Takoda stood up to face me. We eyed each other, and I knew there was nothing I could do to convince him to go home. I embraced him and held him tightly.

"Thank you... Thank you for always being there."

Dark thoughts started to enter my mind. Visions of Susanna's mutilated body in the bedroom. I felt my lips start trembling. *If only I could have gotten there in time...*

"I'm with you to the end," Takoda said as we released our embrace and bumped knuckles. I changed my demeanor and smiled.

Next, we heard a loud smacking sound on the windows of the break room outside the police department.

We heard a muffled yell from a female voice.

"Someone help me! Someone come out here now!"

Hilary was outside the police department, screaming and slapping the windows with her palms. Her behavior reminded me of a mental health patient having a manic episode. Takoda and I rushed out to the front of the building.

"What's wrong?"

"Officer Lawson! I need your help. My future husband is about to make a really bad decision. He and his brother are going to kill that man, Marvin." She was still breathing heavily, speaking fast, and was a little hard to understand.

"Anakin and Mato? When?"

"Any time... They left the hospital together. I don't want them to get in trouble. Can you please go over there and make sure they don't do something they regret?"

"Yeah, we can do that. You stay here. Whatever you do, don't go to them until it's over."

She nodded, weeping.

"I'm carrying his baby... this baby can't grow up without a father. They won't try to kill you guys—it's Marvin they want."

"Nobody is gonna die tonight... Stay here. We'll be right back."

Mato and Anakin were in their vehicle watching Susanna's house. The lights in the house were on, as well as the front porch light outside the home. They were waiting for the lights to go off; then they would make their move. They didn't bring weapons, other than a sharp-bladed knife. Shooting Marvin wasn't going to be enough. What they planned on doing to Marvin made what they did to their father look like child's play. Marvin needed to be made an example of.

As they were waiting, Anakin got a call from Camille and put the phone on speaker.

"The doctors said Aunt Susanna has no chance of survival," she said, sobbing. "Once they pull the plug on the life support, she will inevitably die."

Deep down both of the brothers had known this was going to happen, but they'd been wishing their aunt would somehow pull through. They ended their conversation with their sister all the more convinced that Marvin had to die by their hands. As they watched Marvin's house, they could see him through the windows, stumbling around the kitchen. Marvin would be an easy target. The snow started to fall for a second night and was sticking to an already thick sheet of ice on the ground.

Next, they saw a familiar vehicle recklessly drive into the area. It was their grandpa's truck. Robert Holt sped up to the driveway with the headlights shining on the entire house. Robert's vehicle came to a screeching halt. He got out of the driver's seat, marched over to the passenger door, and swung it open. He grabbed a revolver handgun and cocked the hammer back.

"Is that Grandpa?" Anakin asked Mato.

Mato leaned forward in his seat and squinted his eyes. "Shit, that's Grandpa!"

Anakin and Mato jumped out of the vehicle and started to sprint over to Robert. Instead, they both skidded on the ice and fell. When they got up, their grandpa was at the front door.

Robert Holt was banging the butt of his pistol on the door. He was screaming like a madman. "Get out here, you son of a bitch, and meet your maker!"

There was no answer. Robert hit the door with his gun even harder.

"I'm gonna kill you like I did them Koreans, back in the day, you cocksucker!"

"Grandpa, DON'T!" Anakin shouted.

Robert flicked a glance over his shoulder at his grandchild.

"Anakin? Get out of here, boy! I got—"

A shotgun blast interrupted Robert's sentence. Robert's body flailed forward as the shot hit him square in the back. Robert's body folded like a lawn chair and rolled end over end forward for about five yards. His gun flew out of his hands as he hit the ground. There was a gaping hole that went through Robert's mid-spine and sternum area. Blood poured out of him like water from a faucet. He lay on the cold ground, staring into the sky one final time.

Takoda threw himself into the passenger seat of my patrol vehicle and we headed for Marvin's residence. I turned on the four-wheel drive and kept the speed around forty miles per hour. I found the road that led into the Tribal Housing and spun the wheel left. The tires slid and squealed across the ice. I located the roundabout, dead-end road where Marvin lived, and made another sliding turn.

As I got my wheels realigned and on the road, I hit the accelerator a bit too hard. The back tires spun, and we fishtailed. I let off the accelerator and regained control.

The blast of a gunshot sent my mind to the worst. Takoda jerked his pistol from its holster.

As we skidded to a halt in front of the house, we saw a man lying on the ground in a puddle of blood that stained the white snow around the victim. He was lying on his back, alone. About five yards behind the deceased was a door that had been broken off its hinges.

I radioed dispatch.

"We need medics to respond to our location ASAP. Gunshot victim." I parked the Tahoe, and we flung ourselves out of the vehicle. I hefted my gun up and held it with the barrel facing downward as I assessed the scene for threats.

"Cover me. I'm gonna provide medical care for the victim," I said, then holstered my weapon and rushed to the victim.

Robert Holt, Susanna's father. Goddammit.

I ripped my coat off and wrapped my hands in it. I pressed my coat down on the wound, trying to stanch the bleeding. Takoda stood by, checking the area. I felt for a pulse. Nothing.

"No pulse."

I stood up and yanked out my gun again. Another gunshot roared from inside the house. Same caliber shotgun.

"We got gunshots being fired inside the house. One subject is deceased. Send as many cover units as possible!" I ordered on my radio.

"Wait for cover?" Takoda asked, his voice tight.

"No time. We gotta go in."

———

Anakin and Mato had reacted to the gunshot like trained warriors. Their grandfather was dead, and they both knew it. Anakin snatched his grandpa's gun off the ground.

Marvin Bingham needs to die. Tonight.

Together, they rushed to the front door.

———

Marvin Bingham cowered behind his front door with his beloved twelve-gauge. He saw the hole in the door left behind from the shotgun round. Marvin opened the door to make sure he finished the job. He saw two shadowy figures coming toward him in the night. One gigantic form looked like Bigfoot as it loomed out of the darkness.

Marvin slammed the door and locked it, then sprinted down the hallway to the bedroom farthest from the door. Marvin closed the door, chambered another round, and backed himself into a corner facing the door.

———

Anakin approached the front door and found it locked. Mato pushed Anakin aside and raised his right foot. Mato's heel kicked the door so hard that it ripped it off the hinges. The front door came crashing down as pieces of wood scattered in the air.

Mato entered the house with Anakin right behind him. They edged stealthily down the hall, Anakin with the revolver ready to fire. The hallway was dark. Mato came to the first door, opened it, and Mato lunged in. It was an empty bathroom.

Anakin passed him, sliding farther down the hallway, and checked the next door. The foul stench of Susanna Holt's room wafted out. Anakin closed the door, covering his nose. They turned to the door at the end of the dark hallway.

They paused and shot a glance at each other before moving to the last room. A startling shotgun blast came from behind the door. The shot narrowly missed them, and they both jumped back down the hallway and hid behind the nearest wall.

"I'll kill you all!" Marvin yelled like a madman.

"Fuck you!" Anakin hollered back.

Anakin leaned out from behind the wall and started shooting thunderous rounds into the door, blindly firing at Marvin. Mato and Anakin hid in the bathroom after Anakin ran out of bullets.

"Police department!" came a voice at the front door. "Make yourself known. Drop your weapons and surrender now!"

Takoda and I reluctantly went toward the gunfire.

Six gunshots coming from a hallway to the right: not the shotgun. Takoda and I ducked off toward the kitchen, a few inches to the left of the front door.

I gave a warning that police were there and ordered everyone to lay down their weapons and come out. My voice was loud and commanding, but I could hear a thin slice of fear. I hoped the bad guys couldn't hear it.

We knelt behind a brown laminated kitchen countertop about four feet high. On the other side from where we were kneeling was the refrigerator. I pulled the thick metal door open to use it to cover our position better. The door blocked entry to the kitchen, so we were covered on both ends.

The reality of the situation sunk in. I'd never been in the military or fought in a war. This was new territory. I felt the tremble of my hands as I fought to maintain my grip on my .40-caliber handgun. I wanted to shrink away from the situation to save my skin, but couldn't. It was our job to prevent more violence.

Fear tormented me as I forced myself to stand up and glance over the countertop. Nothing. I heard no movement. The other people in the house were doing exactly what Takoda and I were doing. The tension in the air felt like someone pulling on a guitar string as hard as they could, waiting for the inevitable snap.

I looked back at Takoda and whispered, "Nothing."

I motioned to him that I was going to move toward the hallway area. Takoda nodded. His pale face suggested he was as scared as I felt.

As silently as I could, I closed the refrigerator door and tiptoed along the wall with my gun out, staying as low as I could. I rounded the corner of the wall and spun to face the hallway, gun raised. Nobody was there.

I held my position and motioned to Takoda, using hand signals that we learned during training to indicate the hallway was clear. He snuck out from the countertop and slid along the wall with his back to it, gun pointed downward near his hips. I made eye contact, nodded, and stepped into the darkness of the hallway, feeling my way until I found a light switch.

I flipped the lights on. I felt a shrill down my spine. I inched the door closest to me open. The bathroom.

The door creaked as it slowly swung open. I peeked through the doorway and set foot inside. Nobody was in the room. I slowly backed out. I motioned to Takoda to take a position at the bathroom doorway. I gave another hand signal, advising him I was going to move to the bedroom at the end of the hall.

I crept my way to the door at the end of the hallway. Wetting my lips, I announced, "Marvin Bingham, it's the police. Are you in there?"

"Oh, thank God you're here, Officer! These crazy people are trying to kill me!"

"I know, I'm here to make sure you're safe. I'm coming in, please don't shoot."

I unlatched the door and entered the room quickly. Standing in a doorway or a hall is what we call a "fatal funnel." Meaning if someone opens fire, you are an easy target.

The room was about ten by fifteen, with a single bed, a wooden dresser, and a nightstand. The walls had framed photographs, but there wasn't much in the room other than a place to sleep.

Marvin was completely still in the far corner of the room with his shotgun. His hands didn't shake once. He glared at me with his gun pointed to the ground. For a second, he considered using it on me. He glanced at the gun, then back at me, and then once more at his shotgun.

"Marvin. Drop your gun."

Marvin didn't drop the gun.

"Are you okay in there?" Takoda asked.

———

Out of the corner of his eye, Takoda caught a hint of movement in the bathroom mirror. Behind him, the shower curtain moved. An enormous figure emerged from the bathtub area, his head nearly touching the ceiling.

Takoda's head craned back and swung to meet the threat just as Mato charged like a raging bull. Takoda squeezed the trigger. The bullet went right through Mato's left shoulder but Mato came on, ramming into Takoda, lifting him off the ground, and slamming him into the wall. The impact left a Takoda-size crater in the hallway wall. Mato grabbed the barrel of Takoda's gun and tore it from his stunned grip. Mato tossed the gun down the hallway, grabbed Takoda by the vest and smashed his face with one giant fist. He hurled the smaller man down the hall, away from Marvin's bedroom. Takoda crashed into another wall and fell into a crumpled heap.

———

I heard the crash and ducked out the doorway of Marvin's room. Mato was bearing down on me, breathing heavily. Mato's very presence in the hallway made me sick with panic. Then Anakin stepped out from behind Mato. They'd both been in the bathroom.

"Lawson, leave now and nobody but that piece of shit in there with you gets hurt. You have my word," promised Mato.

I glanced over my shoulder and saw Marvin change his mind about shooting me as he realized he needed me. I tucked my gun in the holster on my hip. I fired a look back at Anakin and Mato.

"Nobody else has to die here. Let me handle this, please." I told the brothers.

"We tried that. It didn't work." Anakin said.

"I don't want to kill anyone. I don't want to hurt you."

"We don't want to kill anyone other than the white man behind you. But we have no problem going through you to get to him," Mato said.

"He's taken too much from us," added Anakin.

"What about your unborn child, Anakin? Hilary came by tonight. She's worried. Leave now and go be with her."

"It's too late now. My child will understand... This man took my aunt and my grandfather. We aren't leaving until he's dead."

"I get what you guys are going through. I truly do, but I can't let you kill a man. He isn't worth it! He's gonna get what's coming to him."

Marvin interrupted, "Hey!"

I glared back at him. "Shut the fuck up if you want to survive tonight."

Marvin stopped talking.

"He won't get what's coming to him," Mato growled. "You know that. I know that. Why can't you let us get true justice for the victim in your own case? I know you want justice like we do. We're on the same side, Officer Lawson."

My gaze went back to the brothers, "Justice for him is living out his days in a prison cell for what he did. If you do this, he wins. Don't you get that? People like him, they bring out the worst in us. That's what makes them feel good about themselves. We shouldn't give him that."

The brothers were done talking, and Anakin stepped in front of Mato.

"Get out of our way or shoot us."

I looked down at the ground and sighed. I gritted my teeth. My fear started to change to anger. "If you want to get to Marvin. You'll have to go through me."

Anakin lunged toward me. I watched his footwork and recognized him as a boxer right away. Even in a cramped hallway, he bladed his feet like a boxer would stepping in a ring. The only advantage I had being in the hallway fighting two men, was that they had to approach me one at a time in a single file line.

Finally, a lawful excuse to let my rage out.

I waited for Anakin. I wasn't as well trained in firefights, but I was well within my comfort zone when it came to hand-to-hand combat. Anakin set foot into the doorway of Marvin's room. I bladed myself like him, left foot forward, right foot back.

First, I sent a distraction blow. I attempted a palm strike with my left hand to the face. Anakin blocked it without much effort. My hand returned to my face like a yo-yo. As my left hand came back to my face, I loaded up a kick with my right leg.

My shin went up between Anakin's bladed stance and cut upward into his groin. *Years of Krav Maga sparring sessions. Lesson One: Never fight fair.* Anakin hunched over at the hips. I grabbed him by the hair and slammed his head into the wall as hard as I could.

As Anakin went cross-eyed and fell, Mato charged at me, slowed by the necessity of stepping over Anakin. I leaped onto him like a koala bear and wrapped my legs around his torso. I positioned my arm around his head and pried his head downward. I attempted to get my forearm under Mato's chin to perform a "Guillotine choke."

Mato tucked his chin, but I had his head, wrenching on his chin. Mato drove us through the bedroom and started slamming my back into every wall of the room. Blood from his shoulder was spilling onto me. I endured the pain and kept my focus on my firearm. If Mato wanted to kill me, he could have reached for my gun, but he didn't. That could change.

I caught a brief glimpse of Marvin in the corner, still hugging his shotgun. He appeared to be having some kind of indecision, but at least he wasn't opening fire.

As Mato thrashed back and forth, the contents of the room went flying. At the first opportunity, I let go of Mato's head and dazed him with a downward elbow strike to the top of his skull. Releasing my leg grip on his torso, I landed on the ground in a standing position.

Mato had enough presence of mind to swing a left hook that would've taken my head off if it connected. I ducked the punch and thwacked him in the kidney, then rotated my hips and landed an uppercut blow under his chin. Mato stumbled backward. I returned my hands to my face with my chin tucked.

Mato spit out some blood before charging me again. He thrust me up against the wall with one arm, placing his forearm on my jugular.

His weight shifted slightly as he reared back to punch me with his free hand. I took my chance.

One solid punch from Mato could put me in a morgue. I placed both hands on the forearm pinned on my jugular and sunk all my weight onto it, dropping into a squat and avoiding the punch in the process.

Mato jerked his forearm out of my grasp and got behind me as I tried to escape my position trapped between him and the wall.

He got one arm around my neck and the other arm behind my head—a standing rear-naked choke.

I gripped the arm around my neck and utilized all my body to drop down, tucking my chin. Mato was squeezing with all his might. My head felt like it was about to pop off. I forced my way down near Mato's legs and wrapped my arms around them.

The only way out of the choke was to take Mato to the ground. I drove my body forward, tugged his legs, and tackled Mato into the wooden dresser. Mato released his grip on my neck as we went down. I fell on top of his legs, and his head bounced off the dresser and to the floor. I crawled on top of him to attempt to keep him down. *That was a bad idea.*

I crawled up Mato like a spider. Mato reached under my leg and reversed the position. He threw my leg up and over and spun my body to my back. My legs went around his torso, I gripped his head and dug my elbows into the traps of his shoulders as his body lay on top of mine. I dragged Mato's head down to my chest and closed the distance.

Mato was growing increasingly annoyed as I held him in an uncomfortable position. I felt his hands pressing against the ground, trying to force himself to his feet. I saw Mato's feet step up near my hips on the ground. He was getting in a squat position so he could stand up and then slam me into the ground. I let go of Mato's head and grabbed the Achilles heel on both of his feet.

I shuffled my feet to his hip flexor area. I pushed with my legs and pulled with my arms. I used Mato's instability against him; the leverage forced him to the ground. Mato fell backward, plummeting to the ground for a second time.

I popped up to my feet, as I had done a thousand times in years of training, just in time to catch sight of Marvin making a break for it. Leaving Mato lumbering to his feet, I raced after Marvin.

I tackled him at the end of the hallway before he could exit the house. The shotgun fell to the ground and bounced into the kitchen.

As I held Marvin to the ground, I felt someone hook grip the backside of my outer bulletproof vest and fling me into a nearby wall like I was an insect. Mato's sheer power made me realize how outmatched I really was.

I crawled out of another crater in the wall, glanced to my left, and saw Takoda unconscious on the ground with a battered nose. Mato was directly in front of me, about to kneel over Marvin.

I popped back up, ready for more. I was breathing heavily, but I was conditioned. If I could stay alive long enough, I knew he would tire before me. Mato spun toward me and I landed two quick and vicious palm strikes to his nose. I felt the crunch, and blood squirted onto the nearby wall. I followed up with a hard kick to the groin. When Mato folded over at the waist, I dropped my weight down and balled up my fist to perform a "hammer strike" to his collarbone, fracturing it. He screamed in agony, his right arm rendered useless.

Sweat was trickling down my face and soaked my uniform.

I was no longer human, I was a wild animal in survival mode. I went to put on the finishing touches when a hard punch cracked me in the left side of my jaw. Anakin had woken up.

Anakin turned to Mato, as I stumbled back a few steps. Some of my teeth felt loose in my mouth and the room was starting to spin.

Another jolt of adrenaline hit as Anakin pulled out a large hunting knife and handed it to Mato, on his knees beside Marvin who was gibbering with fear, motionless. Anakin came at me in his bladed stance.

"Don't do this," I said, panting and rubbing my jaw.

"I'm surprised you're still standing. I know guys in prison that couldn't have kept standing after a punch like that."

Anakin stepped up for a strike, but I hurled myself back just in time to dodge it. The punch fell short a few inches from my face. I attacked Anakin with a flurry of punches, but he sidestepped, ducked, and dodged all of them like Muhammad Ali in his prime. After Anakin dodged my last punch, he hit me twice in the face, and then a bone-crushing shot to my kidney.

The punches came so fast, I couldn't begin to defend. Anakin was at an angle on my body; I turned to face him and he sent another flurry of punches.

I got my hands up, but the strikes were peppering all over my body. My lip got cut open at some point, I couldn't pinpoint when or how. My kidneys were not going to work right for a week. It felt like being stung by a pack of hornets. I stumbled back, doing my best to block. Anakin's stamina showed no signs of slowing down.

I gotta get this fight to the ground. Then I'm gonna beat the brakes off this fucker.

Anakin had me backed against a wall like I suspected he'd done to several boxers throughout his life. He was coming for a knockout blow.

As he loaded the punch, I lunged forward, crashing into him, tucking my chin and putting my elbows up around my head. I controlled his wrist and grabbed the back of his shoulder. I sent a crushing knee strike to his sternum. I wrapped one arm under his armpit, stepped in close, turned my back, hip to hip, and thrust with my legs, lifting Anakin off the ground. I did a "hip toss" and threw Anakin over my body.

Anakin went from standing to flying through the air above me to doing a complete front flip before crashing into the ground. Anakin's back landed on the armrest of a reclining chair before ping-ponging down to the floor.

I was on him. I pinned him down and landed an elbow strike to the bridge of his nose. I kept the top pressure and could feel by Anakin's panicked movements, that he was not experienced in ground fighting. He wasted energy as his body spazzed all over the place. I kept solid chest and hip pressure on him. I had about thirty pounds on him.

Anakin managed to reach up and grab the back of my head. With his other hand, he tried to jam his thumb into my eye.

I closed my eyes and forced my head away before he did too much damage, but that gave him room to try to squirm out of my hold. I shuffled my body and let him move into a more compromising position.

As Anakin rolled to his side, I hooked the arm closest to me, while his other arm was tucked under his body. I pressed down on the side of his face with my other free hand, swung my leg around, and fell to my back while gripping his free arm.

I landed on my back and inertia rolled Anakin to his back as well. With my legs straddled across Anakin's sternum area like a seatbelt, his arm was in between my legs as well. Anakin started to struggle even more. I had him in a perfect submission known as the "arm-bar."

I rotated his wrist so his thumb pointed upward. Anakin was trying to turn and hit me in the groin. I did a sit-up and landed a few short hammer strikes in his face. I jerked the arm between my legs down, I thrust my hips upward. Next, I heard the loud snap of Anakin's arm breaking like a tree branch.

Anakin wailed like a victim of torture. I reversed my position to get on top of him, then punched him again and again in the face. There was blood sprinkling from my knuckles. His arm was dangling to the side.

I warned him not to go down this road with me...

———

While Anakin fought, Mato had his time with Marvin Bingham. He was in a lot of pain, so it took him a moment. Mato held the knife in his left arm, which hurt, but not as bad as the right one. He was fueled by hate and adrenaline. Mato knelt over Marvin. Marvin refused to look him in the eyes as he whimpered.

"Look at me, you pathetic piece of trash," Mato ordered. "LOOK AT ME!"

Marvin was shaking. He gazed up at Mato.

"It's not... It's not what you think," he stuttered.

"I am going to be the last thing you see," said Mato. "This is for you, Auntie."

Mato stuck the fifteen-inch blade into Marvin's abdomen, then yanked out the blade and watched the blood spill out.

"A slow death. It will take hours for you to bleed out, but I will have fun with you until that happens."

Marvin gripped his stomach like he was somehow going to put the blood back into his body, "No! Oh God, no! Please!"

Mato sliced deep into Marvin's cheekbone. Mato sliced into the other cheekbone like it was a piece of steak.

"Death by a thousand cuts for men of no honor."

Marvin begged, he screamed and screamed. Mato didn't care. He'd heard it before. He never cared about the pleas for help. If he was killing someone, they deserved it more than most.

Mato savored what he could at the moment. He shifted the knife down to the trap and was about to stab downward into the flesh of Marvin's shoulder.

Marvin looked up at Mato and knew his chances of survival were minimal. But before the knife entered Marvin's shoulder, a gunshot from Takoda's .40-caliber pistol rang out. Brain matter splattered all over Marvin's body.

I heard the gunshot, leaped off Anakin, and went for my gun. I checked behind me. Takoda was perched over Mato's dead body with his gun still pointed at him. Mato's brains were on the wall and leaking out onto the floor. Takoda stood like a statue. Mato's body slumped over Marvin's.

"That... gunshot... you?" I asked as I could barely get out the words through my heavy breathing.

Takoda looked at me and nodded.

"MATO!" Anakin yelled, realizing despite being nearly blinded by all the blood in his eyes, what had happened.

I whipped my gun toward Anakin. He started to mewl. I imagined it was half emotional pain, half physical agony. I kept my eye trained on him as Takoda shoved Mato's corpse off Marvin. Marvin gasped for air.

"I... need a medic."

"Shots fired, shots fired, two deceased, one wounded. We're gonna need more than one ambulance here." Takoda said on his radio to dispatch.

Anakin got up and staggered in the opposite direction. I pointed my gun at Anakin's back and considered pulling the trigger. Anakin found the back sliding door and slipped out.

Takoda glanced over. "Where'd he go?"

"He ran."

"You're not going to chase?"

I shook my head, then grabbed the microphone for the radio attached to my bulletproof outer vest. "We have one suspect outstanding. He's fled the scene due south out the back entrance of the house. Suspect is a Native American male, midthirties', five ten, and around 175 pounds."

Dispatch replied, "Copy."

After that, every police officer in the next three counties was responding to our location. Suddenly, Jericho Nation was the hot place to be. Takoda had not moved from the spot where he'd shot Mato in the back of the head.

I walked over to Takoda and gently put my arm around his shoulder.

"Come on man. Let's get you out of here," I said.

Takoda flicked a glance, nodded, and placed his pistol back in the holster. Takoda said nothing and trudged out the front door of the house. I knelt and lifted a very bloody Marvin Bingham. I dragged his body from the house, out the door, and laid him out on the ice and snow in the driveway. Marvin yelled at me the whole time, but I didn't care. I told him to keep pressure on the wound, but I wasn't about to help him anymore.

Marvin, you sonofabitch, you deserve far worse than you got tonight.

Police cars from all kinds of agencies started pulling up, and multiple ambulances flooded the scene. The whole neighborhood was lit up by the mix of police and medics' emergency lights. The flashing mix of red, white, and blue could be seen for miles. Chief McCarthy and Lieutenant Fernandez arrived on scene together in a blacked-out 2019 Chevy Silverado pickup.

McCarthy commanded attention without saying a word when he arrived. He was a former UFC fighter with Irish and Native American heritage and had been one of my teachers in the early stages of my mixed martial arts training. McCarthy was in his early forties, five-foot-nine with a stocky 205-pound build. People never dared to say he had little man syndrome because if they had, he would've kicked their ass.

Fernandez was different. He had a laid-back feel to him, but his brain was always working. He could see things others couldn't. He'd been a very successful major crimes detective before coming to Jericho Nation. Fernandez was in his fifties, had dark brown skin, dark black hair, brown eyes, and a short stocky build as well.

McCarthy and Fernandez arrived right after the ambulance took Marvin off to a hospital.

The medics gave Takoda and me ice packs for our bruised faces. Takoda had a nice laceration across the center of his nose with some swelling around it. I had a swollen black and blue jaw, a laceration on my forehead, bloody knuckles, and a black eye. We were seated on the ledge of the front patio of the house. It was around eleven p.m. and the night was getting colder.

Fernandez and McCarthy approached as the Oregon State Police were examining the dead bodies. They placed blankets over the bodies of Robert Holt and Mato. Someone had already put yellow crime scene tape around the house. Neighbors were out and wondering what the fuss was about.

McCarthy stared intently at us and said, "What happened?"

I glanced up at him, but no words came.

CHAPTER
FIFTY-FIVE

Brent Cardwell thrust into Caroline as she lay on her back on the carpet of the living room floor. Caroline moaned as loud as she wanted, knowing there was nobody for miles around. Brent continued to drive his hips into her, gazing down at her naked body.

Caroline's breasts were large and bounced with every thrust. Every time they made love, he couldn't believe he was having sex with such a beautiful woman. Caroline's breasts were fake and had been paid for by the large inheritance she got from her father. The same inheritance paid for the log cabin house.

Brent flipped her body around with ease. She'd told him she loved how he could toss her around like nothing. On all fours, she stuck her firm ass into the air. Brent gripped her hips and took her from behind as she moaned louder. The cycling classes she had been taking had paid off.

Caroline moaned as he approached climax. "Harder, harder!"

Brent did as she asked and smacked his hips against her lean ass as hard as he could.

"Yeah, baby! That's it!"

He gave one last thrust and finished, giving an uncontrollable twitch after the cum oozed out of him. Brent hunched over the back of Caroline's body.

As his face leaned down next to hers, she turned and kissed him on the lips, then crawled forward and lay. Brent flopped down to his back next to her, out of breath. Brent always wore his shirt during sex. Caroline didn't mind.

"Damn, that was really good, baby," she said.

Brent heard his phone start ringing. He couldn't remember where he put it. Brent stood, pulled on his pants, and buckled them as he strolled toward the ringing cell phone. He picked it up off the table and took a second to gather himself.

"Hello, this is Cardwell," he answered like he had a million times throughout his tenured career.

His boss was calling. He was needed to deal with a level five traumatic event in Jericho Nation. A level five was the highest level.

"Where?" he asked. When he heard the address, his heart skipped a beat.

Takoda and I looked up at Chief McCarthy in shock. Both were unsure how to explain what had transpired. We sat on the front patio of Marvin's residence for fifteen more minutes, still frozen in time. McCarthy and Fernandez both supervised us per department policy.

"Are you guys OK?" Lieutenant Fernandez asked.

"Yeah, all things considered," I answered.

"Well, you guys know the drill. We have to split you guys up... Warren, you come with me. Takoda, you go with Chief."

We both nodded.

"See you on the other side, partner," I said to Takoda.

He nodded. He'd been nearly silent since the shooting.

I followed Fernandez to an undercover detective's police vehicle. Fernandez knew all the detectives very well. I felt like I was in good hands with him.

I dropped into the front seat of the detective's car. Fernandez got in the back, and the Oregon State Police Detective got into the driver's seat. I knew the detective, Chad Druery, from back when he was a patrol cop. He had been a cop for twenty years, a detective off and on throughout. He was six-five, 250 pounds, but hadn't seen a gym in ages. It was hard to find time to work out and travel the state working homicide cases.

Druery drove us down to the police department and escorted me to an interview room. Fernandez acted as my representative because our department did not have any legal attorneys on the payroll yet. Our department was very new, only nine years old at the time.

Druery tried to make me as comfortable as he could, but I had a throbbing headache and my ribs had started to ache along with my kidneys. The bottom right corner of my lip was puffed out. I had a bruise slowly growing along the side of my face, which would eventually swell up the size of a golf ball on the right side of my jaw.

I plopped down at a table; Fernandez sat beside me. Chad sat across from us, set a body camera on the table, and pressed the record button. I had a sudden epiphany that I was seated in the suspect chair, with Fernandez acting as my lawyer.

"All right, Warren, I'll be recording this conversation for evidential purposes. It is January fourth, 2020, at 23:27 hours, and we are conducting an interview at the Jericho Nation Tribal Police Department. Can you state your full name and date of birth for the record, please?"

"Warren Lawson. July 2nd, 1992."

"I am going to ask you a couple of questions about the fatal shooting tonight. Is that all right?"

"Yes, that's fine."

"Tell me why you were there."

I explained the details of my case and what led us to Marvin Bingham's residence. I advised him about what we saw upon arrival, the fight that took place, and my actions during the incident.

"So you fought off the two suspects who broke into the home. One of them gets out of your grasp while you're dealing with the other one. While you're in a fight, you hear the gunshot and see one of the suspects dead? Is that correct?" Chad inquired.

"That's correct."

"Did Officer Tehama warn the suspect prior to shooting?"

I pondered this for a moment. The only memory I had was being on top of Anakin in a blind rage, punching him in the face.

"I don't remember."

"You don't remember or you don't want to answer?"

I cocked my eyebrows at Chad. Why was he grilling me on this?

Fernandez interrupted, "Detective Druery, what is your angle here?"

"I'm wondering if the deceased had a proper warning before Officer Tehama shot him in the head. That is the policy at this department, is it not?"

"I'm not sure if you noticed, but the deceased was stabbing a man to death. Officer Tehama stepped up and saved that man's life. Meanwhile, you run your cock holster talking about things you weren't there for."

"Lawson!" Fernandez barked. "Let me handle it."

I crossed my arms and leaned back in my chair.

"It's nothing personal, Lawson. I'm just doing my job," Druery said.

"We know that, Detective, and we're glad you're doing so," Fernandez said. "Officer Lawson did not remember Officer Tehama giving a warning prior to the shooting. That is because Officer Lawson was in the middle of a use-of-force conflict when it happened. It's not indicative of whether or not Officer Tehama did or did not follow proper police procedure."

———

Takoda was getting the same treatment in a similar interview room at a different police department. Another detective escorted him to the Yamhill County Sheriff's Office in McMinnville, about thirty minutes away from Jericho Nation. The questioning was in regard to the shooting, as Takoda expected. If there is a death during a police incident, there will be an investigation, no matter what.

He answered all the questions calmly, and Chief McCarthy sat beside him the entire time. The questions were going smoothly until the detective caught him off guard.

"Did you warn the deceased to stop attacking the victim prior to the shooting?"

Takoda thought about it for a second. The whole event seemed like a whirlwind. His head hurt; his nose kept dripping blood and was most likely broken. The only thing he could remember was getting up from the ground and seeing Mato on top of Marvin, carving his face like a pumpkin. Takoda had pushed off the ground, put the barrel a couple of inches from the back of Mato's head, and squeezed the trigger.

Mato's brain scattering all over the wall kept replaying in Takoda's mind. The violence of a bullet going through a skull at that range is shocking. He'd never shot a man before.

"No. I didn't warn the deceased prior to opening fire."

MCMINNVILLE, OREGON

Chief McCarthy stared at Takoda with wide eyes. The detective had his notepad out and was writing everything down. The interview finally ended and McCarthy escorted Takoda out. All the deputies of the Yamhill County Sheriff's Office had heard about the officer-involved shooting. Heads turned as they left the building. Takoda felt all their eyes on him; all the attention made him feel like the hunchback of Notre Dame. Like everyone was pointing their fingers, silently judging his actions.

Takoda walked out to McCarthy's Chevy Silverado and got in. McCarthy drove, halting at the first red stoplight in the city. It was well after midnight; few people were out on the sidewalks.

"What's gonna happen now?" asked Takoda.

"My personal opinion, from the outside looking in? I think your shooting is justified. I don't think you'll be charged for any crimes," McCarthy said, as the light turned green. "But the family will have grounds to sue our department for wrongful death."

"Because I didn't give him a warning?"

"Yeah... They'll be able to say you didn't follow the policy. Which we all know are guidelines. However, the family will be pissed. They've lost so much recently, Susanna and Robert Holt, and now this Mato guy. We'll be under some heat financially."

"That's bullshit!" Takoda swore uncharacteristically.

McCarthy stayed calm.

"We have your back, Takoda. One hundred percent. I don't give a shit how much money we have to fork out. You did your job and I wouldn't trade you for any cop in the world. Got it?"

Takoda glanced down at the floorboard, took a few seconds to let his emotions come down, then said, "Thanks, Chief."

"Did you guys have your body cameras on during the incident?"

"Yes."

"We'll have to review them. If there was anything you forgot to mention, we'll find it on the body camera footage. If you can let us know now, we can get ahead of it."

"No, Chief, I said everything that happened. I'm not worried about that."

McCarthy nodded and got on the highway to Jericho Nation.

———

Jericho Nation Tribal Police Department

After Detective Druery questioned me, he left, and I remained at our police department. I wanted to wait until Takoda returned. Fernandez stayed with me, and we sat in the break room. I had no appetite, but I forced myself to cook a meal. After a while, Ashley and Cardwell came by. Fernandez let them into the department so they could visit me.

Ashley wasn't very good at hiding the concern on her face. She walked in nearly in tears already. I swear that woman felt all the emotions I never cared to show. As she entered the break room, I rose to face her. She was nearly running and hugged me as tightly as her little body could. I hugged her back.

"I'm okay," I assured her.

She nudged her head back from my shoulder and stared at my battered face, "You don't look okay."

Ashley lightly rubbed her fingers around my face. She pecked every cut or bruise I had on my face as if the kisses somehow were healing me.

Cardwell stepped over and hugged me, too. He hunched down to embrace me. For a moment I felt like a child in his arms and felt this surge of anxiety. His size reminded me of Mato throwing me around Marvin's room like a rag doll. I tensed up for a second, then reminded myself I was with a friend, not a suspect. I relaxed and hugged him back. He knew exactly the emotions I was dealing with.

He inched away from me and looked down with gloom.

"You did the right thing, Lawson. I know it doesn't seem like it, but you did the right thing defending Marvin Bingham tonight. You did an outstanding job, War. I don't know many cops that would have done what you did. Lord knows it would have been easier to let them kill him and arrest them after."

"I didn't want anyone to die. That's all I wanted..."

"That's what makes you a good man."

I nodded and said nothing.

Cardwell placed his hand on my shoulder and asked me, "Do you mind if I give you some advice? From one old veteran officer on his way out to a young cop on his way up."

"No, I don't mind."

"Don't let this change who you are. No matter what happens in your long career. Keep true to yourself. You're a great man, and that's something you should be proud of."

"Thanks, Brent."

I didn't feel like a good man. I felt like a hypocrite. Takoda got wrapped up in the case because of me, and he was going to have to live with his actions for the rest of his life. Takoda begged me to let it go. I should have. Mato didn't need to die. The only person that deserved to die in that house was Marvin.

"What's the status of Mr. Bingham, anyway?" Cardwell inquired.

Fernandez, who'd been standing near the back of the room, sauntered over.

"He's in critical condition at Salem County Hospital. They're unsure if he's going to survive."

"Where's Takoda?"

"Should be here any minute."

Silence lingered in the room. Ashley grabbed my hand and said, "Let's get out of here for a minute."

"Okay... Lieutenant, will you let me know when Takoda gets back?"

"Of course."

———

Ashley and I stepped out into the cold night air. The Bingham residence was a stone's throw away from the police department. We could still see the flashing emergency lights in the distance, lighting up the night sky.

Ashley and I strolled over to the awning near the front entrance and sat down on the cold cement, watching the snowfall. Both of us were wearing several layers of clothing. She rested her head on my shoulder as we watched the light show blended with the flakes of snow in the sky.

"I can't lose you," said Ashley.

"You won't."

"How do you know?"

"I don't, I suppose... I do know it would take a lot for someone to kill me, though."

She smiled. "You're like my real-life Batman."

"The reservation Batman," I quipped.

I wrapped my arms around her and held her tight. Her small body got very cold in the winter.

"Your jaw looks broken," Ashley remarked.

"It's not, or I wouldn't be able to talk right now."

She kissed my bruise again.

I asked her, "How was it on scene? Did you guys have to do the death notification?"

"We were at the crime scene for a little bit... The bodies were covered when we got there. A detective, Cardwell, and I had to go give death notifications to the wife of Robert Holt. The wife was with the sister of Mato, Camille. We told them both at the same time."

"How'd they take it?"

"About as you'd expect from a family that's been through what they have."

"Damn it..." I sighed.

"Do you want to talk about it?"

"Not particularly."

"Can I ask you something about it?"

"Of course."

"Why'd you risk your life for him? For Marvin Bingham?"

I wondered the same thing. All I'd wanted to do since this case started was bash Marvin's face in with a hammer. Next, I pondered how long they would be left at the scene cleaning it all up. The tribal housing community would be stunned for sure. They had not seen that much police activity in years.

Finally, I returned to Ashley's question.

"When I was a kid, I had this cousin... He was more of a brother, actually. Anyway, when we graduated from high school, we went our different ways. Long story short, he went from a straight-A college student to a drug addict. One day he was suffering from a drug-induced schizophrenic outburst. Voices in his head told him to stab a man, so he did... My cousin is currently in the psych ward for the crime."

Ashley didn't know how to respond to me. Her expression told me that this was a surprise.

"Point being, my cousin is on his way back to the real world. Getting better every day... At one point in time, I'm sure someone thought he wasn't worth saving. I thank God that people believed he was. He was a great person, Ashley. I wish you could have met him before the drugs... Anyway, he helped me learn that people are worth protecting. All types of people."

She smiled.

"What are you smiling at?"

"I'm finally starting to figure out why you do the job the way you do."

———

Takoda and McCarthy arrived at the department. Ashley and I went back inside to see them. Takoda moseyed over to the locker room to take off his uniform. I followed. Everyone else was out in the break room talking.

Takoda took off his vest and set it in his large metal locker. Next, he took off his gun belt and hung it up in the corner of the locker.

"Hey," I said. "I just wanted to say—"

"I don't want to talk about it, man. What's done is done."

"If you ever want to talk about it, I'm here."

"Thanks."

I nodded and stood there awkwardly as he put a coat over his uniform and got ready to leave.

"I love you, man," he said. "I would do what I did in a heartbeat if it meant saving a life. You're right. Every person matters, no matter who they are."

"I'm not so sure about that."

"I am. Anyway, I gotta go. I have a very concerned wife at home who needs me."

"Of course. I'll see you later."

———

Takoda returned to his house at around one in the morning. He lived about twenty minutes away from the police department in a small town near the Oregon Coast called Otis. Takoda's beautiful wife, Maria, was in their living room waiting for him, watching TV. Their child, Xander, was sound asleep.

He gazed at his wife's delicate features, her petite body, dark brown skin, and long healthy black hair for a moment, then marched past her to their bedroom. For some reason, he couldn't bear to look at his wife.

The feeling confused him. He loved his wife more than anything on earth. Maria got up off the living room couch and followed him. She saw Takoda undressing for bed. She knew he was tired; he'd worked for nineteen hours straight. Maria shut the door behind her as she entered the room. Takoda turned his back to her.

"Baby, are you okay?" Maria asked.

Takoda didn't answer. He still couldn't look at her. She padded up to him and touched his arm. "Takoda? Can you look at me, please? I love you."

Takoda faced her and saw the trust in her eyes, the innocent look she used to give him before he killed a man.

Takoda had not cried when his father abandoned him as a small child, but he felt something coming on. All the emotions he'd been holding in rushed out of him like a hurricane. A river of tears flooded from his eyes as he sank to his knees and hugged Maria's waist.

"I'm so sorry!"

Maria gripped his head against her stomach.

"It's okay, baby. It's okay," Maria repeated.

Takoda couldn't stop crying.

CHAPTER

FIFTY-NINE

Ashley stayed the night at my house after my shift. After the shooting, Takoda and I were put on paid administrative leave. Oregon State Police Detectives would have to do a complete investigation into the shooting before we could return to work.

When I woke up the next day, the pain in my head and body was even worse than the previous night. I gingerly climbed out of bed. I couldn't sleep anymore. I'd woken up several times to vivid nightmares that left me sweating uncontrollably. Ashley was still sound asleep. I limped my way out of the bedroom to the living room wearing nothing but boxer briefs.

I turned on my TV. The news was on. I knew better than to watch the news. But I was curious about what people said had happened. News outlets had made their way to the crime scene after Takoda and I left.

CNN was on, and there was a group of people on split screens discussing the newest officer-involved shooting in Jericho Nation, Oregon. They slandered us, stating that they learned about Mato having broken limbs to go along with a bullet through the head and shoulder. One broadcaster said that the small police department panicked due to a lack of training and shot a man who didn't need to be shot.

I changed the channel. It was clear that they weren't going to explore both sides of the situation. FOX News was the next channel I switched to—CNN's competitor. I saw a blonde with a southern Texas accent, young and passionate. She was slandering CNN for throwing me and Takoda under the bus. Stating that CNN was only reporting half of the situation. The local news channels were more of the same. I guessed that the local news outlets in Oregon made a pretty penny sharing their newsworthy story to the national news networks.

I flipped the TV off, since the more I watched people argue, the more frustrated I became—these people who weren't there, weren't involved, arguing over what the officer should or shouldn't do. There was no mention that I had fought until nearly my last breath before Takoda was forced to take the shot to save that P.O.S. Marvin's life.

There were video clips replaying Chief McCarthy making a statement to the local news reporters outside the police department in Jericho Nation. McCarthy explained the bare minimum details of the shooting and that Takoda and I were there to prevent two men from invading a home and murdering a citizen. He left out the detail of who that citizen was.

In all the chaos that social media and news agencies bring, McCarthy said on camera that he backed his officers 100 percent. McCarthy reinforced this by saying we'd done everything in our power to keep citizens safe like we were trained to do. I'd seen these things before with other police officers over the years. People would protest, yell, scream, and fight over the next few weeks in the bigger cities around the United States.

I wondered who gave the news reporters the information regarding Mato having broken bones. That was sensitive information. That part of the investigation was not ready to be leaked to the public. Which meant someone was working against us, and I didn't know why.

CHAPTER
SIXTY

Anakin told Hilary to drive until they were well out of Jericho Nation. Hilary drove for miles, listening to Anakin vent. Fleeing Marvin's house, Anakin had hidden in the trees around Tribal Housing and fished his miraculously unbroken cell phone out. As police sirens wailed, Hilary picked him up and they fled before any roadblocks were up.

Anakin's arm was getting worse by the minute. He needed a doctor, but his face would soon be plastered all over the news if it wasn't already. He'd be hailed as a hero by the vigilante-loving people of Oregon. And demonized as a criminal by the rest for the attempt on Marvin's life.

Hilary left I-5 and entered Portland, driving into the slums as Anakin requested. They went through a neighborhood with old brick sidewalks and brick buildings whose businesses had been closed down for years. The houses were built on weak foundations; roofs were crumbling.

At length, they arrived at a two-story, white-painted house with teal doors. Some of the windows were destroyed, and only shards of glass were left. The roof was multicolored and some holes in the roof were covered with plywood. Hilary parked at the curb, next to a brick-paved sidewalk.

"All right, stay here," Anakin said through teeth gritted against the pain.

"Wait. Are you serious?" Hilary protested, "I'm likely to get killed sitting here alone."

"This is IPO territory, babe. If anyone messes with you, tell them you're my girl."

Anakin winced again. He'd bled all over his shirt and passed out several times on the car ride over. A couple of times, Hilary thought he died, only to see him wake back up moaning in pain.

"Will these people help fix you?" she asked.

"Yeah, I'm gonna holla at 'em for a minute... then they'll let you come stay. It's safe, don't worry."

Anakin willed his way out of the car. He crossed the street, staggered up to the house, and knocked with his good arm. A Native American male, wearing all red clothing and a red bandanna around his head answered.

"Yo, homie, you got some heat on you," he said.

"I know. I need the doctor. Can you get him out here? I'm fucked up real bad."

"Yeah, for sure. Come inside. Cops won't come around here."

"Can you send someone to get my girl? She's parked out front, across the street." Anakin pointed over to their car.

Anakin entered the house, which was full of other men, who looked to range from early twenties to midforties. They were all dressed in red-and-black clothing and had tattoos showing their gang affiliation. The same men he and Mato had brought with them to Jericho Nation, returned to Portland after the shooting. They all knew the cops would swarm them like a pack of bees going to a nest, trying to find Anakin.

Anakin found a couch and eased himself down exhaustedly. Several approached him and paid their condolences for the loss of Mato, who'd been a good and loyal member of the gang.

Hilary entered, visibly tense, sat by Anakin, and never left his side. She was the only white girl in the house, but the gangs take care of their own. It wasn't as nice, but it was the IPO version of a police department.

The doctor arrived about ten minutes later. The guys escorted Hilary, the doctor, and Anakin to a silver minivan parked out back. The doctor got into the driver's seat. Anakin and Hilary got in the back together. The doctor was a white man in his late fifties and looked like he was in the wrong neighborhood. Yet he was helping Anakin, so they didn't care what he looked like. He gave Anakin morphine to get him through the drive. Anakin ingested so much that he nearly overdosed. But the pain in his arm finally subsided, after hours of unbearable suffering.

He laid his head down on Hilary's leg.

Anakin's eyes were slowly getting droopy, and Hilary gazed upon him, he was close to falling asleep. Before he did, Anakin said, "They killed Mato, babe... They killed him for that evil white man, Marvin."

"I know baby... I know," Hilary somberly replied.

"The tribal police are dirty—"

Hilary started to disagree, but she knew Anakin was far too high on morphine to argue with, so she just nodded.

"The tribal cops are gonna pay; f' what they did ta Mato," he slurred.

———

Hilary stared at him and saw his eyes slowly shut. Anakin's head rolled to his side. He was completely unconscious. She was the only one, it seemed, who understood the repercussions of revenge. That there were no victories in it. The orange city lights lit up the street as they rode on. For a moment at a time, she could see Anakin's face light up orange and then fade into darkness until another orange street light came. Hilary looked up through the windshield and saw a big green sign. WELCOME TO WASHINGTON: THE EVERGREEN STATE.

DALLAS, OREGON

When Ashley finally woke up, I was in the garage exercising. I had transformed my garage into a home gym with cardio equipment, a barbell, and weight plates. I also had wrestling mats and a heavy bag for my mixed martial arts training.

I was riding a cardio machine called the "echo bike." It's a stationary bike with two levers that you pull on with your upper body, as your lower body pedals. My body ached too much for any heavy lifting so I gave myself a break from my traditional CrossFit workouts. But a burning rage was inside of me. I had to get it out somehow.

Ashley came into the garage and glared at me like my mother would have.

"Warren Lawson. You need to rest your body!"

"I... took some... Ibuprofen," I said, breathing heavily. "I'm good. It's mainly... my head... that hurts."

"That's because you got into a fistfight that destroyed the entire inside of a house last night... Jesus, look at your ribs!"

I was riding the bike with no shirt, wearing black Reebok

sweatpants and running shoes. The bruises on my ribs were multi-colored, from purple to yellow.

"I'm fine."

"No, you're not. Nobody would be fine after that."

"And... to make matters... worse—" I took a breath "—Fernandez called me... today... let me know... Takoda and I... can't continue the investigation... till State Police clear us... of the shooting."

"What happens if you keep investigating?"

"We'd get fired... Also... the media... backlash would be bad... Two cops going rogue... failing to follow... police policy... after a shooting... never looks good."

"What are you gonna do? I know you can't drop this case."

I stopped pedaling. The monitor showed I'd reached my eighteen-mile goal for the day. I climbed down off the bike and grabbed a drink of water.

"I guess I'll have to ask for some help."

I went inside and found a towel to wipe off the sweat on my face. I slipped a shirt on as I explained that the Marvin Bingham investigation wasn't over. There were loose ends—people who needed to be arrested for what they'd done to Susanna.

"Who will you ask for help? You can't ask another cop. Wouldn't that put them in a bad spot?" Ashley inquired.

"I can't believe I'm saying this... but I think you're the best option to help."

"Me? Why?"

"Nobody will expect you to be doing it... also, I can send my brother-in-law with you as protection. He was former Marines Recon Special Forces."

"Okay... but how would it work?"

The good thing about exercise is that it always clears my head. I had let a plan percolate in my head as I was riding my bike in the silence of my garage.

"I need you and Dean to follow up on the media sources. There was a leak from a police officer. That was the only way the networks could've known about Mato's broken bones."

"Why would someone do that? Why would a cop do that to you?"

"A cop who's against us. Someone who wants Takoda and me not to investigate the case."

"Come on, Warren. You're being paranoid."

"Am I? Look outside."

Ashley walked to the window. A couple of Dallas police officers were parked out front. The entire street was filled with news vans.

"All of them here for a story. Takoda's and my story." I said, "How'd our shooting end up on the national news? Nobody cares that much about little ol' Jericho Nation. Something bigger is at work here."

"Holy shit...," Ashley said as she drew the curtain and walked away. "Do you think they're at Takoda's place, too?"

"Yep. Even if we tried to investigate this case while on paid leave, there's too many eyes on us."

"Let's say that whoever leaked this to the press is involved in your investigation. How do we approach figuring this out?"

"I have a friend who used to do stories about me, on my CrossFit accomplishments. I'm gonna reach out. I trust her and she'll be able to tell you who leaked the information in a few days."

"Okay..."

"If you're not comfortable doing this, you don't have to. I don't want you to feel pressured to do it. I'm only asking you because you're so damn easy to talk to. I know people will give you information easily."

"I *am* known to be quite charming," she quipped.

"Ashley, I'm being serious. You don't have to do this. I can find another way if need be."

"If this helps you get the sons of bitches behind what happened to Susanna Holt, I'd do it ten times over."

SALEM COUNTY HOSPITAL

Cardwell rushed to the hospital the next day. He told the nurses he was there on official police business, so no one would guess at his and Marvin's relationship.

He located Marvin and spoke to the doctor outside in the hallway. To his relief, the doctor informed him that Marvin was going to make a full recovery.

Two Salem police officers and a couple of hospital security guards were stationed outside the room, guarding Marvin in case Anakin made a second attempt on his life. And Marvin was under investigation for the death of Robert Holt.

The doctor told him Marvin wouldn't be able to answer any questions for a few days. Cardwell couldn't risk trying to talk to his brother with the Salem police officers by the door. He made his way to the exit.

———

Meanwhile, a few stories below, in Susanna Holt's hospital room, Camille and Emily were by Susanna's side. The doctor and nurses sat down with them in the room and explained the billing information. They explained it as sensitively as they could: the longer Susanna was kept alive by life support, the more money it cost them. Money that nobody in the family had to spare.

But neither of them would make the choice to end Susanna's life. They both imagined Susanna surviving by divine intervention.

Then Camille realized that if Susanna did return to consciousness, she'd learn that her father had been killed as well as her nephew. *Who'd want to return to that news?* she wondered.

———

OTIS, OREGON, TAKODA'S RESIDENCE

Almost a full day had passed since the shooting. Takoda had only gotten out of bed twice. Once to get some food, another time to go to the bathroom. Maria had never seen him like this.

When she told him that news network vans were outside and reporters were champing at the bit to speak with him, Takoda didn't care. He ignored them.

By eleven p.m. they'd given up. Maria came to lie down next to him and attempted to cuddle.

Takoda got out of bed and marched away. Maria at first was offended. Then she practiced patience and did her best to understand the trauma he was going through. It was hard for her to understand, as she was not a police officer. Yet Maria was no stranger to trauma. She had her own horrific past that still haunted her.

In their bedroom, she could hear Takoda shuffling around in the dark. In the background coming from the living room, the TV was playing some sort of commercial.

"Honey, just turn on the light."

Takoda flicked on the light and found his laptop. He sat down on the edge of the bed and switched it on. Takoda picked up his notebook from the nightstand by his bed.

"What are you doing?"

"My brain keeps spinning. I can't stop thinking about this investigation."

"Expecting to find answers on your computer?"

"That's exactly what I'm expecting."

DALLAS, OREGON

Ashley stayed the night for the second time in a row. Having her support me through what I was feeling helped me on a level I didn't know was possible. When we woke up the next day, Dean came over to discuss our plan of action regarding the news network leak.

I told Dean about my friend Alicia who worked as an investigative journalist for the *Statesman Journal*. The *Statesman* was the main newspaper source in the state's capital, Salem. I met Alicia years ago when I was starting out as a police officer. We were assisting Salem detectives on a case that ended up being a big human trafficking story. Alicia's and my paths crossed during the case, and we hit it off for a short time.

To avoid unnecessary conflict, I neglected to tell Ashley that I used to have a relationship with Alicia. She was an incredible woman, and quite attractive. Her charm helped her get a lot of information on stories. Part of the reason I liked her was her tenacity—which was also the reason we broke up.

Dean was on board with the plan; he said he'd help by taking out a couple of cameramen outside my house. I laughed. Part of me wanted to see Dean out there tossing those vultures around like rag dolls, but I knew he was kidding.

Ashley and Dean hit it off, right off the bat. Their dark, twisted senses of humor were a good match. I told them where to meet Alicia and they left the house together. After they left, I got a phone call from Olivia.

"What's up, sis?"

"So... what's going on over there with my husband?" She inquired dubiously.

"Nothing dangerous, I promise. It's just a precaution for Ashley."

"Okay... Have him back home soon, please."

"Will do, sis. How's my beautiful niece doing?"

"Oh, you know still pooping her pants, but cuter than a button."

I laughed and made conversation for a bit longer. She asked how I was doing. I asked that she and the rest of the family stay home until the news vans found a new story. I knew they'd all understand, but call me frequently.

I reassured Olivia I was okay.

Deep down, I knew I wasn't.

———

My house had three bedrooms. I'd ordered a whiteboard from Amazon. When it came, I took it into the spare bedroom, which was empty, with white-painted walls and gray carpet. It was bland, but it was a space where I could think. There was one window, but I had large, dark-colored curtains covering it. I was alone with my thoughts. I started writing important clues about my case on the whiteboard from memory.

Caroline Wilson popped up in my head. She was the doctor in charge of Susanna's care. Next, Monica Hawke, the head of the in-home nursing program. She answered to Wilson.

The Salem doctor who Ashley had introduced me to, looked

over the medical records of Susanna Holt and brought up several health issues. Her feet weren't checked, and her weight loss was not documented. The lack of brain function from her dementia. I wrote out the numbers 0-30 on the whiteboard, remembering the basic knowledge test score Susanna had received.

Emily and Camille advised me that Adult Protective Services (APS) had been assigned the case at their request. Either they were lying for no reason, or it was true. If it were true, why would APS dismiss the case and not dig into it? What would they have to hide? I wrote my thoughts and questions about APS on the board.

Neil Marshal was the next name. How in the world did Marvin Bingham get a defense attorney like him? Neil was an attorney I'd known over the years. The man was a wizard in a courtroom and was not someone to be hired for cheap. Someone was footing the bill on Marvin's behalf.

I tried to connect lines between all these people, but I drew a blank. Dr. Perez seemed to be in the dark about the issues, considering he barely saw Susanna. The medical records he had were the only honest thing I'd gotten from the medical field in this case.

My next consideration was who was behind the news leak. If a cop was behind the leak, maybe the cop was the link between Marvin and Neil Marshall.

Marvin was close with a cop? It fit. A cop who wanted to protect him from prison time. I wrote out another section on my whiteboard: *Who is the cop?*

Another cell phone call came in. To my surprise, it was Takoda.

"Takoda! Hey man, how are you?"

"Hey… I'm hanging in there. Do you have time to come to my house?"

"Of course. What for?"

"I'll tell you when we meet up. I might have a lead on the case."

OTIS, OREGON

I maneuvered around the press outside my house and sped away. A few tried to follow me, but I ditched the tail with ease. Upon my arrival at Takoda's house, I was met by more newscasters trying to get a statement. I politely told them to fuck themselves and made my way to the door. Maria let me in.

Takoda was in his living room, playing the Xbox 360 with his five-year-old son. I wasn't super familiar with games, but Takoda looked as if time with his son was doing him good. I sat on the couch and waited until they were done. Once they finished, Takoda told his son to go hang out with Maria in his room, and she took him away so we could talk.

"It's good to see you, man," I said. "How are you holding up?"

"Not so good. But I'll make it. What's the deal with all the news media everywhere?"

I told Takoda my theory on the media leak. He hadn't been watching the news, so I explained the leaked details and explained how Ashley and Dean were investigating that.

"I think the leak came from a cop."

"It would only make sense. That's the only way they could have gotten those details."

I nodded.

"What if that cop was the brother of Marvin Bingham?" Takoda said.

"He didn't have any family members left in his file."

"Last night I had an idea pop into my head… You know those ancestry.com commercials? I could hear one playing in the background. So I decided to pay the money and do one for Marvin."

"What'd you find?"

"Marvin had a brother. Edward Bingham."

"Yeah, but we couldn't find anything on that name in our system, remember?"

"Right. So I checked the name Edward Bingham again. So maybe the brother died too, ya know, like the parents?"

"Did he?"

"No, nothing. It's like this kid fell off the face of the earth. You know how good I am at finding dirt on people using the internet. Yet, on this guy I found nothing."

A lightbulb went off in my head. "He legally changed his name."

"Bingo, my friend. That's the only logical explanation. And why would someone change their name?"

"Because they're hiding something."

"Maybe hiding the fact that they have a brother like Marvin Bingham?"

"Yep, and hiding it because they had hopes of becoming a police officer one day."

"If a police agency catches wind of any criminal family members—for example, a brother like Marvin—that officer never gets hired. So he changed his name," Takoda deduced.

"How old is the brother?" I inquired.

"Six years younger than Marvin."

"So if he was still alive today he'd be around fifty-four years old."

"Exactly, we're looking for a cop who is fifty-four years old. He has to be someone who was at the crime scene. Someone who knew the scene, and knew about the investigation."

"Lieutenant Fernandez is in his 50s… but there is no way he could be related to Marvin. Unless they were step-siblings."

"Nope, ancestry.com says that Marvin and Edward had the same mother and father."

"All right, that narrows it down. The brother would be a fifty-four-year-old white male."

"How old were the detectives on scene? An OSP detective would have several links to the media. They're always talking to reporters."

Takoda rose, walked to his kitchen, and came back with a fifth of Jameson whiskey. He poured himself a glass, then poured me an even bigger one.

"My detective was no older than thirty to thirty-five range," Takoda said as he sipped. "The nice thing about being on paid leave is I can work while drunk."

"I got interviewed by Chad Druery, and I'm not sure how old he is. He's been a cop awhile though. It could be him."

I took a drink from my whiskey and agreed with Takoda that it was much more fun drinking alcohol and solving a case than doing it sober. Takoda pulled out a sheet of paper and wrote out Chad Druery's name.

"All right, there's one suspect. Chief McCarthy is far too young… What about the forensic people that were there?"

"I can't remember seeing them. We're gonna need to look at the crime scene log entries and see who fits the profile."

"Sounds good, but we're on paid leave and shouldn't be doing what we are doing right now. So how do we figure that out?"

I took another drink of my whiskey. I stood up and sauntered around the house for a little bit. I closed my eyes and tried to recall everything about the night of the shooting. Everything flashed in front of my eyes.

"War… what are you doing, man?" Takoda asked, confused.

"Give me a second to think."

Takoda drank a little more.

"The cop is the brother. Are we sure of that?"

"Positive."

"The same cop brother most likely told APS not to investigate Marvin Bingham when Emily filed the complaint. That's the only reason why we wouldn't be notified. Because a cop already told them to disregard the investigation."

Takoda raised his hand in an *ah-ha!* Gesture.

"That's right. The family tried to get APS involved."

I thought more. "Then there's the doctor who neglected to care for Susanna. What's their motive? That can't be because of the cop too. That doesn't make sense."

"Maybe it was pure negligence and then they hid it after the fact."

"I would have thought that before, but it seems like someone has been covering Marvin's tracks."

"It does seem that way…"

I flashed back in my head to Brent Cardwell hugging me after the shooting. My body tensed up. My body was trying to tell me something that my brain had not yet made the connection about.

"Brent Cardwell is around fifty to fifty-five years old," I suggested. "He's white, and looks a little bit like Marvin, but twice the size."

"The MCRT guy? Ashley's partner? No way!"

I phoned Ashley real quick. After a few rings, she answered, "Hey, honey, I'm safe, I promise." She seemed to need to make me feel comfortable.

"No, that's not why I'm calling," I said.

"What's going on?"

"Did you mention once that Cardwell had a fiancé?"

"Yeah, why?"

"What does she do for a living? Do you know?"

"She's a nurse, I think."

"Where is she a nurse at?"

After I asked the paramount question, Ashley let it resonate for a moment. She said she couldn't remember.

"How do you not know? You ride in a car with him for ten hours a day."

"We just never got around to it," Ashley said.

"Okay, thanks. How's it going on your end?"

"We passed your message to Alicia. Dean is doing recon work on her to make sure Alicia isn't followed or somehow in on this. You failed to mention the woman is flawless looking."

"Must have slipped my mind. Keep me posted, would you?"

"Uh-huh."

"Be safe."

"You too."

"Safe as Trojan condoms, baby."

She laughed and we ended the conversation. Takoda stared at me, as he was anxiously waiting for an answer. I sipped on my whiskey glass. It was going down easier with each swallow.

"You really think it's Cardwell?" he asked.

"We have to figure out if Susanna's nurse happens to also be Cardwell's fiancé. If she is, then we have a common link. A link that ties in why certain people neglected to do their jobs."

Takoda rubbed his tired bloodshot eyes, "Fuck, man, just when I think this isn't gonna get any messier."

"It makes sense now… He was the only cop that night who told me that we did the right thing by defending Marvin. He didn't say that because he was proud of what we did as officers. He said it because he was relieved we saved his brother."

Takoda nodded.

"And Cardwell would know who the best defense attorneys are," I continued. "Which explains how Marvin was able to find Neil Marshall so fast. But I can't see Cardwell or Marvin having enough money to pay Neil."

"A nurse or a doctor could probably help pay the bill," Takoda put in.

"A nurse wouldn't make enough money. Not unless she had a large inheritance somewhere. A doctor could probably afford it."

"What was the doctor's name again?"

I thought back to my whiteboard at home. "Caroline Wilson."

"Who's the nurse?"

"Monica Hawke."

"I got an idea." Takoda took another gulp of his whiskey, finished off the glass, and poured himself another. He went to his bedroom and brought back his laptop with him. "Let's see what I can dig up."

Takoda logged on to his Facebook account and searched for Monica Hawke's name. He looked at her photos. Monica didn't look like she lived a glamorous life. No sign of Brent Cardwell.

He typed in Caroline Wilson's name next. He clicked on her profile and started scanning over the pictures. It didn't take long to find a picture of Brent and Caroline together. The picture was of a memory, from the night he proposed to her and she said yes. The next photo we looked at was of a beautiful log cabin house. In the post, she commented on the photo. Caroline posted that she and Cardwell were proud owners of sixty-five acres of property and a beautiful house in Jericho Nation.

"That's a woman who could afford to hire an expensive defense attorney," Takoda pointed out.

"Cardwell isn't marrying a nurse. He's marrying the doctor," I added.

Maria came out of the bedroom with Xander. Maria gazed at me for an uncomfortable second, and I noticed that she had a hint of bewilderment in her eyes.

"Something wrong?" I asked her.

"No offense, Warren, but your face looks like shit."

My face was still swollen, with bruising that was mostly blue with shades of yellow. I felt my face for a second.

"You're not wrong," I agreed.

I drove back out onto the highway and started heading home. I was feeling all sorts of emotions. Marvin was a piece of trash, and there was no fixing that, but he was what he was. Cardwell was a cop. *He is one of us.* A betrayal of the badge on so many levels was unforgivable. I knew it was him, but in my world, it wasn't about knowing something, it was about whether or not I could prove it.

I decided to call Lieutenant Fernandez. Fernandez made some friends with the FBI during his successful career as a detective. I asked him if the FBI could do a more complete background check on Cardwell. The feds had a lot more resources than we had. I told Fernandez that I believed Cardwell had changed his name in the past, and that he could be Marvin's brother.

Fernandez advised me that I wasn't supposed to be investigating the case, as any supervisor would, but then reluctantly agreed to reach out to his FBI buddies and let me know what they found.

After my phone call, I made it back home; it was near dark outside. I was seeing fewer and fewer news vans in the area, so that was nice. It was easy to breeze by the few reporters sleeping in their cars.

I quickly walked through the brisk nighttime air and into my house. Inside I found Dean and Ashley.

"Your sister is going to kill me," said Dean as I entered the room. My sister might be the one person that man ever feared.

"Don't worry, I'll take the fall. What'd you guys find out?"

Ashley greeted me with a kiss at the door.

"Your pretty reporter friend didn't have all the answers we were expecting."

"What answers did she have?"

We sat down on my couch.

Dean said, "The media is keeping it pretty hush-hush. Those greedy fuckers don't want anyone to know who tipped them. The tip is making stories and they're making good money off a tragedy."

"Vultures, man, fucking vultures," I responded.

"Alicia was able to tell us that the cop was an older male. A big guy, around his fifties, white, and was a local cop who was on scene of the investigation the night it happened."

"Brent Cardwell," I said.

Dean had no idea who that was, but Ashley certainly did.

Ashley shot a look of disbelief toward me. "No… It can't be."

"Did he ever show you pictures of his fiancé?"

"Yeah, I think so. When he proposed."

"His fiancé is a doctor. The same doctor who works at the Jericho Nation Medical Clinic… Caroline Wilson."

Dean said, "All right, I have no idea who the fuck you guys are talking about, but do you need anything else? I got an upset wife who's been left with a six-month-old all day to attend to."

"No, we're good. Thank you for your help. Tell my sister I apologize for making her take care of Laurel alone all day."

"Will do, brother, be safe with all this shit. Call me if you need backup."

"Copy that. Give Olivia and Laurel my love."

Dean nodded and left. The cold breeze chilled the house for a brief second as he made his exit.

"I need you to explain to me how Brent is behind all this," said Ashley.

I started from the beginning and explained it until the end.

JERICHO NATION TRIBAL POLICE DEPARTMENT

The next morning, Brent Cardwell sat in Chief McCarthy's office with Lieutenant Fernandez. McCarthy and Fernandez had not been getting much sleep. Administrative duties were often unsung challenges of the department. They dealt with a lot of the things the patrol guys didn't have the patience for.

"So, as I was saying, Chief," Cardwell informed them, "my fiancé is really torn with all this. The only reason Caroline cleared Susanna's health was because of Monica Hawke. Monica was supposed to be taking care of Susanna, but she failed to do so… As you can imagine, this whole thing is very stressful for my fiancé and me. You both have known me for a long time and have known me to have good character. I came forward with this information as a favor and nothing else. Caroline is ready to accept whatever consequences she gets regarding this issue. She hasn't been able to sleep since she found out about it."

"We appreciate you coming to us with this vital information. It must have been hard for you," responded McCarthy. "Caroline needs to come in to speak with us about the investigation as soon as possible."

"Agreed. She's scared that she'll be arrested for something that wasn't her fault. It's a lot of pressure being a doctor."

"I don't know all the details of Officer Lawson's investigation… As you know, it got cut short after the recent shooting. We thought it might be closed after he arrested Marvin Bingham, but I guess not. When he gets back, we'll work this all out. I promise."

Cardwell rose and shook McCarthy and then Fernandez's

hands, "Thank you for hearing me out on her behalf. I'm sure it will all work out."

"Anytime. Congrats on your retirement. It's coming up soon, isn't it?"

"Yep, next week. I can't wait."

"I bet. Take care."

"You too."

Cardwell left the room. McCarthy and Fernandez waited to hear the doors to the exit shut before they started talking again. Fernandez poked his head out of the office to make sure Cardwell left.

"Do you think Lawson is right?" McCarthy inquired.

"I wasn't sure before… But now I definitely think he's right about Cardwell," replied Fernandez.

"Me too… Call the OSP detectives. Do whatever it takes to get Lawson cleared of the shooting by this afternoon. I'm going to call the DA and have him subpoena the medical records from the Tribal Clinic as evidence."

"Didn't Lawson's report say that the clinic had no medical records?"

"It did. But when they realize that they deleted the documentation, the DA can see about arresting the doctor too."

"Maybe… It's worth a shot. It'll put the pressure on until we can get Lawson back to finish the investigation."

Fernandez left the room to go make some phone calls to a couple of detectives working on the shooting of Mato and Robert Holt. Chief McCarthy dialed the Kirk County District Attorney's Office and spoke to DA Andrew Ketelson.

"Hey, DA Ketelson. Chief McCarthy here. I think you should subpoena Susanna Holt's medical records from the Jericho Nation Medical Clinic. It will help your case."

"With all due respect, sir. I don't tell you how to do your job, so don't tell me how to do mine."

"Listen, I'm doing you a favor. Just trying to help."

"Well, don't."

"You know, it's hard to be nice to you."

"Now I know where your officers get it from."

"Listen here, you little shit. Before I got into law enforcement I used to think of lawyers like a coat. A good coat covers your ass. But that's not the case with you, is it?" McCarthy started calmly, but his voice slowly rose. "Instead, you're turning down a perfectly good tip so you can sit over there and polish up the office with a good midday jerk-off session. Well, you know what, Ketelson? That's not gonna happen. So, stop tugging on your tiny cock, stop spraying man chowder all over your office, and get to fucking work!"

"Okay, fine. I'll do it. Way to set an example for your guys, Chief."

"Yep, no problem. Next time you want to turn down a perfectly good tip for a felony investigation I want you to think of the holocaust. NEVER AGAIN! YOU DUMB FUCK!" McCarthy screamed as he hung up the phone.

Fernandez stuck his head in the office. "Oh, man, you shouldn't have brought the holocaust into it."

McCarthy took a few breaths to calm down.

"I was trying to make a point. I don't need a history lesson right now… That Ketelson is a real prick."

"No, he's just a lawyer."

"Are the detectives ready to clear Warren from the shooting?"

"Yes, they are."

"How about Takoda?"

"Not yet. Still, more with him, I think."

"That's better than nothing. Get Lawson in here as soon as possible."

After Cardwell left Chief McCarthy's office, he drove over to the medical clinic. He stormed in and quickly found Caroline. Caroline was with a patient, but she could see by the look on Cardwell's face that something was wrong. Caroline stepped away from her patient to talk to Cardwell.

"How'd the meeting go?" Caroline asked.

"Not good. They know I'm involved somehow. We gotta go now."

CHAPTER
SIXTY-SEVEN

Ashley and I made a trip out to the Salem County Hospital that day to visit Susanna Holt one last time. The news reporters finally left and found a new story to report on. During all the chaos, I learned that Camille and the rest of the family had just that day had to stop life support for Susanna, ending her life. It wasn't a surprise, but it left hearts broken nonetheless. Ashley spoke to Camille, Emily, and Grandma Halona while we were at the hospital. I kept my distance, given the recent events.

The funeral services people came by and placed Susanna's body on a bed with four wheels, covered it, and wheeled her remains out to their vehicle. Camille and Emily held each other and cried. Grandma Holt sobbed loudly enough for the entire hospital to hear. The sounds of grieving were not unfamiliar in a hospital.

I walked over, unable to make myself keep my distance anymore. I couldn't sit there and let them think that I didn't care. I saw a mother who lost her daughter, then her nephew, and the love of her life in one week. I saw a sister who lost her brother and mother figure. They didn't do anything to deserve that kind of suffering. All that suffering, all that pain, was caused by two brothers: Marvin Bingham and Brent Cardwell.

As I approached, I saw Ashley give me a concerned look. I ignored it.

"I'm sorry for your losses this week. From the bottom of my heart, I truly am. And if you hate me for what has transpired the last few days, that's understandable. I want you to know, I'm gonna make sure we get the people responsible for this. I was too late for Susanna, but I still have time to try and make some part of this right."

"We don't hate you," Camille said, as she used a Kleenex to wipe her nose. "If it wasn't for you, we wouldn't have had any time with Aunt Susanna before she died. We are thankful for you."

Blown away, I told her, "What happened with Mato... was awful. We did everything we could to prevent anyone from getting shot. It was our very last option. We just couldn't stop him."

Camille cleaned more tears streaming down her face.

"It was always hard trying to talk sense to my brothers growing up."

Grandma Holt hugged me and shed a bucket of tears on my shoulder. I didn't know what to do. At first, I stood there awkwardly with my arms at my sides. Then I embraced her.

"I miss them so much..."

"I know you do..." I responded as I gently patted her back.

We stood there hugging for a couple of minutes as she hid her face on my shoulder. I bit my teeth and closed my eyes, fighting off the impulse to cry with her. I had to stay strong. Grandma Holt let go of me and rubbed her red, puffy eyes with her hand.

"You said 'the people who did this.' Does that mean there is more than Marvin who did this to her?"

"I have reason to believe there are multiple people out there that need to be brought in, and I'm gonna do it if it's the last thing I do. I will bring justice for your family."

Emily forced a wobbly grin. "We believe you."

———

It was midmorning by the time I left the hospital with Ashley. I got a call from Fernandez telling me to get back to work. He said I was cleared by the investigation, and that he needed me to finish the Susanna Holt case. He told me about Brent Cardwell's visit, trying to make it look like Monica Hawke was the reason for the medical neglect. Fernandez advised me that he also thought Cardwell was a dirty cop.

I asked Fernandez to call Adult Protective Services (APS) for me while I was en route to the police department. I explained to Fernandez that APS had an open investigation on Susanna Holt and then dropped it. Fernandez told me he'd make the call.

After I hung up I sat the phone down in the center console and kept driving the Dodge Challenger. I glanced over at Ashley.

"I got cleared of the shooting. They need me to go back to work and finish this."

"If you're going after Brent, I need to go with you, Warren."

"No way, that's not safe. You need to stay out of this."

"If you think I'm going to sit on the sidelines when my partner of two years is wanted for assisting in a homicide, think again. He's not just my partner, he's my friend. He protected me like I was his daughter whenever we went on calls..."

I sighed. "We won't have to kill him."

"You don't know that."

I said nothing. A light snow was falling.

"I know where the log cabin is he stays at... He took me to it one time for a lunch break. There's only one way in and out of that place. I bet he goes there sometime tonight. If he sees you, he won't let you enter. But if he sees me... he'll let me in. I can talk him into coming with you peacefully," she argued.

"Explain the log cabin property. Does he have security set up?"

"Oh, yeah. His fiancé is loaded. There are cameras, fences, and gates set up all along the property. His house is at the top of a hill, so if you tried to approach he would see you coming a mile away."

"Typical cop. Of course, he would make the place like Fort Knox with that kind of money."

"I'll follow you to the station in my personal vehicle. Just in case we have to use that idea."

Her idea made a lot of sense. I just hoped I wouldn't regret bringing her with me. My phone rang again. It was Fernandez.

"Got some information from APS."

"What've you got?"

"APS started an investigation, but before they could make a house visit, they received a call from an MCRT unit. MCRT advised them they had already looked into the case. The MCRT unit said that the case was a dead end. APS had no reason to distrust the well-respected members of MCRT so they closed the investigation."

I said, "Exactly like I thought."

"Not exactly."

"How so?"

"The MCRT officer who called APS wasn't Cardwell... It was Ashley Bradford."

———

JERICHO NATION MEDICAL CLINIC

Brent Cardwell waited for a few patients and employees in the hallway to pass by before he continued. Caroline was trying to keep her composure after hearing that the cops were on to them.

"How would they know? There's no fucking way. You're being paranoid," she said.

Brent replied, "I know cops, babe. I've been working with them for thirty years... I know when they aren't showing all their cards. We have to go now."

"Did they say anything to make you feel this way? If we make a run for it, that'll only make us look more guilty."

"If we stay, we give them enough time to get the evidence they need to lock us both away in a prison cell for the next twenty-five years or more. We need to get our shit and head to Brazil before that happens."

Caroline stood there, still unsure.

"Caroline... honey... I need you to trust me. I know this game better than any cop in the county. If you listen to me, we'll be sipping margaritas on a beach in Brazil before they even know what our involvement was."

She rubbed her fingers through her hair and her eyes got big. Brazil had a no-extradition policy for criminals. Caroline had spent her life moving from place to place and felt that she had finally found her home in Jericho Nation. Caroline had dated plenty of losers, muscled-out young men with six packs in her time, but never felt anything for them like she did for Cardwell. Those men didn't possess what Cardwell had: her heart. Finally, she nodded.

"Okay... let's go."

———

AGENCY CREEK BACKWOODS, JERICHO NATION

Anakin's face resembled the rest of his body. Bruised and battered. His arm was in a sling. None of that stopped him from the mission. Anakin had assembled thirty members of the IPO gang, some from Portland, some from Siletz, and the rest from the Spokane, Washington, Indian Reservation. Anakin got fixed up by a doctor at a hospital in Washington, then met up with the Spokane IPO group. They responded to a call to arms he'd put out after Mato's death.

A convoy of pickup trucks escorted Anakin through Jericho Nation and into the backwoods the night prior. They drove miles into the woods on a one-way paved roadway that ran along Agency Creek. The forests around Jericho Nation went on for miles upon miles.

Once they were safely away from any kind of civilization, they drove up a dirt path to an open area in the middle of the forest and parked their vehicles. It was a campsite, closed due to the climate issues that time of year.

The snow was still falling, but the tall trees blocked much of it. As they got out of their trucks, the flakes gently falling around them made it seem like they were in a snow globe. They all walked to the tailgate of one of the pickups and opened it up to see what was in the bed of the truck. What they saw was enough automatic weapons and ammunition for the United States Army.

CHAPTER
SIXTY-EIGHT

I didn't say a word to Ashley about what Fernandez had disclosed. My world was spinning, as I had not suspected that Ashley was involved with Cardwell's schemes. We entered the police department side by side. Fernandez and McCarthy were in the chief's office. I asked Ashley to wait in the patrol room so I could talk to my superiors in private. She sat at my desk to wait.

McCarthy and Fernandez were waiting for me. I strode in and quickly shut the door behind me.

"Why are you shutting the door?" asked McCarthy.

"Ashley is in the patrol room," I whispered.

Fernandez rose from his chair. "Are you serious? Why did you bring her here? Did she hear our phone call?"

"No, but she was in the car with me when you called... I brought her in case we needed to negotiate with Cardwell."

"We are nowhere near having probable cause for Cardwell or Caroline Wilson's arrest. She doesn't need to be here. Not now, and possibly not ever. For all we know, she's in on it."

"What's her motive?"

"Money. Same as most people," suggested Fernandez.

McCarthy added, "I'm sorry, War. This has to be tough for you."

"I don't believe it... There has to be some sort of reason for it."

"Like what?" Fernandez said.

"I don't know, but I'm going to ask her."

I stormed out of the office and went to the patrol room. Ashley was sitting on her phone, doing a 'Facetime' call to her son.

"I'm sorry to interrupt, but I have to ask you something. Right now."

Ashley ended the call. As she looked at me, her face paled. It was time to find out if she was a suspect or my girlfriend.

OTIS, OREGON

Takoda stared out his window and noticed all but one news media van had left. While he was annoyed by their presence, Takoda had to admire their tenacity. The snow on his deck had piled up. He could see about four inches on the fenced-out area of the deck.

Takoda stopped looking out the window. His wife and son were playing a board game together in the living room, the kiddo teasing Maria about being bad at board games. Hearing them laugh made him smile for the first time in days. *Maybe I can retire and spend the rest of my life like this,* he thought.

His next thought hit him like a bowling ball to the face.

Why is that news company still outside?

Takoda walked back to the window and glanced at the van again. It was a white van and on the side of it, it said CHANNEL 5 NEWS.

The hair rose on the back of Takoda's neck. *There is no channel five news in Oregon.*

What national news is on channel 5? Takoda pulled out his cell phone and did a quick Google search. The only news company that refers to them as Channel 5 News was a British News Network channel. There was no way they flew someone from Britain to podunk Otis, Oregon. Takoda dashed to his kitchen and grabbed his car keys.

It wasn't hard to spray paint a van.

His patrol bag was in the closet. Takoda loaded up his knife, gun, and outer bulletproof police vest. He made his way to the door, and Maria noticed a shift in his behavior.

"Where are you going?" she asked.

"Whatever you do, stay here and don't answer the door for anybody. I'm gonna check something out." Takoda pulled on his brown fleece jacket.

"What's wrong?"

"Hopefully nothing." Takoda opened the door to leave, then he stopped, looking over at his family. "I love you guys."

"We love you—"

Takoda hastily left, locking the door and closing it as he stepped into the ankle-deep snow. Takoda got to his car, threw the bag in the back, and started it up. He kept his eye on the "Channel 5" van in his rearview mirror. He had to wait a few minutes for the windows to defrost.

Once the windows defrosted, Takoda backed out of his driveway and turned his vehicle to face the exit. Takoda glanced over and saw a dark-skinned, Native American male in the driver's seat of the van. *You're not the British News Network.* Takoda sped off, and the van followed.

———

Inside the Channel Five news van was a loyal soldier of Anakin's. He drove behind Takoda on the road out of Otis. As he navigated the weather, he made a call to Anakin on his cell phone.

"Save your gas. We're coming to you." The soldier advised Anakin.

"What do you mean?"

"He left the house. We're on the highway heading to Jericho Nation as we speak."

CHAPTER
SIXTY-NINE

Fernandez let me interview Ashley alone in the patrol room. He was wary that I was too emotionally invested in Ashley to make a logical choice. He may have been right.

"Why did APS tell us that you called off the investigation into Susanna Holt?" I asked, trying to keep my voice level.

"Uh, what are you talking about?"

"We got a lead that the family of Susanna Holt contacted APS and asked them to do an investigation. APS says that you called them and told them to disregard the case."

"We're wasting time here. The more we sit here and talk about details that don't matter, the more time we give Cardwell and Caroline to escape."

"Answer my question."

Ashley's face started to turn red.

"So I'm a suspect now? Fuck you, Warren!"

"Damn it, Ashley, it's a simple question. Did you or did you not call APS off the case?"

"I don't remember! Cardwell asked me to do that dozens of times over the past few years. I'm just a therapist, remember? I'm not a cop. If he says that he investigated something and there was no crime, I didn't question it."

"How many times did he ask you to make calls on his behalf?"

"Honestly, I don't know. There were several investigations that went nowhere. We got calls all the time that were bogus. Do you always get calls that end up being criminal?"

"No, of course—"

"Exactly. I sometimes made calls for our unit on his behalf when he was busy with other police work. The mobile crisis response team was put in place for crisis intervention. Sometimes we get calls that don't require the level of training or knowledge that Brent and I have. If I made the call about Susanna Holt to APS, it was because I had no idea what was really happening and I trusted my partner wholeheartedly."

"I want to believe you... I really do, but it's too coincidental."

She shook her head. "Fuck you. I can't believe you are treating me like a criminal."

McCarthy interrupted the interview and strolled into the office.

"That douchebag DA called back and told me he stopped wacking his little pecker and did his job for once."

Ashley glanced at McCarthy, confused. I was embarrassed, but wanted to laugh at the same time. McCarthy seemed to notice Ashley for the first time.

"Oh, you must be Ashley. How are ya, darling? Anyway, DA Suck-My-Dick subpoenaed the files, only to learn that Dr. Wilson has deleted all of them. The DA wants us to interview her, then call him and see about charging her with tampering with physical evidence. We're going to need her to incriminate herself before we can arrest her on that charge."

"Copy that. We need someone to wait with Ashley until we clear her in all this," I suggested.

"Warren, please don't be stupid. You know I am your best shot at arresting Cardwell without an incident."

"I'll take my chances."

Fernandez entered the room. "I'll stay here with her."

I nodded. Ashley scoffed.

"Let's go get this little bitch of a doctor," McCarthy said.

We were making our way to the exit when I saw Takoda walking in. McCarthy and I came to a halt.

"Ah, Christ, what the fuck are you doing here? Trying to give me a fuckin' heart attack, are you?" McCarthy said.

"I think there are some IPO members following me," responded Takoda.

McCarthy sighed and started intensely rubbing his face.

"Are you sure?" I asked.

"No... But something is up. Can I stick with you till I know for sure?"

McCarthy was walking into political suicide, but the safety of his men was more important. He waved us off as if he didn't care anymore.

"Ride with Lawson. I don't like this fucking job anyway."

"Thanks, Chief." I chuckled.

The three of us headed for the parking lot during another snowy afternoon. As we were walking to our snowflake-covered vehicles, Takoda asked, "Where are we going?"

"To find Dr. Wilson. We might be able to get probable cause to arrest her for tampering with physical evidence, according to the DA."

"Finally, the DA is helping out."

"Let's hope it's not too late."

———

Takoda rode in the passenger seat with me, Chief McCarthy followed us in his own patrol vehicle. We made the short, slow drive through the harsh winter elements. The three of us invaded the medical clinic and walked to the medical care department. Chief McCarthy led the way.

McCarthy approached the receptionist with his usual charm. "Hey there, gorgeous, is Dr. Wilson in?"

The receptionist smiled at him.

"Let me check." She trotted off and came back a short time later.

"She left, actually. Went home early. Can I take a message?"

"No thanks. Is that a new hairstyle?"

"It is."

"Looks good. Take care, Lorraine."

She blushed.

McCarthy looked over at us. "They're making a run for it."

"We have to go back and get Ashley," I said. "We need to arrest Cardwell and Wilson before it's too late."

"You won't do a thing. We have no probable cause to arrest either of them... We can't catch them all, Lawson. If we had enough evidence to arrest them, we'd get the SWAT team out here to take them down. If they flee before we get the evidence we need, so be it. Our hands are tied."

"Yes, sir," I replied.

"Your primary concern is to see if Takoda is being followed by IPO members. That is something we can act on today."

Takoda and I nodded. We left the medical department and went back to the parking lot. Takoda climbed into the car with me.

"Are we really going to leave this case alone?" Takoda asked.

"Not a fucking chance."

We went back to the police department, on our way back I saw nothing that was suspicious. I wondered if Takoda was being paranoid—except that I knew better than to question him after everything we'd been through together.

As McCarthy, Takoda, and I entered the patrol office, Fernandez informed us, "My FBI buddy called me. He confirmed that Edward Bingham, the brother of Marvin Bingham, is actually Brent Cardwell."

The three of us nodded. Now we had solid evidence. I noted the date and time we got the information from the FBI in my notebook, along with the FBI Agent's name. Notes for my report to the DA.

"What are we gonna do with her?" asked McCarthy, nodding toward Ashley.

"From what I can tell, we have no evidence to link her to the crime. We tell her to get lost." I answered.

McCarthy and Fernandez nodded.

"Permission to escort her out?" I asked McCarthy.

"Granted. Come right back, though. Although I see no signs of IPO around, be very cautious. They're out there somewhere."

I nodded.

"Permission to escort me out? Warren, I'm your girlfriend, not a fucking suspect! Open your eyes!" Ashley shouted as she stood.

"I don't know that right now."

Ashley stomped out of the office, slamming her feet on the brown linoleum floors. Takoda and I followed her out to the private parking lot at the back of the police station.

Chief McCarthy stood in the office, looking at Fernandez.

"I sure hope she's a criminal... because if she's not. She'll have him bent over with a dildo rammed into his ass for the rest of his days... Am I right, partner?"

Fernandez gave McCarthy a look of disgust. "What is wrong with you?"

McCarthy chuckled, "A lot of things, honestly."

———

Ashley was walking so fast that I had to jog to catch up. I caught up to her in the parking lot near her personal vehicle and grabbed her arm.

"Let go of me," demanded Ashley.

I let go. "We need to go to Cardwell's cabin right now."

"Well, have fun with that."

"I need you to help us."

CHAPTER
SEVENTY

Brent Cardwell and Caroline were frantically rummaging through every room in the log cabin. Cardwell had most of his bags packed and ready to go. Caroline was having a harder time leaving the beautiful home behind.

"Honey, what's taking so long?" Brent impatiently asked.

"I don't know what all I should bring... There's no chance we can stay? Just for one more night?" Caroline begged.

"Damn it, Caroline, do you not understand? The difference between freedom and being caged like an animal is right here right now! Let's get a move on!"

Caroline stopped packing her bags and crossed her arms across her chest, obviously offended.

Cardwell scoffed. "Fine, you stay here. I'll go."

"Can you take a breath? We don't even know if they have any actual evidence to arrest us."

"If they don't, they're damn close."

"I know it's stupid, but I feel so connected to this place... it feels like my dad is a part of this cabin. My dad's inheritance paid for this and I promised myself I would live here forever. It was my dream. And to leave on a whim—when we don't even know if they have evidence against us—is hard for me."

Cardwell inhaled deeply and lowered his voice to normal.

"I get it, baby. I love this place. Lord knows we have some of the best memories together here. But if we stay, we lose everything."

Caroline found herself agreeing once again with Brent.

"I'll get back to packing."

"Good, we need to be out of here in thirty minutes. Pack whatever you can. I'm gonna start loading the Jeep."

She nodded and ran up the stairs. Cardwell had a couple of bags set out by the door. He grabbed two black duffel bags and made his way to the Jeep. As he put the bags in the back tailgate of the vehicle, the zipper on one of the bags came open. Poking out was an award he'd won years ago: the medal of valor award from 1997. A small golden plaque with laminated letters. His name was on the award for courageous acts when he was on the Oregon State Police SWAT team. He'd breached a house during a long and tenuous hostage negotiation.

A husband had gone crazy and held his family hostage after a domestic disturbance. Cops responded to the call and one officer took a bullet in the bulletproof vest upon arrival. SWAT teams were called out and Cardwell's breach team went in, Cardwell in the lead.

They found the dad with a knife to a little boy's throat. The kid looked about eight years old. Cardwell saw a tiny bit of blood start to drip from the boy's neck. He lined up his AR-15 assault rifle at the suspect's head. Cardwell squeezed the trigger and a long, thin AR-15 round went right through the suspect's forehead.

The suspect went down, and the boy survived. Cardwell went for the boy and made sure that he was okay. The boy was crying.

Cardwell remembered holding the eight-year-old in his arms, reassuring the child that he was okay.

His mind came back to the present and he started to shake. He felt nauseous. The world started to spin. In all his years as an officer, he had never felt this.

Cardwell grabbed onto the Jeep to avoid himself from falling.

What is happening to me? This doesn't happen to me... I'm a SWAT veteran. Is it a panic attack?

He screamed up at the sky, hoping that this would all be over soon.

If we do get away with this, can I live with what I did after the fact?

———

JERICHO NATION TRIBAL PD

Ashley was pissed but she agreed to help us and we left the police station. She drove her Toyota 4Runner with determination in her eyes. I could see then, how much she cared about what happened to Susanna Holt. Takoda and I folded the back seats down and lay down so we couldn't be seen. Takoda had his police vest and gear on, ready to go. It was cramped in the back, lying down with our arms squished together.

"Are you sure you remember where this log cabin is?" I asked.

Ashley kept her eyes on the road. "Yes. He was very proud of it."

"Do you have any questions regarding the plan?"

"Nope."

"Good. Thank you for doing this."

She didn't respond.

———

A pickup truck full of Native American males dressed in red sat outside the police department. The soldier in the front passenger seat phoned Anakin and reported that they had been driving back and forth and were unsure what the tribal cops were doing. They'd seen a woman leaving the police station.

"Was she in a police car?" Anakin inquired.

"No. A Toyota 4Runner."

Anakin was at a different part of town with a group of soldiers. The IPO was covering each corner of Jericho Nation.

"Follow her. If they think they are being followed, they'll try to sneak the cops out of there without us seeing. They could be trying to trick us."

"On it."

"Call me when they stop somewhere."

W e lay in the back of Ashley's 4Runner in silence, feeling every bump in the road. I was disobeying a direct order from Chief McCarthy. Plus, Takoda being at work could result in him being fired. Ashley could get hurt. I'd hoped that this plan would work because if it didn't, I was going to need a new job. Maybe even if it did. Takoda and I stared at the gray inner roof of Ashley's vehicle.

"Listen, Takoda... I just wanted to say—" I craned my neck and started to explain. "I made the wrong call trying to protect Marvin that night."

Takoda spoke softly, "You didn't make a single bad call that night, you hear me? You did everything right and did all you could to protect *everyone*."

"But—you made the sacrifice that night. Because of me. I wish that had never happened. I wish I'd put aside my pride and listened to you, to spare you of that."

"I'm with you till the wheels come off, bro. I'd do it again in a fucking heartbeat. You want to know why?"

I looked on and waited for Takoda to finish.

"Because it was you making the choice, Warren. You're the best man—and cop—I've ever known."

Debatable. But...

"Likewise, my friend," I said.

Takoda nodded, and whipped out a couple of magazines to check if they were full. I did the same. We had three fully loaded magazines of .40-caliber pistol rounds holding sixteen rounds each. I'd grabbed our AR-15 assault rifle from my patrol vehicle as well. I had three magazines that were fully loaded, each holding thirty rounds apiece. Takoda had his AR-15 and the same amount of ammunition. The rifles laid on top of our bodies, both set to Safe and one magazine loaded into the weapon. Our .40-caliber pistols were in our holsters located on our right hips. Fully loaded with one round in the chamber, ready to go. Also on our gun belts were department-issued tasers: left hip.

"He's a former SWAT team guy. Cardwell will have expert training with firearms. Our best chance is getting in close enough to surprise him. If I get my hands on him before he can get to a weapon, that'll be our best shot," I said.

"Let's hope this Trojan horse idea works and Ashley isn't working for the suspect," he said in an undertone.

"Keep an eye on her," I whispered back. "Unfortunately we won't know what side she's on until it starts."

"I think she's with us. I think her feelings for you are real."

"Yeah, but she's been working with Cardwell for two years. They have a bond."

Takoda nodded.

I spoke loud enough for Ashley to hear me.

"Explain the layout of the house one more time so Takoda knows."

Ashley was leaning forward over the steering wheel with her eyes squinted, trying to see through the pouring snow. She turned the vehicle slowly to the right and then started to explain, "Well... it's big, like really big. It's about five hundred or so yards away from the highway in the middle of the woods and on a massive hillside. It's surrounded by giant green trees everywhere and he has a security system setup. There's a gate remotely operated from inside the house so if we want in, it has to be because he allows it.

The cameras at the gate were very high-tech from what I can remember."

"Anything else you can tell us?"

"I only went there once. I can't remember all the rooms or the layout. I remember there is a living room and kitchen near the front door."

"Is it one story, two stories, three?"

"Two stories, I think," she replied as she glanced in her rearview mirror. "Hey, I think we're being followed."

"How do you know?" Takoda cut in.

"There's a truck that's been following us since we left the police station."

"Everyone in Jericho Nation drives a truck... that could be anyone. Can you see the driver?"

"I can barely see anything in this snow."

The snow was falling so heavily that it was obstructing every angle. We were forced to drive at speeds of ten miles per hour due to the icy roads, added on with the growing inches of snow. It was the worst snow day in Jericho Nation in quite some time.

I looked at Takoda, "You think it's them?"

"No idea. There was a 'Channel 5' news van outside my house today. It was the only one left. I did a Google search and found that Channel 5 News is a British News Network. There isn't a Channel 5 local news in Oregon. I left my house, called a county cop to keep watch of my family. When I got to the police department, the van kept driving and I haven't seen it since."

"Maybe they switched vehicles and are following in the truck?"

"I have no idea... It'll be another thing we'll have to keep an eye on."

"We're almost there," from the front seat.

"Are you ready for this?" I asked, hoping I was talking to my girlfriend and not another threat.

Ashley took a deep breath, and was silent for a few seconds, then responded, "I'm ready."

I felt the weight of the vehicle shift as we made another turn. I heard muffled sounds of the gravel underneath the tires crunching and crackling. Our speed slowed as we bumped all over the road. The gravel road had several potholes which rocked Takoda and me all over the place. We grabbed onto the side panels of the vehicle to avoid rolling into each other.

Our feet slid down the back trunk door as we climbed the hill. It was difficult to remain lying down out of sight and not lean up to check where we were. For all I knew, Ashley was driving us into the middle of the woods where Cardwell would ambush us. The reality set in that Takoda and I were quite possibly riding to our deaths. I wondered if twenty-seven years was long enough to experience a full and complete life. The inside of the vehicle went completely silent.

The silence led me to a train of thoughts. I thought about my dad living without his youngest son. My mom crying at my gravesite, my nieces who never got to know their Uncle Warren. I should have been spending time with them, instead of risking my life. If I were to survive this, there were no promises that any of the people who were behind Susanna Holt's death would be convicted of their crimes. That was up to the lawyers and judges of the Kirk County Courthouse.

Next to me was the most loyal friend I could ever ask for. I felt I never deserved a friend like Takoda. I knew he was a mess after the shooting. Yet, there he was, lying beside me, ready to battle to the death if need be. They don't make friends like Takoda Tehama anymore.

But I'd made a promise to Susanna's family that I would bring them justice. I don't make a habit of lying to people. Regardless of my fears, and feelings toward our justice system, above all else... *I made a promise.* A man's got to keep his word.

"All right, we're at the gate. No talking from here on out," Ashley told us.

My hands trembled. I braced myself with a deep exhale and closed my eyes.

Brent Cardwell was trudging more bags to the front door. He looked out his window and saw a vehicle at the bottom of the hill near his gate. Brent walked over to the security video monitor and brought up the surveillance footage from a computer. Ashley buzzed the intercom.

"Ashley?" Brent answered over the gate call box speaker.

"Hey, partner. I need to talk to you for a second. I'm really worried and I'm here as a friend. Can I come up?"

Caroline stepped downstairs and saw Brent in the living room area speaking on the laptop to Ashley.

Caroline blurted out, "Who's that?"

Her demeanor was obviously not happy that they had visitors.

"It's Ashley," Cardwell informed her. "She's not a cop. Don't worry, we can trust her. She won't turn me in."

Caroline sighed and trekked back up the stairs. Cardwell hit the button on the computer security system to say, "Sure, come on up. We're about to leave, though."

Brent pressed the button to open the gate. As it swung slowly open, Ashley drove through, crawled up the hill, and parked the 4Runner. Ashley hopped out of the driver's seat and shivered in the cold winter air. Brent met her at the front door. Ashley walked up the porch and approached Brent with a friendly hug. She stepped back to look at her old partner.

"What's going on, Ash?" asked Brent.

Ashley sighed. "I heard some bad things about you."

"From War?"

She gazed down at the ground, "Yeah."

"What'd he say?"

"He said you were Marvin Bingham's brother..."

The snow was blowing sideways and making its way to their faces even under the awning of the front porch.

"Oh, Ashley... You must be so confused. You deserve an explanation. I owe you that much. Come inside and I'll make it clear for you."

Brent opened the door, and she stepped inside. Multiple bags were piled up near the front door.

"Going somewhere?"

"Yeah, vacation. Caroline is upstairs packing."

"Where are you going?"

"Brazil, actually... Gonna get out of this cold weather."

"Sounds nice." Ashley forced a smile. "What's going on, Brent?"

"Truth is... I am Marvin Bingham's brother." Brent turned his back to her and faced the window. "As much as I want to sit here and tell you that Warren is spreading lies about me, I can't do that. Warren is a good man and you deserve to be happy."

"So it's true?"

"It's true... Whatever he said... it happened."

"Then you have to turn yourself in, Brent."

"Is that why you're here? To talk me into turning myself in?"

Ashley recklessly stomped over to him next to the window, "I'm here because you've saved my ass more times than I could count and protected me from things I could've never handled alone. I'm here trying to return the favor."

"But I don't deserve to be arrested. I was doing what a good brother should do. I've given enough sacrifice to be owed one mistake—though I know that isn't how Warren sees it."

"No, it's not. I don't want you or him to get hurt."

"Are they coming?"

"Who?"

"Don't mess with me... you know who."

"Warren and the cops? No."

Cardwell paused for a second and assessed Ashley's face like cops do. "You're a good friend. You've been like a daughter to me," he said softly.

"Then listen to me. Trust that I have your best interests at heart. If they arrest you, you know that doesn't mean shit unless you get convicted."

"Maybe... Caroline, on the other hand. Well, that's a different story. I can't live without her, Ashley. I really can't."

"Brent, please..."

"You have to go now. I'm sorry."

———

While Ashley talked to Cardwell, Takoda and I slipped out of the back door of the Toyota 4Runner. Takoda and I used the vehicle to conceal our location from the front door. Both of us held our AR-15 assault rifles at the low ready position, with the gun barrel pointing downward.

"You stay here and watch the front. I'm gonna try to sneak around and find a back entrance. I'll radio you when I get in position," I said.

He nodded, "I don't see any more surveillance cameras on the property."

"Me neither. The snow probably covered any camera on the property by now."

I raised my weapon and moved toward the wall of the house. The garage was a separate building at the end of the driveway, about twenty-five yards from the front door. Takoda and I shielded ourselves behind the wall of the garage. On the right was the front door entrance to the home. On the left was a path that appeared to run around the outskirts of the property.

Takoda took up a position on the right side, checking around the corner to keep his eyes on Ashley at the front door. He could barely see the door from the outside and the snow prevented him from seeing through the windows of the house.

I tramped through the snow, going left and around the outskirts of the property. I'm usually a fast runner but sprinting in the accumulating snow was difficult. I stayed close to the walls of the residence, hunching down and staying out of sight of the windows.

Takoda called dispatch prior to our arrival and asked them to ping his cell phone location. The residence was not registered in the DMV database. If this encounter went south, at least they'd know where to find us.

I rounded the corner to the west side of the house, where the back door was located. So far, I had not been detected. I didn't feel good about what we were doing, but it had to be done. It felt like we were playing chicken, waiting for someone to open fire so we could call the cavalry. We were out on a limb that was about to break.

Low crawling to the door, I found the handle and cracked the door open silently. I overheard Ashley and Cardwell talking. I honed my listening skills as my brother-in-law, Dean, had taught me, pinpointing their location the best I could. I closed the door.

I used my radio to let Takoda know I was in position—the signal for him to make his way to the front door.

––––––––

Ashley pleaded as Cardwell gripped her arm and forced her toward the front door.

"Brent, listen to me: just come down to the station. I'll drive you down myself. It'll help your and Caroline's cause! I know you know this."

"This is the hill I die on, Ashley. I won't live in a prison cell or let my name get dragged through the streets after all the good I've done. I'd rather die than let that happen or see my beloved suffer the same fate."

Ashley's eyes filled. "Please don't do this. We can fix this!"

"I'm sorry it has to end this way."

Cardwell grabbed the handle of the front door. As he swung the door open, he saw Takoda approaching through the snow, rifle sights set on him. Ashley was standing directly between Takoda and Cardwell.

Cardwell grabbed Ashley, yanking her behind him, shielding her from any potential gunfire. He heaved Ashley to the side, and her little body hit the ground and rolled out of the line of fire, into the living room. Cardwell reached into his waistband and tightly gripped his 9mm Glock pistol.

"Don't!" shouted Takoda, continuing to move forward.

Takoda's finger went to the trigger, waiting until the last possible second to fire.

———

I snuck from the back door down the hallway, advancing slowly to make sure I didn't make the wooden floors creak. I heard what sounded like Ashley crying nearby. I passed a bathroom and a stairwell to the second floor.

The living room was at the end of the hallway. Cardwell stood in the light by the front door. The hallway was dark. I proceeded into the living room and heard Takoda shouting. I saw Ashley to my right, lying on the ground, her eyes wide with fear.

I raised my AR-15 and aimed it at the back of Cardwell's head from ten yards away.

"Cardwell, drop the gun now!"

He hesitated and instead of raising the gun and pointing it at

Takoda, he held it down at his side. Takoda stood on the porch, just left of the door so we could avoid a potential crossfire.

"I always knew I'd go down in a blaze of glory... I just didn't expect you to be the one pulling the trigger, War," said Cardwell softly.

"It doesn't have to be this way. Cooperate with me. Let me get your side of the story," I replied.

"Don't pull that cop bullshit on me, I know all the tricks. It's not gonna work."

The next moment felt like it progressed in slow motion. My eyes found Ashley's ashen face and wide eyes at the same moment I heard the sound of a shotgun being cocked directly behind me. *Caroline.*

Ashley shouted my name as loud as she could. I plunged to my left, toward the kitchen, amid the thundering shotgun blast.

I landed and did a shoulder roll under the dining table.

Am I hit? My body felt good. I had leaped out of the way a second before the shot.

I swiveled toward Caroline and saw the gun slip out of her hands to the ground. Her knees buckled and she collapsed.

I glanced behind me. No Cardwell at the door. I army crawled out from under the table with my rifle trained on Caroline. Tears started to stream down her face.

———

Takoda stared. One moment, Cardwell was standing in front of him. The next, the renegade cop had a hole the size of a basketball through his body, which spiraled through the air and onto the front deck. He crashed face-first to the wooden decking, cracking a piece of wood.

———

I got to my feet. Cardwell's body lay on the deck. *Dead before he hit the ground.* Caroline wailed loud enough for the entire state of Oregon to hear her.

Ashley froze where she lay. She had not moved since Cardwell had shoved her out of the line of fire. She was staring at her old partner in disbelief, not able to fully comprehend what had happened.

I kept my AR-15 trained on Caroline as Takoda approached, knelt next to Cardwell's body, and placed two fingers on Cardwell's neck. Takoda looked at me and shook his head.

"God, no! No, no, no!" screamed Caroline.

She grabbed the shotgun, cocked another round into the chamber, and placed the barrel of the gun under her chin, her finger on the trigger.

I cast the AR-15 aside, closing the distance between me and Caroline, leaping toward her, and forcing the shotgun down. As I knocked the gun out of her hands, a round launched into a nearby wall, nearly decimating Ashley. Ashley instinctively flinched, curling into a ball as the gun went off. The gun spun across the floor, sliding across the living room. Caroline tried to crawl after it, but I wrapped my arms around her, pinning her arms to her sides. As she squirmed and shouted at me to let go, I got to my feet, hefting her up with me, and dragged her away from the gun.

She kicked and swung her body the whole time, but she was not big enough to cause me issues. Takoda secured the shotgun by dislodging all the bullets and putting them in his pants pocket.

"Let me go, you fucker! Why couldn't you just leave us alone!" screamed Caroline.

Takoda came over to help restrain her. We forced her to the floor. With her stomach on the ground, we pried her arms back and I placed handcuffs around her wrists.

We let her bawl and flail on the ground handcuffed. She rolled over to Cardwell's body and rested her head on him, sobbing.

I said to Takoda, "I gotta contact dispatch. You have to get out of here before other police agencies see you here."

Takoda nodded and started to march out of the residence. In the distance down at the bottom of the hill, he observed several vehicles. Takoda couldn't quite tell who they were, due to the conditions. I heard a loud beeping sound near the video security monitor.

Ashley's voice came alive. "Guys! What's that?"

Caroline was sniffling, lying sideways on the ground. "Someone's at the gate."

I walked over to the security monitor, but the camera was completely covered by snow. I hurried out to the front door with Takoda. I saw him leaning forward, his eyebrows furrowed, hoping it would help him see farther. I re-entered the home and hit the 'talk' button on the security monitor.

"Who's there?" I asked over the gate call box.

"We're here for the dirty tribal cops," a voice said. *Anakin.*

———

Anakin stood outside the vehicle, speaking into the monitor. Behind him were his IPO soldiers with what they felt was a righteous cause.

There was no reply from the speaker. No reply was needed. They were in the house.

A soldier approached. "You think this is some safe house or something?"

"I don't know... but trying to get into that house is gonna be a bitch. We gotta assume they've got guns."

"We can do what we did to that biker gang a few years ago. Remember that? They tried fuckin' us over on that drug deal. Then they fucked with Camille at that bar, and we burned their house down?"

"Then when they came out, we picked them off like flies."

"Yep... Those white biker scum learned not to fuck us on drug money or mess with our family that night. Time for these tribal cops to learn the same lesson, boss."

Anakin nodded, then walked to the tailgate of a pickup. Anakin stood up on it, so all his men could see him. "All right, everyone listen up! These tribal cops are as dirty as they come!

They protected a white man who brutally killed my aunt and then they shot Mato for delivering what that bastard had coming!"

His men shouted, signifying their agreement.

"We're going to burn that house to the fuckin' ground! When they flee, we're going to pick them off. I need groups of four to five men on all corners of the house. We're going to have to move quickly. They're probably calling for backup as we speak." Anakin gazed at his men proudly and then continued.

"I won't lie to you. Some of us might not make it out of this. If you guys want to go home, I'll understand. This is as ride-or-die as our line of work gets. But if you stay, we'll have payback for our brother, Mato! We'll die legends to our Native people around the country!"

Not one of them left. Mato was their brother and the IPO was their family. This was how they would honor his death. Mato would have done the same if one of them was killed by dirty tribal cops.

An army of voices shouted, "FOR MATO!"

Takoda came back inside and closed the front door. Ashley got up and dusted off some pieces of wood that landed on her after a shotgun round nearly hit her. Caroline was lying on her side on the floor sobbing.

"I guess you weren't wrong about someone following you, Takoda," I said.

Takoda responded with a single word.

"Fuck."

That pretty much summed up the situation we were in. I went back outside. The snow had let up enough that I could see six or seven pickup trucks at the bottom of the hill. The men resembled ants in that distance, moving around the gate, fanning out around the property.

I walked near Cardwell's body and grabbed his 9mm handgun

that had fallen. Back inside, Ashley was trying to stand up, but nearly passed out and had to sit back down on the couch. I handed her the 9mm.

"Do you know how to use this?" I asked.

She stared at the gun, frightened. "No."

"It's really easy. All you have to do is point and squeeze the trigger." I checked the firearm to see if there was a bullet in the chamber. The gun was loaded and ready to go. "Do not squeeze this trigger unless you plan to kill someone, got it?"

Ashley nervously nodded her head up and down. I tried handing her the gun but her hands were trembling so bad, she nearly dropped it. I knelt next to her in the living room. I gently grabbed her hand.

"I was wrong to question you," I said. "You're the best thing that's happened in my life since I can remember. You saved my life by warning me that Caroline was behind me. I'm sorry I got you into all this, but I am gonna get you out. We're gonna survive. Do you believe me?"

She said nothing, but she nodded.

"I need to hear you say it."

"I believe you."

"Good." I kissed the knuckles of her hand. Ashley's hands started to shake less. I handed her the gun.

Caroline's whimpering subsided when she saw me handing Ashley a firearm. "What's happening?"

"There are men at the gate. I counted twenty-twenty-five, maybe more. They're fanning out around the property. Which means the IPO is coming to kill us."

"The IPO?" Ashley repeated.

"Indian Power Organization. It's a criminal organization. Similar to the mob, or biker gangs. People you don't want to cross. The other night, we killed one of their men."

Takoda gazed out the window and dropped his chin to his chest when he heard me explain to Caroline and Ashley. Caroline panicked. "Oh, my god. They're gonna kill and torture us like the Mexican cartel! You should have let me kill myself!"

I ignored her and turned my attention to Takoda, "Can you take Ashley and Miss Wilson to a room upstairs? I need to call in backup."

"Copy that," replied Takoda.

Before they went, I said to Ashley, "Put your back against the wall, pick a room with one entrance, and face that entrance with the gun. If anyone comes through that door, you shoot them until they're dead. Got it?"

"Got it."

Takoda had his AR-15 slung around his shoulder. Takoda and I switched our radios to a secure radio channel so we could communicate. He grabbed Caroline and pulled her to standing, then escorted her up the stairwell. Ashley followed with the 9mm. I stayed on the bottom floor and looked out the window. The snow had stopped. It was time to call in reinforcements.

JERICHO NATION TRIBAL POLICE DEPARTMENT

McCarthy and Fernandez rushed out into the parking lot. They glanced around. Their two most trusted officers were nowhere to be seen. McCarthy anxiously asked Fernandez, "Where the fuck did they go?"

"Their patrol vehicles are here."

"Call them."

Fernandez called Takoda. No answer. Next, Warren. No answer.

"They aren't picking up. It goes straight to voicemail."

"God fucking damn it. Lawson just couldn't leave it alone!"

"You think he went after the doctor?"

"Yep. And Cardwell."

"Shit..."

McCarthy and Fernandez dashed back into their office and logged onto their computers. They typed in Cardwell and Caroline's names to see their listed home addresses, frantically jotting down every listed address.

They met up in the hallway and compared notes. Cardwell's was in Salem, Wilson's in Willamina.

"Maybe Ashley is driving them to the Willamina address?"

"It's possible."

"Let's go see."

They left the department in a Chevy Silverado pickup. Once on the highway, McCarthy punched the gas pedal. McCarthy was eager to have words with Lawson for not following a direct order. As they drove, the radio scanner went off.

"Attention all units. Code 0. Officers in need of assistance!"

The dispatcher listed the coordinates and put out an exact location. The dispatcher explained that Warren and Takoda were under attack at a log cabin on the outskirts of Jericho Nation.

McCarthy executed a U-turn in the middle of the highway, causing other vehicles to slam on their brakes, slide, and honk their horns.

"Ah, go fuck yourself. I'm the chief, you cocksucker!" McCarthy shouted from inside the vehicle.

Fernandez had his pistol in his lap. He'd seen enough of these calls. He knew exactly what he was driving into.

"I've been jonesing for a good fight," McCarthy said. "Time to go kick some fuckin' ass. Show the young bucks how it's done!"

"Chief..."

"Yeah?"

"You're fucking batshit."

"Oh, yeah, I am!"

CAROLINE WILSON'S CABIN

Takoda came back down to the first floor after getting Ashley and Caroline settled in a room with Ashley protecting the door. I picked up my AR-15 as I waited and contemplated a plan. The sun started to peek through the clouds outside the cabin.

"Looks like they're surrounding the place. They must think we won't have backup for a while to be acting this ballsy," Takoda said.

"Seems that way," I replied. "I need you to get to the story above and provide cover fire. I'm gonna go out there."

"Are you crazy? You'll die."

"The best defense is a good offense... I'm gonna take this fight to them."

"Warren, you know what this means, don't ya?"

"Yeah, Takoda, I do."

"It's either them or us. Don't think about anything else right now."

I nodded.

"Give me your handcuffs. I'm gonna need them."

"What are you gonna do? Arrest them all?"

I stared blankly at Takoda for a moment.

"All right." He said as he pulled out three sets of handcuffs and handed them to me. I stuffed them in my tactical pants pockets.

"Get to the top floor in a good position to see most of the angles of the house. Radio to me when you're in position."

"Will do. See you on the other side, brother. There's no other way I'd rather go out."

"We aren't dying today."

Takoda gave me a wry smile and then left back up the stairs to the top floor. I went out the back door with my rifle at the ready. I knew the IPO soldiers couldn't make it around the entire property in the amount of time that they'd been there. I ran toward the forest on the west side of the house, about four hundred yards away.

I was faster than most college athletes, so I knew I could beat Anakin's men to that part of the forest. Once I arrived, Takoda contacted me via radio to advise me that he was in position.

I found a thick Douglas fir and took cover behind it. I focused on controlling my breathing after sprinting four hundred yards in a little over a minute. As my breath steadied, I readied my rifle. If someone saw me running, they'd know where I was in the woods. I remembered what Dean had taught me, drawing on his special forces training. We'd train in the woods on the acreage my parents owned. He'd set up a target for me and I would move through the forest, shooting the human cut-out targets twice in the chest, and once in the head. Dean had explained military tactics. I was going to need them that day.

I inspected the ground for footprints in the snow. The only ones were mine. I jogged deeper into the woods, farther from the house, and waited. Along the way, I shuffled snow over my tracks. The bad guys would have to show up sooner or later.

I crawled up in a tree and a short time later I saw a group of five men underneath me. All of them carried AK-47 rifles. Bullets that would rip right through my bulletproof vest. I waited for them to walk past me, heading toward the house. I checked to make sure that they were the only group in the area. *They were.*

Silently, I climbed down the tree like a spider. My grip strength was crucial; holding on was a challenge due to the ice buildup. When I dropped to the ground, the crunching of the snow made a sound. I ceased all movement, terrified. My rifle was slung behind my back. I quietly grabbed the rifle and positioned it on the front of my body. *No reaction. I'm good.*

I approached the group of IPO members diagonally and from behind. I closed the distance and was about fifteen yards away from them. I clicked my gun from 'safe' to 'fire.'

I called out, "Police SWAT Team! Stop right there or we'll shoot all of you where you stand!"

All five of them were standing side by side and froze. One of them started to turn to glance over his shoulder.

"If you turn around, you will be shot. Stay facing away, toss your weapons away from you onto the ground, and raise your hands!" I ordered.

The five IPO members stood still, contemplating their next moves. Suddenly they threw their guns to the ground about ten yards in front of them.

I had five sets of handcuffs. I pretended to talk to other people who weren't there. "Cover me as I arrest these scumbags."

As I approached, I patted them down individually, looking for any other weapons. I walked down the line of IPO soldiers, placing handcuffs behind their backs, and around their wrists. I told them to sit on the ground and they did as I said.

I trotted out in front of them with my gun pointed at the ground. "Gentlemen. You have walked into a trap. Inside that house are about fifteen more members of our finest Oregon State Police SWAT Team. Your fearless leader is leading you on a suicide mission. We don't want to kill all of you, but make no mistake about it, we will if you force us. I need you to call your leader and tell him to pull his men back or we kill you all here and now."

"Fuck you, pig!" one of them yelled.

I glanced past them as if I was looking at a SWAT team behind them armed with rifles. "Have it your way... Kill them all."

After my pretend conversation, I turned as if to march away. One of the men begged, "Wait!"

I stopped, "Yes?"

"I'll make the call."

"Stand down!" I hollered to my pretend friends.

I glared at the cooperating IPO soldier, "You better not screw me on this, or so help me God, I will bury you where you sit."

"Okay, okay, I won't."

The man told me where his cell phone was in his pocket. I grabbed it for him, dialed Anakin's number, and let him explain the situation.

Five down, twenty to go.

———

Anakin was at the front gate, waiting for a phone call from each group once they were in position. Anakin had his most trusted adviser and three other soldiers with him.

"What the fuck is taking everyone so long?" Anakin asked. "They should be calling me with their positions by now."

"We may have to retreat, boss. The cops will be here any time," his adviser bitterly replied.

"Fuck that, we have them pinned in the middle of nowhere. Backup won't be here for hours with this kind of weather."

"Boss, I hate to say this, but you're being blinded by rage, not honor."

"Oh, yeah? Did your brother get his bones broken and executed by the police? Yeah, didn't fuckin' think so. These cops need to die if it's the last thing I do."

Anakin's cell phone started to ring. "Finally, some good news."

He answered the call.

"Hey, you guys good? What part of the property you on?"

There was a pause.

"What the fuck did you just say?" Anakin shouted. Another brief silence, followed by, "Shit!"

Anakin paralleled a mentally ill patient talking on the phone. Anakin's feet were stomping on the ground like a child not getting his way. All of a sudden he stopped freaking out and his body went still.

His voice mellowed. "Lawson?"

CHAPTER
SEVENTY-FIVE

I listened as the IPO soldier called Anakin and told him everything I wanted him to say. After the message was given to Anakin, I stole the phone.

"I have five of your men, Anakin. Don't make me take more."

"Lawson?"

"If you want me, leave your men out of this. I'll tell my men to stand down and you and I can finish this. None of our men need to die."

"You itching to break my other arm or something? *Fuck* you, trying to fight me knowing I'm crippled. I'm gonna kill you and your friend."

"That's fine. Just leave your men out of it. They are walking into a trap. There doesn't need to be any more bloodshed."

"You tellin' me there is a SWAT team in that house?"

"Yep. We have some of the best snipers in the world all over the woods. As soon as I tell the commander to fire, all your men go down. We knew you were coming... Why do you think Officer Tehama led you here? Do you think it's a coincidence that we're away from any civilians in the middle of nowhere? Think about it, Anakin. Be smart and turn yourself in."

"Let's say I believe you. I ain't cuffing up, so I got a counteroffer for you."

"What's that?"

"I got five guys with me, they all got felony warrants. Us five want a shot at you and your friend. You agree to letting the five of us take a shot at you and your partner, I'll call off the rest of my guys. You also have to promise that we won't be shot as we approach the house."

"I'll tell my SWAT unit to follow your guys to make sure you hold up your end of the bargain. Once your men leave, so will mine."

"I'll make sure I stay out of sight when my men leave. I want my shot at you and Tehama."

"You'll have it."

"A'ight. It's a deal then. I'm gonna have fun with your bitch ass."

"Meet me at the cabin in ten minutes. The deal expires after that."

"Get ready to meet your maker, motherfucker."

"Looking forward to it."

I ended the call. I escorted the IPO soldiers a safe distance away from their weapons and handcuffed them one by one to nearby trees. I seized all their cell phones and threw them in random spots around the woods. I advised them that an officer would be there to pick them up shortly. I also told them if they started yelling and compromised an officer's safety. They'd be shot by a sniper and then darted off toward the cabin.

"Golf 103, what's going on out there?" I heard Takoda's voice in my ear via a radio earpiece.

I was racing back too fast to answer until I got to the rear door of the log cabin.

"Golf 103, do you copy?"

I opened the back door and entered the log cabin. I alerted everyone by shouting, "It's me! I'm back!"

Takoda hurried down the stairs. "What the hell did you do? I can see their men retreating."

"I got five of their men on the west side of the property, then I convinced Anakin to back off."

"You killed five of their men?"

"No, I caught them off guard and surprised them. They surrendered and I put them in handcuffs. They're all handcuffed to trees out there."

"So why are they retreating?"

"They think we have a SWAT team and that they're walking into a trap."

"Holy shit, I can't believe they bought that."

"We're not out of this yet. I made a deal with Anakin."

"A deal?"

"He's coming with five men. His dying wish is to take a shot at us. He believes that when his men leave, so will our make-believe SWAT team."

"Shit, Warren, five against two is still not very good odds. Not to mention if he does get the upper hand, there will be no SWAT team shooting him."

"No shit, Takoda. But it's better than fighting an army. I did the best I could, given the circumstances."

"Are they coming right now?"

I looked at my wristwatch, "They'll be here in three minutes. Get in position."

———

Takoda hiked back up the stairs and knocked on the door of the room Ashley was in.

"Don't shoot. It's me, Takoda. We have five subjects planning on attacking. Stay ready."

Ashley's nervous voice shouted, "Okay."

Takoda continued on down the hallway. He found a bedroom facing east, with windows that covered every area of the house except the west side. Takoda positioned himself behind a tall wooden dresser and a king-size bed. Takoda propped himself into a sniper position, resting on the dresser on the south side of the room, with the bed on the east side, looking through the scope of his rifle. Through the optic rifle scope, he could see five men climb the gate and enter the property. All five were armed. Anakin in the middle was holding a pistol by his hip.

———

I positioned myself in the kitchen. I flipped over tables, opened a single window, and knocked the fridge and couches over for additional cover when the bullets started to fly.

"You got a plan here?" Takoda asked on the radio.

"Yeah. Don't die. Call out their movements for me. I'll cover the east and west entrances. You cover the north and south side of the house."

"Copy that."

In the distance, I saw the five men climb the hill about two hundred yards east of the house. I felt a bead of sweat come down my forehead. My skin felt blotchy, and I wanted to scratch until the skin peeled off. My heart rate was one hundred sixty beats per minute, easy. In my head, I could hear drums thumping as I saw the warriors step into the arena. There was no going back.

I said a quick prayer.

"Dear Lord, forgive me for my sins. Please keep Ashley and Takoda safe. Amen."

I crossed my heart and gazed up at the big man in the sky, hoping he heard me. I gulped on a lump in my throat.

One hundred fifty yards away, the men started to spread out. Anakin stayed walking straight toward the front of the house with his arm in a sling and a pistol in his other hand.

One hundred yards out, Takoda advised me that two men went toward the north and south sides of the residence.

Anakin was fifty yards away, one minute until our deal

expired. He stopped walking. He checked his surroundings for a second. Takoda let me know that he lost sight of two men on the north side of the house, most likely making their way to the back entrance on the west side.

Thirty seconds left on our deal. Anakin held up his side of the bargain.

Time was up. It was time to fight.

As soon as the time limit for our deal ended, I opened fire. Not many people knew this about me, but I was an expert-level rifleman. Dean told me I shot better with the AR-15 than most special forces soldiers in his old unit.

I put that training to good use. I saw Anakin's smug, arrogant face and knew he didn't expect to be shot without warning by the police. He was wrong. I fired once. The bullet went through an open window and lodged in the meat of his right hip/pelvis area. One of the most painful spots in the human body to be shot.

The AR-15 bullet pierced his skin and lodged in his hip bone, rendering Anakin's hips about as mobile as a ninety-year-old World War II veteran. He collapsed to the ground, falling on his broken arm, unable to stop his fall. I heard his screams of pain from inside the house.

His men saw the muzzle flash come from the bottom floor of the home. It drew their attention to me and they started blasting rounds my way. I dashed to the refrigerator on the ground and climbed into it for protection. Bullets tore through the windows. The barrage of gunfire was deafening. It took everything I had not to curl up in a ball, close my eyes and hide forever. I heard porcelain cups in the kitchen cupboards get torn apart. Shards of wood and glass were landing in every part of the house.

"I got two men hiding behind a bush on the south side. One down on the east side of the house and two men in an unknown location." Came Takoda's tense voice on the radio. In the background, I could hear him returning fire from the second floor.

I didn't respond. I laid my rifle up and positioned it in the back part of the kitchen counter, should I need it for a long-distance shot later. I crouched down and started moving toward the back door in a squat. I looked like I was doing a frog crawl exercise to stay out of sight. I advanced to the hallway and stood up, drawing my pistol. I moved down the hallway, pointing my pistol at the door.

Nobody was making an entry, but that would change. I locked the back door, so they would have to kick the door to force their way in, making a lot of noise. I went to the right side of the door and waited in a blind spot. When the door opened, I would be momentarily covered by the door as it swung open.

I listened. Footsteps. Boots in the snow. The door handle jiggled. Five seconds later, the door was kicked off its hinges and came crashing down into the hallway.

Holy shit, that was some kick.

The two IPO soldiers entered. One went right, the other left toward the stairs. The one on the right was surprised to see me a few inches away, around the corner. I grabbed the barrel of his AK-47, swung it up, and cracked the soldier in the face with the barrel. Blood spurted from his nose as I moved past him, pointing my .40-caliber pistol at the other soldier.

Soldier number two started to pivot to shoot me. I was three feet away. As he turned, I squeezed the trigger and a bullet ripped through his right shoulder. I raised my left leg and kicked him with the heel of my foot into his sternum, a Muay Thai push kick. He stumbled and fell to his back, hitting his head on the stairs. His AK-47 dropped to the ground in front of him.

The first soldier still had a hold of his AK-47, had stemmed the blood from his nose, and was rearing his body around to blow me away. With one hand I grabbed the muzzle of the AK-47 and used a hammer strike with the butt end of my pistol. I smashed up his bloodied nose by hitting his face three times consecutively, then ripped the AK-47 from his hands. Blood from his nose got on my hand and the bottom of my pistol.

I hurled the AK-47 out the back door and into the snow, then lunged for the second AK-47 that was lying on the floor of the hallway. The second soldier, lying on the ground, kicked my knee out from under me. My knee buckled for a minute, but I caught myself on the wall with my arms. I turned to point my pistol at him as he got up, but he closed the distance and punched me in the face.

I stumbled backward, straight into the arms of the first man. He attempted to put me in a headlock, but I brought up the pistol in my right hand and pointed it at his head without looking.

The second soldier, face bloodied, grabbed the wrist of the hand holding the pistol and twisted it downward. Ligaments in my elbow made a popping sound as I tried to keep hold of the gun. He balled -up his fist and struck downward on the inner deltoid muscle of my right shoulder. My arm made another cracking sound. I screamed in pain and dropped the pistol next to the AK-47.

I was facing a couple of men that were the same size as me and well-trained. I thrust my head backward, smashing my skull into the nose of the man holding me. He lost his grip on my head, and I smashed downward with my fist into the other guy's groin. *You can never go wrong with a groin shot.* As his body folded forward, I twisted my hips and landed an upward elbow strike square to his mouth. Then I pivoted for a fast and effective palm strike into the second man's face. He stumbled back.

Free, I kicked the AK-47 and pistol to the side as hard as I could. The guns slid down the hallway about ten feet. Soldier number two recovered and lunged at me. I sidestepped him with a jab punch to the face. We circled and switched positions in the hallway, so his back was near the door, and I was in the hallway.

I stepped back down the hallway, toward the living room. I had one healthy arm; the other dangled at my side for the time being. My left hand was up near my face. I bladed my stance and waited.

I could move my right arm, but not very well. The two soldiers regathered themselves and noticed the two loaded guns behind me. They wondered for a moment if I was going to grab one and use it on them.

They charged me together. I lunged back and then stepped forward. I straightened my spine, put my weight on the front leg to balance, stayed light on my toes, rotated my hips, and performed a Muay Thai snap kick on the knee of the guy in front. His knee buckled and he went down like a tree falling. The other one moved in. He had blood leaking from his nose and down his chin. He looked like an undead zombie.

He leaped over his compatriot and started attacking me with punches. I stepped backward; the punches were clearly a distraction, as he was not putting much power into them. Then he rushed, trying for a double-leg takedown tackle.

I sprawled backward and took him with me. His body fell underneath me, my chest on top of his back. I wrapped my forearm under his Adam's apple, his head in my armpit. I put the sharp end of my forearm into his throat and grabbed my right wrist which was under the throat with my left hand. I tugged upward. *Guillotine choke.*

Six seconds and he'd be out. But by the fifth second, Soldier number two was back. I had to release my grip and refocus my energy as he let out a war cry and tried to punch me. I blocked it, tucking my chin and covering my head with my elbows and arms up. I stepped back, behind the prone figure of the nearly unconscious soldier. The second man came over to his friend, blading his hips as I did to him. He wanted to show me his kicking skills, clearly.

He had a strong kick, as I'd seen when he kicked down the door. The problem was, he kicked too high, trying to show off. We weren't in a Muay Thai gym, we were in a street fight. Kicks were risky in a street fight. You had to pick a good location on the body, or they could be easily countered.

The second man kicked toward my ribs. I absorbed the shot;

my bulletproof vest made the strike less painful than it could have been. I caught his leg and held it in the air, then shifted it to the side of my hip, drove my lead leg to the outside of his body, and got my rear hip under his.

As I kicked his ankle, my free arm went across his chest and hauled downward. Both his feet went out from under him and he hit the ground hard, slamming the back of his head into the wooden floor and knocking the wind out of him. The adrenaline coursing through me made me completely forget about my injured arm.

We were inches away from the AK-47 and my pistol. I grabbed the guns and threw them as far as I could out a nearby shot-up window. I heard gunfire all around me, but I couldn't focus on anything but the two men I was fighting.

Kneeling next to Soldier Two, I punched him in the face, then jammed my thumb into the gaping bullet wound in his shoulder. I stared into his fearful eyes as he yelled in pain.

Soldier number one was coughing but regathered his breath. I rose to face him.

He'd remembered a pocket knife. He yanked it out and flipped it open. *I should have just killed these fuckers with the AR-15 when I had the chance.*

———

Takoda was in a firefight upstairs. He was trading gunshots with two soldiers outside the house using vegetation to conceal themselves. Takoda knelt behind the dresser and reloaded a fully loaded magazine into his rifle. He peeked out the window and didn't see anyone. The reflection of the sun on the snow momentarily blinded him. Then one of the men rushed to the house. Takoda took aim. But the second man stayed behind and provided cover fire for the guy storming the cabin. Takoda had to duck behind the dresser as bullets sprayed all over the bedroom. Takoda knew that it wouldn't take long for the soldier to reach the side of the home and be out of view. If that happened, Warren would be in danger.

Takoda glanced back out the window. The soldier was twenty yards from the cabin. Takoda fired five rounds from his AR-15. The burst of fire dropped the soldier to his belly, but the soldier who was providing cover fire kept blasting. A bullet hit Takoda and he fell. He didn't know where he had been hit, only that he was thrown to the floor. Takoda felt blood trickling down his cheek. He touched his cheek. His hand was covered in blood.

———

Ashley was sitting in the back corner of a bedroom with Caroline Wilson. Caroline had been hiding in the closet of the bedroom since the shooting began. Ashley was exhaling loudly, her chest rising and falling. She was sure that she was having an anxiety attack. Ashley had provided therapy for many patients over the years who suffered from anxiety attacks. She knew exactly what she was feeling.

The barrage of gunfire was foreign and chaotic. Ashley had ridden with law enforcement for two years and seen her fair share of hectic scenarios. But Cardwell had always kept her well removed from danger. Now Ashley was not well removed. Bullets were tearing the house to shreds. It felt like only a matter of time until an IPO soldier came charging through the bedroom door. The panic set in even more when she heard Takoda shout in pain, in the next room.

"Stay here," Ashley said.

"Where are you going?" asked Caroline.

"Takoda is hurt. Can't you hear that? He needs our help."

"We won't be much use to him dead. He can handle himself."

"All the more reason for you to stay here."

Caroline didn't argue that point. Ashley gripped the 9mm Glock and hurried out of the bedroom.

She closed the door behind her and started talking to herself, "I can do this, I can do this, I can do this."

Ashley crouched down in the hallway and called out. "Takoda! Are you all right?"

Takoda didn't respond.

McCarthy and Fernandez located the gravel path just off the highway that led to Caroline Wilson's cabin. Fernandez had instructed McCarthy to turn off the police siren so they could make a silent approach. The overhead emergency red and blue lights flickered noiselessly as they drove.

They saw two pickups full of IPO soldiers about to exit the gravel pathway and turn onto the highway. McCarthy and Fernandez intuitively knew that the pickup was fleeing the scene of a crime. McCarthy came sliding across the asphalt and halted right in front of the lead pickup. The two pickups were lined up in a single file line. Fernandez and McCarthy were ten yards in front of them.

McCarthy grabbed for his custom-made all-black AA12 semi-automatic shotgun that rode with him everywhere. Only the chief of police could carry that powerful force of machinery. The AA12 was propped up in between the front driver and passenger seats, secured in a locked, upright position.

McCarthy pressed a button to release the gun and got out of the truck. Fernandez jumped out of the passenger side with his American-made .45-caliber ACP pistol. Fernandez raised his handgun at the truck. Both of them used the already open doors to cover their bodies from enemy gunfire.

Fernandez called out, "Everyone out of the car with your hands up!"

McCarthy had a twenty-bullet circular magazine attached to his AA12 shotgun. It would take five rounds to take out everyone in the truck in front of them. Fernandez saw a door fling open on the driver's side. He saw the barrel of an AK-47 peeking out of the truck door.

"GUN!" he shouted frantically.

Fernandez shot the driver square in the forehead, killing him instantly with one bullet. The rest of the IPO members were drawing their rifles and attempting to climb out of the vehicle.

McCarthy opened fire and bodies fell. He sprayed booming shots all over the vehicle, killing every IPO soldier in the vehicle before they could get a round off. The bullets of the AA12 shotgun tore through the lead truck, making it look like Swiss cheese. The gun was ear-splittingly loud and intimidating to the enemy.

The IPO soldiers in the second vehicle were covered by the lead vehicle. The occupants bailed out of the truck and returned fire. AK-47 rounds started peppering McCarthy's patrol vehicle. Fernandez and McCarthy ran to the back tailgate of the vehicle and hunkered down.

McCarthy reached for his radio microphone, "Dispatch! This is Golf 1! We're under heavy fire here. We need a rapid response SWAT team, now!"

I saw the knife in the IPO soldier's hand. I watched to see how he was holding the knife. A person can tell you a lot by showing you which way they face the blade. He held the blade down toward the ground with his thumb on the very bottom of the handle.

I thought about going for my AR-15 in the kitchen. AR-15 rifles are good for long-distance but can be tough to get a shot off at close range. That's why I used the pistol instead of the rifle when they invaded the home. Also, if I ran for the rifle, he would follow me to the kitchen and likely stab me before I got a shot off.

His body language told me this guy knew what he was doing.

I had an X26P yellow-colored Taser in a holster on my left hip. I pulled it as I stepped away from him and into the living room/kitchen area.

I could shoot him with the Taser prongs from a distance. Too risky. Tasers don't work like they do in the movies. You have to hit them perfectly to immobilize them. Connecting two probes, one in the top part of the body, just under the head, and the other probe in the lower abdomen/low back area.

Tasers also don't incapacitate someone instantly. Once the electric shock ends, the suspect is no longer in pain and is still a threat. A long shot with the Taser could leave me vulnerable to a knife attack. The guy was only three feet away. Baggy clothing can also protect the subject from the Taser prongs making skin contact. Due to the cold weather, he was wearing layers.

I pulled the taser cartridge off and tossed it to the ground. I had my Taser ready for a drive stun' approach. I held the Taser in my injured right arm down by my hip. Judging by the bladed stance, and what I learned throughout the fight, I expected a distraction strike, followed by an attempted stab with the knife. *Standard Krav Maga weapons combat training.*

My prediction was correct. He feinted right and then lunged forward with his lead foot. He tried to attempt a snappy kick, upward and between my legs. I hopped back on my toes, and the kick missed my groin by an inch. I countered the attack by reaching down with the Taser and zapping his kick leg for a painful second.

He grunted and stepped away, shaking off the Taser shock. We circled. Caroline Wilson's shotgun lay abandoned on the floor. I knew it wasn't loaded, but he didn't. I expected one of the two of them to go for the gun. My AR-15 was hidden for the moment in the kitchen

He feinted left, then attempted a jab punch with the hand not holding the knife. I efficiently dodged his punch by stepping to the right, then zapped his collarbone with the Taser. He stumbled back and I took two steps away from him. I kept my eyes trained on the knife. I needed to keep my distance until I had a moment to strike back. My opponent realized his distraction strikes weren't going to work. He took a different approach with the knife.

I noticed him turn the position of the knife blade. He changed to holding the blade upward toward the ceiling in a more standard grip. He charged. I sidestepped and he ran past me like a bull chasing a red flag. He attempted a wild slash toward my neck, but I ducked underneath it and shuffled away.

Growing frustrated he yelled, "Come on, motherfucker! Come at me!"

I ignored him, staying with my game plan. I kept circling him like a UFC fighter in a cage fight. He feinted left again, then lunged right, and tried an under swooping stab to my stomach. I leaped back and grabbed the knife hand wrist with my right hand, stopping the knife's forward momentum. With the Taser still in my left hand, I cracked him in the face twice.

With his knife hand controlled, I lifted his arm and turned while stepping close to his body with my back to his chest and the knife arm on my shoulder. I reached up with the Taser and sent a bolt of electricity into the hand holding the knife. The electric shock forced the knife to fall to the floor.

I kept his arm on my shoulder and pivoted around him, turning toward the side of his torso. I folded his arm into the shape of a modified C and pinned his wrist against his lower back.

My Taser hand now rested on the back of his neck, with my forearm bladed against the neck. I jerked his head downward and sent a crushing knee strike into his sternum.

He quickly turned to face me, aiming to get his arm out of the uncomfortable position it was in. I pressed the taser against his chest and squeezed and held the trigger, driving his body backward and into a wall. I landed a crushing knockout elbow strike to the mouth, causing a tooth to fly out.

To my surprise, he was still standing, though he appeared dazed. The window next to us only had broken glass on the edges of the window sill left. I planned to use it. As long as he was still standing, he was still a threat. I reholstered the taser and slammed his face into the windowsill, dragging his face against the shards of glass, cutting up and decimating the whole side of his cheekbone.

He yelped as blood gushed from his face. I chucked his body to the ground like a rag doll. Pieces of glass were still stuck in his face. Soldier One was making an unpleasant ear-piercing squeal. I rolled his body to his stomach, latched onto his back, slid one arm around his throat, and the other behind his head. He flailed as if he knew what was coming, but he wasn't strong enough to defend it.

I wrapped my legs around his body, sinking the heels of my feet into his hips. I thrust my hips up and applied pressure to the neck: the "rear-naked choke" as it's called in Brazilian Jiu-Jitsu. He tried to turn, but my legs held him as we rolled together. We landed on our sides. Six seconds passed, and he was down for the count.

As I shrugged his body off me and stood up, I heard the second man cock the shotgun.

I faced him, putting my hands up as if I was afraid.

"Don't shoot," I said, breathing heavily. He was about five feet away from me on his knees, with the gun aimed to kill.

"Go to hell, pig!"

He squeezed the trigger. *Click.*

I smiled. His grin went to a grim, hopeless look. He started to get up, but I tackled him, and we rolled end over end, near the fireplace area of the living room. The shotgun fell from his grasp and slid across the floor.

I landed on my back, with my opponent in between my legs, often called "the guard" position. His upper body was on my chest, and he pushed off my abdomen to throw a punch at my face. I blocked the punch with my forearms. Putting one heel on the outside of his left calf. In one fluid movement, I hooked my foot against his right hip, did a sit-up, and hooked my arm under his right armpit.

My legs scissored, as I pulled him to the left side, where he dropped to his back. I mounted him with my legs straddling his torso. He bucked and turned his hips to get out before I could get a good top-mounted position.

I shifted to a side-control position, with my chest mounted onto his, driving downward, with my feet sprawled behind me. From his back, he sent an elbow strike into the side of my head, right into my ear. He popped his hips up and started to slide away from me.

Ears ringing, I switched positions and let him shrimp away as I rotated to straddle his legs. I cradled one of his legs with mine, put my feet on his hip, and quickly wrapped my forearm under his heel, his toes in my armpit. I squeezed my thighs, pinched my elbows to the side, let my chest fall to the floor, and rotated his heel to the roof. His knee ligaments tore, making a popping sound. More screams. I shifted again, straddling his legs with my back to his upper half. I gripped the already injured leg by the ankle and viciously jerked it up to chest level while squeezing my thighs. He would not be able to walk for a very long time.

More high-pitched shouting, more gunfire around the house. I rose and stomped his jaw, rendering him unconscious.

———

Ashley, hearing a commotion going on downstairs, was torn between helping Warren or checking on Takoda. She figured Warren could handle himself, and clearly, he was still fighting. Takoda, on the other hand, was silent.

"Takoda! Are you okay?" she yelled as more bullets ripped into the upper story of the house.

As soon as there was a pause, she sprinted into the room Takoda was in. He was lying with his hand on his face. A bullet had come close to hitting him square in the head. Instead, it had grazed his face, causing a large laceration on the side of his cheekbone.

"Ashley, get down!" Takoda managed to grit out.

Ashley ran to the window with her gun. One of the men outside was helping up a wounded soldier.

"Fuck you guys!" Ashley roared as she started booming off shots that were nowhere close to hitting anyone.

Takoda got up, reloaded his third magazine into the AR-15, and stood up to cover Ashley. They fought side by side shooting from behind the moderate cover of the wooden dresser. Ashley's wild firing gave Takoda a second longer to focus his aim. He set his sights on the man he'd previously shot, who was being helped by another man. Takoda focused on taking one perfect shot, instead of pulling the trigger several times. He squeezed the trigger. The AR-15 bullet tore through the skull of the wounded soldier on the ground.

The IPO soldier had a moderate-size bloody hole in his head. Like a robot that was disconnected from a power source, he collapsed and died instantaneously. Takoda turned to point his rifle at the second guy, who was aiming at the house, targeting Ashley, who had stepped out from the cover of the dresser, a rookie mistake. Takoda threw himself over to Ashley and jerked her to the ground behind the dresser. The IPO soldier unloaded fifteen shots into the room. Ashley fell on top of Takoda for a brief awkward moment as the dresser protected them from the bullets.

"We have to get out of here," Takoda said. "Our cover is torn up."

Ashley nodded and they bolted from the room and rushed back to the bedroom Caroline was in. That room had one window, but it faced the south side of the house and was covered by a dark-colored curtain.

Takoda walked over to the window and gently moved the curtain. Takoda saw the IPO member approaching, looking up at the room they'd just vacated.

Takoda slid the curtain open enough that he could reach the

window and slid it open sideways, feeling the cold winter breeze from outside.

Takoda controlled his breathing. He wasn't a sniper, but he knew plenty of former snipers who stressed the importance of breathing during a shot. His target was twenty-five yards away. There was a lull in the battle.

The IPO soldier appeared to be limping and may have been wounded. He was dedicated; Takoda gave him credit for that. Takoda set his rifle sights on the soldier's center mass. *Shoot once and do it right.* He fired. The .223-caliber bullet went right through the IPO member's heart.

———

Anakin was covered in snow. His shot-up hip was throbbing. But pain had been par for the course on his long journey for justice for his Aunt Susanna. After several failed attempts, he fought his way to his feet, foaming at the mouth. He was so angry. Every step toward the house was agonizing, but he was close to finishing the mission. He raised his .19-caliber Glock in his good arm and labored on. He was still twenty yards away after what felt like an hour. Anakin started firing off rounds one-handed.

He knew that the shots were not going to hit anyone; if they did, it would be pure luck. His plan was to get close enough to the house that he could use the flare and lighter in his back pocket to burn the cabin to the ground.

McCarthy and Fernandez were in a firefight from hell. After the two cops got the jump on the IPO members in the lead vehicle, the rear vehicle had the advantage. McCarthy and Fernandez were pinned down, trying to fire shots to hold off the suspects. The group started to spread out along the tree line near the highway. The huge evergreen Douglas fir branches nearly brushed the ground, providing excellent cover for their movements.

McCarthy glanced over-the-top of the tailgate. Some of the IPO soldiers had vanished. He and Fernandez squatted down side by side behind the torn-up Chevy Silverado. There was no traffic on the road due to the weather conditions.

"Well, you wanted a good fight. I'd say you have one," said Fernandez.

"This isn't a fight. This is a fucking war zone."

Bullets started coming from all directions. They couldn't hold their position much longer.

I heard a smaller-caliber gunshot coming from the east side of the house, just after I knocked out the second man. The shots were smashing through completely random areas of the house. I ducked down and started low crawling to my AR-15 in the kitchen.

The bullets stopped. I deduced that Anakin was bursting off shots from his pistol. Reloading was going to take him a while with a broken arm. I stood back up, grabbed my AR-15, darted out the back door, and went after Anakin...

———

After Takoda took the final kill shot, he kept his eyes on the fallen to make sure they stayed down. Movement came from the closet area. Ashley, rattled by the gunfight, hastily pointed the 9mm Glock at the closet and pulled the trigger.

Luckily, Ashley was out of bullets, because Caroline was hand-cuffed and hiding in the closet. Takoda walked away from the window and slid open the mirror glass door to the closet. Caroline flopped out, along with a black duffel bag of cash. The bag was slightly open. A couple of hundred-dollar bills fell out.

"Holy fucking shit! How are you guys not dead? How am I not dead? What the fuck is happening?" Caroline frantically shouted.

They heard Anakin's Glock 19. All three flinched out of sheer muscle memory, but for a change, the gunfire wasn't directed at them.

Takoda checked the magazine for his AR-15. Twenty-seven bullets left. He handed it to Ashley.

"Take this and for the love of God, do not leave this room."

"This gun is bigger than I am," responded Ashley.

"It works the same as the others. Point and shoot. It's loaded and ready to go."

Ashley nodded. "Where are you going?"

"I assume the gunshots downstairs are aimed at Warren... I'm gonna go down there and help him."

———

Anakin's gun was empty. He threw it to the ground like a sack of trash and continued limping toward the house. Fifteen yards away. Anakin dug out the flare and the lighter. He lit the top of the flare and a flame ignited the red-colored torch.

Ten yards. Close enough to throw the flare through a window and set the house on fire. He was shocked that nobody had shot him yet. Why had he not been taken out by a sniper? In the distance behind him a couple hundred yards away, he heard a gun battle echoing through the hills. The fucking Tribal Cop had set up his men to be ambushed. Renewed rage flooded him. A dead white man was lying on the front porch. He paid no attention to him.

Anakin got ready to toss the flare in the house. His arm started to wind up like an NFL quarterback.

The metal barrel of a gun pressed against the back of his head.

"Drop it."

———

I sprinted around the house after the gunshots stopped. AR-15 in hand, I looped around the garage and hugged the wall, passing Ashley's SUV. I rounded the corner of the garage. Anakin was closing on the front porch where Cardwell's body was lying. He was holding a flare that had a flame fuming from the top.

I crept up behind him. I had to get to him before he set the house on fire. I tiptoed until I got within arm's reach of him and pushed his head with the barrel of the AR-15.

"Drop it." I took a couple of steps back from him to avoid a wild attack.

"Fuck you."

"You throw that flare in there, you die."

"I know you won't kill me. It's not your style. You would have killed me twice already if it was."

"The love of my life and my best friend are in that house. Trust me, if you try to throw that flare into the cabin. I'll remove your head with a bullet."

"Funny how our loved ones change us and make us do the most savage of things."

"I guess so. Drop the flare."

Takoda came out the front door with his .40-caliber pistol pointed at Anakin. "Two of your friends are in here and still alive."

Barely.

"If you burn this house down, they die. You won't kill your own men, Anakin."

Cardwell's body was riddled with bullets from the gunfight. Takoda stepped around him.

Anakin stayed frozen, the flare still burning in his hand.

"I..." Anakin's voice cracked and he fumbled his words, "I just... miss him... I miss my mom. I miss my aunt. I miss my grand-father..." His eyes started to fill with tears. His lips trembled. "I wanted to do what was right. I want justice for my family."

"One of the men responsible is lying dead next to Officer Tehama. After this is over, I'll make sure Marvin Bingham either lives the rest of his days in a prison cell or gets buried. You have my word."

"Your word ended with my aunt, grandpa, and brother dead."

"I know it did... but you said it yourself. I'm not a killer. I didn't want anyone to die in this, especially your family members. But this time—this one time—I'll make an exception. Marvin Bingham goes down, one way or another."

"Why are you giving me a chance? Why not just kill me?"

"Because I understand you, Anakin. Had I been in your shoes, I would be standing where you are right now. You have a kid on the way, and I want you to know your child."

Anakin gripped the flare. His body stiffened, and a vein in his temple started to throb. *Live for his son or die for Mato...*

He dropped the flare into the snow, where it fizzled out. Anakin settled to his knees and put his hands behind his back. He choked back a sob.

I motioned with my hand to Takoda to move in on Anakin. I kept the AR-15 trained on him. Takoda holstered his pistol. He zip-tied Anakin's hands behind his back and then patted him down. *No other weapons.* He had to attach multiple zip-ties because of Anakin's lack of mobility with his broken arm.

Behind us was a flurry of gunshots being exchanged out near the highway. This wasn't over yet.

An IPO soldier ran through the woods, trying to find a good angle on McCarthy and Fernandez. He got to a spot where he could see them, but the Latino guy was blocking the white guy. The soldier remembered the Latino cop shooting his comrade as they attempted to flee. He raised his rifle and aimed at Fernandez, about thirty yards away.

Fernandez and McCarthy were still taking fire from one soldier who stayed with the line of pickups at the gravel road entrance.

The IPO member snugged his rifle against his shoulder and aimed for the neck/head area. Next, he focused on the trigger pull.

Fernandez was giving as good as he was getting, in terms of trading gunshots. It was a miracle that neither one of them had been shot yet. Their luck was just about to run out.

SEVENTY-NINE

I left Takoda with everyone at the house and ran as fast as I could toward the highway. I had to prevent further loss of life. Too many had died because of this case.

As I approached the hill, I picked up speed, hard-charging the steep decline. The sun was starting to turn the snow to slush on the ground. I slipped and went tumbling down the hill.

Luckily, my fall came to a stop by the gate. I popped up to my feet and scaled the gate without issue, but I didn't realize until I was on the other side that I'd dropped my rifle somewhere during the fall. I didn't have time to go looking for it. I had my taser on my left hip though. I dropped down about five feet from the top of the gate and continued toward the firefight.

I was about a hundred yards away, following the path to the highway. The ground was starting to flatten out, making it easier to run. My legs were starting to fatigue; my lungs were burning. *This is what you train for, don't stop.*

A quarter of a mile away, I could see the firefight: Chief McCarthy's patrol vehicle shot to shit. But, obviously, they were still alive, or the gunfire wouldn't be continuing.

I grabbed my portable radio and changed the channel from the private frequency Takoda and I were using, to the main frequency. Radio reception was poor, but I was close enough that it might work. Holding the radio high in the air to get a signal, I grabbed my microphone and said, "Golf 103 to the units in the firefight by the highway. Come in!"

Fernandez's voice came on, as well as a chaotic sound of crashing and gunfire nearly drowning him out.

"Lawson! Lawson! If you can hear me, we need you to flank these guys! I've lost sight of a subject who moved into the forest southwest of my location. We have no protection from that direction! We need some help!"

"I'm on it."

I saw the positioning of their vehicle and how they were using it to shield them from the hail of bullets. It was moved slightly to cover from a straight-on attack and a diagonal attack from the northeast direction. The problem was, the vehicle bladed itself more toward that direction, leaving them vulnerable from the woods to the southeast.

Fernandez was like a father to me. He'd taken good care of me when I was a young rookie... I had to think quickly, or I'd lose him. And I had no gun. I faced northwest and scurried into the woods.

I was racing past trees like I was the DC Comics character The Flash. I had never run so fast in my life. I leaped over bushes and branches at knee height without breaking stride.

I was looking for a needle in a haystack and I was running out of time. I stopped, looked around, and saw nothing. I was breathing heavily, but I had to keep going. I was nearly out of energy, but I couldn't admit it yet. I arrived deep enough in the woods and darted up the tree line heading back due east, toward the gunfire.

I figured the shooter would be facing northeast to shoot Fernandez, so his back would be to me. A somewhat competent shooter could make a twenty-thirty-yard shot with an AK-47, so I deduced that the shooter was that far away from the firefight and had planned my approach accordingly.

I could jog a mile in five minutes. I could run a hundred meters in seven seconds. Added some debris in the way, it makes it ten to twelve. I could close the distance of twenty-five yards in two to four seconds.

The man was dressed in red, hunkered down behind a tree about thirty yards from Fernandez. His finger was on the trigger. I was too late...

T he IPO soldier heard the trampling of what sounded like a bear behind him. *Are bears common in Jericho Nation?* He paused and turned to look behind him.

———

I was going to kill him. That was my plan when I realized I was too late. I was done trying to save people.

Marvin Bingham finally changed me into a killer.

But then something happened. The IPO gang member didn't fire on Fernandez.

I hit him like a semi-truck. We nosedived down a hill and tore up some vegetation on our way down to the highway below.

We plummeted through branches, logs, and underbrush. The woods spat us out onto the asphalt. Both of us were groaning in pain. He'd lost his AK-47 somewhere along the way. We were both scratched and bleeding. I crawled on my hands and knees, covered in blood, and hit the guy as hard as I could with a punch to the face. He was out cold.

I reached for my radio to let Fernandez know I took care of the blind spot, but my radio was lost, too. I collapsed panting. My shoulder felt dislocated from the fall, but the adrenaline coursing through my veins made the pain manageable. It's amazing what adrenaline can do.

The gunfire was still happening; my guys needed me. I tried getting up, but my world was spinning. The gas tank was empty. I tried to push off the asphalt to stand up, but instead, everything went black.

A group of SWAT team guys who looked like Navy SEALs was standing over me when I opened my eyes. It was hard to understand them, but they looked worried.

Eventually, I made out, "Are you okay? Officer Lawson, are you okay? Are you hit?"

"No... not hit," I mumbled.

Three guys got me onto a stretcher and carried me to an ambulance. I was fading in and out of consciousness. Everything hurt. I stared up at the roof inside the ambulance.

I slurred out, "Get... Ashley and Takoda... out..."

If he answered, I didn't hear it. I hadn't slept well since I saw what Marvin did to Susanna. The images kept me awake, followed by the images of Mato's brain matter on the walls after the shooting. The stress finally caught up with me.

CHAPTER
EIGHTY-ONE

I found myself in a hospital bed. My police uniform had been taken off. It lay in a heap, covered with dried blood and dirt, in a chair in the far corner of the room. Ashley had fallen asleep in a chair next to me, lying half across my lower body with her head on my legs. My upper body was propped up by the bed a little bit. I nudged her with my hand.

Ashley woke up, yawned, and smiled at me. The side of her face had an imprint of the blanket. Outside the window were the city lights of Salem. It was night, and the city sounds were humming at a normal pace. The hospital room had a monitor with a slow, consistent beeping sound.

"I told the doctors that it was normal for you to have a slow heartbeat. They thought you were dying when you got here," said Ashley.

My gaze fell on the heart monitor. My BPM or beats per minute was at thirty-six.

"Nights at your house, I remembered lying on your chest and hearing how slow your heart beats."

I grinned and thanked her for informing the medical staff so they didn't perform a needless surgery. I was already sore enough.

Ashley told me that what was left of the IPO guys surrendered when they saw the Oregon State SWAT team. They were taken into custody without further incident.

They found Cardwell's body and had questions about who killed him. Ashley, Takoda, and Caroline all gave statements to the Oregon State Police. Caroline confessed to accidentally killing the love of her life and was taken to jail by detectives when they arrived at the scene. Caroline would later plead guilty to the negligent homicide of Susanna Holt. She was sentenced to ten-fifteen years of prison.

Ashley warned me that I would be getting interviewed by Oregon State Detectives about the shootout. My family was outside the hospital room, waiting to see me. I asked Ashley what had happened. I wondered if I had gotten shot. Turned out I had suffered a concussion and was severely dehydrated. I noticed a tube connected to the veins in my arms that were pumping fluids into me. My shoulder was dislocated, and I had several torn ligaments in my elbow.

Takoda was quickly cleared by medics; he made it out all right. He had a laceration on his face and got shot through the hand. His hand function was going to be minimal for a while, but other than that he was okay.

Fernandez and McCarthy survived unscathed. Fernandez wouldn't ever know how close he was to losing his life. Had Fernandez lost his life that day, I doubt the SWAT team would have arrested the remaining IPO soldiers. They would have all died for killing a cop. Luckily, God was on our side and that didn't happen. The department's fearless leaders were on paid leave along with Takoda and me, leaving the police force to be led by Sgt. Rod Mollahan until further notice.

The local news was all over the story, calling the shootout a modern version of the gunfight at OK Corral. Ashley thanked me several times for keeping her safe. I told her I couldn't have done it without Takoda. Her next question was interesting.

"There were men in the house... IPO guys. They were badly

beaten but left alive. There were five guys handcuffed to trees outside the house. Also, that Anakin guy was safely taken into custody. Men that should have died by all accounts. People that you would have been more than justified in killing," Ashley said.

"What's your point?"

"Why didn't you kill them? From where I'm sitting, the choice not to kill those men landed you in a hospital bed. But something tells me that you'd do it all the same if you had to do it again."

"I told you why I don't kill. Even the Marvin Bingham's of the world."

"It's more than that... You told me once that it was for your family and what happened to your cousin. They would have understood killing those men coming to slaughter us today... The men inside the cabin—" Ashley paused as she pictured them. "One guy's face was brutally disfigured. The other guy had no leg cartilage left."

"Those men had it coming and they're lucky to be alive..."

"Warren, I want this to work between us. And if it's to work, I need to know who you really are. I know you're not a boy scout, and I'm perfectly okay with that. I need to understand you. I need to understand this no-killing rule. I want an honest, loyal man."

I sighed, looking everywhere except in her direction. Truth was, I had never told anyone about that side of me. The darkness that hides within. After everything she'd gone through with me, she deserved an explanation.

"Are you sure you want to know?" I inquired.

"Positive," Ashley replied firmly.

"I do everything I can not to kill—for myself. It's not for the suspects. It's not about saving lives unless it's those I care about. I avoid killing people because I know myself. If I kill someone, I'm afraid a part of me will like it."

Ashley sat still.

"There's a darkness lurking in me. Itching to get out. Clawing from the inside... Whispering, *Let me out*. But I won't let that darkness win."

"Tell me where that darkness came from."

"I've always had it…"

"What happens on the day you have to kill someone to survive or save a loved one?"

I pondered that for a few seconds. "I'm sure that day will come. Some guy will get the jump on me, and I'll have to resort to my gun. I guess it's a good thing I'm dating a therapist now. Hopefully, she can help me keep the darkness at bay."

Ashley smiled and then kissed me on the lips while I lay in the bed unable to move with all the tubes and wires connected to me. My mom interrupted the kiss and made it as awkward as possible.

"Oh, wow! You must be the girlfriend! I can come back another time," she quipped as she winked at me.

My bruised, black-and-yellow face turned red, as we were both completely embarrassed. Ashley jumped off me like I had the bubonic plague when she heard my mom's voice.

I said, "Ashley, meet my mother."

We all shared a laugh. My dad came in a few seconds later, followed by Olivia, Dean, and baby Laurel. I held Laurel and visited with everyone.

Later, Keith, Kelsi, and their daughter Kaylee came. I got to hold Kaylee next.

Kaylee told me, "I wuvs you Unk War-War. I wuvs you so much. Please, no more hurt."

For a two-year-old, she was very good at conveying her love and concern for her ole Uncle War-War.

———

After the gun battle at Caroline Wilson's cabin, Takoda discovered Caroline Wilson had been hiding in a closet for most of the shootout and stumbled out of the closet along with a large duffel bag of cash. Takoda later totaled the contents at $75,000.

Takoda figured that Caroline either inherited the money or that it was money accumulated from something criminal. Either way,

Takoda had a better use for it. Instead of seizing it for the department. With the help of Ashley, he smuggled it into her Toyota 4Runner before the rest of the cops arrived on scene.

While Warren was at the hospital, Takoda grabbed the money out of her vehicle and drove back to Jericho Nation, where he phoned Hilary, Emily, Camille, and Grandma Holt. They met at Grandma Holt's house.

Takoda parked in the driveway and took a deep breath before getting out and entering the residence. It'd been a long day, but he felt that he needed to talk to the family.

He entered the house while holding the duffel bag full of cash. Hilary, Emily, Camille, and Grandma Holt were all in the living room area. Takoda set the bag in the center of the room and stood next to it. All four of them were seated on a couch or cushioned reclining chair.

"I want to say thank you for meeting me like this. I know the events of the past few days have been hard on all of us, and more so on you guys than me. I wanted to inform you that Anakin was brought in alive. He was not among those who died in the shootout today."

Hilary let out a huge gasp. "Oh, thank God."

Takoda nodded in agreement. "You guys have every reason to hate me, yet you agreed to meet me under such odd circumstances, and I appreciate that. As you can see, I brought you a gift."

"A gift isn't going to bring back Mato," Camille interrupted bleakly.

"I know... I wish it could. Believe me, I do. I'm not asking for forgiveness, because I don't deserve it. All of you have been through hell. I'm here doing what Officer Lawson would do if he wasn't in the hospital right now... In fact, Officer Lawson is the sole reason Anakin and many others survived today."

Takoda let those words resonate for a few seconds. He looked around the room like a great public speaker giving a speech on television. Camille's demeanor changed and Takoda continued his speech.

"I can't change what has happened no matter how badly I wish I could." Takoda's voice cracked and his eyes welled up. "But maybe... I can help make the future brighter for all of you."

Takoda brushed a tear from his face with his sleeve. He knelt next to the black bag, and unzipped it, showing the stacks of bills. Their eyes lit up. Takoda regathered his emotions and said, "If you want it, this money is yours. I don't think you guys need hand-outs, nor did you ask for anything. However, there's $75,000 cash here. Enough money to pay for high-end lawyers that you'll need to sue the tribal medical clinic and hospitals for neglecting to care for Susanna. Money that'll help Hilary's future child live outside the reservation and away from gang life. Money that can change the future for everyone in this room and their loved ones for years to come."

Hilary, Camille, Emily, and Grandma Holt all glanced at one another. They didn't say no. They didn't say anything, which Takoda took as a yes.

"Well then, I guess it's settled. Best of luck to all of you and thank you for your time."

Camille stood up from the couch and rushed over to Takoda. She gripped him intensely and hugged him.

"Thank you..." she said softly, as she pressed the side of her face into his chest.

Takoda hugged her back and said nothing. Takoda left the money for the four of them to split up among themselves. He strolled outside and saw the full moon shining bright. He pulled his wallet out from his back pocket and opened it up. Takoda found a picture and looked at it as he stood outside in the snow.

He wondered what would happen because other police agencies knew he was involved in another shooting while being on paid leave. Time would tell. He didn't care about his job. Takoda didn't think about the events of the past week. He was focused on the people whom he loved very much in the photo he was staring at: Maria, Xander, and him at Disneyland a few years prior. In the picture, he was kissing Maria on the cheek. She was smiling ear to ear, her brown eyes showing the intense love she had for Takoda. Her hair was down to her shoulders and blew in the wind. Xander was in the background making a disgusted face. Grossed out by Mom and Dad sharing "cooties."

Takoda couldn't help but smile wider than Maria was in the photo. It was time to go home.

EPILOGUE

I t didn't take me long to figure out that I was in the same
hospital as Marvin Bingham. The next day, I was hydrated
enough to be able to walk around. I was also on some
wicked awesome painkillers. I was moving at a snail's pace, but it
was better than doing nothing.

Marvin's room was a couple of floors above me. My family was
still waiting near my hospital room, but I told them I had something to do alone. I found the elevator, heard the ding of the
opening doors, and entered. When the doors closed, I pressed the
button for Marvin's floor.

It was hard to avoid all the cops who came to see me. Cops I'd
never met were there telling me that I did a great job. I slowly got
past all my brothers and sisters in uniform and made it to Marvin's
room.

There were a couple of cops on guard duty. They were young
Salem PD officers, around my age. One of the cops knew me from
the news stories.

He stopped me at the door. "Are you Warren Lawson?"

"In the flesh."

"What do you need, sir?"

Sir? I'm twenty-seven years old.

"I saved that guy's life." I pointed at Marvin. I noticed he was awake, watching something on the television. "I was hoping we could talk privately for a few minutes. Kind of a sentimental thing. You know how it goes."

The two cops glanced at each other, and shrugged, "Sure, whatever you need. Let me know if you need anything else. We'll be right down the hall."

"Thank you."

After the two Salem cops sauntered off, I entered the room for one last showdown with Marvin Bingham. I saw a stitched-up scar on the side of his face, left by Mato's knife.

It was time to put this case behind me.

Marvin looked flabbergasted to see me standing in front of him, looking worse than he did. I limped my way into the room, closed the door behind me, and sat in a chair directly next to his bed. Marvin was sitting upright. We looked at each other eye to eye. In the background was more news on the shootout in Jericho Nation. He knew what had transpired. He knew it was all because of him.

"Officer Lawson, to what do I owe the pleasure?" Marvin grinned.

His grin pissed me off beyond all measure. How could he smile knowing that all those people died because of his actions? *Because he isn't human.* Marvin was a demon sent from hell to torment the weak.

"Shut the fuck up and listen, because I'm only gonna tell you this once," I replied.

His smile went away. I glanced behind me and made sure that nobody was within earshot. "First. The news hasn't reported it yet, but your brother is dead. He died in the battle yesterday. I would say sorry for your loss, but you're such a worthless sack of shit that I don't even wanna do that."

For the first time, I saw emotion from Marvin when I gave him the news about Cardwell's death. Like someone had just told him his dog died. A part of me wanted to apologize for the unprofessional tone, but then I remembered Susanna Holt.

"You have two choices. Option one: You will go to your

attorney when you heal up and plead guilty to murdering Susanna Holt. You will do your time in prison and also plead guilty to manslaughter for shooting Robert Holt."

"Wait a minute! I was defending myself when Bobby came to my door!" Marvin proclaimed.

"I don't give a fuck. Let me finish telling you your options before I don't give you an option. Do you get what I'm telling you?" I was clenching my jaw.

Marvin shut up and nodded.

"Option two: Which is the one I'm leaning toward right now. This option allows you to go to court and plead not guilty. We can put the family through the torture of trial and hope you get convicted. You may or may not end up a free man when it's said and done. You should know that Caroline Wilson has already told the cops everything and pled guilty to being an accessory to Susanna Holt's death. Which might help your case, but doesn't exactly clear you either."

"Option two, I want option two," Marvin begged.

"I'm not done."

"Okay, okay, sorry."

"There's a catch with option two."

"What's that?"

"Let's say a jury finds you not guilty and you're a free man."

"Which is likely to happen."

"Oh, I know it's likely to happen. Which is why I need to tell you the catch."

"Go on."

"If you're found not guilty after putting the family of Susanna Holt through the trauma of her death for a second time... I'll have to step in."

"What are you gonna do? Kill me? You don't got the balls."

I glanced over my shoulder. Nobody was around. I leaped out of my chair and wrapped a single hand around the front of Marvin's throat and squeezed. I pinned him against the inclined bed. He thrashed around, but I held him in place.

"The more you flail, the quicker you lose breath. Now calm down."

His eyes showed discomfort, he was unnerved by the calmness in my voice as I choked the life out of him with ease. Marvin stopped flopping. I kept my hand on his throat but released the pressure enough so he could breathe.

"Make no mistake about it Marvin. I will fucking kill you. As soon as the jury finds you not guilty on some bullshit technicality and puts the blame on Dr. Wilson. I will flip your switch in the slowest way possible. I will bury you in the woods where nobody will find you. Nobody will come looking for a scum like you. I will rip you apart, piece by fucking piece for what you've done."

I released my grip on Marvin's throat, he gasped loudly and I stood over his bed, looking down at him. "That's the catch with option two: I will make you feel what Susanna Holt felt if it's the last thing I do on this planet."

Marvin was rubbing his throat. His breathing was rapid and he looked like he was about to have a heart attack. I'd never wanted to kill someone so bad. The darkness within me was whispering again. *"Let me out."*

Marvin was coughing, but he forced out the words, "I'm sorry."

You don't get to be sorry, Marvin. My hand launched around his throat in a millisecond and crushed down.

"What do you say, Marv? Option one or Option two?"

He held up a single finger, signifying to me that he chose option one. I let go of him and watched him gasp for air.

"Too bad. I would have liked killing you. Oh, and if you screw me and try to get out of this option, this deal won't come again. Do you understand?"

He nodded his head up and down.

"Good. Eat shit and die in prison."

I left the room and swung the door open with Marvin still regaining his breath behind me.

THE LAWSON FAMILY FARM

One month later, I found myself on my parent's deck staring at the stars. Marvin had pled guilty to the DA's office for torturing and killing Susanna Holt, as well as the negligent homicide of Robert Holt. He had been sentenced to twenty-five to life in a federal prison.

I received the news from Takoda on a cell phone call. He and his family were doing well. He was telling me a story of a date night with Maria that made me laugh. He sounded more optimistic about life going forward, even though he and I were both still on paid leave.

I, on the other hand, felt the opposite.

I ended the call and my dad joined me on the front deck of their house. We'd decided to have the whole family over for dinner that night.

Ashley was inside cackling with my mom and grandma, getting to know them. I heard my grandma's laugh as my dad opened the front door to come outside. My grandma had always called me Tiger since I was a kid. I never understood why she called me that, but she had called me that from the day I was born.

Now she was drinking wine with Ashley, my mom, Kelsi, and Olivia. Laurel and Kaylee were playing, having the time of their life. I loved my grandma's laugh. It was contagious, like my mom's.

I needed a minute after talking to Takoda. Memories of the case flooded my brain, and it was hard not to have a breakdown that would ruin a rather perfect night. I had this guilt that wouldn't go away and I didn't know why. All I could think was, why was I lucky enough to keep my family when the Holt family lost half of theirs?

Flashes of the case started entering my mind more intensely.

Every horrible visual was sneaking its way into my emotions. *How am I going to live with this?*

"Hey, son. Are you okay?" asked Dad.

I heard another wave of laughter coming from inside the house. My grandma's laugh above everyone else's.

I stared at Dad and said nothing. The emotions I felt closed my throat. Police sirens sounded in the distance. Tears welled up in my eyes.

Before I could choke down the tears and man up, he crossed the distance between us and put his arms around me. He held me like he hadn't since I was a little kid. Like he didn't plan on letting go anytime soon. For once, I could let go, and let someone else be strong. For once, I was the one being protected from the evil in the world.

ACKNOWLEDGMENTS

Thank you to all my friends and family who took the time to read my novel before I got published and for all the feedback you guys gave me. Without you, this book would not have happened, and I feel blessed to know each and every one of you!

Thank you to my editors. Karen Brown and Virginia Herrick. You guys are amazing!

Stacey Smekofske. Thank you for all your hard work to get this novel published and for helping me through the process. You are an incredible human! You work so hard to help promote the stories we authors want to share with everyone. I don't know how you do it, but I am sure happy you do.

Thank you to my family. My mom, my dad, brother, sister, nieces, nephew, stepson, aunt, uncles, all my cousins. I have a massive family, but all of you are like my immediate family. Thank you for always being in my corner. I love you all so much.

Thank you to my wife for your unwavering support throughout this lengthy process. You supported me every step of the way and I couldn't do this without you. I love you with everything that I have.

ABOUT THE AUTHOR

When Tyler is not writing books, he is a martial arts practitioner and a competitive CrossFit athlete. He practices Brazilian Jiu-Jitsu, Krav Maga, Boxing, and Muay Thai.

He competed in the sport of CrossFit, before blowing out his knee in 2021. Like most Crossfitters, he would do the "Crossfit Open." A nationwide test of fitness that introduces some of the hardest workouts in the world. In 2019, Tyler placed in the top 1 percent of the world, which was not enough to make the famous CrossFit Games, but he was proud of it nonetheless. In 2021, before injuring his knee, Tyler competed in a CrossFit Competition involving the fittest Law Enforcement Officers in the world. He was the 29th fittest Law Enforcement Officer in the World that year.

Tyler is also a certified Defensive Tactics Instructor for police officers in the state of Oregon. When he is not doing his own training, Tyler works with Police Officers or civilians who want to learn how to stay alive in verbal, physical, or deadly use-of-force conflicts.

Tribal Honor is Tyler's debut novel.